THE DEVIL'S GARDEN

OTHER BOOKS BY RALPH PETERS

OTHER BOOKS BY RALPH PETERS

TWILIGHT OF HEROES
THE PERFECT SOLDIER
FLAMES OF HEAVEN
THE WAR IN 2020
RED ARMY
BRAVE ROMEO

THE DEVIL'S GARD

THE DEVIL'S GARDEN

· · ·

RALPH PETERS

AVON BOOKS ◆ NEW YORK

This is a work of fiction. Names, characters, places,
and incidents either are the product of the author's
imagination or are used fictitiously. Any resemblance
to actual events, locales, organizations, or persons,
living or dead, is entirely coincidental and beyond
the intent of either the author or the publisher.

The views expressed in this book are those of the author
and do not reflect the official policy or position
of the Department of the Army, Department of Defense,
or the U.S. Government.

AVON BOOKS
A division of
The Hearst Corporation
1350 Avenue of the Americas
New York, New York 10019

Copyright © 1998 by Ralph Peters
Interior design by Kellan Peck
Visit our website at **http://www.AvonBooks.com**
ISBN: 0-380-97362-6

Library of Congress Cataloging in Publication Data:

Peters, Ralph, 1952–
    The devil's garden / Ralph Peters. — 1st ed.
        p.   cm.
    I. Title.
PS3566.E7559D48   1997   97-28603
813'.54—dc21   CIP

First Avon Books Printing: February 1998

FIRST EDITION

QPM   10   9   8   7   6   5   4   3   2   1

To the Foreign Area Officers of the United States Army:

"Regiments of One"

But inordinate ambitions are the soul of every patriotism, and the possibility of violent death the soul of all romance.

—William James, "The Moral Equivalent of War"

THE DEVIL'S GARDEN

CHAPTER

■ ■ ■

Her dark hair hung heavy with filth. Sores ripened over her skin, red welts on larval white. After mastering the shock of the daylight, her eyes stared as if sightless, although sudden movements made her pupils track. She was young, not twenty, with good bones sharpened by her decay. Layers of clothing clung to her as she squatted, and her smell spread more harshly than that of any animal. As Kelly watched, the madwoman jerked once, then clawed at the life in her scalp. Exposure to fresh air meant nothing to her. A cone of sunlight thrust down and made another cell for her in the middle of the grove, suspending her in the summer's deep, hot beauty. The other women, those whom the war had touched only on the outside, retreated back into the shade, their children driven out of sight. Kelly stood between the keepers and the kept. The young woman cawed once, a motor reflex and not an attempt at communication.

"How long," Kelly asked through her interpreter, "has she been like this?"

The clean-shaven young man, a thoroughly citified being,

spoke nervously to the refugee women. They flocked together in the half cool under the trees, their thick bodies and burned faces shrouded in worn floral cloth and headscarves. The women would not look directly at the interpreter, or at Kelly, but they chewed the air with speech.

"They say," the interpreter told the American, "you must take her away right now. Before the men are returning." The interpreter's name was Yussuf. Sweat glassed his forehead. He had tried to feel his employer's breasts early in their partnership, when she had dozed off during one of their long rides in the fuming Russian-built jeep, but she struck him hard on the side of the face with her fist and he never bothered her that way again.

Two shots pocked in the distance, followed by a third. But that was someone else's confrontation.

"Tell them," Kelly said, "that I need more information. Her name. How long she's been in this condition. And they need to tell me what happened to her."

Kelly believed she already knew what had happened to the young woman. She had been in the country five months and had seen enough for five lifetimes, none of it in the textbooks. But she wanted to hear the words. She wanted to crack these people out of their medieval idiocy. She had been to this refugee settlement several times before, inventorying needs that led to endless arguments back at the WorldAid office in Baku. Aid was ninety percent politics and ten percent real effort. And that was before it collided with the local genius for corruption. At times, Kelly suspected that the only reason she did not quit was because she would have been embarrassed to go home a failure.

The settlement, one of hundreds in a country with over a million displaced persons, was a roadside cluster of worn tarpaulins and sod huts, with burrows dug into the earth for the animals and the winter. These refugees had camped within artillery range of the front, expecting a swift return to their homes in the mountains, but each time Kelly came back, the settlement betrayed further signs of permanence. The front had gone stagnant and the soldiers sauntered dull-eyed through the towns, alert only to the passage of females. Dysentery haunted the children.

The male refugees, who made all of the decisions, had been unwilling to deal with a woman on any matters they considered significant, until they learned that Kelly was from the United States. Then they complained feverishly that America was against them because they were Muslims and did not help them in their just war. Kelly did not have the heart to tell them her country did not even know they existed. As they developed a sense of her, the men alternately closed themselves off in silence or made wildly unrealistic demands. The women decorated the background or smiled, gold-toothed and wary, when Kelly surprised them at their chores.

They had kept the madwoman hidden during Kelly's earlier visits. But today was different. None of the men were about. They were off at another rally full of lies that would end in meager handouts. The women literally pulled Kelly from her jeep, dragging her toward a bump in the ground that resembled the pithead of a poor mine, while other women hurried a rigid human shape up out of the darkness.

The settlement was one of the worst, pitched under a ravaged copse of trees, its water drawn from a roadside ditch that gathered waste and the chemical fertilizers from the neighboring fields. The luckier refugees in the camps up the road lived in boxcars or old military tents, and some even had intermittent electricity to power the television sets they had rescued before saving the family photographs. The boxcars were infernal in summer but preferable in the winter, when the wind swept down from the mountains. The latrines were always too close to the living areas. The Turkish-run camps were clean enough and not bad, with basic medical care and even schools, but the others, those run by the Iranians or the incompetent Saudis or the Baku government, resembled balls of human yarn. The best that could be said of them was that they had kept the cholera to a minimum this year, but the summer was not over.

Kelly looked into the cluster of women with anger and disgust. She was stubborn and she wanted the admission to come from their lips. Why did you bury one of your daughters alive?

After a few opaque exchanges, Yussuf gave up again. Yussuf was forever giving up, a man for whom sustained effort was impossible. Especially on behalf of a woman. Kelly hated to rely on him. She hated relying on anyone. But she had not learned enough of the language to communicate this kind of information on her own. There was no time to study, barely time to sleep. And Yussuf was regarded by her organization as the best of the local hires.

Perspiration snagged on the grit down her back, and her thoughts quirked briefly to the need to take better care of her skin. Everything was so difficult here.

"They say, 'Go,'" Yussuf told her. "They say you must take the girl and go away at this moment. Or everything is very bad."

Kelly turned her face to iron. "Listen to me. I want you to tell them that they could go to prison for this. All of them. For keeping her like that. Even this godforsaken country has laws against shutting human beings in holes in the ground."

But Yussuf wanted to debate. "Please, Kelly-*hanum*. You *know* what has happened to this woman." He pointed off beyond the screen of trees toward the mountains that rose suddenly from the plain. As though the mountains themselves were responsible. "*They* use her the bad way. It makes great shame on the family."

"The word in English is 'rape.' And just because a woman gets raped doesn't mean you have to bury her alive."

The interpreter blushed and lowered his eyes.

"It is a great shame on the family. It is, I think, better if this one is dead."

A few months earlier, she would have exploded at anyone who said such a thing.

"I need to know her name. Just that. All right? And how long she's been like this. Only those two things. I can't take her away if I don't even know who she is."

"I think she has no name now."

"She has a name."

"I think her family does not want her to have a name."

Kelly sensed her nostrils flaring. In the brown shade, the women whispered to one another.

"This is fucking sick," Kelly said.

"What?"

"I said I want her name. Tell them to give me her name. Or I won't take her."

She was bluffing. She was going to take the young woman. As far away as she could. They would drive through the night to the International Red Cross camp at Sumgait, where the air was as wretched as the care was competent. Slopped along a ruined shoreline, Sumgait was diseased with industry, a Soviet legacy. The children of the workers of the world choked with asthma and paraded deformities. A pogrom in Sumgait, supposedly triggered by the beauty of an Armenian girl, had begun this war. But the refugee camp was good.

Yussuf would complain. The young woman would soil the jeep, which, to his credit, he kept very clean. And Kelly anticipated her own squeamishness during the upcoming ride, the fear of contagions great and small. Nothing had prepared her for this.

She looked at the young woman whose life had been ruptured forever. Imagining her against the backdrop of a high, drowsy valley. Tending sheep. No, that was man's work. Carrying water up from the stream. Maybe knotting rugs. And dreaming of her marriage. Before the war set one village to slaughtering the next.

Yussuf was frustrated with her. But Yussuf was always

frustrated with her, and Kelly did not give one shit. He was well-paid.

There was something else now, though. The surge of fear in her translator-driver-bodyguard-watcher reached her like scent. "Kelly-*hanum*. You must listen. *Please.* If you do not take her away right now—"

The eyes of the refugee women changed suddenly and they flocked together. A big fist smashed the interpreter to the ground.

The men were back.

More and more of them. As if drawn by an alarm.

Dark, quick and unsmiling, the men flooded down from the road. The boys among them swaggered, honorary adults for the duration of this encounter.

An elder with a black cap plunged into the midst of the gathered women, lashing about with a switch. The women squealed and ran. He chased the slowest of them, swinging at heads and faces.

No one touched Kelly.

And Kelly did not move.

The men closed in on her, forming a ragged oval that also included the madwoman and Yussuf, who had opened his eyes only to close them again. He remained curled up on the earth.

The old man with the switch approached her and Kelly flinched. She could not help it. But she did not back off. The old man had hair the color of cigarette ashes and black eyebrows over gun-muzzle eyes. Despite the monstrous heat, he wore his shirt buttoned to the neck under an old cardigan, with a suit jacket drooping over everything else. He cracked his lips to speak, then turned abruptly, stalking off and calling an order to someone else. The ring of men tightened.

A younger man who looked far less confident approached her. He shouted at her in his mountain dialect, voice breaking, and he waved his hands. Kelly sensed that had he tried to hold still, he would have been trembling.

She was afraid now.

Two of the men pulled Yussuf to his feet. Kelly had a growing vocabulary in the language, and she caught the words for
"automobile" and "whore," but could not connect them. She
did not know whether "whore" applied to her or to the
madwoman.

Shaken, Yussuf looked at her with an expression that said,
Please, do not be foolish now. "They want to know what you
have done to this woman," Yussuf said carefully. "They want
to know if you have bewitched her to make her a prostitute
in the city."

"What *I*—" Kelly looked at the men. Turning from face to
identical face. Then she looked down at the young woman,
who seemed oblivious to the change in the atmosphere. It was
a lunatic world and for an instant, Kelly felt like laughing.
She certainly could not imagine the madwoman accomplishing
much as a hooker. Not without a lot of rehab.

"Tell them," Kelly said calmly, "that she's sick. I intend
to take her to a camp where she can be treated. To make her
well again."

"I think we must go now," Yussuf told her.

"Tell them what I said, goddamn you." Voice of ice, heart of
fire. "Tell them I'm not afraid of them."

She hoped she had inherited her father's gift for credible
lying.

Yussuf spoke to the men. For all Kelly knew, he could have
been talking about sports or the weather.

The elder who had thrashed the women had lingered at
the edge of the crowd. Now he stepped forward again and
gave a stony command to the young man who had done the
shouting.

Other men called out encouragement.

Yussuf looked terrified.

Before Kelly could speak or act, the young man drew a
knife from his waist, turned, and bent over the madwoman.
Her head jerked back and blood streamed down over her chest
as if it had been splashed from a bucket. Her eyelids fluttered.

Her murderer let go of her and her chin fell. Then she collapsed onto the ground.

Kelly did not scream. She kept her mouth locked shut as she fought to hold the contents of her stomach halfway down her throat. She closed her eyes, felt dizzy, then opened them again.

The world, viciously hot even under the trees, paused in exhaustion. Even the flies calmed. Everyone simply watched as the girl's blood pulsed out, its pressure soon easing to a seep from a gash so deep it had exposed the bone at the back of her neck.

"My God," Kelly said.

The young man who had done the killing woke at the sound of her voice. He rushed toward her, knife still in hand. He screamed at her, screaming and screaming, as he stood in front of her. Tears throbbed from his eyes.

She was not afraid anymore. He was not going to kill her. She sensed that the play was over. Inside, she felt an emptiness greater and darker than the mountains of Karabakh. The Black Garden.

In the background, at the edge of a cornfield, a tiny old man in a cloth cap trotted by on a donkey, tapping its hindquarters with a stick, heedless of the world's drama.

The young man threw down his knife and staggered away. Then there was silence.

"You're all bastards," Kelly said in a shrunken voice. "Your fathers were bastards. And their fathers were bastards." Her voice rose with each word. Suddenly, she was shrieking at them, "*Mur*derers . . . murderers . . . murderers . . ."

Yussuf got her to the car. No one followed them. Except the mouse-colored sedan that had been trailing them on and off through the day. There was nothing unusual about that. The government monitored the aid workers constantly and clumsily. When the sedan had picked them up in the morning just outside Yevlakh, Kelly merely assumed it contained more watchers watching to make sure Yussuf did an adequate job of watching her. The surveillance team had disappeared for a bit, probably taking a nap in the shade for the hottest part of the day. If the war ever picked up again, it would have to wait until both sides had lunch and a snooze.

"*They* could've stopped it," Kelly said, partly to Yussuf, partly to herself. "The shits."

"Kelly-*hanum* . . . I think there is nothing anyone can do."

"Oh, shut up." She was determined not to weep in front of this man. Not in front of any man. Not here. "So tell me. What happened?"

"They had to kill the girl."

"*Why?*"

"Because you are knowing about her. There is too much shame. These are mountain people."

She was crying now. "God*damn* this place. You ought to join the twentieth fucking century, you know that?"

Yussuf, who had been so afraid, lost his own temper now. "Miss Kelly, you are not listening to me. The girl dies because you are never listening. You believe the brother wants to kill his sister like that? With the knife? You have made great shame for the family. The girl cannot go in front of strangers like this. Her brother will break his heart now. The father will die of the shame."

Kelly tasted vomit. "Stop the jeep."

"We are driving away."

"*Stop the goddamned jeep.*"

Yussuf slammed on the brakes. Hating her. But she did not care. She burst from the vehicle and ran down an embankment the height of a child, heading for a bit of shrubbery that had been skipped by refugees scavenging fuel. She noticed the mouse sedan stopping not far behind the jeep, closer than most tails ever came. But she did not care anymore. She rushed through brambles, ignoring all the warnings about the vipers, and the dry stems snapped and stitched through the legs of her trousers.

She began to puke before she reached the first cover. Horribly dizzy, buttered by the heat. She reached out for invisible supports. As soon as she thought she had finished, she began to vomit again.

She had to sit down. There were small thorns, but she could not change her position. She dropped her head toward her thighs. The killing was only now coming real.

She heard voices back at the roadside, one of them Yussuf's. Then there was a shot and the interpreter's voice broke off in the middle of a sentence.

Adrenaline lifted her to her feet. But two bearded men had already rushed down the embankment behind her. Kelly tried to run, but she slipped in her own vomit and fell facedown into withered briers. Then she felt their hands.

Heddy twisted to face him and braced herself on an elbow. The dark counterweight to her blondness emerged from the sheets, wet and glistening in the lamplight, with the guarded flesh swollen to show a pink-gray sliver, a rooster's comb on a hen. Spillage glazed the top of her thighs and glued down the high trails of hair she did not shave, since there was no clean place to swim in the country. Below the rigor of her shoulders, her breasts piled, uncharacteristically heavy at this angle. Crisp, almost prim in public, she was shameless in the managed light of her bedroom, a delight to him and to herself. Heddy's voice made Burton think of dark flannel, a perfect accessory to the handsome looks German women substituted for beauty. He liked her best without perfume, a day unwashed and sexed out, with good jazz in the background. The way she was now: pale-eyed, satisfied, and thinking about herself.

"The ambassador wants to marry me, Evan," she said in the Brit accent veined into good Hamburg girls. "Should I have him?"

Burton smiled. Of all the women he had known, Heddy had the most sophisticated sense of theater. The sweat from his back had slimed the headboard and he pulled away to pile up his pillow. Taking his time. When he was comfortable, he put a hand over the woman's shoulder and said:

"Listen to this cut. Then we'll talk."

In the amber light, wintered by a big Siemens air conditioner, Charlie Parker played "Bloomdido" for the ghosts of Baku. Burton imagined the saxophone's valves burning the man's fingertips. Forty years before. Bird died and a soldier was born. Stream of life. And all that shit.

He already knew about the German ambassador's proposal. There was not much that occurred on the dip circuit that he did not know, because his Azeri counterparts loved to laugh with him over the foibles of his kind. To the Azeris, every non-Russian paleface belonged to Burton's tribe, and the shared laughter respected and mocked him at the same time. It was that kind of a place. He wished he knew a quarter as much about the closed world of the Azeris as he did about the infidelities and black marketeering of the diplomatic community.

The track ended with a report of drums recorded flat—the old Verve sound—and Heddy rose from the bed, white flesh. She turned off the compact stereo without taking the disc out.

"Bird lives," Burton said. He had given her a half-dozen jazz recordings to lure her into that part of his world, but the music was too spontaneous and disordered for her. Heddy was a gal with a plan.

A plan in which he had been pleased to play his part.

It was ending now.

She stood before him for a moment, offering him her nakedness, the good health that stood out here, in this lovely wreck of a city, and the hips just a size too wide for a classicist. She brushed her straight, business-cut hair back from a collarbone that carried a narrow scar from a ski vacation that had not gone according to plan. He could smell her deeply, like butter gone off, and it quickened his instincts before his body was ready. He found her eyes—northern warnings of intelli-

11

gence—and slipped into the minor key of a loss for which he was not quite prepared.

"I'll miss your conversation," he said. "And your body."

She smiled, almost motherly, and sat on the edge of the bed. His eyes drifted down over the goodness of her body, then came back to her face.

"We wouldn't have to make an end," she said, her voice smoke. "Helmut knows about us. He doesn't mind. Really." Heddy's gigantic water purification unit grunted in the background, a monster out in the kitchen.

Burton shook his head. "I'd mind. I gave up on sleeping with other men's wives a long time ago. I play fair."

"Nobody plays fair."

His smile eased. "I try. Have I ever been unfair to you?"

She showed her strong white teeth. "You force me to listen to jazz." Her fine accent slipped and she pronounced the last word "chass." Heddy trying to be funny, ending up German. The Germans were a people with a great deal going for them, but the closest they got to humor was a bathroom joke told in a beer garden. Burton's enduring image of Germany hailed from his days as a lieutenant in the Eighth Infantry Division, two decades before, when he and his friends had hiked through the Rhineland autumn. At a village wine festival, he had gone to the john in the community hall and encountered a self-absorbed German sitting on the crapper with his plus fours down, eating a mammoth sausage.

Deutschland.

"So," she continued, her tone lightly seasoned with impatience, "you believe I should marry him? You don't care?"

"Yes. I think you should marry him. And no. You're wrong. I do care. But I care on a realistic level."

"I'll miss our sex." She said it in a way that told Burton she did not really believe he would abandon her bed forever. "But we shall still be friends. *Why* do you think I should marry him?"

Burton almost laughed. "Hedwig, I think you should marry

him for the same reasons you think you should marry him. He's rich. He's well-connected. And all he asks is that you decorate his life. With some discretion. In return, you'll be the belle of Bonn, with a *Familiensitz* up on the bluffs back in Hamburg. *And* a vacation home in Tuscany, thanks. You hit the lotto, baby. Ten, fifteen years, and you'll be an ambassador yourself." He shook his head gently, in mock admiration.

"He loves me," she said.

"Lie down. Please. I just like to look at you like that."

She did as he asked, rolling onto her belly and up on her forearms. The posture spread her flesh, deforming the contours of her body in a way that was unaccountably erotic.

"He truly does love me, you know."

"Yep."

"*You* don't love me."

"Nope. And you don't love me."

"I don't love him, either," she said.

The lamplight gilded her rump. With the music gone, the streaking of cars and the sudden thrill of horns described the night beyond Heddy's shutters.

"I wish I loved him," she said. There were tears in her eyes, a phenomenon rare as a comet.

Burton slipped down beside her and took her in his arms, appreciating the gift of her company with redoubled intensity. "No, you don't," he said in a comforting voice. "You don't wish you loved him. That's not what it's about, Hed. Nor do you wish you loved me. Not really. Because the one thing you do not want in a marriage is a contest of wills."

"We have wonderful sex."

"Yep."

She tightened against him.

"That's a start, as you Americans say."

"No. When you're twenty, it's a start. At forty, it's a lifeline with nobody on the other end."

"You needn't be so hard, Evan."

"I have to start breaking the habit of you."

13

"Not yet."

He paid her the tribute of a sigh and smiled. "I guess not yet."

She passed a hand down over him, reaching for the reliable. "How do you think of us, Evan?"

His smile grew. Feeling her touch, letting things work. Thinking. "I think of us as survivors. Lucky enough to have shared a very nice lifeboat for a while."

"I think you'll miss me. I believe you'll miss me a great deal."

"I told you I'll miss you."

"Then show me. How much you'll miss me."

He was perfectly willing to do that. He angled to kiss her, feeling her full warmth against him, body warmth in a machine-chilled room with the hot, thick night beyond, a layered life in a city that smelled of oil, garbage, and sweat. Her mouth was stale from sex and thirst, and he wet her lips with his tongue, then kissed her sincerely. No lie. He would miss her very much. Heddy's bedroom carnival. And her flannel voice reciting poetry as they lay in wine and darkness. *Die Frauen von Ravenna tragen . . .* The plain good company of her over coffee.

Someone knocked at the door of the apartment.

It seemed distant and ignorable at first. But, after a pause, the fist tried again.

Burton drew slightly away from his lover. "An ambassadorial visit?"

"They'll go away," Heddy told him, closing their bodies together again. "I don't want to answer."

But the visitor would not go away.

"Better see who it is, Heddy."

She looked at him. Her green-gray eyes were incandescently selfish. But there were some things, he knew, about which she would never lie. That was her Lutheran hangover. "You go. Please. It's late."

"If it's—"

"It's not him. He knows better. Please. It's late."

He nodded. As an attractive Western blonde, Heddy had excited more than her share of neighborhood attention. And after a bit of wine, the local males could talk themselves into fantastic imaginings. She had struck one admirer who followed her home, giving him an attaché case full in the face, knocking him down the stairs and into the hospital. Anyway, Burton figured he was good at opening doors. Part of his job.

The banging came again, almost destructive in its force. Burton tugged on his jeans, working to fit in the awkwardness of his anatomy while Heddy watched and giggled like a teen-age girl.

"Come back soon," she said.

He went barefoot over the hallway Shirvan, switching on the light and finally getting his zipper up. Baku was a city of complex and sometimes sudden enmities. Before he undid the locks, Burton picked up the baseball bat he had given Heddy to keep behind the door.

It was his NCOIC from the embassy, Sergeant First Class Spooner. Wearing an embarrassed face.

"Boss? Sorry for coming after you like this. We got a sensitive one. Didn't want to pass it over the cellular. All the ears out there. I mean, I guess they'll find out soon enough, but you know . . . Jeez, it's a bitch parking around here. There some secret to it?"

"What's up, Spoon?"

"That senator's daughter, the do-gooder?"

Trost. Kelly Trost. Oh, yeah.

"Yeah?" Burton said.

"Somebody grabbed her ass."

"What?"

"She got kidnapped."

Burton's first thought was that he was going to miss Heddy very much.

*   *   *

15

August is a terrible month in Washington, D.C. The District is at its most southern in August, when the ghosts of the old swamps rise up from the asphalt and the air pushes down on your shoulders like swollen hands. The days are long and the heat has a Baptist tenacity and the twilight takes a long time to work.

A weaker man would have driven in air-conditioned comfort from the underground garage to the backslapper restaurant over on K Street, but Senator Mitch Trost relished displays of strength. He left his key staffers behind in his suite in the Dirksen Building: the office den mother, Ruby Kinkiewicz, and a pack of very ambitious kids hunched over tomorrow's laws during what should have been a Congressional recess. Ruby was great because she was plain, desperately hard-working, ferociously protective of him, and never a temptation. The perfect chief of staff. Above dark trees, the dome of the Capitol drew the late, orange sunlight.

He walked down between the lawn and the street with his suit jacket slung over his shoulder the way he remembered his dad walking down from the Schuylkill County courthouse, posture just fine and an occasional jewel of sweat heading for his bow tie, an aristocrat among his coalcracker constituents. Like his father, Senator Trost did not perspire extravagantly and he even found the evening heat something of a comfort, its scents evoking tableaux from his childhood and youth, the Mahantongo Street lawn parties where the coal-money crowd held off the future with Manhattans or whiskey sours, then the scrubbed feel of the girls who had contested his early desire. Mitch Trost cared passionately about his broken state, and he romanticized it all the more as he visited less, in love with its past, bored by its present. He read John Updike out of loyalty and reread John O'Hara out of love, never dated any woman who was not at least five years older than his daughter, and knew more about wine than he would ever let on to the voters back home in the anthracite hills or down in the Dutchie lowlands.

After so many years, Trost considered Washington, not Pottsville, his real home, and he regarded the time he actually spent in Pennsylvania not as a pleasure but as a soldierly duty. Begging for votes from back-country yonkos who recalled not his voting record on the Hill but his record as a running back for Penn State. Then there were the Dutchies, who still hated to flush the toilet for the water it cost, hard-working and sour, their women like oxen. And the miners without mines, the steelworkers without mills, the farmers on a permanent grump, all of them lost in a world they no longer understood, television more real to them than their own lives. Except during hunting season. Mitch Trost was as different from them as a man could be, yet he understood their needs and wants—he regarded himself as the last good union man in either house— and he had the knack of speaking to them. They were family, but a family loved most easily from a distance.

Washington was home. Trost had been in the city for almost two decades and he saw it as few others did, with connoisseur's eyes inherited from a failed-artist mother and with the calculation of an appropriator of the city government's funds, as a moralist and as an impassioned lover. He regarded things and people attentively, and had a gift for remembering them. After three drinks he still could have described in detail the searching tourists and evening joggers, the frazzled staffers and the homeless he passed on his stroll. Approaching the juncture of Constitution and Pennsylvania, one of the noble intersections of the world, he offered an old-acquaintance glance to the parent-and-child buildings of the National Gallery, where he sometimes met women over the lunch hour and where he had fallen in love with the long-dead wife of Richard Brinsley Sheridan. He passed horseless old George Meade— lucky bastard of Gettysburg—and the iceberg of the Canadian embassy.

In front of the steak house of the moment, a woman's legs startled him as they emerged from a blue Lincoln. She had young skin in the deepening light and white hair cut in a bob, and she wore a short, black, let-'em-eat-cake suit that paid no regard to the town's dreary dress code. Swift to judge, Trost found her admirable. Until a shaggy, terrible head emerged from the driver's side, nearly falling over the parking valet. Trost nodded a gentleman's greeting to his colleague. The encounter, the deplorable waste of a woman's flesh, put Trost off his stride for a moment and it did not help when, just across the street from the National Archives, a scarecrow in a filthy T-shirt lurched from the Navy memorial to hustle him for spare change. Trost, who believed firmly that the homeless were victims only of their own dissolute behavior, gave the man a look none of his constituents would ever see. The senator was tall and still athletic, and the beggar waited until he had gone on several paces before calling:

"Shit, motherfucker."

But there were tourist girls in shorts and halter tops, some gross but others lithe sponsors of memory, and the automobileness of the air was fading, and the heat felt tired of itself. By the time he reached the Willard Hotel, where a sloven family tumbled from a Range Rover with Connecticut plates, the guttering day felt delicious again, and the walk past the White House lifted his heart. You never knew. You really never knew.

He turned off Pennsylvania, second shirt of the day still fresh and surprisingly dry, and marched past the unfathomable loonies with their protest signs spoiling Lafayette Square, willing himself anonymity until he reached the safety of Connecticut Avenue. He left a note in the Army and Navy Club for a retired four-star, then pushed on past lightless think tanks and closed-for-the-day coffee shops, past street kiosks pushing five-buck fantasies of Africa and junker cabs whose drivers knew neither the city nor its language. Bookstores, banks, and brokerage houses, all sleeping. K Street thrived during business hours, then emptied quickly. The few other pedestrians he encountered were either lost or angling from their cars toward restaurants.

Trost paused for a moment before entering Prime Rib, although the doorman had already recognized him and hastened to do his duty. It still was not quite night, but the freshness was there now. Perfuming a sweated city. For all the baggy suits and the dull muchness of government, he found Washington romantic, humid with opportunity.

Washington, capital of the world. He knew there were less appealing parts of the city, but he felt no need to go there. Let the mayor pretend. Trost's Washington was a pale, fan-shaped wonder, its base fixed just east of the Capitol, the left border touching National Airport and the right reaching up Massachussets, past the cathedral, to the land of dinner parties and the wives of expendable friends. Wonderful city, soaking in power, vivid by day and monumental by night. It had addicted him as no single woman had ever done, not even the wife who had fixed his attention for five years or so before holding him in law for another ten.

Capital of the world.

Pulling on his jacket and shooting his cuffs, the senator plunged into the air-conditioned splendor of the restaurant. He smiled but did not really listen to the greeting from the captain. He was a pol now, and a good one, waving, greeting, modulating pauses, touches, and words. Taking his own good time, he made a triumphal procession of one as he headed toward the table where this season's woman waited.

"Laura," he said finally, smiling down. "And how is the most beautiful woman in our fair republic?" He bent to the offer of her hand, but did not quite kiss it.

"Hungry." She had a cigarette-stained voice of the sort that would be lost to the rising generation. She no longer smoked, but she had done so long enough to shape the movement of her forearms over a table setting. Her life was a finely sculpted thing, and she had perhaps five more years of great beauty in her. Ginger-haired, she brought an autumnal intensity to the things that mattered most, and while he did not love her, he valued her enough to accord her fidelity for their time together.

Never less than perfect on display, her clothing moved with her as though it craved the feel of her skin. She was a malleably sexual, molten woman in private, ready to find pleasure in an extended range of activities. Her only rule was no gadgets, and that was one of his rules, too.

"You should have ordered something." He adjusted his chair. "A bite to keep the tummy well-disposed." He liked the restaurant for its insider clubbiness, but the seating was very close and you had to speak accurately. For beginning relationships, he preferred 701, both for its convenience to the Hill and for the distance between tables.

"So. Are your lunatic friends going to keep you in session permanently? Or are we going to get some beach time?"

"Laura, my beloved." He looked at her, forever judging afresh, this time contented. "We have elected a Congress of reactionaries bent on revolution and a President who longs to be a revolutionary but adores the status quo. That, my darling, is a prescription for frustration. But pay it no mind." He leaned across the table, seeking her scent, and he timed his words to beat the approach of the wine steward. "It is my intent to make love to you by moonlight on the remotest beaches of the Outer Banks."

"One beach will be fine. Christ, there's that shit MacCauley."

Although Trost agreed with the sentiment, he would not have expressed it within hearing of the next table or the restaurant staff. Still, he turned and looked, with the wine steward half blocking his view.

The steward launched into a spiel about a single case of a very special Gevrey-Chambertin, but MacCauley, the number two man at State, a friend of the President and a spectacular fool, made it plain by eye contact and his expression that he had not come for dinner. He sliced through a crust of lawyers by the bar.

Trost was not one to underestimate his own importance, but it struck him as a bit unusual for an arrogant bastard like

MacCauley to be his own messenger boy. He could not imagine for the life of him what this could be about. MacCauley was the Administration's point man for its colossally failed Russia policy, which consisted primarily of handing newly independent states with unpronounceable names back to Moscow. While he despised MacCauley for his blue-ribbon combination of arrogance and incompetence, the man's portfolio was not one of much concern to Trost, since the Russians bought nothing from his state and built nothing in his state. But MacCauley, clumsy between the tight tables, clearly had something on his mind.

Then Trost made a connection. And the sweat the summer heat had failed to draw prickled along his back.

Oh, God. No.

"Mitch . . . Senator . . . I'm . . ."

Out of breath. For God's sake, man. You are out of breath. Calm down. Let's not make a show.

"Shall we go on outside, Drew? We need to have a talk?"

"If you please, Senator."

As they maneuvered back through the crowd, Trost minimized the socializing. His heart whacked at the walls of his chest. The front doors opened and the lolling parking valets scuttled out of the way. The heat amplified after the brilliance of the restaurant's air-conditioning. A police cruiser shot by, blue light churning. The two men stood on the sidewalk by MacCauley's chauffeured Lincoln, both of them nervous but only one showing it.

"It's about your daughter," MacCauley said at last.

The briefer waiting in the Secretary of State's seventh-floor conference room was a thirtyish woman with a married-to-her-work look. Her dreadful red suit was dark at the armpits. She reminded Trost of Ruby Kinkiewicz twenty years before, and he immediately trusted her more than he did Drew MacCauley.

"I'm afraid the information's still sketchy, sir. But as I said, there are no indications at this time that your daughter has come to physical harm."

The senator nodded. "Driver took a bullet up the nose," he said. "And my daughter's last known location is a stone's throw from where a girl got her throat cut. Doesn't sound friendly."

The analyst looked pained. Not just because she had so little to offer a powerful man, but because she hated to do an inadequate job. Trost pegged her as one of those little heroes who make the government go but never go anywhere themselves.

"Sir . . . the only blood at the site where the car and driver were found seems to have come from the driver. It appears that whoever shot the driver wanted to kidnap your daughter, not harm her. But . . . frankly . . . we don't have enough information to draw firm conclusions."

Trost studied the woman. Waxy skin even in summer. Serious eyes. "Your given name, Miss Rains?"

"Virginia, Senator."

Trost could always manage a little smile. "A great name and a great state. Well, now, Ginny. How about telling me what you really think? What's your gut tell you?"

She looked briefly at MacCauley, in love with her work and fearing the loss of the beloved. But she made the right decision.

"Sir . . . it's really too early to tell. But I'd bet on a kidnapping."

"Because she's my daughter?"

The analyst shrugged. "That certainly sets the stage. The region's such a mess that it could have been anybody from bandits out to make a few bucks to terrorists looking for a hostage trade. We may just have to wait for the kidnappers to come up on the Net with their demands."

"If it *is* a kidnapping."

"Yes, sir."

"Funny thing. To find yourself hoping your daughter was kidnapped. When that's the best option looking at you."

"Yes, sir."

He turned to MacCauley and spoke with the jocularity of a cobra. "I thought your people were going to keep an eye on Kelly for me. What's that ambassador's name?"

MacCauley's facial features remained poised and posed, but his eyes were unsteady. "Kandinsky, Senator. B-team, I'm afraid. I've had trouble making him grasp the greater contours of our policy." MacCauley did not quite meet his guest's eyes. "One of those junior types we had to draw on to fill the new embassies when the Soviet Union came apart on us."

Trost made a mental note that the ambassador was probably all right. He could imagine no greater recommendation for a foreign service professional than being on Drew MacCauley's shit list.

"In the department's defense," MacCauley continued, "Kandinsky's got a very small staff and a damned big mission. Azerbaijan's the linchpin state to all those oil and gas issues you've been hearing about. The president over there has delusions of grandeur and I've had the devil of a time trying to bring him to an accommodation with Chernomyrdin. But Kandinsky *was* asked to keep an eye on your daughter. As staffing allowed."

A slight change in the analyst's expression caught Trost's eye. "Something to add, Ginny?"

She glanced at MacCauley again. And again she made the right decision. Trost took another mental note: Have one of the staffers keep tabs on her, make sure MacCauley doesn't screw her.

"Sir . . . the Azeri government was perfectly aware that the daughter of a U.S. senator was doing relief work in their country. The station chief reported that the security ministry kept a pretty good handle on her whereabouts. Tails and that sort of thing. Probably some phone monitoring."

"Doesn't look like they did a very good job."

"It's not an exact neighborhood," the analyst said.

"Well," MacCauley told the room, "I have to tell you

frankly, Senator. That whole region was better off when the Russians were calling the shots."

Trost looked at the man. His regard caused his host to draw back physically. "Tell me, Drew," the senator asked, "how would you feel about the Russians calling the shots in your neighborhood? Strikes me that property values have gone down a bit in Chechnya over the last couple of years. I pronounce that right?"

MacCauley reddened.

Trost turned his attention back to the analyst. "Tell me, Ginny. Just what *is* the local government doing to get my daughter back?"

"Sir, I don't have all the details . . . by the time word filtered back to Baku—that's their capital—the government had shut down for the day. Our ambassador had to track officials down at home, or at parties . . . or in private locations. But the embassy reports the Azeris are jumping now. They don't want to do anything to jeopardize U.S. support. And Ambassador Kandinsky will be going up to Yevlakh personally in the morning." She looked at her watch. "It's morning over there now."

"This Kandinsky a good man, Ginny?"

"Yes, Senator." She looked warily at MacCauley. "But he really *is* operating on a shoestring."

Trost sat back. "Well, maybe we need to send him a little help. Who are our experts—I mean the *real* experts—on that godforsaken place?"

The analyst and MacCauley exchanged glances. Then Mac-Cauley said, "Well, Senator, you know with all the cuts we've been taking, with the downsizing . . ."

"Ginny? Who do we have that knows anything about that place?"

She regarded him earnestly. "I guess I'm it, Senator. As far as State goes. Although the embassy staff has a better day-to-day feel for things, of course."

"Would it pay us to send you over there to help find my daughter?"

Trost watched the muscles in her face, the thoughts in her eyes. No fear. She wanted to go. Hungry woman, hungry for anything. Fine grades and failed relationships in grad school, then set adrift in a sea of nasty little cheats. And asses like MacCauley. The senator thought he knew her answer in advance, so he was surprised when she said:

"I've served in that country, Senator. I helped open our embassy. I just came back a few months ago." She looked away from his gaze. "As much as I hate to admit it, a woman comes up against brick walls. You just knock your head against them. It's still a man's world out there."

Trost smiled so faintly that a camera would not have captured it. "It pains you greatly to say that. Does it not?"

The analyst had a defeated look. Trost did not want her to feel defeated already. The fight was just starting.

"Senator, it pisses me off beyond description."

"You're honest, Ginny. Rare thing in this town. Ever need a job, you come on over to my office. Meantime, tell me who the best-qualified males are. To go over there and dig up Kelly."

He was instantly sorry for his choice of words. He believed in luck, which he viewed as a fragile thing.

"Well, frankly, the best man's already on the scene. At least, the best one I know. He's an Army lieutenant colonel"—she smiled, thinking something private—"but he's really more of a—"

MacCauley cut her off. "Really, I think we'll want to minimize the military's involvement in this."

"Drew? Why don't we hear our expert out? I happen to be very impressed with her judgment." He turned his attention back to the young woman with the eternal dark circles under her eyes. "Tell me more about this lieutenant colonel of yours."

She shifted as if trying to find a way of standing that would make her more confident. "He works at the embassy. As a temporary military representative. We don't actually have a military attaché there because of . . . but that's beside the point. His name's Evan Burton, and he's been in every ditch in the region. Knows everybody, speaks the languages. He's . . ."

Trost smiled more openly. "He's exactly who you'd like to be. Right, Ginny?"

She blushed.

"So," Trost continued, "you think this wild man of a lieutenant colonel's the one to find my daughter?"

The analyst nodded. "He knows how things work. When I was at the embassy . . . whenever I had a problem, he'd fix it, or explain . . . he used to make me so damned angry." She looked Trost in the eye.

Suddenly, a terrible thing happened. Trost felt tears burning. He had just flashed on Kelly as a little girl, running to him with a smile of unguarded joy.

The senator took a moment to compose himself, touching his eyes with a handkerchief with a blue monogram. Then he said, "Well, Drew, I'm sure we can put this lieutenant colonel to work on the case. Give him a free hand and everything. Along with all our other efforts, of course. I'll talk to the Sec-Def about it, make sure we're covered on that front. And I'll give the chairman a ring."

"If that's what you want, Senator."

"That's what I want." He thought more lucidly again. "NOIWON out on this?"

"Every terminal worldwide should have the report by now. Everybody'll have their ears to the ground."

"Word's going to get out. Always does."

MacCauley shrugged, unsure how to answer.

Trost focused his mind on business. "We'll have to prepare a statement for the press."

"We can handle—"

The senator held up his hand. "No. My office will take care of it. E-mail you a copy." He considered the analyst, who truly did look weary. "Just to make sure our collars and cuffs match. Anything else?"

MacCauley and the analyst shook their heads.

Trost stood up. He felt battered. "You know," he said in a quieter voice, "my first impulse was to rush over there and get my hands on the problem. Get on a plane tonight. Just to be closer to Kelly. But I suppose I should at least wait and see what these bastards want, find out exactly what happened. I suspect I can bring more guns to bear here in town than I could out there at the back of beyond."

MacCauley started in with some bullshit about giving diplomacy time to work, but Trost walked away, paying the man no further attention. He had been thinking out loud, an uncharacteristic action. But nothing felt the same now. He felt unusually alone. Helpless. He wondered where his daughter had been taken, who had done it, how she was being treated. It struck him that Kelly was the only thing in his entire life he had been able to love unselfishly and enduringly.

For the first time in as long as he could remember, Senator Mitchell Trost was afraid.

CHAPTER

. . .

Burton sat with the ambassador on the rooftop patio of the American embassy. At seven in the morning, August was bearable, but you could already feel the sun getting ready to hit you like bad news. Both men were in their shirtsleeves. Drinking bad coffee to beat down the lack of sleep. They knew they had to return to the issue of Kelly Trost, but their mutual weariness held the world in suspension. Drink the coffee. Suck in the last coolness. Rally the inner troops.

The embassy had been the mansion of a financial buccaneer during Baku's first oil boom. The Reds came and made it a clinic in which there was never any medicine, then a library in which the books were inaccessible. Sited on the ridge that curled around the old city, the embassy had a privileged view of the bay that gave you the Caspian blue but hid the mud flats spiked with antique derricks and the ecological desolation just around the headland. With a breeze down from the Caucasus to shift the oil smell, Baku looked and felt pleasantly Mediterranean in the morning light. It was a place where every appearance tricked you.

The ambassador could fool you, too. Almost six feet tall, he gave an impression of smallness, with his fox face and the feeble mustache twitching under the loose nosepiece of his glasses. He smiled with the left side of his mouth and his voice chipped at the air. You might have cast him as the clerk who watched the pennies so closely he missed the theft of millions. Yet Burton judged him to be the gutsiest diplomat with whom he had ever worked. Kandinsky was the kind of man opponents would always underestimate until he had them sublimely outmaneuvered—the perfect ambassador for a region where nothing was quite what it seemed.

Burton gazed past a stained apartment building that blocked a slice of the view and watched a sea-tug tow an enormous oil platform toward the heart of Asia. He sipped the gringo coffee the embassy imported and said:

"Really think the Russians will let that oil come out through here?"

The ambassador did not answer immediately. Cheap china clinked and Burton looked at the man, whose glasses had perched at a mad-professor tilt. They had both worked much of the night in their overlapping worlds.

"Our little Russian brothers don't much care for the idea," Kandinsky said in a slowed voice, "but if we're really good, we can shove it down their throats." He took another sip of the coffee.

"Are we really good?"

The ambassador smiled his lopsided smile and readjusted his glasses. "We'll find out. Russians hate the thought of losing the money, losing control. And they truly hate the prospect of one of the backwaters of the old empire hitting the jackpot while the Kremlin can't pay the grocery bill." He drank and smiled, and his glasses listed again. "Jealousy is the most fundamental of Russian characteristics. Closely followed by greed. Peasant culture. Rest of it died in the camps."

"I've never believed the Russians would let a pipeline leave the Caspian. Not if they can't control it."

Kandinsky put down his cup. "That seems to be your favorite song these days, Evan. If I didn't know you better, I'd suspect you of defeatism. By the way—mind if I hold onto the Dexter Gordon disc a little longer? Catherine adores it." He reset his glasses. "Anyway, we'll see. I'm more worried about our own government than I am about the Russians at the moment. Pipeline decision's coming in October. I'm afraid Mac-Cauley's going to have us in bed with the Russians again. Which is a prospect I find as morally repugnant as it is strategically futile. You know, I've really got to get these glasses fixed." He took off the frames and regarded them with concentrated sorrow, as if a friend had let him down, then he leaned closer to Burton. "Speaking of getting in bed, Evan . . . I'm not one to pry into the personal lives of my staff. But I would be grateful if you could be just a *bit* more discreet with Heddy Seghers. My colleague the German ambassador has sent out invitations to an engagement party—I don't suppose you've received one?"

Burton looked at the ambassador without answering.

"I'm not telling you to join a monastery," Kandinsky went on. "Just use the back door or something. Helmut's head over heels. And we need him on the pipeline team, Evan. I'm looking for an ideal score. Azerbaijan: one, Russia: zero. And local independence preserved, thank you." He looked at Burton with an expression that had turned inscrutable. "By the way . . . think you could find out from Heddy where he stands on the EU development loans?"

Burton laughed. "Thank you for making your position so clear, Mr. Ambassador."

"I try to do my duty. Which brings us to the point. The girl. The missing Miss Trost."

Burton's cell phone rang. But it was only the office driver reporting his return with a topped-off vehicle.

"Everybody I could track down was drunk or in the dark or both," Burton told the ambassador. "Wonderful world of Azeri Islam. Prez is out of town for the CIS meeting. Akhmedaev's up on the cape with his mistress, so I couldn't bother him. I think the other players are ducking us until they figure out the position they want to take. They've got the little guys jumping, but that's a circle jerk." Burton waved away a fly. "The big guns absolutely do not know how to handle this one. They're in a panic. And an Azeri pol in a panic does the same thing his ancestors have been doing since Alexander the Great dropped by for the weekend: He disappears."

"Help them out, Evan. Show them how to handle it. Point out that Senator Trost could kill their pipeline deal deader than Lenin."

Burton drew his sunglasses from his shirt pocket and put them on, softening the world. "*A Lenin zhiv, tovarisch posol.* I'm going over to the Interior Ministry. Ambush Hamedov when he shows up for work. Every dirty thread in this town leads to the good general. And he owes me."

The ambassador snorted. "As you owe me. Preferential study visa for that lying bastard's nephew."

"Price of doing business, sir. And I admit a soft spot for Brother Hamedov. He always lives up to his rumors."

Kandinsky nodded. "I suppose none of us is a model of probity out here, Evan." He put his glasses back on and looked off toward the sea, his profile unheroic. "The future of continents is being decided right here in the middle of Bumfuck, Nowhere, and the department's worried about hurting the feelings of every drunk in Moscow." The ambassador turned his crooked glasses and dark circles toward Burton. "You have any idea how many cables I just ignore?"

"Trost isn't on any of the key committees for the pipeline," Burton said. "Or am I missing something?"

The ambassador shook his head. "Mitch Trost probably never heard of Azerbaijan. Until his daughter decided to come out here and save the world." He touched the edge of his glasses, straightening them for an instant. "But the Senate's a lot like Russia, Evan. It's a feudal society. All personal allegiances. If we can't ship Kelly Trost home with a smile on her face and an FDA seal on her little blond rump, he'll start a wave that'll drown the pipeline, Azeri independence, and at least one frustrated ambassador. And he'll do it without breaking a sweat." Kandinsky worked his lopsided smile into one cheek. "Then he'll move on to things he thinks are truly important."

"What are you going to do?"

"Go up-country. Stand on the last-seen-alive spot. Show the flag." He stripped off his glasses as if sick of them and gave Burton a milky gaze. "God knows, you're the man to go, Evan. But if I don't put in an appearance and give them good cable on it, we'll have more help out here than we need. And I expect the press to hit town by sundown. Sniffing for blood." Kandinsky gave up on blindness and put his glasses back on. "Meanwhile, you check out General Hamedov. And any other newly democratic, reform-minded thieves you can grab by the sleeve. I'm convinced that everybody in this place knows who-what-why-when-and-where five minutes after Fanny drops her knickers. We just have to crack the code." He sat back, with the day's heat avalanching. "That ride up to Yevlakh is getting to be one of the dullest drives on earth. Like commuting across Utah. But that's where all the action is. Any contacts up there I should talk to?"

Burton thought for a moment, with the penal humidity tightening his collar and making a noose out of his tie. "No, sir. To be honest, they wouldn't talk to you. Gunslingers, and proud of it."

Kandinsky nodded. "Guess I'd better drop in on the station chief, then hit the road. Just wanted to touch base, see if you'd turned over any lucky rocks." He stood up, drawing Burton to his feet as well, then hesitated before leaving. "And, Evan. Please. Help me keep the DCM out of trouble on this one. I've loaded him down with other projects, but he's itching to get out front and make a friend on the Hill. Have Sergeant Spooner or somebody keep a discreet eye on him in their spare time. I want to know if Arthur starts getting too chummy with the press."

The Deputy Chief of Mission was Drew MacCauley's watchdog in the embassy, dispatched to ensure Kandinsky did not do any sudden harm to the Administration's "Russia First" policy. The commissar system was alive and well.

"Roger, sir."

The ambassador smiled. Everything about him was slanted: his smile, his glasses, his thin shoulders. "Bothers him that you don't wear a uniform. I had to point out to him that it's State's own policy out here. I think he's afraid you'll be mistaken for one of us."

"God forbid," Burton said.

Burton sensed the identical tone of their thinking about the DCM, a hippo named Arthur Vandergraaf who hid from the heat in his office and composed endless "Eyes Only" messages on his computer. Certain of his skill and slyness, he hinted clumsily to the Azeris that they should deal directly with him if they really wanted to tap the sources of power in Washington. Completing the package, he had roaring bad breath and a perky, savage wife whose ambition dwarfed continents.

The ambassador made a time-to-go gesture. "Don't be afraid to bang on the desks with our Azeri brothers. I'll back you. Make sure they understand the ramifications."

Heat coming down like John Henry's hammer. Traffic fumes from shoddy engines browned the air. Another day in paradise. Well offshore, the oil platform under tow still provided the focal point on the horizon.

They walked across the patio to the door that led to air-conditioned safety and the stairs.

"Trost girl's not a bad kid, from what little I've seen of her," Burton said. "Self-righteous, bit of a smart-ass. World according to grad school. Positively glows with belief, though. Wants to save the world on her summer vacation." He breathed air that had been poisoned for a century. "I'm on her side, you know."

The ambassador paused with his hand on the door latch and looked at his partner in strategy. "We all are, Evan. At least, I hope we are. But she's a long way from home. And in way over her head."

Two men sweating in the hard sobriety that follows a sleepless night.

"Bet she's scared shitless right about now," Burton said.

The ambassador's face looked unusually old and vulnerable in the hard light.

"If she's still alive."

The Ministry of Internal Affairs occupied a building where nothing quite worked. An arch carved with vines hinted at the region's heritage, but the rest of the exterior was Stalinesque bulk. You went in and hit the Soviet ghost-warp, with dank halls where the light had been soaked in varnish and the smell hinted at public toilets. Only the bosses had air conditioners and the heat mulled. Secretaries loitered like hookers to the music of a lone manual typewriter. The young officers had post-Soviet uniforms that did not fit, while their superiors wore suits from a thirties gangster film. The best offices had personal computers on prominent display, but Burton had never seen one being used. The elevators were used as storage closets.

It was a marvelous place, an informal museum of the bad old days when the world had been simpler, if less interesting. One key difference now was Burton's unescorted presence. Half a dozen years before, he would have been shot for nudging past the guards. Now they greeted him with lazy respect as "*Podpolkovnik Boortan*," bound by long habit to Russian military titles.

A bad painting of President Aliev stood watch where the main hallways converged, and Burton offered the old survivor an offhand salute as he passed. Aliev was an old KGB hand the Russians had putsched in to get rid of Elchibey, who had been talking too much Islam. But Aliev underwent a Pauline

conversion to Azeri patriot that had frustrated the boys in the
Kremlin for several years now, and the old man had survived
two Moscow-sponsored coups against him, declaring all the
while that Azerbaijan was going to pump its own oil and keep
the profits and the Russians could bugger off. Aliev even had
the West convinced that Azerbaijan was tilting toward true
representative democracy, which was about as likely as the
Saudis running Bar Mitzvah tours to Mecca.

It was not yet nine, and Burton expected to wait at least
an hour in Hamedov's outer office before the general arrived.
But this was an age of surprises. Just as he crested the stairs
and turned toward the general's office, the door opened and
Dick Fleming came out with Hamedov smiling behind him.
Fleming was an oilman with contracts and contacts everywhere, a Euro-accent, and a U.S. passport. Heddy described
him as the kind of man who could make a woman shudder
just by walking past her desk. The general had a friendly grip
on the double-expat's upper arm.

When he spotted Burton, Hamedov lost his smile.

"Colonel *Burton*," Fleming said, quicker than the general.
He wore a gray suit the color of a deep-sea fish, while
Hamedov, a slave to post-Soviet fashion, wore a double-
breasted purple number with a polka-dot shirt, a white tie, and
a bulge under his left armpit. Beefy, with black hair greased to
his scalp, the general looked like a bouncer in a Third World
disco. An utter contrast, Fleming was detention-camp thin,
with hair and skin the color of paraffin. The oilman put Burton
in mind of the kind of guy who bargains with cheap whores
for a discount. As a character summation, Fleming was *persona
non grata* at the embassy, thanks to his taste for bribery and
an aptitude for lying to the ambassador's face.

"An unexpected pleasure," Fleming continued. "And here
to see our friend the general." He offered his hand insistently,
and Burton gave it a perfunctory grip, then wished he hadn't.
"Well, business, business. What do we Americans like to say?

'Hundred miles an hour. This train never stops.' My regards to our ambassador. Tell him not to work too hard."

"You're going to come to a bad end, Fleming."

The oilman smiled. "Race you there, old boy."

"Evan, my great friend," Hamedov said, his voice slower and eyes sharper than the oilman's. "I think I know why you are coming to see me."

"Yes, well," Fleming said, still smiling. He had craggy nicotine chops that told you his first visit to an American dentist had come as an adult. Although the embassy was not allowed to keep files on U.S. citizens, Burton knew the man's original name was "Vlaminck," that he had been born in Liège, and that he lied about having a degree in economics. "I'll let you two military men talk state secrets. If there's no money in it, Dick Fleming's not interested. Stars and Stripes forever, right, Burton?"

The oilman pumped off down the steps, leaving Burton and Hamedov facing each other with two of the least sincere smiles in history.

"My good friend," Hamedov said, taking Burton by the upper arm as he had his previous guest. "I am so relieved to see you. I was afraid I would not be able to reach you on the phone. I pledge to you the full of my cooperation. But you must come inside."

Hamedov had been a junior captain when the Soviets pulled out not half a decade before, but he had the good fortune to have been born in Nakhichevan, as had both Presidents Aliev and Elchibey, as well as a third contender, a Russian puppet named Mutalibov. Nakhichevan was a very small territory separated from the rest of Azerbaijan by a forlorn, well-armed strip of Armenia, but it produced big men. Hamedov had also had the good sense to stick by the government when the mafia crowd from Gyandzha launched a near-thing coup, and he had the even better sense to stay off the Karabakh front lines, where reputations were lost but never gained. All the while, the new general developed business connections, about which he bragged, with Russia, Turkey, Iran, and Israel, as well as with the pipeline consortium. On some days he was a general, on others a businessman, and he had reportedly shot a man to death in a nightclub because the victim would not let the drunken general dance with his wife. Hamedov was the perfect Post-Soviet Man: Everybody knew him, everybody owed him, and sensible people feared him.

The general had a large office with high windows, stained red velvet drapes that were always three-quarters shut, and a green carpet dotted with burn marks. Smoke ghosts floated lazily down the long room. A computer sat entombed in dust, the fax machine never worked, and the Panasonic television was usually tuned to the bingo-hall glamour of the local station even when official guests were in the room. This morning, though, the room was silent and Burton could hear the traffic sounds from the boulevard and the general's breathing. There had not even been a secretary or bodyguard in the waiting room.

Hamedov offered Burton a seat at the conference table that abutted his desk, then bent to the cabinet behind his chair. The general lifted out a tray with cordial glasses and a half-empty bottle of brandy, placing it under a big framed photo of President Aliev.

"Mr. Fleming has an ulcer, you know. He cannot drink like a man. And he has no woman. I do not know why he bothers to remain alive."

Burton noted that the brandy had an Armenian label. Ethnic hatred never stood in the way of a good drink in Baku.

Hamedov handed Burton a glass. He knew Burton would take only a token sip, but it was part of the ritual allowing the general to knock a couple back. Like the Russians, the Azeris could drink phenomenal amounts of hard liquor and continue to function.

The general drank the brandy as a shot, sighed, and said, "First I must ask you. Is this a serious thing that you have said to me last week? You will retire from your army?"

Burton let the brandy touch his tongue, then put the glass down on the table. "Next June. Twenty years. Time for life number two."

"But this is a wonderful thing! You must think about my offer. How much money we could make together! What partners we would be!"

Burton smiled and shook his head. "I told you, Hassan. When I pack it in, that's it. I'm going to just walk away from it. Literally. Backpack with a change of shorts and socks and a couple of books. I'll send you a postcard."

"But you could become a very rich man in Azerbaijan. You speak Russian, Turkish . . . you know many secrets. There would be everything for you."

"I think I might take up the saxophone."

The general waved his square chunk of face back and forth like a flag of surrender. "But this will be such a waste. With no money and no position, how will you make the women come to you?" He brightened. "You know, there is a woman I wish you to meet. She is half-Russian, but a very nice girl. Not one of these Russian women with so much paint. You will like her."

It was Burton's turn to grin. "I never sleep with agents. Not even if they work for a friend. Besides, I hear all the Russian girls want to marry businessmen now."

"Oh, no," the general said seriously. "That was last year. Now they wish to marry a husband from the mafia. More money."

"Well," Burton said, calculating that he had let the banter go on long enough to be polite, "I've come to talk to you about a woman, as a matter of fact."

Hamedov dropped his smile. He put down his emptied glass and began to pace, cracking his knuckles as he went. He looked out of a window at the old town across the boulevard.

"What are we to do? What are we to do now?" He waved a paw, then went back to working his knuckles. "We wish for our American friends to be happy. We wish for good business. And now some terrible enemy has taken a revenge on us . . ."

"Who do you think grabbed her?" Burton asked.

The general turned to face him with an exaggerated expression of disgust. "Who can have done this? You wish to know the view of Hassan Hamedov? *I* think it is the Armenians. They will do anything. They have no morals. The Armenians would even steal a woman."

Burton kept his smile at the level of a polite suggestion. "Hassan-*bey*, I have too high an opinion of the Azeri army and of your own subordinates to believe that the Armenians could slip through your lines, kidnap a girl your agents had under surveillance, then get away."

The general made a conspiratorial face from a silent movie. "The Armenians are devils! They are capable of anything, so long as it is evil. I tell you that America cannot trust them. It is a great foolishness." Firecracker pop of a knuckle.

"I'd just like to go over a few other possibilities with you," Burton said. "In case it wasn't the Armenians." He looked up at the general. "Any chance it could have been Iranians?"

The general's eyebrows caterpillared up and down. Groucho Marx, professional wrestler. He took out a battered pack of Marlboros, offered one to Burton although he knew the American did not smoke, then lit one for himself from a silver desk lighter in the shape of a Grecian vase. "I tell you, the Iranians are terrible, too. But they are our brothers, of course. I do not think they have taken Miss Trost. They are not so good at these things as America believes. You know their women come here to work as whores? In Baku, where no one knows them? Then they return to Iran and make a good marriage as a virgin. Never trust an Iranian. They are the Armenians of Islam."

"Could it have been some Iranian faction, though? Or any kind of religious fringe element?"

The general dropped into his big chair, exasperated, working his cigarette hard. "Those people are the worst. Nothing but trouble. I think it must be better in America, where there is no God. These religious people are all liars and thieves in the night. But they would only make a kidnapping of a man. They do not believe anybody would pay enough for a girl."

"Is it possible that somebody followed her? From the refugee settlement where the girl was killed? Maybe they took her as an act of revenge?"

The general shook his head fiercely, rising again to head back to the brandy bottle. "I tell you, Evan-*bey*, nobody on this earth is worse than those country people. They are nothing but bandits. Every one of them. Sometimes I don't know why we must fight for them in this war. They would betray you for a handful of *pilaf*." He drank another shot and sighed. "I think there is no chance they have taken Miss Trost. They are all afraid of the police. They are only brave in their mountains. They are like lost sheep now."

"The Russians?"

Hamedov grunted and flopped into his chair again. "The Russians are capable of anything. *Anything*. The Russians are animals. But why, I think, will they take Miss Trost? The Russians want to be America's friend so they can take your money and so that you will look away when they kill Chechen grandmothers. I think any man is a fool to trust the Russians. But why will they take away Miss Trost?"

"You tell me, Hassan-*bey*. Your knowledge is far beyond mine."

The general ran a paw over his chin, smoothing out the alcohol sweat. "You know what Hassan Hamedov thinks? I think maybe Miss Trost has a lover. Maybe she has gone away with her lover. Azeri men are very charming." He dropped his cigarette butt on the carpet and wiped his nose on his sleeve.

"What about the dead driver?"

"Maybe this is a *jealous* lover. Maybe Miss Trost has had two lovers. Maybe more. You will excuse me for saying so, but your women have the energy of lions."

"I met Kelly Trost a few times. I never got the impression sex was her top priority."

The general smiled, spreading the whiskers that had already counterattacked after his morning shave. "How can a man of experience such as yourself say so foolish a thing? All women want sex. That is all they think about. And money, of course."

"Let's just scratch the lover theory for now."

"But you can never trust a jealous lover. The men of Azerbaijan have great passions."

"I think we could trust him not to follow her all the way to the front lines." Burton refused to smile anymore. "What about a dissident Azeri faction? Maybe the Gyandzha crowd? They'd like to embarrass President Aliev."

Hamedov spit on the carpet. "Those scum. Nobody is lower. They are worse than the Armenians. Worse than the Russians. They are traitors. Filth upon the earth. But they could never have taken Miss Trost."

"And why is that?"

The general made a gesture of breaking something over his knee. "It is because we have broken their backs. They are finished. Nothing is left. Only some human filth that we have not taken the bother to clean up. Besides this, they do not want more attention from America. They wish to take over the government, to sell America the oil. But first they must not make America angry. They think the CIA will come, and your Marines, and then they will never make a coup. The vermin of Gyandzha are not the ones who have taken Miss Trost."

"Maybe a rape-kidnapping?"

The general sat up straight. "The men of Azerbaijan do not rape. They have no need. All of those stories the Armenians tell? All lies. *Lies.* Terrible lies that smell like the sewers of Yerevan." The general made a disgusted face. "And I, too, have seen Miss Trost. She is not the beautiful movie star."

"She's presentable. Just out of grad school and going through her I-want-to-be-unadorned-so-I-can-find-truth phase."

"What?"

"And she's blond. That's always a good sell locally."

"She is too much your boy named Tom."

"So who did it? One faction trying to embarrass the other? A plot within a plot?"

Hamedov smiled and lit another cigarette. "See? You are thinking like one of us. You could be my greatest business partner. Here in the Trans-Caucasus, everyone lies. Except the men of Nakhichevan. So . . . I think it is anyone who could have done this."

Burton raised the flat of his hand. Okay. Let's stop the bullshit. The room was hot and scented with brandy and smoke, but Hamedov had not thought to turn on the air conditioner, a Turkish-made machine that had been working during Burton's last visit. Was the general trying to sweat him out?

"I know American politics can seem very complex," Burton said. "Even contradictory, Hassan-*bey*. But let me share something with you. Something very simple and clear: The father of Kelly Trost is Senator Mitchell Trost. You know that already. But I would fail in my duty to you as a friend if I didn't tell you that Senator Trost is an extraordinarily powerful man. He has the power to determine votes in Congress. He even has the power to block many of the actions of our President. He certainly has the power to block U.S. backing for something as minor as an oil pipeline. And if the United States does not back the Trans-Caucasus pipeline, the Europeans will get cold feet. Everybody will go back to the Russians and the pipeline will go north. The independence of Azerbaijan will not get the international support and attention it deserves." Burton paused as if he were reading poetry aloud, then added, "And the oil money will go straight to Moscow."

The general opened his mouth to speak, then restrained himself. He laid his half-finished cigarette on the edge of the table and cracked his knuckles again, sweating into his collar. Suddenly, he rose and strode over to the air conditioner, turning it on and cursing. Then he stood with his back to the window, making his face very dark.

"What must we do? How can we help our American friends? I have already told you we will do anything . . ."

"We need to find Kelly Trost. And she needs to be alive when we find her."

The general shook his head. When he spoke, his voice was less confident and it sounded far more honest. "If I knew who has done this . . . they would cry out for the mercy of death." He came back to Burton and sat down again, forgetting the cigarette that was burning into the table. His face was earnest. Or it had the appearance of earnestness, which was all Burton expected. "I will tell you a thing now that I believe you do not know." His eyes were brown and warm and deadly. "Yes, we had Miss Trost under the surveillance. A car with two men has followed her. And these two men are discovered where they have gone to rest and eat their lunch. They are dead, these two men. With bullets in the head. It is a shame to my service. I have had to explain this to *my* president, who is most unhappy, before he will fly to the CIS summit." He waved his butcher's hand. "I think the men who have done this are not afraid of us. This makes me very worried for Miss Trost."

Burton laid his jacket and tie on the passenger seat of the jeep, clipped his cell phone to his belt, then told his driver to go back to the embassy and wait for him to call. He needed a bit of time alone. Thinking time. Besides, the driver was on Hamedov's payroll and Burton was not in the mood to be monitored too closely.

He walked down Istiglaliyat Street with the old citadel wall on his right, a relic of the days when Baku had been a khanate and pirate's nest. To the left, sagging enclosed balconies and struggling trees shaded the side streets. From a block away, everything looked picturesque. Seen close, the exteriors were shabby and buttressed with garbage. When you walked by the houses in the morning, the doors stood open for the coolness and the women sat gold-toothed in kitchen caves, slicing the ingredients of the midday meal into enamel bowls. Burton liked to walk the back streets, to listen and learn and enter this other world to the degree an outsider could, and usually the city's foreignness intrigued him. But now, after a sleepless, useless night, the old fortress walls looked like bulwarks against modernity and the streets had a repellent, huckster feel. He watched as a narrow-hipped young man dropped a bottle into the gutter.

At the edge of a dappled park, pensioners sold off their libraries and heirlooms—shabby bits of nothing—and unemployed toughs loitered. Kiosks offered to change money or sell you molten ice cream. No veils here, women with nominal jobs wandered about in light cotton dresses, their high heels a cherished torment. By the fountain, two long-haired, sweat-soaked Scandinavians ate sandwiches from paper balanced on their knees, and a young mother, Scheherazade in jeans, pushed a stroller off toward the poetry musum.

The thought of the poetry museum, a unique institution so far as Burton knew, softened him toward the Azeris again. They might have picked up bad habits from every one of the countless invaders who had passed their way, but Burton gave handicap points to any people who maintained a national museum dedicated to their poets. Even if half of those poets had been appropriated from old Persia. Burton had done his time sweating in that museum, struggling to read the script in rooms where the windows never opened. Nizami of Gyandzha, too, was a refugee, a poet who had idealized an age when Persian princes might fall in love with ivory Armenian maidens. Burton found Nizami as soothing as slow jazz, music spun of words, jamming on eros. In his spare time he translated Nizami, largely for himself but wondering if he might not someday publish a collection of the poems:

Recall the white form in the water,
Woman born of roses,
Perfuming the spring . . .
Father! Behind far mountains,
I have found a love unbounded!
My horse's hooves are hungry for the road . . .

A Slavic woman with hair dyed chemistry-set blond pulled Burton back to reality. She wore the cheap, hard-colored clothes that Russian girls mistook for sophistication and she made him think of Kelly Trost, although there was not the faintest resemblance between them. Baku was a small town when it came to foreigners, and Burton had run into Kelly Trost several times at parties or embassy receptions. She was the sort you had to like even when they pissed you off, a young woman whose commitment to saving the world was sincerely meant, although much of it was really a commitment to her image of herself. Reflexively anti-military, she had not annoyed Burton much, since he read her attitude as a phase. He even suspected that she might become an interesting woman in ten years.

If she lived that long.

How many cards was Hamedov holding back? Burton was convinced that if the general really did not know who had kidnapped the girl, he was hell-bent on finding out. And the appearance of Dick Fleming, the point man for Scumbag Oil, needed to be filed for later consideration. Although the general had his finger in plenty of pies, and there was no logical reason to connect Fleming to anything other than good old-fashioned thievery.

The frustrating thing was that Burton did not know where to start. This was a country where the Israelis and the Turks teamed up against the Russians and the Iranians and nobody trusted anybody outside of his own family. The locals killed each other for arcane reasons that had festered for generations. And the stink in the air was the smell of oil. Hundreds of billions of dollars' worth of oil just waiting to flow to market. Baku was Gold Rush California with a Soviet hangover, and every bankrupt with a passport was in Baku trying to pass himself off as the next Armand Hammer. Anybody could have grabbed Kelly Trost. And they could have done it for reasons so stupid, or naive, or cynical, or convoluted, that no marginally rational human being would guess what it was all about until it was too late.

He ached for the kidnappers to go public with a set of demands or make contact with the embassy and stake their claim. Once they gave him a target, however slight, he could use his machinery of contacts, call in the debts owed him. He felt as though, given any kind of a grip, he could squeeze out the answers. And bring 'em back alive.

He turned into a cafe on the corner of Nizami Street, just across from a new private bank with a hardwood-and-glass facade that imitated Europe. This part of Baku wanted desperately to belong to the outside world. Boutiques sold Turkish knockoffs of Italian fashions, business firms advertised their vague purposes with sharp graphics, and a miniature supermarket priced its imported goods in hard currency. But the draw for Burton was the Cafe Des Artistes.

The cafe was gorgeously air-conditioned and striking to the eye: Central Asia colliding with a fifties diner and struggling to pass itself off as a Parisian cafe. With Viennese pastries, hamburgers, and kebabs.

He ordered a Turkish coffee and mineral water from the main counter, then went to the pastry stand and picked up a dish of profiteroles half submerged in chocolate pudding and sprinkled with ground pistachios. Self-conscious about his weakness for chocolate, he usually came to the cafe alone, designating it Official Thinking Place Number Four. Only Heddy really knew how badly he was hooked on the cocoa bean, since he used her to import German Ritter Sport bars—the proletarian revolution in fine chocolate.

He took his time, rationing the flavors, forcing himself to think through the weariness.

It really could have been Armenians out to embarrass the Azeris.

Or it could have been Iranians or Russians intent on showing the U.S. Government that Azerbaijan was unsafe at any speed and a bad place to invest your pipeline dollars.

It could have been Azeris doing a double sting on the Armenians.

She could even have been grabbed as a fuck toy for some back-country strongman with a yen for something blond.

Terrorists. Patriots. Yahoos. Take your pick. Kelly Trost might just have been a target of opportunity, not a premeditated grab at all. An apple plucked from a roadside tree.

Burton spoke to the empty chair across the table. "Just keep your ass alive, kid. I'll find you."

He treated himself to another cup of coffee, wondering whose office he should haunt next. It was a poor way to go about it, begging for crumbs from officials who probably did not know a damned thing, but he was not a detective by trade and he did not know what else to do. Then the old man came in and captured his attention.

He wore a shaggy Caucasian hat despite the heat, and his clothing combined discolored trousers and a Western-style shirt with a long belted robe. His beard and exposed hair were yellow and white, and his face had the texture of a raisin. Just down from the mountains, maybe to buy his son out of the military, he seemed shocked by the changes since his last visit to the city.

He stood before the counter, hands in his belt, face upraised. Trying to read the menu posted above the wall of rugs. If he was literate, he had probably gone in his lifetime from Persian script to Cyrillic. Now his aged eyes confronted a Latinized alphabet borrowed by a people aching for a Europe and America they knew only from videos and magazines. Studying the list of offerings and prices as though it were holy writ, he looked fragile and ancient and lost in time.

Burton was about to offer to translate for him, perhaps cornering the man into what could have been an interesting conversation, when he found himself on the floor.

The bomb blew out the windows on the Nizami Street side and carried enough force to rearrange the interior of the cafe. After a moment's silence, the screams and moans began, and Burton did a quick inventory of his body parts.

Then the shooting started. Weaponless, Burton flattened himself on the floor, shouting for everyone else to get down.

Automatic weapons and pistols dueled out in the street. Intermittently, a sequence of bullets chewed into the rugs on the walls. Burton saw blood nearby, but it was not his. A woman crawled across the floor, shrieking.

Full-scale battle.

Men shouted in the street, their words clear in the brief lulls that punctuated all shootouts. Burton's first instinct had been to judge it another coup attempt, but the language had a different feel.

Gang business.

More bullets tore up the restaurant at standing height, and Burton turned to scramble for better cover. Then he saw the old man.

His mouth was open and his eyes shone in wonder. He turned as if doing a slow-motion whirling dance, the skirt of his tunic billowing as his hands interrogated the smoky air.

Burton launched himself, intending a tackle. But he was afraid that knocking the old man down might do more damage than a bullet. So he lifted him like a child and ran through the debris, carrying him behind the trench of the pastry counter.

"Get down," Burton told him, gesturing in case his words would not be understood. But the old man had awakened from the shock. He understood. Instead of taking cover, he drew a dagger from his belt and made for the door, calling out what

could only be curses in some mountain dialect. Unlike the low-land Azeris, the hill tribesmen never backed away from a fight.

This time, Burton got him from behind by the shoulders and pulled him down hard. The knife dropped.

"Listen," Burton said in his best Turkish, "we'll fight later. They have guns."

But the fighting was already over. A few last shots pocked from down the block, and sirens rose. The cafe was noisy with fear and confusion, and there was some blood, but Burton did not guess the human damage to be severe. Flying glass caused superficial head wounds. Lot of blood, but not much harm, so long as you did not take it in the eyes. When he wiped his hand over his own face, the fingers came away bloodied.

Unneeded, he headed for the street.

The cafe customers had been lucky. The street and sidewalk were cluttered with writhing bodies. Friends, relatives, lovers emerged from cover, calling out names and wailing in discovery. At the edge of the plaza, a security man in olive fatigues and a black beret emptied his magazine into a twitching body, holding the weapon one-handed. The target jerked as if given electric shocks. Blood spread over the pavement as if a tub had overflowed.

Somebody had hit the bank. The newly renovated building showed a smoking cavern at street level. Bits of furniture and clothing lay everywhere. Burton thought he was looking at a chunk of blackened building material when he realized it was a limbless human torso.

Bank job. On a crowded street. Where you couldn't even park a getaway car because of the pedestrian zone.

A mother ran back and forth, clutching a bundle of bloody rags that held her infant. Her mouth was a cartoon of a scream.

Burton, too, had been shocked. By the blast itself, then by the idiocy of it all. But he made himself snap out of it.

Before he could move, the old man in the robe came up beside him, *kindjal* in his hand again. But he held the weapon loosely and ineffectually, and his expression showed that this sort of violence baffled him far more than the menu had done. In the mountains, cruelty always had a purpose.

He spoke to Burton, looking for a kindred spirit, but Burton could not understand the dialect. The old man's eyes were Circassian blue, touched with glaucoma, and bewildered.

Burton smiled weakly at the old man and said:

"It's Chinatown."

Then he left the old man's side and made a tourniquet of his belt for a quivering, legless girl who would not find a husband now.

CHAPTER

Mitch Trost valued exercise and the psychological armor of routine. He rose for the last coolness. After paying the tax on his prostate, he pulled on his running gear, flicked on the coffeemaker, and stretched on his front steps before launching himself into the green-and-black shadows of Georgetown.

Apparitions of Kelly followed him down to M Street and across the bridge onto Pennsylvania Avenue, where the summer-term students from GWU were dragging each other home after Friday night parties. Two girls still young enough to disregard self-preservation looked right through him. The prettier of the two wore a ring through one nostril and had dyed her hair obsidian, but Trost had no difficulty picturing her as a suburban housewife ten years hence. Kelly, to her great credit, had never been seduced by the superficials of rebellion.

Perhaps, Trost thought, it would have been better had his daughter been more trivial. Better a pierced navel at home than a bullet over there in Shitsville.

No. No bullet. He could not allow himself even to think that.

He followed the avenue past the Old Executive Office Building, its gray stone blushing lavender and rose, and wondered where his daughter was as he passed the White House. He would return from his run, eat, and dress, then face a grumpy press corps whose weekends would have been spoiled. Then he would try to reach anybody else who might have the power to help. He envisioned a day of disappointment and frustration, hating his powerlessness to break the world to his will the one time it truly mattered.

He retraced his steps of the night before along Pennsylvania, then jinked up Seventh Street, unwilling to go all the way to the Capitol this morning. He made the Chinatown Gate his turnaround point. A black man with spikes of hair and torn Army trousers slumped against the metro entrance, waking in slow motion, and an early bus stopped with a grunt.

The house would be empty when he returned. Laura had wanted to spend the night, to offer him comfort, which was a woman's way of moving in for the kill. He adored women, but they fit into a space with distinct boundaries, and he valued female companionship only during the florid initiation of relationships or when women he had underestimated caught him off guard. Men fared little better in his life, for that matter, and Mitch Trost had thousands of acquaintances but no close friends—although several men believed they were each his sole confidant. In women, he valued a sort of exclusive availability, in men reliability and utility, and, jogging past the hideous bulk of the convention center, he wondered if he had not followed a policy of containment toward his own daughter, too, the one human being he had always believed he loved beyond measure.

What in the name of God was Kelly doing over there anyway? What was she trying to prove? Fiddling about with a bunch of dirty buggers who no more wanted to better themselves than a hillbilly with his trailer paid off. She was a pretty enough girl, if no beauty, and she had brains and talent and she could have come to work in Washington or taken over the management of her mother's horse farm out in Fauquier County, or done any damned thing she wanted. What had he done wrong? He had tried to play by the rules of fatherhood, and had convinced himself Kelly and he were friends. He had even pretended to consult her on his vote whenever social legislation came up, and he had not touched one of her college friends, despite the bluntness of their availability to him.

The sheer cementness of H Street revolted him, and he turned up toward Massachusetts, with its trees and decaying embassies. Sweating his way around DuPont Circle, he ignored a "Don't Walk" command. In front of the Starbucks, a bald man with a row of silver earrings and a motorcycle jacket sat cross-legged on the ground, weeping and clutching a large velvet slipper to his breast.

Trost ran on through thickening air, through light rich as flesh. The city was up to its Saturday morning yawns now, and the senator followed Embassy Row for a few more blocks, cutting left at the Ritz-Carlton to catch the bridge over the Rock Creek Parkway. As soon as he reentered Georgetown, his legs began to ache, an old horse sensing the barn door. He kept himself in good shape, out of pride and convinced that a man's life was over the day he no longer appealed to women. But his pace had slowed over the years.

He would have to see MacCauley again, and that was never a pleasure. Mr. Potato Head from the CIA was out of town, but the deputy dogs would bark more freely for that. The Chairman of the Joint Chiefs had connections in that part of the world, and he might be able to bring local resources to bear. The man could get the military intelligence side of things running at full speed. The White House needed Trost's vote this week, so, as a minimum, one of the moral dwarfs would call over to express the President's concern and the First Lady's sympathy. Krem would probe him, wondering if there might be a positive spin in direct Presidential involvement.

Trost followed a line of grand old townhomes with alarm system signs displayed prominently in their miniature yards.

He was going to abuse his position, milk it for all it was worth, and he did not give one damn about the ethics involved. Kelly was more important. Confronting a mental image of her being abused by brown, vaguely Arab men, Trost shivered as though the temperature had plunged fifty degrees.

A door opened and a woman in a blue robe stooped to pick up her newspaper.

The tall houses and trees here kept the cool longer than in the rest of the city, and Trost was sweaty but not drained as he broke stride and began to walk. A block ahead, his home waited: a decidedly empty place this morning. Three stories of Philadelphia-style red brick facade, plus a basement archive and library, it had been built by a Union general who retired to defraud veterans through bogus railroad shares.

He stretched on his front steps again, feeling his body's resistance, feeling old. Kelly was all that there was. Without her, pointlessness. No lover's threatened loss had touched him a tenth so deeply.

He picked up his newspapers and worked his house keys out of the little pouch fitted in the waist of his running shorts. When he opened the door, the coffee smell fell on his face like a veil and the alarm system beeped. He drank mineral water first, rehydrating, bringing the bottle with him as he came back out to the foyer to peel off his running shoes and his socks.

Hung on a wall just inside the doorway, the family pictures of his father's rough-cut Dutchie forebears mingled democratically with the Main Line Quakers and fakers into whose hermetic world the old man's political stature and bank account had allowed him to marry. Actually, that was not correct. His father had not married in. His mother had married out. With her illusions of artistic talent, she had, he knew, embarrassed her bloodline. And his father, an aristocrat born to a semiliterate family that had hacked a fortune out of anthracite, had married against the advice of his mentor, the governor. Married for love. It meant that his father never moved beyond state senator. His mother had been steely in her selfishness, physically fragile, arguably insane, and beautiful in a manner that wanted a portrait, not a photograph. Kelly, with her swimmer's muscles and quickness, her jeans, T-shirts, and activism, was as far removed from her grandmother's universe as blood could let her go.

Now she had been removed from him, too.

He poured himself a cup of very dark coffee and noticed the light on the answering machine he kept in the kitchen. He poked the play button and listened, expecting to hear Ruby Kinkiewicz's voice telling him about a press query or sharing a new bit of information, but the caller was male and unknown. Trost alerted: his home number was unlisted and very carefully guarded.

The voice was middle-American, more confident than intelligent, with a businessman's hasty rhythm: "Senator, this is Bob Felsher of Oak Leaf Oil. I apologize for calling you at home, but we just want to help out, if we can. Our company rep over in Baku hunted me down on my boat and filled me in on the incident involving your daughter. Senator, we're very well-connected in that part of the world, and we have people and access where the U.S. Government doesn't have a presence. Been there longer than the embassy. I've told our man over there, Dick Fleming, to drop everything else and see if he can't help find your Kelly. If you can find the time, I'd like to fill you in on our view of the situation and what we might be able to do to help." He left a private number with a prefix Trost recognized: Potomac, Maryland, home to many a serious campaign contributor.

Trost's first reaction was outrage. His phone number was a secret just one step down from the nuclear release codes. How on earth had this man Felsher gotten it? Trost did not even believe he had ever met the man, although, in Washington, it was impossible to be sure. But oil was not one of his issues, and he tended to go straight party line on energy bills. At most, the guy would have been a handshake in a receiving line or an introduction in a hallway.

Ruby would never have given the sonofabitch his number. And if one of the staffers had done it, he or she would never do it again. Simmering, Trost peeled off his wet shirt, dropped it on the floor, and took his coffee upstairs toward his shower. But he made it only halfway. He stopped and looked around his home in sudden confusion, transported to rooms impossibly foreign. His world had blown apart, and the extent of the destruction hit him like a fist.

He sat in a good chair and wept.

"I weep ten thousand tears to think I must disappoint you, Mr. Burton," Fahrad said, "but I have heard nothing of this girl."

Burton nodded and waited. The hotel room harmonized one ugliness with another, old pasteboard furniture set against walls marked until they resembled an abstract-expressionist painting. The adhesive stink of the plumbing met Fahrad's dinner of goat cheese and the air conditioner moaned and blew heat. A bottle of Iranian pop had the sullen fizz of toxic waste.

Fahrad always had the same room in the Hotel Azerbaijan and the same view of the Soviet-gothic Palace of the People's Powerlessness and the boatless quay, with its cranes in the background like a fringe of dead trees. That meant the Azeri secret police would have the walls wired. Maybe the Russians, too. Or they might be working the same listening post, since the formal hostility between the two governments had not severed the old security service ties.

Let them listen, Burton thought. I want them to know this one's serious.

Fahrad touched his beard like a character from a black-and-white film, kissing the air with his lips. Flies raisined the cheese. "I tell you this. As a friend. I do not believe the Government of Iran has done this kidnapping. I cannot speak for every Iranian person, but, as a friend, I believe I can assure you our government has not done this. You see, the clever people in Teheran—not the religious ones, who have no proper education, but the clever men—they know we must deal with America again. I think it will not be this year. But the time is coming. And these men want to shake the hand of America, not to slap the face." Fahrad smiled, teeth white and straight in the frame of his whiskers. "You will laugh, Mr. Burton. But these men still hope the great pipeline will go south. It is the shortest way, you know. Through Iran to the Gulf. And it is the best economics. This oil—it is not for Europe. Your own oil people say it will be for India, for China, for the expansion of the Asian market. Why should this oil go to the Black Sea? What sense is this? Should your country and mine do something so foolish because a handful of yesterday's mullahs and the lobby of Israel still want to make hatred between us? What is better for peace than good business?"

"Fahrad, my brother . . . if you don't object, I'm going to share your insights with our ambassador," Burton said. The ambassador already knew this particular riff by heart, of course, and Washington was no more going to let a major pipeline go south through Iran than the President was going to enlist as a private in the Army. But Fahrad, the shabby merchant of nothing much, was an Iranian diplomat in mufti. Since U.S. officials were forbidden to talk to Iranian officials, Teheran had, as usual, found a practical way to send messages to Washington. Telling Fahrad Adjami that he would report the conversation to the ambassador was the price Burton paid for getting the information he wanted in return. "I would be grateful, though, if you would use your contacts to gather any information you can on the whereabouts of Kelly Trost."

Fahrad shooed a fly from his block of cheese and it flew past Burton's face and into the bathroom. The Iranian's hand returned to his beard. "I swear it. Out of my friendship for my American friend. The moment I return to Tabriz, I will ask everyone I know. And the bazaaris know everything. If an Iranian . . . or a Kurd or one of these Turks . . . has touched this senator's daughter, I will return immediately to tell you of it. Better still, I will telephone to my friends here, and they will bring the message to you immediately." He looked into Burton's eyes. "I believe I am right that the Government of America would be grateful for Iran's quiet help in this matter."

Burton touched his hand to his heart. "A lifetime could not repay my gratitude."

"A lifetime can be long or short. As Allah wills. You have cuts on your face. I think you must be more careful."

"I was downtown when the bomb went off at the bank. I caught a little flying glass."

The Iranian's hand stopped at the tip of his beard and he smiled. "And if my whispers are correct, you have not even had the time to finish your sweet?"

Burton's face did not change. Everybody in Baku spied on everybody.

"It wasn't a very appetizing sight," he said.

The Iranian shooed another squadron of flies and cut off a slab of cheese with a kitchen knife. He extended the white rectangle at knife point. "Will you eat now?"

The lobby howled with squalid maleness. The cheese had been good, but salty, the crust of bread that accompanied it dry, and Burton bought mineral water—that, too, from Iran— out of a refrigerator an ambitious local had set up in an alcove. Plastic bottle sweating in his hand, he pushed out into the twilight, nodding to the hotel's security guards, two young thugs with cast-off uniforms and Israeli submachine guns. He crossed the boulevard to the seaside promenade, heading for Charley's American Bar and Grill, where the here-for-the-duration expats linked up with the locals who wanted their money.

A typical Saturday evening crowd decorated the park by the water. Ranks of young men strolled along in clean shirts, their imaginations outstripping their romantic possibilities, and young women—never alone—paraded arm in arm, feet slow and eyes quick, with an elder trailing them like a detective. The lighting along the waterfront made an old-time carnival of the fresh darkness. There were even a few rusting kiddy rides. For pennies, you could buy ice cream that would make you shit blood for a week, or good kabobs sizzling on tin grills. Old men played chess in the shadows and a few slivers of neon, hints of a distant, desired life, colored in the gaps between dusty trees. The Azeris were well-behaved, solemn in their joys, and the occasional eruption of a knife fight was far more likely to be over a point of honor than a result of drunkenness. Just before you got to the Maiden's Tower, there was one good restaurant with jazz not quite bad enough to keep him away. Burton strolled through echoes of "Mood Indigo" played through blown speakers and dropped his emptied water bottle in a trash bin.

He did not trust anybody here, but he accepted Fahrad's take on things for the moment. Back in Washington, the analysts would likely jump to the conclusion that the Iranian government was behind the kidnapping. But Burton did not buy it. Fahrad was right. The Persians were financially on their butts and the bearded bastards were still hoping against hope that the pipeline would go south, bringing them oil bucks and strategic leverage. People here lived rich fantasy lives and walked over quicksand. If there were any Iranians in it, they would be free agents.

Charley's American Bar and Grill would never be the target of a bombing. It was a curtained-off enclave in the basement of a big sports hall that now served as the headquarters for an American oil services company—platform builders and pipelayers, an outfit that could not lose, no matter who won—as well as housing a mafia-owned Scandinavian furniture outlet and video-rental shop, a woman's clothing store that specialized in astonishing undergarments and was owned by security services officers, and a luxury auto sales dealership reportedly in the president's family. The parking lot mixed old Volgas with new Volvos, Chaikas with BMWs and Jeeps, and there were enough milling bodyguards to form a platoon. A weightlifter beside the front door prissed in a burnt-orange, double-breasted suit with a lump under the left shoulder large enough to be a light artillery piece.

"Looking good, Shamil," Burton told him. "The girls can run, but they can't hide."

"I introduce you to good girl," Shamil told him, but Burton was already inside and heading for the stairs. He could hear the noise from the bar already—Texas laughter, North Sea crude jokes, Parisian declarations, and universal bombast. Charley's was Rick's from *Casablanca* for the nineties, where polo shirts substituted for Bogart's white dinner jacket and the in-crowd played oil deals for hundreds of millions instead of roulette for a handful of francs. Roughnecks from camps down-country complained of the vipers, and a man with an Armani jacket and a soaked forehead wailed that all of the filters expressed in from Frankfurt were of the wrong density. Charley's offered Western liquor and beer, curries and burgers, and the walls back from the curtains were covered with pastel caricatures of the clients. Burton was up there. He had been beside Heddy, until he asked Charley, a son of the Lone Star Republic by way of Pakistan, to move his picture to a less confrontational spot. The staff were Indians, Paks, Irish, Azeris—well-intentioned, forgetful, flirty—and slightly out-of-date rock from a Jap stereo made up for the lack of a piano jockey. It was a place where a patient man with a little money in his pocket could learn a great deal.

Burton worked the crowd at the bar, where the oil boys with big biceps and bigger bellies herded three-deep. None of the drill-till-you-drop crowd mentioned Kelly Trost to him, but a foreman cursed the local government for yet another rumored import-tariff hike on seabed exploration equipment. Didn't they know they were cutting their own throats? Couldn't the ambassador do something? In the background, a grunge band whined on compact disc. A Kuwaiti out of the University of Texas fit a Tuborg draft into Burton's grip, telling him for the hundredth sad-eyed time how much he missed Saturday nights on Sixth Street.

"Ah, the women of Austin," Burton's interlocutor said, "with this golden hair so big and beautiful! They are not afraid of you!" His expression dreamed away continents. "I am born to be a Longhorn!"

Finally, Burton got his lower ribs in against the bar and asked the chief barkeep and watchdog what the rumor mill had to offer on Kelly Trost.

"Fook-all, since you're asking," Eamon half shouted in his ear. "Gang-raped and dead in a ditch, they tell me. Who carved up your face?"

"Who's 'they'?"

"Mostly Bernard. Little French shit she wouldn't give it to. Wishful thinking, you know? Fooking frog don't know a thing. They never do. Bad business, though. Innit? Kelly's your good enough sort."

"She ever hang with the local bloods, Eamon?"

The barkeep laughed. "Too much of the queenie for that. Give the wogs a handout, but none of your sweet kisses. Don't think she'd even do an Irishman, though I never asked. Never one for your serious sort, not me. Enough of that back in Dear Dirty. 'But what does it all mean, Eamon dear?' 'Means I just bloody fooked you, and there's the sum of it.' Heddy's not by, if you were on the edge of asking. Fooking reporters slithering in, though. Boogers all questions, but they don't listen to your answers. Never tip, your journalists. All shite."

"How about Razim?"

" 'The Prince of Thieves?' Owes me a fooking new carburetor, for which I was fooking daft enough to pay him in advance. He'll come by, though. Early, innit? Tell him I pick out his ice cubes with my left hand."

"Thanks, Eamon."

"Ho, Evan. You're still six inches over for a Welshman. Big mick must've got the old girl going down to chapel."

"We grow 'em big in the States. An Irishman's dick can get three inches long in Boston. What's got a hundred feet and four teeth?"

"Piss off."

"Line waiting for a Dublin pub to open."

"Piss off before I do ya."

Burton took a table where he could sit with his back to the wall and he ordered the curry of the day from Leila, a local waitress who wore heavy makeup and blue jeans. Burton had long since figured out that Leila did not mean to flirt but was the prisoner of genetic programming.

A small man with a limp who had become something of a mascot to the expat crowd shuffled over to Burton's table. Balding, with a mouth that hung open as he moved, he reminded Burton of the happy camper in Munch's painting "The Scream."

"*Bey-effendi,*" the little man said as he slowed his approach.

"Talaat-*bey,*" Burton answered. The beer was almost gone and it had made him very much aware of his lack of sleep. "Have a seat."

The little man shook his head as if it would be too dangerous. He existed in a universe of imagined dangers. Instead of sitting, he used the opening to curve around the table until he could share his diseased-gum breath with Burton. He bent close.

"I have most secret information," he said in the local dialect of Turkish. "It is about the woman. The Russians have taken her. She is already in Moscow. They have made her a captive in their most secret underground headquarters. Where they keep the machine that makes the earthquakes."

Burton believed that the little man believed every word of it. In a perverse way, Talaat was a sanity check, delineating the most outlandish concoctions of the regional imagination. And he could be funny as hell. Once, just for a hoot, Burton had cabled in one of little Talaat's fantasies to his masters at the Defense Intelligence Agency, only to be horrified by an excited follow-up query mentioning that the report had been included in the President's daily intelligence brief.

"Talaat-*bey*," Burton teased as he took out his wallet, "you're the most valuable spy in Baku."

The little man raised his hands in horror, waving them back and forth like a chorus girl. "Oh, no. No, *no*. Not a spy. You must not say such a thing, *Bey-effendi*. I am only the lowest of your servants."

Burton gave him the equivalent of a dollar and watched him shuffle off, wondering how many of the marvelous rumors that seasoned the city actually originated with Talaat.

The noise level rose back at the bar. A moment later, Razim, another local legend, appeared after running the gauntlet of oilmen. He had promised some of them tires, others awaited helicopter parts or antiquities. Razim, a born smiler with a basketball of flesh under his discolored linen suit, assured them all that they would be satisfied the next day, and he had the magic to pacify men who had cursed him a moment before his appearance. The trick, of course, was that Razim always came through in the end. He had been a black marketeer, if more quietly, under the Soviets, and he was a black marketeer now. His ancestors had probably been black marketeers under Darius and Cyrus.

Depending on whom you listened to, Razim was either incalculably wealthy or living from one grubby little deal to the next. Burton was one of the few foreigners who had ever been invited to Razim's home, a modest compound in a suburban village where his kinsmen kept sheep and light artillery. Burton genuinely liked the Azeri, who was remarkably intelligent, adored the old Glenn Miller tunes Stalin had tolerated, and could recite classical poetry by the hour. But Burton had no idea whether Razim honestly reciprocated the feeling, or secretly despised him, or both. On the practical level, Burton steered all of his embassy's need-it-right-now materiel requirements to Razim. Razim paid him back by anticipating what America needed to know.

And Razim knew there was serious work at hand. He extricated himself from the evening's more prosaic business and headed for Burton, arriving at the table just as Leila laid down the plate of curry.

"Bring me a mineral water," Burton told her. He nodded toward the approaching Azeri. "And a Coke for my friend."

Razim did not drink alcohol, and Burton suspected him of being religious without any public flapping about it. One more reason to be drawn to the man.

Burton stood up and held out his hand. Razim took it and put his free hand on Burton's shoulder.

"Evan . . . you have blood on your face."

"Right. I had a ringside seat at the bank bombing."

The Azeri's brows condensed. "But you are in good health?"

"Dandy."

Razim sighed. "Are these not terrible times? When there is blood in our streets at noon? When men have fallen so low that they kidnap women with whom they are not even in love? But you must sit and eat, Evan-*bey*. Sit, and I will tell you everything."

Burton smiled, and sat, and ate. A memory of Lahore's musty alleys winked at him as he tasted the curry.

Razim adjusted the generosity of his body on the small chair, fended off a petitioner, and began:

"Now, Evan-*bey*, I know what you are thinking. You must tell me if I am a fool, but I do not think so. You are thinking, 'They would not keep this girl near where she has been over-powered. And since they would not risk bringing her to Baku, where no secret remains a secret, there are only two possibilities: They have taken her north, into the Great Caucasus, or south, into the Talysh country. Perhaps even to Iran. But where should a man look first?' Is that not what my friend is thinking?"

Chewing, Burton smiled with a closed mouth. Yes. That was what he had been thinking.

Razim broadened his smile to show a gold tooth and gold crowns. "You see how well I know my friend? But it is because we think alike. We are brothers. So I will tell you. I do not think they have taken her north. Why is that? Because I do not believe the Russians have taken her. They could kidnap such a woman to advantage, but they do not have the imagination. They are like petty criminals, your friends the Russians. They never think beyond the next trivial advantage. I cannot explain how they produce masters of chess." Leila brought the drinks and Razim immediately drank half of the Coke. "I think the people who have taken her are foolish people. And the most foolish people are the men who turn religion into politics and politics into religion. It hurts my soul to speak this, but I wager that she has been taken by men who misconstrue Islam. Wait and see."

"Something to eat, Razim? Curry's good today."

Razim made a politely dismissive gesture, then touched his stomach as though it were made of the thinnest crystal. "I eat too much. I love the fruits of the earth the way a young man loves women. I must be more cautious." He lifted his hand higher. "The heart, you know. Perhaps you will make me take exercise with you? But we will talk of that another time. This poor girl. I have helped her find batteries for the relief vehicles after they have been stolen." He held up his thumb and index finger, shaping them into a tweezers. "And I have not taken a sliver of profit, do you know that? How could I take money from someone who has come to help my countrymen who are too greedy to help each other? How the Russians have ruined us! Only the mountain people still have virtue." He finished the Coke and cleared his throat. "My friend, I think these things: I would look first in the Talysh country. Up in the hills. You know what a wild place it is. Almost a state of its own. What a perfect place to hide the girl! If they are threatened, they run across the border into Iran."

Burton touched his mouth with a paper napkin. "Why not take her straight to Iran?"

Razim pulled his bushy eyebrows together. "I have asked myself this. But I think this only happens if the kidnappers are Iranian secret police, and I do not think that is the case. I do not think Iran wants trouble with America just now. And it would be much harder to keep the secret in Iran, where everybody is afraid, than in the Talysh Hills. You have been to the Talysh country. It is a wild place, a place as terrible as it is beautiful."

Everything Razim said made sense, and Burton had worked through most of it on his own. But Razim seemed so sure of himself, Burton wondered if there might not be more to it.

"Okay, Razim. Say I want to check out the Talysh Hills. Where do I start?"

Razim's smile waxed again. "Here is where your brother Razim is of service to you. You know how those people are. Backward, still living in their clans. You must start with the big man, the one who knows everything. The man who says yes or no to everything, from marriages to blood feuds."

"Which one of the clans do I start with?" Burton pictured the hills that rose coolly from the coast, their northern sides green, the southern slopes burned brown.

Razim stroked the air as if smoothing out invisible folds. "Oh, I think there is no question about that. You must start with the chief of chiefs, Haji Mustafa Galibani."

Burton felt gravity tug on his expression. "Galibani? Razim, that guy's the heroin king."

His friend shrugged and drew back his smile, looking down at the checkered tablecloth. "Evan-*bey* . . . people make many claims. Who knows what is true? I only tell you that Galibani is the man you must deal with. He knows everything that happens between Lenkoran and the occupied zone."

"I take it you know him."

Razim shifted his weight. "A man in my business meets many people. I have enjoyed Haji Mustafa's hospitality."

Burton was accustomed to the talk-around-it mode of doing business in this part of the world. But he was tired now. "Are you telling me . . . that Galibani *wants* to see me? Give it to me straight, Razim. We're pals, right?"

The Azeri moved around in his seat again. "Evan, my

friend . . . I say to you . . . perhaps only this man can help you. That is my offer to a friend. Perhaps Galibani wishes to talk to someone. Perhaps you are the best person. And perhaps there is not so much time." He was not making eye contact now. "You know how these people are. They make a deal with one person, but they are always wondering if there is a better deal to make with someone else. Their only loyalty is to the family. To the clan. Promises to strangers flow like a river. Maybe Galibani thinks you could offer more than these dirty kidnappers. If they happened to pass through his territory."

"All right, Razim. Sold. I'll go down in the morning. He still have that mansion on the hill above Lerik? The one that looks like a fort?"

That surprised the Azeri. "You know it, then?"

"God's country. One of the beautiful places on this earth."

Razim warmed again. "Is it not, my friend? My mother was Talysh, you know. Or perhaps you do not know. A marriage to erase a stain of blood. Very unusual."

"You're an unusual man, Razim-*bey*."

"I think from you that is a compliment."

"Meant as such. So tell me. Is he really a *haji*? Or is it just a name?"

Razim sat back. Burton tried to catch Leila's eye to order another Coke for his companion, but she ducked between two Scandinavians in wilted business suits.

"Has he been to Mecca?" the Azeri asked the ceiling. "Who can say? I have heard that he is absolutely devout. Others say he never went farther than the brothels of Beirut. Before the civil war, of course. But he is respected on his own lands. And the government fears him."

"Razim, the ambassador's going to shit a brick when I tell him I'm going down-country to visit Galibani."

"The ambassador likes you, Evan. You are the only one he trusts. He will forgive you. And doesn't he want the girl back? But here is the beautiful Madame Heddy!"

Burton looked up: Heddy working her way through the crowd at the bar, killing the roustabouts with coolness. There was no way Razim could have seen her with his back turned. Razim smiled like the cat that ate the entire Russian eagle.

"How did . . . all right, Razim. Explain."

"I have heard her voice. A man like me must know how to listen. You listen in your own way, Evan. That is why we are such friends."

Heddy smiled and waved.

"Okay, Razim," Burton said quickly. "You're going to set up the meeting? With Galibani?"

"With your permission. I will tell him you will see him . . . shall we say tomorrow afternoon? If you leave early, that is enough time. And you must stay overnight. Haji Mustafa's hospitality is as it used to be among the Talysh. Before the Russians came, with their piggishness. When men understood their responsibilities."

"Men never understand their responsibilities," Heddy said, her Turkish quick and exact. "Am I interrupting a very interesting conversation?"

Burton rose to his feet, a bit late. "Every conversation with Razim-*bey* is an education," he said. "You look worth fighting over, Heddy."

And she did. Tanned, her hair pale and precise, she wore a short midnight-blue dress cut to show off her legs and mask her hips.

"I think our ancestors would have made great wars over such beauty," Razim said, rising heavily and bowing. Then, for just a moment, Burton could feel Razim's brain at work, a precision instrument. The Azeri continued. "How sad it would be not to see two such people together. But I must go. Evan-*bey* has given me a wonderful commission and I must work very hard."

Heddy gave the two men a what-are-the-little-boys-up-to-now smile.

Saying farewell, Razim put his stubbly cheeks against Burton's face, a common enough gesture of friendship to pass as routine, but, with his warm, wet smell pressed to his friend's cheek, the Azeri whispered, "Be careful with Galibani."

As Razim lumbered off to do business at the bar, Heddy took the seat he had occupied and asked, "All right, Evan, what did he whisper to you?"

Burton smiled. "That you're the best-looking piece of ass this side of Malibu."

"Come on."

"Ohne Ableitung."

"And your President's a faithful husband."

"Now, now, Hedwig. Be diplomatic."

But her smile was already gone, so Burton dropped his. She began to speak, then stopped, so Burton said, "I thought we weren't going to be a public item anymore. You do look great, by the way."

"Oh, stop it. Damn it all, Evan. I want to ask you something. A favor."

"Ask."

"Come home with me tonight."

Burton figured he was getting old. A lovely woman whom he desired and liked had asked him to go home with her, and all he wanted to do was catch up on his sleep. He thought of the long, hot drive down the coast in the morning. But he only said:

"What's the matter, Hed?"

Suddenly, tears rose in her eyes. She fought them. "They've ordered me back to Bonn. Tomorrow. 'For consultations and advice.' I don't know what it's all about, Evan. I'm afraid Helmut's cooked something up. To keep you and me apart. I didn't think he—"

Against his better judgment, Burton reached out and closed a hand around her nearest wrist. "Probably just standard diplo-bullshit. You'll only be gone a couple days." He grinned. "Listen, let's turn it into a secret mission. You can go up to

Cologne and bring me back a box of Leonidas chocolates. Then I'll really owe you."

"Don't joke."

"I'm not joking. Those are serious chocolates. You know my darkest secret."

She pulled her wrist away.

Burton didn't get it. Heddy was one of the most controlled women he had ever known, at least in public. Now the tears began to escape.

"I don't want to make a scene," she said. "This is awful."

"Want to leave?"

She shook her head. "That's worse. Then they'll all see."

"Heddy, I've been playing twenty questions with everybody and his brother today. And I'm tired and slow and confused. Is there something I'm missing here?"

She looked up at him, her eyes darkened by the tears. Gray as winter seas.

"I *love* you. Damn it all, Evan. I *do* love you. I hate this. I don't want to marry him. And I don't want to go back to Bonn."

"Dry your eyes and let's go back to your place."

"I knew I'd find you here," she said. "I know you, you see."

"Everybody knows me."

She could not stop crying. "I know you in a different way. Better than any of them. I would even listen to jazz for you."

"Heddy . . ."

"Do I look terrible?"

"You look beautiful. Just a little damp around the eyes."

"Will you really come home with me?" She looked at him, and she truly did look beautiful. "I panicked. I was afraid I would never see you again."

"You need time to think . . . sort things out."

She raised her voice a bit too much. "I *don't* need time to think. I *know*."

"Dry your eyes and we'll get out of here." Burton tried again to flag Leila, this time to pay.

But there was more to come. Sergeant Spooner was rushing through the bar crowd like the angel of death in a plague year. Swollen with news, he looked like he wanted to shout, and only military discipline kept him from broadcasting his secret to every patron in Charley's.

Breathless by the side of the table, he included Heddy in the charmed circle of those with a need to know.

"Boss—sir—they called the embassy . . . the guys who kidnapped the girl . . . she's alive . . . they say she's alive and they got her . . . some yo-yos calling themselves the Sons of Salvation . . . they got her and they want to make a deal . . ."

Burton looked up at him, wondering for an instant whom he was going to have to disappoint tonight.

No question who it would be.

Heddy. Who deserved better than this.

"All right," Burton said. "Sit down, Spoon. Get a grip. So what do these buggers want for the girl?"

The NCO sat down and everything about him sagged.

"That's the problem," he said.

CHAPTER 4
· · ·

"They're lunatics." The ambassador pushed at the nose-piece of his glasses. "What *planet* are these people on?" He was almost shouting. "There's no way the U.S. Government could meet a single one of these demands."

Kandinsky had abandoned a reception and his tie hung in disarray, shirt collar opened. Burton had never seen the man so distraught. The ambassador looked at the Deputy Chief of Mission, whose bulk punished the office sofa, then at Burton. Suddenly, Kandinsky collapsed inward. He hunched over his desk, face in his hands for several long seconds.

Glasses at a cartoon cant, he told Burton, "All our work. This could spoil it all."

"Mr. Ambassador . . . I've got a prelim cable ready to go on it," Burton told him. "Just need your release." He held out the paper a second time. The first time he offered Kandinsky the cable, the ambassador's outburst of emotion had stopped him.

Kandinsky nodded. Burton laid the paper on his desk. The DCM strained to see the contents, although it was impossible to read the cable from where he sat. Giving up, the big man glowered at Burton: All the paperwork goes through *me*.

As the ambassador scanned, Burton looked down at the old Kazakh carpet Kandinsky's wife had found for her husband's office, which was a surprisingly humble space. The carpet's design appeared bold and obvious, unless you looked very closely and knew what you were looking for. Then there were meanings hidden in every shape, messages in each hue, signs and codes woven into the wool. Burton thought about the demands the kidnappers expected the United States to meet as a precondition for Kelly Trost's release. Their outlandishness told him a great deal about her captors, as well as making him worry all the more about the girl's chances of survival. But the very extremity of the demands made him wonder what else might be hidden behind them, waiting to explode.

The ambassador read slowly. Very tired. He took his glasses off, then put them on again.

"Good God, Evan. What are these people all about? 'Sons of Salvation.' Do they really imagine for one moment that the United States would cut all ties with Israel? Or force it out of the UN? Or use military force to drive the Armenians out of Karabakh? Or pay some undefined 'Islamic Council' a one-hundred-billion-dollar indemnity? These people can't be serious."

"This is nothing but a prank," the DCM put in. "A red herring." His face looked like a wad of chewed-out gum. "*I* don't believe this nonsense has any connection with the real kidnappers. Monkey business like this doesn't merit a cable."

The ambassador ignored him and continued looking at Burton through his canted glasses.

Burton shook his head. "Mr. Ambassador, I think the bad news is that they're entirely serious."

"That we'd withdraw all our troops from the Middle East and deny government positions to American Jews?"

Burton nodded. "Just the boys from the Dogpatch mosque on a rhetoric bender. No idea how the world really works. All they get is satellite TV and barking mullahs. Which does not make for clarity of intellect. They probably had a ball making up the demands, trying to outdo one another in pissing off the Great Satan." He thought for a moment. "Wouldn't be surprised if a ringleader or two had a half-assed Western education. Just enough to be dangerous. Pol Pot's poor dating record at the Sorbonne. That sort of thing."

"Mr. Ambassador," the DCM said, "that's all idle speculation." He sat forward and the sofa cried out in agony. "The fact is, we have no proof of anything. We can't go off half-cocked when there's so much at stake."

Kandinsky looked at the man with an expression of mixed annoyance and indulgence. "And what do *you* recommend, Arthur?"

"Wait a bit," the DCM said. "Let the situation develop. Get our facts straight."

"I'm not sure Kelly Trost would share your patience," Burton said.

Arthur Vandergraaf grunted. "Let's not lose our perspective. Miss Trost is only part of the equation. We're talking about the future of our Eurasia policy here." He wrestled in the wet clutch of his shirt. "While Miss Trost—and her father—have my profound sympathy, it's our professional duty to maintain our objectivity. If these demands hit the *Times* and the *Post*, to say nothing of *The Wall Street Journal*, this mission will be the laughingstock of Washington. We can't risk our policy on one crank call."

"Evan?"

"Arthur . . . may be right." The DCM winced every time Burton referred to him by his first name, so Burton always made a point of doing so. "No guarantees in this neighborhood. But my bet is that the call was the real thing. In this neck of the woods, even the government leaders have a skewed notion of international realities. Except Aliev, and he's God's own exception. Mr. Ambassador, I have no problem believing that a six-pack of fundamentalist yokels could talk themselves into the belief that they can change the world by grabbing a senator's daughter." He smiled sourly. "Bet they aren't even sure what her father does or what a senator is. They probably just heard through the rumor mill that she's the daughter of somebody important in the U.S. Government. And they fantasized from there."

"Preposterous," Arthur said. "But *since* we're all jumping to conclusions, let me offer my con*sid*ered opinion: This is patently the work of a highly organized group. Has to be the Iranians. Teheran's behind this. Official effort. That phone call was bogus from start to finish."

"Arthur," Burton said, "if it comes out that the Iranian government is running this as a clandestine op, I'll never disagree with you again."

The ambassador regarded both men. "I'm releasing the cable. Don't see where we have a choice. We can't withhold information on this. And I wouldn't want to." He focused on Burton. "But I have to tell you, Evan . . . I *don't* find these demands terribly credible. Arthur may be right on this one. Or maybe we're all wrong at this point. Anyway, send the damned cable." He scribbled his initials on the upper margin of the paper. "But I'm going to call back to Washington and do an informal caveat. Buy us some time." He shifted his eyes from one man to the other, glasses seesawing. "Meantime, what do we do, gentlemen?" He turned to Burton again. "Evan, there wasn't a damned thing up at Yevlakh. Waste of time."

Burton had considered keeping the next morning's destination to himself until his return. It was easier to gain forgiveness than to get permission for an unorthodox approach in the diplomatic world. But Kandinsky was under a lot of pressure, and Kandinsky was a good man. Who relied on *him*. The ambassador needed to know which trees his staffers were shaking before the coconuts started hitting heads. Burton only wished Vandergraaf were not in the room.

"Sir," Burton began, "first thing in the morning, I'm going

down-country. Unusual lead. It's sensitive, so I'll leave my driver back and take Sergeant Spooner with me. You may not hear from me for a bit—I'll be outside the cellular net. Heading down to Lerik. Got a visit set up with Mustafa Galibani."

Despite his body's dedication to gravity, the DCM almost jumped to his feet. "Now *wait* a minute. Just wait a *minute*. No representative of this mission can afford to associate with a known drug lord." He raised his chin, making him look like Mussolini posing before a crowd. "Galibani's the most notorious man in the region. Our German allies would never forgive us. That man traffics most of the heroin that hits Berlin from this part of the world. Why, they're seeking extradition even as we speak." He settled back into the sofa with a disgusted, dismissive look. "And what if the *press* got wind of it? I've already fielded two calls from reporters fresh off the plane and snouts already down in the dirt. More to come, I guarantee you."

Burton looked to Kandinsky. "Sir . . . I'll keep it as low-profile as I can. But right now it's the only lead I've got. I can't promise that anything's going to come out of this. But I damned sure do not want to sit quietly by the telephone while none of us knows where the Trost girl is or what's happening to her." He looked down at the splendid rug, then slowly raised his eyes to meet the ambassador's. "If anybody gets wind of it, you can tell them it was an unauthorized trip. Spank me. Put a letter in my file. But let's not sit on our butts while Kelly Trost is out there wondering when in the hell the cavalry's going to show up."

The DCM pruned his face. "Do spare us the melodrama, Burton."

The ambassador held up his hand: Peace, brothers.

"Evan," Kandinsky said, "I've got mixed feelings about this. To say the least. Galibani's not the sort we want to be associated with." He nudged the bridge of his glasses with his index finger. "However . . . I agree that we can leave no stone unturned. None of that 'unauthorized mission' nonsense, though. You're going down there with my approval." He raised his eyes behind his disintegrating glasses. "And good luck."

"I protest," the DCM said.

"Noted. Tell me, Evan. Honestly, now. You don't think there's any chance Galibani would grab you . . . do you? I wouldn't want two hostage situations on my hands."

Burton was not completely sure himself. "I've got something of an invitation. I think. And the Talysh take the laws of hospitality seriously. He'd probably wait till I got back to Baku before he put the hurt on me."

"Sheer romanticism," the DCM said. " 'Talysh hospitality.' Galibani's a thug and a murderer."

Kandinsky looked immeasurably weary. And the show was just beginning. He rocked back in his chair and wiggled his mustache as though a fly had come at his nose.

"I'm a little ashamed of myself," the ambassador said, as though he were alone. "My first concern should be the welfare of that girl. And I find myself thinking about *my* policies coming undone, *my* plans being frustrated. Odd, isn't it, to find out just how selfish we really are?"

Senator Mitch Trost sat in the basement of his Georgetown home, sifting through family photographs. Outside, the evening light had begun to gild the rooftops, but he had lost track of time. In the back of his mind, he remained alert to the doorbell and his expected visitor, but the rest of his being dissolved into remembrance.

Kelly with her friends from the swim team in college, a medal around her neck, her womanliness toned down by the intensity of the sport, her muscles a threat to men of his generation. A younger Kelly at Sidwell Friends, alternately earnest and daffy. On a school-organized trip to China, posing with an inconsequential boy against a backdrop of majesty. Kelly as a toddler, her mother kneeling beside her, smiling and almost likable, propping up her daughter as Kelly strained to walk.

Yes, her mother. Janet, whom he had married because her father had been a cabinet member, and because she was ornamental, and because he had been far more ambitious and naive as a young man than he was now. There had been sufficient passion to allow him to rationalize the mercenary side. They had fucked well enough to get his attention and hold it for half a decade. Janet, the beauty other men desired. The second time around, she married a real-estate developer and fellow member of the horsey set, and seemed to have found contentment as a bitch.

Following his divorce, his margin of victory at the polls had been the slightest ever. But he recovered from that. As he recovered from everything.

And now. Kelly. So blessedly unlike her mother, barring the fondness for horses. Kelly, who read and thought about the world, who was as hungry for life as her mother had been for status. He stared at an alternate take of Kelly's graduation picture in a paper jacket. You could see both families in her. But she had his eyes.

And she had his heart. He had wanted a son so badly, had struggled through the later phases of the marriage, making love to a woman for whom he felt less and less, wanting only a son from her. Until the night they fought for the thousandth time and she misstepped, mocking his folly, telling him she'd had her tubes tied immediately after Kelly's birth. It was the only time he hit her, the only time he had ever raised his hand to a woman. Because she had made him into a fool and stolen more than a decade from his life. Today, he and Janet were comfortable with each other socially, and there was no awkwardness when the hallmark events in Kelly's life brought them together in front of a camera. There they were in Charlottesville, the three of them. Smiling. The mother beautiful and dead inside, the daughter straining to leave the tomboy behind, wonderfully alive.

He recalled how he had read ''The Owl and the Pussycat'' to his little girl, only to be horrified the next day when she danced happily in front of him, singing the rote-learned lyrics to a disco song celebrating same-sex promiscuity.

The doorbell rang at last, and he rose. His knees were stiff from sitting cross-legged on the floor and he went up the basement stairs slowly, confident that his guest would wait. Later, Laura would come over, insistent upon draping him in her beauty. But now his guest was a man he had never expected to see in his home, a man of whom he had not heard until that morning.

Trost opened his front door, surprised at how much of the daylight had fled. In that other country, where strangers held his daughter, it would be almost dawn.

The stranger in the doorway smiled, then thought better of it. He looked as average as could be in a town of excruciatingly average human beings. Mid-fifties, with a paunch and a horseshoe of graying hair surrounding his bald pate. He was the kind of man who sweats intolerably, but, despite Saturday and the heat, he had put on a suit, a counterpoint to Trost's worn polo shirt and khakis.

The man thrust out his hand. "Bob Felsher, Oak Leaf Oil. An honor to meet you, Senator. I'm a big fan."

Trost felt the wet palm against his own, registered the man's inability to maintain the initial strength of his grip. "Come in, please, Mr. Felsher."

"Sorry it took so long, Senator. It's a good way down from Potomac. Even on the weekends. And then the parking around here . . . wife and I never come to Georgetown because of it."

"I was not counting the time, Mr. Felsher. On the contrary, I'm grateful for your kindness in sharing your weekend—you have a family?"

Felsher smiled with unmistakable pride. "I do indeed, Senator. Wonderful family. Wonderful wife. Two kids I wouldn't trade for love nor money. Jack's a lawyer, and our Jackie's premed." Then his guest caught up with himself and tamed his smile, remembering the reason for his visit.

Trost led the way upstairs to the formal study where he received guests.

"Fine place you got," Felsher said. "'Elegant's the word. What're these houses up to now? Mil and a half, about? Incredible, isn't it? Wouldn't want to live in the city, though."

"Please have a seat. Can I offer you a drink?"

Felsher waved away the offer. "Wouldn't want to inconvenience you." He sat down in Trost's favorite reading chair.

Trost took a seat as well. "Mr. Felsher, I have had a frustrating day. I won't burden you with the details, but the bottom line is that no one seems to know who has my daughter or where to start looking for her. Despite plenty of sincere good intentions. They have left me . . . clutching at straws." Trost smiled, inviting his guest to smile with him. "Now there has been one development of which you are likely not aware. Something quite recent. The kidnappers—or someone who claims to represent the kidnappers—phoned our embassy with a list of outlandish and impossible demands." He stared at a bookcase, unable in his helplessness to look another human being in the eye. "These . . . bastards . . . if you will pardon me . . . expect the United States to—"

"That's all right," Felsher said, smiling. He had the smile of a salesman with a very good product. "I know all about the demands. Lot of nonsense, I'd say."

"But . . . the press release . . ."

His guest maintained his smile, but it was condensed now, matter-of-fact. "As I mentioned in my phone message, Senator, we're *very* well-connected over there. Not much happens that our man Fleming doesn't know about." He made a peculiar gesture, as though smoothing invisible sheets. "You know how it is in those parts. Spread a little cash around, folks tell you anything you want to know."

Surprised, Trost put his guard up, changed his approach. "Well, good. Saves me getting angry just repeating all that crap. But—mind if I call you Bob?—I really do have to ask you something directly. Given my position in this town." He cocked his head to the side, an artist considering a perspective. "Without question, I'm grateful for your offer of help." And he was. His day had been wasted on hasty meetings with empty-handed men, from generals to sullen White House staffers. And the press had been heartless. There was so much nothing in the air that he had phoned Felsher in desperation, looking his number up in the phone book after deleting the answering-machine message in anger, hoping he recalled the name correctly. "But senators learn to be skeptical. So kindly do not be offended by my directness." He looked his guest in the eye now. "Just what is it your organization gains by helping me?"

Felsher frumped his chin as though this was a fair question that merited a sound answer. "Well, Senator, I have two responses to that. First, we genuinely want to help. And we find ourselves in a unique position to do so. Naturally, a major player like Oak Leaf looks for any opportunity to build goodwill." He chewed his cheek for a moment and his face reminded Trost of a kicked-in basketball. "The second answer . . . well, that's more pragmatic. We've already put a lot of money into the region. And the pipeline decision's coming up—you've probably heard all about that by now. Well, we just don't want that decision distorted by extraneous events—I do not mean that disrespectfully, not in the least. But we want the pipeline route selected on its business merits—within the strictures of our foreign policy, of course. We . . . would hate to see anybody, whether some renegade bunch of clowns or a troublemaking government, sway the decision of the United States Government on this one."

Trost looked at the man. Felsher had the eyes of a hound dog and the jowls of a Watergate defendant. He struck Trost as someone who would preserve his essential mediocrity through any success, making the dependability of his averageness the launching pad for further successes. He would threaten no one, and would outlast them all. Sneaky fucker, too.

"Bob, I appreciate your frankness. Always the best basis for a relationship. Wish there were more plain-spoken men in this town." Felsher's double chin quivered, as if preparing a response. But Trost pushed on. "Now, I'll tell you honestly . . . this pipeline business was nothing but a faint echo to me. Until yesterday. And suddenly, it's central to my life. But I am not in a position to make a decision or a commitment. I am . . . distracted. To say the least. My heart and soul are focused on getting Kelly back. And my mind seems to be lagging a good distance behind."

Felsher waved his hands. Wide, stubby hands. "*Please*, Senator. We're not looking for any kind of commitment. Nothing of the sort. We're on the public record as believing that the pipeline should transit Azerbaijan and Georgia, en route to Turkey and the Med. Absolutely consonant with the avowed policy of the Department of State. Everybody knows that. No secret there. We just don't want local events to prejudice anyone against an essentially wise decision. We're not trying to sway your vote. Swear to God. We're just trying to make sure . . . trying to ensure . . . that disconnected events . . ." He was sweating despite the air-conditioning in the house. "I mean, we don't want anybody else swaying your vote, either. On a level playing field . . ."

Trost wanted to put the man out of his misery. "Bob . . . I have always sought to cast my vote objectively." He was aware, even as he spoke, that this was untrue. But he wanted to mean it, genuinely did mean it on some level.

His visitor leaned closer. "Senator, our man on the scene— that's Dick Fleming, good man, good man—he's concerned that this is all some third-party plot designed to divert that pipeline." Trost could see the veins under the man's eyes, the wear on his skin. "You know yourself, Senator . . . when we're talking tens if not hundreds of billions of dollars, folks start reaching for desperate remedies. Everybody wants a piece of the action over there . . . your Iranians, your Russians . . . throw a dart at the map and you'll hit a nest of nationalist schemers or religious fanatics or mafia types . . . or all three. It's like stumbling into a rattlesnake convention. We just have to keep our heads clear."

"And," Trost said in measured tones, "we have to bring my daughter back."

"Absolutely. That's what this is all about. Of course. You see how our interests coincide? It's politics at the most practical level. We suspect your daughter was kidnapped to make Azerbaijan look bad, make the place look hostile, unstable. To move that pipeline route. So we want your daughter back safe and sound, too." He turned his face slowly from side to side. "Kelly's fate and the future of Oak Leaf Oil are intertwined. And we're going to do our damnedest for you."

Trost sat back and nodded. Sure. Why not? Nobody else had any ideas. Bring Kelly back alive and you've got my vote for eternity. Roll your dice.

He rose, drawing his visitor to his feet as well. The senator thrust out his hand first this time.

"Bob . . . I stand in your debt. I appreciate everything and anything you can do to help bring Kelly back home." He experienced the man's soft, wet grip with unaccountable intensity. And a connection snapped inside him.

Trost let go of his guest's hand and sank back down in his chair as if his legs could no longer support him. He covered his face with one hand, then with both hands. Shuddering. Unable to master himself. He did not cry. He felt suspended, shocked, the opposite of emotional. It was as though he had lost control of his muscles. His intestines quaked.

After a frozen moment, his visitor laid a hand on Trost's shoulder. It was a horrible feeling. The senator could not bear for anyone to see him like this. No one could be trusted to see him like this. But he could not gather himself.

"It's going to be all right," the man said in a baby-talk voice. "Don't you worry, Senator. You just trust old Bob Felsher."

The world had fractured and Trost could not put it together

again. He could not see properly. He could not even restrain his speech in front of a stranger.

"I don't know where she is," Trost said, clutching himself and rocking. *"I don't know where she is."*

It was horrible. She had not slept in two nights. Each time she tried to clean a spot against the wall, the bugs found her again. And it was cold. The day between the two darknesses had been brutally hot, with the room's lone, small window shut tight near the rafters. But the temperature plunged as darkness fell, and vermin sought her warmth. She ached for the next day to begin. Her prison seemed at once hallucinatory and more real than anything she could remember.

How much longer could this night go on?

The first night, a woman veiled in black had brought her porridge and water, but the water made her sick within hours and Kelly soiled the stall in which they had chained her. Later, the woman delivered a slops bucket. But she gave Kelly nothing with which to clean herself, and no one came to empty the bucket, and her stomach hurt so badly she could hardly move and did not even care about her nakedness when the frantic need came to relieve herself again. Between cramps, she curled up on the floor and sobbed.

She considered herself a capable, rational person, but she had already begun to drift into minor delusions. Her skin reported creatures even when there were none, and she imagined hands intimately upon her. Figures, their humanity blurred, moved at the periphery of her vision. Yussuf, her driver, lay in front of her with the top of his head blown open, refusing to die, blaming her. But he disappeared when she tried to touch him. She emerged from the bad drunk of sleeplessness and sickness, only to tumble backward again. The day had been a scorching, fetid twilight, the nights a cold sewer. Dehydrated, she worried about going mad. But iron sanity prevailed.

In the beginning, she had feared rape, the region's favorite contact sport, and subsequent death. Her bearded captors seemed utterly unmoved by the murder they had committed, yet they had been almost Victorian in the scrupulousness with which they handled her. They hurt her only enough to let her know they were capable of hurting her a great deal more if she made it necessary, then they left her to her fear. With Yussuf's body lying face-up in the road, the men had gone through a grim, curiously polite comedy of trying to fit a healthy, five-foot-seven American woman into a car trunk too small by half. Finally, they settled for cramming her down under a blanket in the backseat, warning in cartoon English, *"Not moof. We keel you."*

She had cowered and gagged under that blanket, breathing its residue of sweat and motor oil, as they drove on and on without stopping at any of the capricious military roadblocks that punctuated the trips of every relief worker. Once, they let her out of the car to take care of herself in a shit-studded green spot in the desert, and she could tell by the position of the setting sun that they were driving south. Toward the Talysh Hills. Or Iran.

Much later, the car struggled to climb a long mountain road, gears shrieking, until they stopped for the last time and new voices and hands led her from the car with the blanket still over her head. They guided her, stumbling, into a building, and a strong hand forced her head down each time they crowded through a doorway. Finally, they pulled away the blanket and chained her like a beast.

Her prison was very different from the refugee camps. Emptied of animals, the shed still stank of them. It was a permanent place, built of stone, fitted to a larger building. There was even electricity. Whenever the veiled woman appeared, she flicked on a bare overhead bulb that stabbed Kelly's eyes. In this part of the world, an electric light in a cowshed meant a great deal of prosperity and, probably, the nearness of a town. Somehow, the notion that a town might be nearby seemed reassuring.

Why were they doing this to her? Ransom? Politics? Revenge? No other relief workers had been kidnapped, as far as she knew. And her father was no world figure. His interest in foreign affairs had been limited to a summer with a Brazilian woman who had frustrated the household's sleep with screeching orgasms and had queried Kelly with bewildering nonchalance about her high-school "lovers."

Her father. He would move heaven and earth to help her. The thought comforted her intermittently, only to leave her feeling weak and frustrated and angry.

It was always her father.

She could not escape him even now. Nor did she want to escape him this time. She wanted him to come get her, and she could not help wanting it. She felt immeasurably alone and discovered cravings so fundamental and unglamorous they had never before entered her life.

She loved her father and liked him and just wanted a life of her own. She had hated him all the way through ninth grade. After he had walked out on her mother. But he was impossibly seductive to voters, women, and dogs, all of whom followed him blindly, hind ends wagging. Daughters were easy.

Her father could not be resisted without the benefit of a whole lot of distance. She had loved and resented him, and she had been terribly jealous. Then she watched her mother remarry awfully. Chuckie had a sprawling horse farm that ran on inertia and he never missed a chance to paw at his step-daughter. When she complained, her mother told her, "Honey, he's just trying to make you feel like family." Meanwhile, her father paced his campaign to win his daughter back. With his relaxed elegance—he was the only man she had ever known who looked sexy in a bow tie—her father treated her as a grown woman when she was not, and made her laugh with his imitations of his colleagues. Despite their scarlet willingness, he never slept with the college girlfriends she brought home for a visit. She gave him big points for that. She and her father had become pals, and it all would have been fine, if only he had not been so overwhelming.

He plagued her with help. And when his efforts rested, the zillion people who owed him and adored him reached out to take care of her without being asked. She lived in a monstrous cocoon of privilege, and the boys and men she had taken into her life never seemed consequential for long. Her father was too much. Gigantic. With his Paul Newman smile and manners inherited like family silver. Now, in this dungeon, the thought of him made her cry with anger and hope and confusion.

Swimming had been so good. It had been the one thing at which her father could not help her, something of her own at last. He had been proud of her, of course. But he could not fix the races, could not rig the clock. Even her failures were valuable to her. Because they belonged to *her, her, her*.

Lying on the stable floor, she wished she could dive into a clean pool now. To immerse herself. To dive in and shape her body smoothly and let the water strip her clean. She imagined that, somehow, she would be safe in the water, and healthy again.

Giving up swimming had been the only real sacrifice she had made to come to Azerbaijan. Where an entire sea was diseased and there was cholera in the tap water.

She swept a silk-legged creature from her ankle.

Without warning, the light went on and the woman shuffled in. She had to be old. She was stooped, slow, her quickest motions imprecise jerks. Kelly looked at the veiled black form moving toward her through shocked eyes and screamed:

"What do you want? What do you want from me?"

She thought she had screamed. Wanted to scream. But her voice was a withered croak. The old woman put the food down prematurely and scuttled off. In her haste, the woman had placed the bowl and pitcher out of Kelly's reach. The lights went off again.

Kelly strained to reach the water, clawed at the air. But the manacles grabbed the bones of her ankles and the chain would not give at all. She imagined armies of small black life racing toward her food, swarming over it, thickening her water.

She gave up, let herself lie stretched out on the floor, weeping again.

The daylight refused to return, and each time she thought she might sleep, something bit her and made her contort with exaggerated panic. Her ankles were scraped raw. Finally, she began to wail, making a dry, nasal sound that would not stop.

The door opened, and the light hurt her again. She could not look up at first. Ambushed bugs scattered over the floor.

A man entered. He said nothing, but as her eyes learned light again, she found him watching her with his arms folded. Like her kidnappers, he wore a neatly trimmed beard and a white shirt buttoned to the neck. The shirt seemed to her the cleanest thing she had ever seen. It made her dazey. And it made her cry all the more. She had never seen such a beautiful shirt.

Her visitor was a young man, slender and not tall. He had good features, but his eyes reminded her of the things that crawled over her in the darkness. Nothing in his demeanor said he was the least disturbed by the conditions in which he found her.

Unexpectedly, he smiled. With small, regular, very white teeth. The sight made Kelly aware of her own teeth, which were painted with scum. The man reached into a pocket in his baggy trousers and produced something small and brown.

It was a Snickers bar.

He lobbed it between her knees. She wanted to be proud, to show her defiance. But her hands would not obey her. She tore at the wrapper, aware of the filth on her fingers, revolted even as she hurried the food to her mouth. It was home, it was familiar, it was everything she needed. She could not think beyond it. She felt as though she had been dying of hunger.

But her system did not want the chocolate. Not yet. Her mouth would not take it. Her tongue, gums, throat were dry as sand.

"Water," she begged, unable to chew. Then she remembered their word: *"Su."*

Her visitor understood. He reached down to bring the pitcher closer to her and they both saw that the bowl of porridge beside it was writhing with vermin. Kelly shut her eyes, trying not to spit out the chocolate paste in her mouth.

The young man shouted a word. Kelly believed it was a woman's name: *Yasmin.* Jasmine. A joke of a name in this place. His voice was confident, full of superiority and ownership, the voice of a boy from the top frat transplanted to another culture.

The woman in black hurried in and the young man turned and struck her where the veil covered her cheek. She fell against the wall and Kelly expected her to break like glass. But the woman recovered immediately, as if such treatment harmonized with her life. The young man gave a series of commands and the woman grabbed the bowl and pitcher and hurried out.

The young man calmed immediately, as though emotions were a matter of choice, and said in English:

"She is a foolish woman. Such people must have many supervisions."

He spoke each word distinctly, as though reciting in class.

Kelly still could not swallow, could not speak. Her intestines were on the verge of another mutiny and she did not want to shame herself in front of this male. But only part of her really cared.

She felt as though she should rage at her captor. But she was too tired. The best she could manage was a sense of humiliation.

The young man thrust his right hand away from his torso. The gesture had no meaning in Kelly's world. "This is a bad place," he said slowly, as if reciting a prepared speech. "But such is the suffering of our people because of America. This is how *they* must live."

The woman returned with the pitcher of water, but bearing

no food. This time she set the vessel down so that it almost touched Kelly's knee and she nodded a quick bow, then rushed back to the safety beyond the door.

Still clutching the candy bar, Kelly grabbed the pitcher and drank, washing her mouth empty and clean. Then she gasped, spilling water down her chin and onto her neck and chest. As soon as she caught her breath, she drank again, eyes closed, not wanting to see anything that might have remained in the water. The liquid tasted sweet and decayed.

When she had drunk, she ate the candy fast, piggish and uncaring. She imagined that somehow the caramel texture would bind up her guts and slow the panic of her bowels. And she was afraid that her tormentor would snatch the candy away from her before she could finish. The chocolate was stale and melted to the wrapper, and its smell melted into the smell of her waste and her surroundings. But she did not stop until she had finished it.

"You see how our people must live?" the young man asked when she was done. "But without such kindness as this chocolate? Not even for little children?"

Kelly half heard the words. She wanted to eat more now, real food. And to wash. Above all, she wanted to sleep undisturbed.

"All of these most terrible conditions," her visitor went on, "come because of your father. He is a very bad man."

Kelly alerted. She felt her brain rushing back to life.

"Your father makes the children sick. He is the warrior of Israel and the great enemy of Islam. He is the lover of the Jews."

Kelly did not understand. She did not even begin to understand. This had to be some mistake.

Maybe it was all just a mistake?

"Your father makes the genocide"—he pronounced the word with a hard *g*—"against Islam people." He smiled in satisfaction. "So now we have taken his daughter."

"Please . . . I don't know what you're talking about. My

father is Mitchell Trost. He . . . doesn't know anything about foreign policy . . ."

The young man laughed with one hard, dismissive sound. "You think we are the fools? We know everything. Now your father must pay. America must pay. No more Israel. We will make the peace."

Kelly searched her memory for any remote connection her father might have with Israel or Zionism. She did not even know if her father had so much as dated a Jewish woman. Well, probably. But he tended to go for the lanky Anglo type. Redheads. And he thought New Jersey was a foreign country.

"*Please,*" she begged. "My father is Senator Mitchell Trost. All he cares about is federal grants and union shops and stuff. He doesn't know anything about all this."

The young man looked down at her with theatrical disdain. "We know everything. You cannot make lies with us. I have been to the university."

"*Please.*" Kelly tried again. "This is all some kind of mistake."

"You are a whore of America," her visitor told her matter-of-factly. Then he turned his back and left.

He forgot to turn out the light, and Kelly got her first good look at the creatures that lived with her by night.

Knowledge was not always a desirable thing.

"I witnessed the most peculiar thing just now," Bob Felsher said as he sat down to his reheated supper. "I saw a United States senator break down. The man totally lost control."

"That's interesting, dear." His wife bent to load the dishwasher on the other side of the mammoth kitchen. It was the maid's day off. When they had begun their lives together, their first apartment would have fit into this single room. Easily.

He ate for a bit, enjoying the food without paying it great attention, thinking. His wife sighed and rummaged under the sink.

"Isn't it something, though?" he asked her. "How far

we've come in life? I mean, we've worked hard for it, God knows. But just think about it, Ellen. This house. The kids. Everything. Back when we started out—you ever think we'd get this far? What a wonderful country this is." He cut another bite of roast and turned it in the gravy. Good old-fashioned cooking.

"I count my blessings every day, hon," his wife said. "The Andersons called to ask if we're free for a get-together next Saturday."

After he swallowed, Felsher said, "We'd better go. He's in tight with the Hill. But . . . just think about it a minute. How many people get to see a United States senator go to pieces before their eyes?"

"He was probably upset," she said, sitting down across the table from him. "I picked up the video you wanted. I had to pay full price, though."

When he finished eating, Felsher rinsed off his plate and put it in the dishwasher while his wife went into the den to turn on the big-screen TV and load the VCR. It was a pleasant routine, and he considered that he led a very pleasant life.

They watched *High Noon*, a favorite of his and as it was rewinding, he put his arm around his wife and said:

"That's the problem with this country today. Nobody's willing to stand up for what's right. Nobody cares about doing the right thing. It's all me, me, me."

"Isn't that something," she said.

Bob Felsher went to bed in a particularly satisfied mood and put his arm around his wife, molding his belly to the small of her back.

"Love you, Ellen."

"I love you, too."

But sleep did not come to him immediately. The truth was that he was as excited as a child. Not just because he had seen a senator break down in front of him. It was better than that. Bob Felsher had a secret. And nobody else in the entire country knew it.

CHAPTER

There are some things you do not forget. In the last days before the war went into its long stall, as the Armenian offensive herniated the country, Burton had been an observer on the southern front. Unarmed, he watched as a people who had suffered terribly for centuries burned the towns of a people who had not been important enough to suffer grandly before this, and the calculated nature of the violence twisted inside him until he did not think he could bear to watch anymore. A human landscape that had blossomed over millennia dissolved. The Armenians were much the better soldiers, and they had learned to plan, while the Azeris drank and blustered and fired off their weapons too soon. Then they ran away. The better units tried to shield the refugees, but the Karabakh troops outflanked them and shot them down, shot the survivors, shot the wounded.

Earlier, with fortune on their side, the Azeris had done the same thing up in the mountains. Then the reequipped Armenians broke into the lowlands determined to create a dead zone around their ancestral homes. For Burton, who liked and respected the Armenians, and who liked and indulged the Azeris, the butchery was as hypnotic as it was unnecessary, and he felt covered in filth as he watched on, knowing, in a deep way he could not defeat with logic, that he was staring into a mirror. The Azeri collapse was the last nudge that turned him from the long road his life had taken.

He was on a more mundane road this morning. Leaving Heddy's bed, where he had stolen an hour from duty, Burton climbed drowsily into a small Russian-built jeep driven by his NCOIC from the embassy. They drove south in orange light, rounding the headland where the road hugged the cliff above the old oil fields. It made for an ugly start. The famous wilderness of derricks was disappearing as scavengers sold off the old steel, but the earth lay black and brown and poisoned where a century of oil had been dredged. It would have been a challenge to pack in more ecological devastation per square mile than the succession of turn-of-the-century oil barons followed by the vanguard of the proletariat had managed to do. Driving past the stretch of ruined earth chilled him unreasonably every time he had to head south.

The road curved back from the sea and the oil wastes, with the headland steep on their flank, then lowered and stretched along a bay. The rising water level had overrun a complex of beach facilities, stranding rusted pavilions in the sea. The city's middle class still swam there on the weekends. Burton would not have put his toes in it. On the landward side, white flats smooth as bedsheets stretched toward the hills, and boys by the roadside hawked big sacks of salt their families had harvested. Scuttling figures tended breakfast fires in front of tents. To the south, the new oil machinery loomed hugely, the superstructures as menacing as alien craft, occupying land and sea.

Where the salt flats ended, a graveyard of military equipment spooked under dead hills. Some of the carriers and tanks had been shot through, but more had been wasted because a recruit had not known enough to check the oil and his officers had been too enraptured with themselves to bother. There was sufficient reparable gear to equip a regiment, plus a few spare battalions for the starved army, but the Azeris were content to let it all rust, guarded by a pair of sleeping boys. Once, when Burton had come down to count the hulks in response to a DIA message insisting the vehicles belonged to a combat-ready unit poised to launch a counteroffensive, a child with a uniform and a rifle had shot one round at him, then begged a cigarette, content that he had carried out his mission.

Then came the boxcars. Lined on sidings, flagged with washing, dozens of them teemed with refugees. There were over a million refugees strewn throughout the country, tucked into folds in the landscape, people of remarkable fatalism and patience, waiting day after day for a miracle to carry them home to their melon fields and herds. In the early days, Burton had stopped to talk to them whenever he could, to glean their stories, to learn these people. But he could not bear it anymore.

Instead of becoming accustomed to suffering, he now felt shamed by any tolerance for human misery. He was no longer the right man for his job, no longer detached and effective, and he glimpsed himself as a particularly useless creature this morning, hiding behind routine and the restrictions of his position. He was almost glad the Trost girl had gotten herself into trouble. The situation, for all its confusions, offered him the sort of clear goal for which he had been starved.

There are some things you do not forget. And Burton would never forget the afternoon he first suspected he would leave the Army. The Karabakh troops had shoved the unit with which he was moving out of a railroad town on the Iranian border. In truth, it had not taken much of a push, since the Azeris had grown accustomed to being beaten and usually ran after the first vanity of shots. It was not his fight, but Burton had been ashamed as he clung to the side of a jeep, fleeing with the moon-eyed officers whose soldiers had thrown down their weapons to run more quickly. The colonel, a well-connected man of endless complaints and no qualifications, stopped behind a hillock a kilometer from the last buildings, anxious to rally enough of his troops to protect himself and his loot, preening heroically now, since the Armenians never pursued until they had rendered the settlements they seized permanently unlivable. It was a war of amateurs who preferred hatred to efficiency.

Burton had lain in the scrub grass on the rise, the sandy soil brilliant with ants, watching the town's destruction through a pair of Soviet-surplus binoculars. The Armenians shot the captive males of military age, randomly beating or shooting any other townspeople who had been paralyzed by the velocity of the attack. The shots rang out clearly, but the human sounds were little more than a murmur, washed out by the distance and the grunting of military machines. Burton lay on the earth watching mouths open in soundless pleading before the rifle butts came down, and he saw the first fires bloom, and black smoke stained the sky. He had seen it all before, but never from so clear a vantage point.

A gang of men in black uniforms stormed into a house at the edge of the settlement, ripping off the door. They tossed chairs and utensils and clots of fabric out of the windows, emptying the house like a pocket. Then they drove out a white-haired man, thumping him through the doorway with the flat of their weapons, poking him with the barrels. In this silent movie, the soldiers laughed exaggeratedly, but it was impossible to read the expression on the old man's face. Then one of the soldiers dragged a young girl out of the house by her hair.

Burton would never know exactly how old she was. From her size, he guessed twelve or thirteen. But she might have been small for her age. Young enough, though. You could tell by the awkwardness of her limbs. The old man raised his arms as if begging God. A big boot put him down. The soldiers did not bother to strip the girl—both sides were shy of nakedness. They simply put her on the ground with her skirt up and her undergarments ripped away and took turns. Each time a soldier finished, the girl tried to cover herself, rolling onto her side, until the next man pushed her belly over a crate or flattened her in the dust. Burton watched, and did nothing, full of legitimate excuses, and his binoculars wavered only once, when the last man finished and shot the girl three times in the abdomen with a pistol. They did not bother killing the old man. Not long afterward, the Armenians sent a mortar round out into a nearby field and the Azeri colonel decided it was time to resume his retreat. He offered Burton a place in his jeep and a drink from his bottle of brandy.

Burton remembered that girl penitentially now, as he often did. She had no facial features in the reality of his experience, but he imagined them for her. He saw her dark, loosened hair cascading as the soldiers handled her, the bared legs so thin they were no more than slivers, and her tiny black shoes. He saw the custard rumps of the soldiers as they topped her, trousers let down only to the knees. And he saw himself among them.

At first, he struggled to rationalize his discovery, to armor himself with the lessons of history. He knew that men would always make war and that decent societies needed to be protected. It had taken over a year for him to face what he had realized on that afternoon: that he could no longer regard soldiering as a moral profession. Not for himself. You could be an honest soldier only until you realized what soldiering really meant.

Even when he could no longer hide from his new awareness, he refrained from grand gestures. Instead of resigning, he resolved to finish his twentieth year of service, to take the pension he had earned. The blood money. He imagined a pilgrim's path before him, and he told himself that he would need money for that, and he was not willing to give up everything. The truth was that he was lost. To others, he knew, he appeared the most certain of men. To himself, he seemed foolish and unknowing, except that he knew he wanted no more part of the business of violence, no matter what code or tradition dignified it. To Lieutenant Colonel Evan Burton, it was as though he had been one of those rapists. One of the glorified criminals who washed their hands in blood and dried them in a flag.

"Mind if I ask you a personal question, sir?" Sergeant Spooner said. Windows rolled up, they had passed through the purgatory cloud from a mammoth cement plant, emerging in scrub desert under a blue sky tinged green.

Burton lowered the glass again and hot air punched in. "Can't tell you until I hear the question." He knew it would be about Heddy. Spooner had a crush on her twice the size of Cleveland and he always found a way to raise her as a topic when they traveled together.

"Well . . . I don't know . . . you know, boss, I just can't see that girl of yours marrying that cum-bucket ambassador. She really going to do it?"

They entered a village of roadside compounds where children watched the world from wooden gates. Nearly every family had turned entrepreneurial, serving the trucks on the Iran run from plywood stalls by the highway. Time-warp refrigerators stood white as bone in the sun, powered by tapping the overhead lines. Cigarettes, pop, cans of beer. Melted candy and bread. Commerce.

"So rumor has it," Burton said slowly. "It would be a very good marriage."

Spooner made a disgusted sound. "Aw, come on. That guy don't look like he ever figured out your dick's for more than just taking a leak."

"Helmut Hartling is a distinguished diplomat."

"It's a waste of a damned fine woman. If you don't mind me saying so."

Burton smiled to himself, sure that Heddy would not go to waste, but not at all certain she would ever be happy.

Up ahead, a woman stood by a flimsy table lumped with purple.

"Look like grapes to you, Spoon?"

"All that fruit's going to kill you," the NCO told him. But

he pulled off the road, content with the pattern of their jour-
neys together. Whenever a road trip had to do with sensitive
matters, it turned into the Burton and Spooner Show. Burton
would do his Mr. Health Club routine with the fruit-sellers,
and Spooner would bide his time. Then, on the return trip,
with business done, Burton would drive and they would stop
now and then for Spooner to buy a cold beer from one of
the Islamic stall-tenders for whom religion had collapsed into
superstition and a repertoire of physical duties.

The grapes were fat and dark, cracking open, pungent. The
woman who offered them smiled, her belly a careless bulge
under gypsy colors. A little boy monkeyed against her leg,
naked from the waist down. Burton settled the price, then
asked if he could wash the dust off the skins. He followed the
woman into a courtyard daubed with chickens and ancient
machine parts and waited while she drew water from a well.
He dipped the grapes in the bucket, dipping his hands, too,
into the lovely coolness, then took the big soaking bunch back
to the jeep, leaving a trail of fallen fruit behind him. He broke
off a laden stem and offered it to his partner, but Spooner
made a face and ran a hand back over his chopped hair.

"Water on 'em would rip my guts open for a week. Don't
know how you do it, boss."

"You get used to it." They pulled back onto the two-lane
thread that connected different worlds, Moscow and Teheran.
"A man can get used to just about anything. That's the good
news, and the bad news."

"Back to what we were talking about, though. I mean . . .
I might as well be honest. I kind of picture you and Heddy as
a team. You're good together. You make her smile the way a
guy wants to make a woman smile."

The grapes were sweet and bitter-seeded, and their meat
was thick and wet. Yes, Burton thought, and I cannot even
talk to her. And I know things about her you will never know.

"Heddy's great, Spoon. But she mixes up what she wants

with what she needs. Given time, she'd figure out that I was the greatest disappointment of her life."

"I still think you're good together."

"It's all jazz, pal. Can't hold onto it. Here and gone. Sure you don't want some grapes?"

Spooner shook his head—he was a Southerner of the bone-faced, bad-toothed sort that had frustrated the career of many a Union commander. "Last time? When you talked me into eating that melon? I near died. So anyhow. You're really serious, right? About getting out of the Army? Haven't changed your mind?"

"I keep telling the world. But we live in an age of disbelief."

A big Iranian truck, its driver bearded and capped, passed a boy on a donkey.

"I wish just once you'd explain it to me. I mean, you got a big career ahead of you. Everybody says so. You could be a general."

"We're all dust in God's eyes, Spoon. Want a Coke?" Burton reached back between the seats to the little cooler that kept them hydrated on the road.

"I'll wait. You know, I just can't figure you out, boss. Not for the life of me. You got this drop-dead gorgeous woman who'd swim the ocean for you. And you just walk away. You got a career other officers would stab their buddies in the back for—if you'll excuse my way of putting it. And you just flat-ass want to walk away from that, too. I mean, what are you going to do with your life?"

Burton smiled, amused at the perfection of the question. They entered a town where irrigation canals and roads intersected. A huge, crumbling bus terminal dwarfed the houses, their gardens jungled with fruit and vegetables. There would be another long stretch of desert, with gray hills rising to the west, then the countryside would green and the houses would become bigger and more frequent, and the water would be close again, and the hills would become the mountain barrier that funneled nomad armies and now diesel trucks along the coast.

"What am I going to do with my life?" Burton said, tasting the question like fruit. "Told you, Spoon. I'm just going to walk. Put on a backpack and go. I'm a walking man."

"Come on, sir. You got to have some plan. Grown men don't do things like that."

But *he* would, Burton thought. His far-flung assignments had left him with old pays barely touched, with fair investments and a half-pay pension. He figured he could travel for a very long time. To see if he couldn't learn something, after all. To try to make some sense of things. He was mature enough to know that revelation was as likely to hit you in McDonald's as in Tibet. But he told himself he was not hunting dramatic revelations. He just wanted to understand a little more about the world and the men and women in it, including himself. To see if God really was in the details.

"Music?" Burton asked, unwilling to talk anymore. Spooner meant well. Younger by five years, he looked and acted a decade older than Burton, and he had the good NCO habit of wanting his officer to be the best and wanting the best for his officer. Burton valued the man and took care of him. But there were some things for which he could not find the words.

"Yeah, music time, I guess."

Burton took out a coin. "Call it."

"Heads."

It came up tails. "You win," Burton lied.

"Steve Earle."

"You got it."

Burton leaned back over his seat to the jumble of cassettes they stashed in a brown paper bag. Spoon had rigged a stereo system so that the speakers were hidden from thieves and the player could be snapped out and stuffed under a seat when they parked. Spoon was a country music fan, which was almost a requirement for an NCO, but, blessedly, his tastes included the new country that had an edge and the old music with its toothache honesty—not just the Nashville assembly-line stuff. Together, the two men had driven to the end of the world and back, listening to Johnny Cash walk the line and John Coltrane describe a love supreme, as nations withered around them.

" '*Git*-tar town,' " Spoon sang along, grinning and pressing his foot to the accelerator. But when the song was done, the NCO reached to turn down the volume.

"So . . . I guess you already got a plan, sir? To get the girl back? From Galibani? I mean, if he's got her?"

Burton gave a one-syllable laugh. "Christ, Spoon. I not only don't have a plan, I don't have a clue."

"I just thought maybe you knew something you weren't telling. You're like that, you know?"

Burton just smiled. And suddenly he realized why he had been thinking about the raped girl back at the front. It was part of the web of fears he had for Kelly Trost.

As if reading Burton's mind, Spooner said, "I got to tell you, sir, I'm worried about that girl. Decent kid, seems like. And, to tell you the truth, she always struck me as the kind who'd be a knockout, if she'd just let herself. Hate to see all this end bad, you know?"

"Five demerits for sexism, Spoon. Your sympathy is not supposed to be enhanced by the victim's attractiveness."

Spooner tapped a hand on the wheel, keeping time. "Ain't that horseshit, though? Like it isn't natural to feel sorrier for, like, Michelle Pfeiffer than for one of them lesbo professors? You can't change human nature, boss. Not even if you pass a law. Not even if you pass a whole bunch of laws. I mean, if the good Lord didn't want us to like some women better, why make them better-looking?"

The highway doglegged into the desert and power lines marched across the horizon. It would be an hour before they returned to the sea.

"Seem fair to you, Spoon? That the way a person looks determines the way a person lives?"

The NCO made a face as though Burton had tried to sell him a mule dressed up as a horse. "Like I'm Brad Pitt or something. Since when has life been fair?" He shook his head. "All this feminism stuff. As if you can bully a fella into wanting what he don't want. Just you tell me why is it all them big writers and folks got a theory why normal people are guilty of something?" He grunted. "Hell with 'em, anyhow. I figure men and women are just going to keep making babies and having fun doing it. No matter what the books say."

Sergeant Spooner, Burton thought, was the banana peel on which intellectuals unhappy with God's burlesque had been slipping since the first artist conned the first female grad student into posing nude for a cave painting. But there was more to Spooner than the man let show. The NCO had organized embassy volunteer support for an orphanage where the children had been living in bestial circumstances, and he slaved at the place in his shreds of spare time. Although he found the standard-issue tough-sergeant image as comfortable as an old pair of jeans, there was no meanness in Spooner. He just suffered from the male inability to admit to acts of kindness.

The NCO turned up the volume on the cassette player, only to turn it back down a moment later.

"I don't know," he said. "Maybe I *am* a sucker for a pretty face. Maybe I'm stupid and unfair and backward and everything. But this whole business with the Trost girl just eats me up. I mean, here she is trying to help these people out. Maybe she doesn't get it exactly right, and maybe she gets snooty sometimes. But she's *trying*, for God's sake. And they grab her butt and do God knows what with her. It just isn't right." Spooner set his face hard. "I'd just like to see the kid survive so she can wade through all the bullshit young folks are up against these days and get her head on straight. I just want her to *live*. And I feel helpless and useless and dumb as a rock. You know?"

Yes. Burton knew.

*   *   *

Haji Mustafa Galibani's youngest son—felicitous proof of his enduring virility—ran toward his father with an expression that mixed budding delight with fear. The plump boy's pantaloons billowed down from the puzzle of knots his mother had tied into the waist and he moved with choppy steps that had not yet begun to expand into manliness. The child spread his white-clothed arms to embrace his father and, with a squeal, closed them around the man's thigh.

Galibani patted the boy on the head, then slid his hand down to a shoulder. The child's bones felt fragile, innocent, and Galibani decided that such a casual gesture was not enough. He lifted the boy in his strong arms, contented with the good weight of his flesh and blood. Soon the boy would be too big to lift, and he himself would become too old. The son would lift the father. The thought filled Galibani with a honeylike sadness.

"Now, now," the man said, "what's this? Where's Baba? You should be with Baba."

"Baba's bad." The boy's expression cinched around a remembered fear.

Galibani smiled. "And why is Baba bad? I thought Baba was the one you liked best after me!"

His son shook his head. "Baba's bad. Baba's mean. I don't like him anymore. Can I have a Snickers?"

Galibani was slowly growing concerned. The boy's baba, his minder, was not supposed to let the boy out of his sight. Ever. But the man was nowhere to be seen. Galibani did not like little mysteries of this sort. He enjoyed great challenges, but problems of detail infuriated him.

"You have not eaten the good food. How can I give my son a Snickers when he has not eaten his good food yet?"

The boy smiled. "You can do everything! Everybody says so!"

Ah, Galibani thought. Perhaps he'll be a political leader. The boy knew what to say as surely as did a clever woman.

He lowered his son to the floor, then took his hand, bending down. "Now . . . where's Baba?"

The boy pointed toward the big-screen television and videocassette recorder that dominated one wall of Galibani's combination office and receiving room. "I want to see *The Lion King* again."

"Someday *you* will be the king of the lions. Now . . . where's your baba?"

"Baba's bad. I want a Snickers."

Galibani's question did not require an answer now. The boy's guardian had appeared in the doorway, face scrubbed of any expression above humility.

The boy followed his father's gaze, then tugged on his fingers. "Baba said he was going to put me in the donkey shed. Baba said there's a devil woman in there and she'd eat me up."

Galibani kept his eyes steady. And he saw that the little man in the doorway understood, clearly, that he had done something wrong. He had a hump on one shoulder and a grotesquely swollen ear, and now he bent lower than usual.

"You're hurting my hand." The boy began to cry.

Galibani took his son into his arms again. Tutting, he carried the child across the room to the minder.

"Take him to his mother. Then come back to me. Immediately."

The guardian's eyes filled with terror. Yes. He knew, indeed, that he had done something wrong. And whoever had told the man about the girl had done something wrong as well. All this deviousness would be brought to account.

Galibani had no time to spare for this petty treachery. It was noon, and the Americans might arrive at any time, although he suspected it would be an hour or two before their vehicle climbed to the hilltop. He had been thinking—thinking was the thing that made him a great man—and he had not finished his contemplation. The issues involved were complicated, and things had to be managed to maximum advantage. He was certain he could indebt at least two of the concerned parties to him, and perhaps more. But it was also folly to attempt to ride too many horses at once.

The terrified little man reappeared. His face was simple and trustworthy, but Galibani knew that no man or woman could be trusted forever. You could extend their trustworthiness only through a combination of fear and obligation.

"Take off your shirt," Galibani told the man.

Quivering, looking up, then looking away again, the man did as he had been told.

"Turn back the corner of the carpet. Farther. Stay away from the television."

The little man looked at him one last, desperate time. His mouth shaped a word, but failed to make a sound.

"Here. In front of the table. On your knees."

Again, the little man obeyed.

"Stretch your hands out to the table." Galibani took off his belt and wrapped his fist around the buckle. The weight of silver studs tugged the leather band downward.

"Please . . ." the kneeling man said, ". . . I meant nothing, Excellency—"

The force of the first lash drove the man belly-first onto the floor.

"Get up," Galibani said calmly. "On your knees. Don't touch the carpet. Who told you about the girl?"

The cringing man pulled his body back from its stone bed. *"Bey-effendi* . . . everyone knows . . . even in the village—"

Galibani hit him harder this time, drawing blood just below the unsightly protrusion of the man's shoulder. Galibani had always had a charitable inclination toward the crippled and unfortunate. He helped them publicly, had even taken this one into his household. Now he charged himself with folly. The man's soul was probably as deformed as his humped back. Perhaps Allah had wanted to punish him. And who was a man to interfere with the Will of God?

The man had collapsed again, but Galibani did not wait. He struck him a third time, enjoying the good stress on his muscles, bringing his arm back over his shoulder before plunging his entire body forward. The leather landed with a gunshot crack. Then he straddled his son's minder. The little man protected his face and head with his hands as best he could, whimpering, and Galibani, who hated weakness in men, struck him two more blows.

"Who told you about the girl?"

The man cried like a woman. "*Yasmin*," he said, his sobbing distorting the name. "*Yassssminnn.*"

"Get up. Get out of here. Don't get your filthy blood on the carpet."

The man scuttled off with his shirt balled in his paws, whining, his back glistening red.

Haji Mustafa Galibani had acquired a useful degree of religion and its vocabulary with the changing times, and he was proud of the notion that he contemplated Allah and the Prophet, Peace be unto Him, for hours at a time, although all he really did was daydream over an unread Koran. He had not actually made the Haj, but he had traveled as far as Abu Dhabi on business, and he was flattered by the title that had fallen to him after a bit of prompting. The world had moved under men's feet, and the centers of power and profit had shifted, and he had built mosques in three of his bigger villages in the past three years. He had come to consider himself a man whose life was consonant with true religion, and he relished dispensing justice to his people even more than he had in the past. In retrospect, it seemed remarkable to him that so many of his actions even during the Soviet days undoubtedly had been pleasing to Allah. In a sense, Allah had always been with him, guiding his hand.

Of course, the household staff would know about the girl. And the village. What a foolish man he had been! Greed was the downfall even of the mighty! He had not wanted to hold the girl here, his instincts had been against it. But he had made a rash decision, concerned that if he did not personally control the captive, these madmen would exploit his hospitality and protection, then abandon him without profit. All promises were dust. And the religious radicals were unholy idiots. Left alone, they would squander the fruit of their efforts, while he, Haji Mustafa Galibani, saw a dozen ways to profit from possession of this particular young woman. He laughed aloud. They had not even understood who she was.

They were fools, and fools were always dangerous.

Upon his return that morning from two days of not unpleasurable business in Lenkoran, he had been appalled at the conditions under which they had been keeping the girl. He had ordered that she be bathed and cleanly dressed and treated with decency. They claimed to be religious men, but they treated a pretty girl like the lowest of beasts—a thing which not only might bring about needless quests for revenge, but that could devalue her trading worth. Fanatics had to be watched with a gun ready in your pocket. Haji Mustafa Galibani intended to profit enormously by delivering the girl to the right party at the right time, while letting the radicals— who soiled the teaching of the Prophet, Peace be unto Him— pay the just price of their actions.

And there were so many possibilities. Everyone wanted the girl. He had been wise enough to see opportunity when it settled on his roof.

The thought should have pleased him. But his day wore a complexion of bitterness. What if some fool dropped a loose word around the Americans? The man from the embassy, Boor-tan, had a reputation for cleverness. Perhaps it had been folly to invite him here? What if he were forced to kill him? And to do so while the man was a guest? Perhaps he had been too impatient? The thought that he might have erred enraged Galibani. He wiped the wetness from his belt with his hand, secured it around his waist, and stamped out of the room.

He told himself that he had to make certain that his instructions regarding the girl were being carried out. But the truth was that he wanted to look at her again. She reminded him of Sharon Stone. Certainly, the girl did not have the full beauty of the actress, or the glamour, but even degraded by filth she was young and Western and very blond. Galibani had never possessed a Western blonde, only false Russian blondes who turned out to be as black as their souls. He knew he would be man enough for a Western woman, all of whom wanted nothing but brute sex and who could not be controlled by their weak males. It angered him peculiarly to think that the girl in his power had probably already had many, many lovers, despite her youth.

In the sage judgment of Haji Mustafa Galibani, the video *Basic Instinct* perfectly captured the decadence of the West. Women who did not have a firm hand laid upon them turned into ravenous creatures, prisoners of sexual appetite. They were too weak to resist the constant prickling of their flesh. Although Galibani had never been west of Kiev, he knew that all of the women of Europe and America betrayed their husbands, reveling in unimaginable orgies. All of the films of Sharon Stone were instructive in this, and he imported pirate editions from Istanbul or Warsaw as soon as they became available. But *Basic Instinct* remained his favorite. It was unthinkable that women could be indulged so, and the shamelessness of the actress, her squandered beauty, made him want to cover his eyes in horror. He had watched the film more than twenty times.

Galibani strode through the labyrinth of the home his sweat and cleverness had built. Bodyguards, relatives, servants . . . everyone leapt from his path, aware that the day had not been a good one so far. He opened doors and slammed them behind himself, shoved aside curtains, cursed at the resistance of the air. Finally, he entered a low corridor with storage rooms on either side. A rough-hewn door led to the rear pasture, both a practical measure for animals quartered here in winter and one of the irregular exits placed so that he could flee his own home in an emergency. On a chair by a door at the far end of the corridor, a man with an unkempt beard held an automatic rifle across his lap. A younger man sat cross-legged on the floor nearby. He was bearded as well, but his facial hair was delicately trimmed and his attention had been submerged in a book, an embossed Koran. When they saw Galibani, both men jumped to their feet and their mouths opened.

Galibani forced them aside without actually touching them. The reader began to protest. Before the man could shape sufficient words, Galibani tore open the door to the rear shed that had become a young woman's prison.

The girl squatted white-fleshed in a round tub as Yasmin poured water over her shoulders. The moment Galibani appeared, the old woman dropped the pitcher from her hands onto the floor and it smashed. She stepped backward, covering the nakedness of her mouth.

The nakedness of the girl, who had been sick, was different. She tried to stand, to cover herself, then collapsed into the shallow water, curling forward, hiding her breasts, her face. But Galibani had seen her, the shocking paleness of her, the glistening paleness. And the color of her.

The last rein snapped and his emotions ran. He averted his eyes from the girl, but stepped forward quickly and grabbed Yasmin, the traitor, the old whore, the liar. In his hand, the ancient woman's arm felt brittle as straw. He snapped it, and she screamed. The girl screamed, too, and the voices of the other men rose in a hubbub behind him. Galibani ignored the noise, dragging the old woman out of the shed by her broken arm.

He beat her down the hallway with his fists, kicking her when she fell, then planting the flat of his foot in her back. Grunting, he picked her up only to beat her down again. Her bones disintegrated and her screams collapsed into gasps. Startling him and enraging him all the more, the younger of the two men tried to restrain him, but Galibani knocked him away, shouting curses. He fell astride the old woman, scuffing his knees, and took her skull in one hand, smashing it onto the floor again and again. He was no longer disciplining an old slut of a servant, he was beating many women, all women, his wife, unreachable actresses, the girl in the tub. He hunched his back and, with an enormous growl, snapped the old woman's head backward. Bone popped and splintered, and the life went out of her. After giving her two more reflexive blows, he straightened himself, panting, beginning to realize what he had done.

The old woman had been with the family a long time. This was a bad end. But it was not his fault. She had brought it on herself. Women were forever bringing things down on themselves. They were beguiling monsters. He raised his hands, then his eyes, heavenward, but saw only a spiderweb in a corner of the ceiling.

From another world, he heard whimpering. Slowly, he realized it was the girl. Whose nakedness he had witnessed. He recalled her with veracity. The tautness of muscle and skin. The fabulous color of her. The hair of an actress. He did not remember her face.

Abruptly, he turned on the two men from the side of the fanatics, the fools who had begun all of this.

"Cover the girl. Give her something to cover herself. Bring her a bed." He thought for a moment. "Then bind her to it. Cover her mouth. Until I say it can be uncovered."

The younger man, the one who had been reading the Koran, began to speak, then stopped himself.

Galibani left the hallway, stepping so that his boots did not come into contact with the shriveled corpse. He retraced his steps through the house and threw himself into the big chair in the shadows behind the big desk. Only then did he notice the blood on his hands. He wiped the knuckles on the sides of his dark trousers. Then he shouted. He did not even form a word, but a terrified servant appeared in moments.

"Bring me my son," Galibani cried. *"Bring me my son!"*

It was terrible, the fate the old woman had brought upon herself. Such things should not happen. Not in his house.

The boy appeared in the doorway, his baba hunched behind him. The boy giggled, with two fingers in his mouth. It was as if he were the only being in the household who had no sense of what had happened. Or perhaps it was that he knew he need not fear. Not ever.

"Leave him," Galibani told the crippled man. With doubtful eyes, the minder shuffled off.

Galibani smiled and opened his arms, spinning around in his chair. The child laughed and flung himself across the room. They kissed each other repeatedly, and the hands that had recently done other business caressed hair, shoulders, back. Galibani told the boy to cover his eyes, then he reached into a drawer of the desk and produced one of the brown-papered candy bars the size of a box of cartridges.

"Open your eyes," the father commanded.

The boy clapped his hands, then seized his prize. "*Sneee-kehrs,*" he declared. His father helped him tear open the packaging, then sat him on the flat of the desk.

"Now we will watch a film," he said. "We will watch a wonderful film together."

The boy did not even turn around.

With practiced gestures, Galibani turned on the television, switched from satellite reception to the VCR, then inserted a film. It had not been fully rewound, but that did not matter. Father and son knew the plot by heart. Galibani turned up the sound, but not so much that he would not hear an approaching vehicle, and he took his seat again, holding his son against his chest as smears of chocolate coated the child's face and cascaded onto both of their shirts. When the candy was finished, Galibani held the boy tightly against him, cheek to cheek at first, until the boy complained of his whiskers, then against his chest. They watched the wonderful colors and miracles of *Aladdin,* and tears touched the father's eyes as he pondered the cruelty of life and the perfidy of the flesh and the transience of mortal splendor, and the son laughed, and they waited for the arrival of the Americans.

CHAPTER

■ ■ ■

Heroin built the houses on the outskirts of Lenkoran. Soviet architecture pigged the center of the port, while the surviving colonial buildings moldered behind ferns in the side streets. But only the poor or the stupid or the honest, who were usually one and the same, had to bear the slave-market humidity downtown. The suburban ethic had arrived.

Out past the uproar of the bazaar, three-story homes rose from the compounds that lined the road. Vegetables substituted for flowers in the gardens, a legacy of lean times, but new BMWs glinted beside the irrigation ditches. Within a grandfather's memory, tigers had shopped here for human flesh. Now tin roofs curved and flashed skirts of silver lace that made the houses resemble pagodas, and deep, cool porches kept the interiors in permanent dusk.

Spoon pulled over where a roadside baker offered wheels of *lavash* from his oven. As the jeep climbed out of the jungle glades into the hills, the two men tore off warm, oily strips of the bread, dusting their laps with crumbs and waking their appetites. They rose through villages prosperity had not yet touched, where ragged old men in flat caps ambled by the roadside. The wild growth thinned with every curve until the first meadows opened up around them and small flowers, pricks of color, fringed the cuts where the road went through.

"Chow call?" Spoon asked.

Their route slipped into a vale of trees crotched between two limbs of a mountain and they stopped to eat properly. Below the road, a stream tumbled into a gorge where farm children ruckused, splashing the air. The two companions chose seats in the humming shade.

They had gone separate in their thoughts and spoke only the words necessary to cut off slabs of white cheese and share a bag of tomatoes, their fragrance thick as the scent of roses. The bread was still faintly warm and gorgeous, and mineral water from the cooler cleaned their throats. A long green insect alighted on Burton's forearm, then lifted off again, and a woman gauged the visitors from a hillside garden. With the food scrapped aside, both men knew they needed to move, but sensed they were not headed toward anything pleasant.

"You know, boss," Spoon said finally, "those cuts on your face make you look like an Indian on the warpath."

Burton smiled. "Well, we're in Indian country now."

Spoon looked around lazily. "Beautiful place, though. The sky."

Burton nodded. "Even better higher up." And he became the officer again, the spoilsport. "Boots and saddles, partner."

Built to survive the Soviet pretense at roads, the jeep performed like a mule, complaining but climbing steadily. The roadside trees grew fewer and the meadows steeper. The hamlets through which they passed, with their terraces of square, small-windowed houses, had learned over centuries to be wary of travelers, but the smaller children ran out to the fences at the sound of the vehicle. Male or female, the kids were shorn like recruits. The bolder waved. The Americans waved back, smiles ambassadorial. Far above the road, just below the high ridges, the summer shacks of herdsmen semaphored washing.

Across a valley, a world away, a kerchiefed woman carried a yoke of water cans down a steep path, heading for a hidden stream. At a switchback reached after an hour's climb, the view behind them thrilled until it blurred into the heat-haze of Lenkoran and the sea. With the next curve, the earth and sky opened.

Spoon instinctively eased his foot from the gas pedal. Ahead, between lesser mountaintops, a massif of orange rock marked Iran, a smuggler's landscape. To the right, the hills fell away toward villages and dark ravines. Flocks preened under the sun and desert banded the horizon. On the left, the mountains tumbled toward them, meaty with trees. You could see the effects of sun, wind, and weather with yes-and-no clarity, all of the northern slopes green and alluring, the southern exposures scorched and panting, bare. In the foreground, the town of Lerik clutched its hillside. Ramshackle and lively, family compounds circled a few blunt buildings of the sort inflicted on frontiers by imperial bureaucracies short of cash. Above the town, a big house and compound dominated the hilltop. Its outbuildings stretched down to a wall high enough to double as a fortification.

Galibani's joint. Burton had seen it from the road before, but had never been invited inside.

They drove into the town. School-age children yelped in the streets and women bent under great loads of kindling or balanced baskets of melons on their heads. The older women, clothing black as a lawyer's heart, stopped to stare at a presence that did not belong to their streetscape. The younger women's clothing was colorful, if well-worn, reminding Burton of Kurdish dress, but sleeker and less oppressive. The vehicle jalopied noisily through the streets. A young man in a hand-me-down suit waved as his female companion drew her kerchief forward. Animal corpses hung from a butcher's balcony and a policeman, his authority meaningless here, narrowed his eyes at the visitors as if he might convince them, at least, of the dignity of his uniform. Then they began to climb again, passing the last compounds, the trained vines and privies, until they entered the no-man's-land between the town and Galibani's sanctuary.

At a roadblock, guards with automatic weapons and bad manners demanded identification. Both Burton and the NCO held up government-issued diplomatic passes with photographs, but refused to relinquish them into the hands of the guards. The guards balked until Burton told them in his renegade Turkish that he was a personal guest of the Haji and that he would not allow his dignity to be soiled this way, that he would turn around and leave. Of course, the guards already knew whom to expect. They had hardly looked at the ID cards. The toughness and demands were part of the ritual, of the endless bartering for psychological advantage, that was as endemic to this world as gut worms.

The guards retreated into childlike smiles and accommodation. Burton passed over two of the American cigarettes he kept in the vehicle for just such occasions, then Spoon bullied the jeep through first gear into second, leaning into the steering wheel as if trying to help the vehicle master the steepness of the road.

"I just hope," the NCO said, "that they're still smiling on our way out."

Kelly fought as they tried to tie her down. When she realized they were not going to hit back, she struggled even more ferociously, punching and kicking. Her two guards, the young man who had lectured her on injustice and his older companion, had attempted to cope with her by themselves, but they were soon forced to call for help. Two other men arrived, dirty-faced, stinking of the barnyard. They were no help at first because they were afraid to touch her. Then they began to grip her with too much enthusiasm. She kicked one of them in the face, bloodying his lip, and when he came back at her, he hurt her in ways the others would not notice.

The new phase of her captivity had begun when two

women Kelly had not seen before brought her a pair of baggy trousers and a smock. She still felt ill. And a new terror had come with the violence she had witnessed. She stumbled in putting on the clothing, jigging one-legged across the floor. Just far enough to see into the hallway, where the old woman's body lay unmistakably still in a puddle of blood. Kelly screamed. Then the men came back, and she screamed again, covering herself as best she could, and the young man who spoke English repeated, "There is no worry, please, there is no worry."

Dressed, she cowered in a corner. Dizzy, stomach twisting. The women brought in a wooden bedframe laced with rope. Arms folded, the men watched the awkwardness of the women's struggles. Finally, the women covered the bed with a striped, pulpy bag. The room had been swept before her bath, but they swept it again now, stirring up more of the choking dust and driving small creatures into local migration. Nothing was clean. They had not washed the floor and it was still horribly stained from her sickness. But the room looked neater. The older of her two guards grunted his approval, and the young man said something Kelly could not understand, then they all left her alone.

For a beautiful, hopeful quarter of an hour Kelly sat on the bed, grasped by an unexpected happiness. Just to be able to have all of her body off the floor. She began to imagine that she would be treated better from then on. Then the men returned with several lengths of rope that might have been used to tie cattle.

Kelly shouted, "No," as best she could, but her throat was dry again and the sound that left her mouth was a rasp. Still, she found surprising strength in her body, as if the sickness had called a time-out. She wrestled out of the ropes they looped over her wrists and ankles, rising up only to be pushed down again. She hurt her elbow on the bedframe, but did not stop struggling. Then the reinforcements came in.

Finally they had her spread-eagled on the rumpled mattress, each of her limbs tied snugly to a different corner of the bed, the ropes chewing into ankles already raw from the manacles she had worn for two nights.

"Bastards," she told them. "Scumbag fucking bastards." But they did not understand, and despite herself, she began to cry. The rape fear had flamed up again, but she quickly realized that they would have pulled off the baggy trousers before tying her if they were going to do that. It almost felt like rape, though. The way she imagined rape. They had pushed her down to a new level of helplessness. She sensed that she could not yet control her bowels, and now she could not even use the bucket, could not flick away the bugs. Why on earth had they let her clean herself, only to do this? She crashed. For the first time, she felt an utter absence of hope. When her tormentors left the room, she let her face clown into deep sobs, and she said, "Daddy . . . please . . . Daddy . . ."

The sobbing made her nose run, and she could not blow it or wipe it, and she gagged a little, thinking, Please, don't let me die like this . . . please, somebody help me . . . She cried, then she could not cry anymore, and she waited for her body to betray her or for the creatures from the floor to discover her helplessness.

With a spasm of fear, she thought again of the big man who had stormed in, who had seemed so amazed at her nakedness. He had killed the old woman. For nothing. How could death be such a casual thing to these people? Before her abduction, she had believed herself jaded, pushed to the edge of experience, but now there seemed to be something horrible and new with every passing hour. This world was immeasurably different from the place described in the precincts of her education, where humankind was inherently good and needed only to be freed from Western oppression or from inexplicable dictators, and where women would soon liberate themselves to soar above the male squalor of history. The big man with the monster eyes and the bowling-ball fists had walked in and killed an old woman without warning or language or any sort of hesitation. The ease with which death happened here was still unbelievable to her, the way a broken limb can take hours to register fully on the mind. This simplicity of death was a thing she did not want to accept, and it would have been unthinkable to her professors. She felt as though she had been lied to all her life.

Once she got past the flush of struggle, she realized that nothing that had happened to her so far seemed quite so horrible as the big killer's eyes taking in her nakedness. Not even the clumsiest or stupidest of the boys and men who had entered her life had ever managed to reduce her that way.

With jarring suddenness, the young man who spoke English came back and stood at the side of the bed. Contemplating her. He smiled, showing his precise white teeth, and she could not bear it and looked away.

"Do not be afraid," he said in an oiled voice. "Please. We are not animals." He took out a rag and wiped her mouth and nose.

Hating herself for it, Kelly began to cry again.

"We are not animals," the young man repeated, as if trying to convince himself. Then he rolled up the rag like a kerchief and lowered it over Kelly's mouth. Despite the outraged twisting of her head, he managed to tie it off at the back of her neck.

"You must be quiet now," he said. Then he reached down and stroked her hair.

Abbas tried to return to his reading of the Koran, but could not concentrate. The girl would not leave his thoughts. He realized that all Western women were whores and damned, but he wondered if it might not be possible to teach one of them about the bounty of Allah and the splendor of a life lived according to the Law of the Prophet, Peace be unto Him. Perhaps *this* girl was not so much of a whore. She fought men like a lioness. Perhaps she had not had so many lovers. For a moment, he imagined his sister instructing the girl in gentle proprieties.

.

His thoughts shifted and anger swelled in him. Galibani was a dog. It had been foolish to attempt to deal with such a man. He was not a true haji, but a thief and an exploiter of the poor, hateful in the eyes of the Prophet. The chieftain's insolence was unbearable. Worse, Abbas realized that he and his illiterate companion with the rifle were almost as tethered as the girl.

When the revolution of the Word arrived, all of the Galibanis would pay. The revolution in Iran had been imperfect, smeared with corruption, but they had learned from it. You had to exterminate *all* of the enemies of true religion. You could not compromise, could not bargain with them. You had to kill them all. The next revolution would be pleasing to Allah.

He thought of the girl again. She looked better now that she had been washed, and he sensed how lovely she might look with proper care, proper clothing. Perhaps she was not a whore at all. Perhaps she was even a virgin. He resolved that he would never allow Galibani to touch her.

It was embarrassing, of course. Humiliating. Their contact in Baku had misrepresented the role of the girl's father for purposes that still mystified Abbas. A telephone call that morning, twice broken off, had finally informed him about the descriptions of Senator Mitchell Trost in the international newspapers. The American was not the great Zionist and man of limitless power whom the kidnapping's guarantor had made him out to be.

Still, the father was powerful enough, and America was guilty. He would have to pay for his daughter's return. He would have to make America pay. America would have to right its terrible wrongs against the children of Islam, to stop its satanic genocide.

All the same, Abbas thought, their "great friend" had lied to them. And what else had he lied about? What other discoveries would there be? Vague possibilities chilled Abbas. Perhaps the man was even an agent of the CIA or the Russians?

When the revolution arrived, he, too, would have to be killed. Their "protector" in Baku deserved death even more than did Galibani.

And yet Abbas did not know to whom else he might turn. Over the past two days, almost all of his co-conspirators had faded away, their promises of help and declarations of courage weightless. They had done everything wrong. *He* had done everything wrong. Now he was little more than a prisoner himself.

Helplessly, Abbas thought yet again about the girl, recalling his glimpse of her nakedness, the shamelessness of the un-shaven hair, the white breasts like clouds. The Koran in his lap slipped and closed itself. He had known women, of course. He was a man. But a woman had never come to him of her own accord. In his trips by car to France, carrying the heroin, he had stopped with his companions in Turkish bordellos, and he had visited women for money in Teheran, too, when he had been at university. Twice he had needed to go to a doctor. In France, too, he had had a woman, a Moroccan who he thought wanted to go with him because she desired him. There had been a row about money and a man with a knife.

He dreamed of rescuing Kelly Trost from the precipice of sin and of the gratitude she would lay at his feet. Certainly, a man could never marry such a woman. But perhaps they could have a great love, a love of the irresistible sort condoned in the old poems. Perhaps they could live a poem together.

He remembered the feel of her hair under his hand and shuddered.

"An honor to my humble house! An honor!" Galibani cried. He bowed slightly as Burton emerged from the jeep, then thrust out his hand Western-style. Sweat gave his big mustache the shine of anthracite. He was a head taller than the average Talysh, with the chest of an ox and hands like boxing gloves. He wore a too-small polyester shirt that would have passed for high fashion in the Soviet days and a suit jacket over baggy hillman's trousers. Black hair grew through the gaps in his shirtfront. Bouncing on imported running shoes, the chieftain reinforced the handshake with his left paw and Burton noted a big Breitling watch on the man's wrist. The watch shone golden, hedged on both sides by tufts of hair. "You are welcome in my house!"

He squeezed Burton's hand just hard enough to demonstrate his strength.

The big man released him, ignored Spoon, and executed a quick half-turn. He spoke quickly in the local dialect. A fat little boy had been dawdling in the background. Now he ran up to Galibani, giggling happily.

"*This*," Galibani said, "is my youngest son! The pride of my life. You know that I have many grandchildren, Colonel Burton? Fourteen grandchildren! I swear it! And yet I have made a son so young. Is it not a marvel?"

"*Mashallah*," Burton said. "He will take after his father. The mountains will shake at his approach."

His host laughed magnificently. But the truth was that Burton did not think the boy looked even remotely like Galibani.

The heroin king of southern Azerbaijan took Burton by the arm, and Burton smelled horsey sweat.

"Now . . . I am terribly disappointed. I am told you have eaten! In the glade, in that beautiful place where the road hides. You wound my feelings! How I would have fed you! I have killed my best lambs! And my American guest has eaten mere bread and cheese. Tonight we will eat the lambs."

The child dusted along beside them, miffed that his father ignored him now. Some of the retainers in the heart of the compound wore Western clothes, while others stuck with the traditional dress of the mountains. No guns were in evidence, but Burton suspected weapons were never very far away.

"Would my guests rest privately for a moment? Does your vehicle need fuel? Is there anything you would have of this simple host?"

"Haji Mustafa," Burton said, "I crave nothing but the

honor of your time. My companion and I ate a poor lunch because we knew your dinner would be a feast."

Galibani laughed again, and his son tugged at him. Suddenly, the big man swept the boy up into his arms, tossing him and catching him, making him laugh and shriek. It was no minor feat, since the boy had plenty of pork on him.

"But, Colonel Burton, they tell me you have no wife. You must marry! I will find you a wife. A wife fit for an American colonel! You must have sons. Every man must have sons. A healthy son is pleasing to Allah. There is no better thing on this earth."

Abruptly tired of playing, Galibani set the boy down and called to a retainer with a hunched back. The man scuttled over like a crippled horseman.

Galibani led the way to a faded awning where bottles and glasses had been set out. He waved to Spoon now. "Your driver, too, must have refreshment. But he is not an officer?"

"American sergeants are higher in rank than Russian officers," Burton said, and his host howled with laughter.

"I am told this man does work worthy of the Prophet with the orphans of Baku."

"Your intelligence network is perfect."

"I am proud to be the host of such a man. In my lands, he will be as a general."

Spoon loped up to them.

"Sergeant Spooner, Haji Mustafa Galibani, king of all the eye can see." Burton spoke in English, but Galibani smiled anyway, taking the sense of it.

Galibani lifted a bottle of brandy in one hand, a bottle of white Georgian wine in the other. "What gives my guests pleasure?" he asked.

"A little wine, please," Burton said, and Spoon nodded along.

"You know," Galibani said, "these religious madmen are beyond my understanding." Overfilling the first glass, he spilled a bit of wine and grunted. "I am a man of sound religion, a man who contemplates his beliefs and cherishes the Word of the Prophet, Peace be unto Him. But there is no stricture against wine in the Koran. Such things are also gifts of Allah. Wine is praised by all of the great poets of our history . . ."

"The wine of her lips is like unto the wine of the good earth," Burton quoted, *"both transport the drinker toward the Divine."*

Galibani smiled, but Burton doubted he really knew the reference. The three men toasted the eternal friendship of the Talysh and American peoples. Galibani drank the wine like a shot of cheap whisky. He retopped the glasses of his guests, then refilled his own with brandy. Burton proposed a toast.

"To the deep honor of the Talysh, who would never allow harm to come to an innocent woman."

Galibani's eyes glinted before he drank, then he put down his emptied glass. "I think this is a very clever toast, Colonel Burton. But I am told you are a very clever man."

"In your domain, I am the humblest of fools."

Galibani laughed again. He laughed as punctuation, the way some men nod their heads, and he took Burton's arm. "Your sergeant will excuse us, but I think we must talk alone. Come. I will show you the beauty of this country."

The old chieftain led the way out through a door in the side of the courtyard wall, and he and Burton followed the perimeter of a corral where good horses pranced. The wind came straight from God's lungs at this elevation, and it was cool and carried the scent of the horses. Despite the brilliance of the sun, the air chilled Burton's forearms and iced the wet in his armpits. A guard opened a door in the outer wall and they emerged into a meadow that reminded Burton of hiking in the Alps. He had known Germany and its border mountains as a lieutenant, then again as a captain, and he and Heddy had vacationed there twice, climbing into Austria the last time, high above Scharnitz, where you could pause to make love in the firs.

Two bodyguards with rifles followed at a respectful distance, scanning the earth as though the low grass hid assassins.

In another minute, they reached the true crest of the hill, and Galibani paused, letting Burton come up by his side.

"I think Heaven must look like this," Galibani said, sweeping his hand from the Iranian massif that had been recolored gray and mauve as the sun shifted, on to the distant plains, and back to his forests and meadows and the mountains with their tops swept bald by hard winds. It was the kind of view that has too many details. All you could do was let the glory of it soak into you. "Have you ever seen a more beautiful place?"

No. Burton had seen many beautiful places, from the Himalayas to the Grand Canyon, and he had never known a landscape more humanly compelling. A herd of sheep moved over a hillside like a cloud fallen to earth, and distant water cans clanged. The earth and sky seemed to embrace in a long, slow rhythm. It was a beautiful, hard place, and a thousand conquerors had watered it with blood.

Without speaking, Galibani began to walk again, recrossing the ridge and strutting down into the valley where the road, well below, wound toward Lerik. Burton followed, memory flickering with other places and long-gone women, but his concern for the kidnapped girl returned to spoil the mood. He ached to get on to the subject of Kelly Trost, but he knew that he could not rush Galibani. The chieftain *wanted* to talk. That was the whole point of inviting him here. But Galibani would begin in his own good time.

The older man slowed, letting Burton come up beside him again.

"I think perhaps I should visit America. I have heard that America is very beautiful."

"Some parts of it are more beautiful than others. To me, it's beautiful." Then he quoted, *"A man will always love the barren hills where he was born."*

"Were you born in 'barren hills,' Colonel Burton?"

Burton smiled, thinking of the lush green summers of upstate New York, of the deep, cold lakes. "No, Haji. It was very green. With good farms and hills soft as women."

"And what is your state?"

"New York."

Galibani made the face of a man who has gotten a bad oyster. "But New York is a city. I am told it is a terrible place, though very rich."

"There are two New Yorks, Haji. There is the New York where people come to make money and reputations, and then there is the New York where people come to make love. I am a son of the second New York."

"Perhaps I should visit this New York. Where everyone makes love. I will come to you for a visa."

"You might like Arizona. Many would disagree, but I think Arizona is the most beautiful state."

"But what of California? All of the movie stars are there. It must be the most beautiful."

Burton thought of the golden women with gold on their minds and of the men who could not be taken seriously. "California is a world of its own."

"I think I would love California. I would like to meet your Sharon Stone. Tonight, we will have a video."

"Of all the women in the world," Burton said, "right now I'd most like to meet Kelly Trost. Our missing friend must be very frightened. We can only hope that she is in good health."

Burton had been unable to pass up the opening, but he caught the immediate change in Galibani's mood. The chieftain had been putting off the topic, perhaps still wrestling with his angle on it. Now annoyance came off his skin like heat. But it faded quickly. And the ploy worked.

"Certainly," Galibani said, "if a man of this country took her, she would be in good health. We Talysh do not hurt women." He paused, and Burton sensed a resurgence of bad temper. "But I do not think any of my people are involved. I would know."

"You know all that happens, Haji."

"Most things, most things. But . . . listen, my friend. I heard about this . . . misfortune. And I thought, 'Haji Mustafa, you must help. This is a matter of honor. The daughter of a great man of America, a young girl who has come to this country to help the people, she has been stolen by bandits or murderers or who knows who.' So, very quickly, I said that I would like to speak with you. But here is the problem: I do not know how best to help you."

"The best way would be to find the girl. To set her free."

Galibani nodded. "But this is a very complex matter, I think. It would take many resources. And there would be risks." He paused and looked Burton in the eye. Burton was six-foot-one, but the older man still looked down on him. "I am an old man and, *Inshallah*, not too much of a fool. I would take these risks for America. But I must ask myself, 'Haji Mustafa, what risks would America take for you?'"

"Whoever found the girl would earn the gratitude of the United States."

Galibani smiled and began to walk downward again. The meadow was very steep now, and the grass slippery, but the chieftain walked with unthinking confidence in his Reeboks. "But what is gratitude in this world? What does it mean, my friend? Understand—I do not speak of money. Money is as unimportant as the blades of grass. But allow me to ask . . . what do you think of an independent country of the Talysh? We are an oppressed people. And there is oil in our sea. What would your president think of an independent Talysh Republic?"

The answer, Burton knew, was that his president had never even heard of the Talysh people and the Secretary of State would faint at the thought of another splinter state on the Caspian, right bang up against Iran and, oh, by the way, headed up by Big Daddy Heroin. It did occur to Burton that he was being offered a chance to alter the course of history and make Drew MacCauley's life a nightmare in the process, but he suspected the Talysh people, as well as Azerbaijan and America, were better off just the way things were.

"I think this is an interesting concept that deserves further thought," Burton said in his best State Department imitation. "But there might be problems."

Apparently, Free Talyshstan was only a straw man, because Galibani agreed, too. "Yes, there would be problems. Perhaps this is only a possibility for the future. But . . . there is another matter. The great pipeline. The pipeline that will take the oil through Georgia and Turkey to the sea. Must it take such a foolish route?"

"The route hasn't been finalized," Burton said slowly.

"Yes! Good, good. You see, I think this would be a foolish thing. Would it not be wiser to bring this pipeline through the Talysh country, then through Iran to the sea?"

"Well . . . such a route has been considered. But the United States and Iran are not on friendly terms."

"But that is nothing. Nothing! The Iranians will do anything for money. I know them. They, too, want this great pipeline."

"Haji Mustafa . . . I cannot lie to you. The United States will not support a pipeline that goes through Iran."

They descended further, and the chieftain sulked. "All right. But it could go through Armenia. Don't worry about these Azeris. The Talysh and the Armenians can be friends. You can still make a pipeline here."

And from here right on through the no-man's-land of burned villages and ruined cropland, Burton thought. Right through a war zone. Sure. Where do we sign up?

"That's a very interesting idea. I'll tell my ambassador about it."

"Good. A good thing. Then there is another matter. Besides the pipeline, which would bring great prosperity to my poor people. America could help me with these damned Europeans. They make great trouble. The Germans, especially. They accuse me of terrible things, of making narcotics and smuggling them into their countries. They try to wound me, an innocent man . . ."

"Haji Mustafa, there are rumors . . . perhaps you should take greater pains to confirm your renowned honesty."

"*Rumors!* And that is all they have, these Europeans. They are only little people. Little people believe rumors. Haji Mustafa Galibani is a businessman, a father to his people. Look." He waved his hand again. "Where are the poppies? What do you see? Sheep. It is a poor country. Poor and beautiful. I will tell you the truth. All of these drugs are a problem made by the Europeans. Perhaps it is true that one bad Talysh man or another sells these narcotics now and then. But it is the Europeans that want them. And none of this is a problem for America. Your drugs do not come from here or from Iran or even from Afghanistan. And are the Europeans your friends? They are nothing but weaklings and prostitutes. I say, if they want to destroy themselves with these narcotics, it is a sin, but it is *their* sin. It is not my problem. It is not America's problem."

"Still . . . I don't see exactly what America could do to help you."

Galibani stopped and waved both arms. "But they are your servants! They do what you say. America could say to these Germans and the others, 'Stop these lies about our friend Haji Mustafa. He is a good man. Stop trying to punish him for a thing he would not do in a hundred years!' "

Considering it, Burton decided that the idea was not so far-fetched. The old bugger might get the CIA to bite. But he was not going to go for it.

"I think," Burton said, "that you have nothing to fear. The Europeans are prisoners of their laws. They couldn't punish an innocent man."

Galibani sent the Europeans to perdition with a couple of fingers. "But you see my predicament, Colonel Burton? I want to help America. But what help would America be to me?"

It was, in fact, a very good question. This was only the latest in a string of circumstances Burton had faced for which none of the rule books or classes back at DIA prepared you. You had to make policy with your fingers crossed and one eye closed. And sometimes you had to do things you did not like.

"All right," Burton said. "Let me tell you what I *can* do. What I can promise. I will personally inform you, from my lips to your ear, if the Germans or anybody else seem to be closing in on you. If they have something up their sleeve. No, I'll do even better. You haven't mentioned the Russians. But they're after you. That's right. I know you have protectors in Moscow. But not every Russian likes the soaring number of heroin addicts staggering down the Arbat." He held up a hand. "It doesn't even matter what's true and what's not. The Russians believe you supply a fair proportion of the heroin that wanders up their way. They'll kill you if they get the chance, Haji. Although I don't think they'll go too far out of their way to do it just yet. They've got their hands full across the mountains. But the day will come. What I can do is this: keep my ear to the ground, give you a warning. *And* I'll get you out of here in a pinch and get you a visa to a country that won't extradite you. *If* you can deliver the girl."

They were nearing the road. A stolen military truck, faintly repainted, groaned uphill under a load of crates. There was a back trail into Iran from Lerik that had been used for smuggling down the centuries.

"All of this," Galibani said, "may never come to pass. What if I were able to help you, to bring this girl to you . . . but then never needed your help?"

Burton smiled tightly. "Then, Haji Mustafa, we would both know that Allah truly smiles upon you. And you would have done a righteous thing."

Galibani nodded, but his expression made it clear that he was unconvinced and disappointed. Still, he would think on it.

"But here is what I wanted to show you," Galibani said, voice brightening again. He pointed to a fountain tucked into a draw off the side of the road. It bore a mosaic of President Aliev's face that looked as though it had been made of the colored stones from the bottom of a goldfish tank. The likeness was unmistakable, though.

"I have done this," the chieftain said. "In recognition of the heroic deeds of our president, who is my good friend. I have paid for an artist to come from Tbilisi."

Amused, Burton said, "But we were just talking about an independent homeland for the Talysh. You said you were oppressed."

Galibani cupped his hands and drank the splashing water, unfazed. "This is special water. You must try it. It is cold from nature. It comes from the heart of the mountain."

Burton lowered his hands and head. The water was, indeed, cold and marvelous in the mouth. It was a land of hidden riches.

"President Aliev is a great man." The chieftain picked up the subject again. "If he were not the president, he would support the independence of the Talysh. I know this in my heart. Anyway, a president is just a king for our times. And it is never bad to erect a monument to the king."

Burton drank again, loving the sweetness of the water. It was probably pure. At the higher elevations, you could drink from the springs that ran fast.

"Come," Galibani said. "We must return. I will make a feast, if you will accept my humble hospitality. You will want for nothing."

With a nod, Burton fell into rhythm with the older man's steps. No choice but to see this through. A tantrum would not help.

"But I must ask you a difficult question," Galibani said. "Please. In your opinion, who is the most beautiful, Sharon Stone or Kim Basinger? I think that *Basic Instinct* and *Nine and a Half Weeks* are the greatest films of all time. But who is the most beautiful?"

Burton almost laughed. At the thought of a beauty contest between two hack actresses out here at the back of beyond.

Which movie was worse? Hard to say. Yet this was the part of his culture that quickened the world's appetite.

"I'm more of a Juliette Binoche man myself," Burton told him.

But the chieftain was serious. He stood erectly in his running shoes, with the wind rippling his thinning hair and flapping his jacket, a tough paradise for his backdrop. Almost somberly, Galibani said:

"I would like to possess such a woman just once."

CHAPTER 7

• • •

Heddy left the Cologne-Bonn Airport in a taxi that was not a taxi at all. She gave the driver no instructions, and he asked no questions. Everything was clear and well-planned, as precise and geometric and killingly dull as the waning countryside and lumped housing developments flanking the Autobahn. It was Sunday in Germany, a prison of a day, and she felt as though her blood had been drained on arrival.

It was a fine day, weather-wise. The sun was having an uncharacteristic fit of generosity and the few clouds off to the southwest, over the Ardennes, were easily dismissed. The brown Rhine glittered as they crossed the big bridge. Green hills spotted with villas pressed a fine old town against the river, and all this was home and dependable and startlingly lonely. Automobiles passed swiftly and correctly, their alert occupants rushing from one regimen to another, desperate to squeeze out all the juice the week owed them. She knew these people, their habits and prejudices had contoured her life. She had despised them, of course, after the fashion of the times, laughing in the company of her girlfriends and clever men over "Herr Meier," but she had never really questioned her belonging. Now she felt foreign, at once privileged and ship-wrecked, observing her heritage through the eyes of the man she loved.

Her driver turned off on one of the Bonn exits, and clean, equitable streets rushed toward her. They entered a neighbor-hood where uniformly white homes with garden walls faced rows of townhouses. Cobbled streets grumbled under the tires. The notorious house where an aging general had shot his leftist lover before killing himself appeared and drifted behind, and its ghosts were the only hint of passion Heddy could imagine for this smug, safe world.

She had always been practical, her life shaped by the bar-barian ambition she kept nicely concealed and by her ability to think quickly and work hard. She believed she had made good choices, and her private life had been one of freedom preserved and pleasures managed. Her lovers had been serious men, usually older and accomplished at this or that. She had never been one for vacation affairs or blunt flesh mechanics. Then she met Evan, whom she had seen at first as innocently American, delicious and undemanding. And she learned that she was not a good judge of men at all, and that she did not know herself, and that passion not only existed but addicted.

A part of her wished she had never met him. He had ru-ined so much, not least her peace of mind. Helmut, on the other hand, was the partner of whom she had dreamed: distin-guished, brilliant-mannered, and confidently rich in a style that took generations to achieve. He had phoned his household staff in Bad Godesberg to open the place so she would not need to stay in a hotel. Tomorrow, she would wake to coffee served in Jugendstil silver and a view of the Rhine. Then there was the Hamburg home, with its Biedermeier interiors and the garden where a poet shot himself for love during an outbreak of cholera.

Although she presented herself as a Hamburg girl, Hedwig Seghers had been born in Bremen, with its mists, brick, and

monotony, and her family moored there until her father's pro-
motion swept him into a shipping headquarters across the flat-
lands in Hamburg. She had grown up with intellectual
privileges a deck above her family's charter and a discipline
that buoyed her through the wake of the *Grosse Freiheit* with
no danger of capsizing. Her family's anonymous middle-class
home sat barely a kilometer from Helmut's family mansion,
but it might as well have been across an ocean in the days of
her girlhood.

Now she had been invited inside. And she wanted to go.
The only thing holding her back was an idiotic, unreasonable,
laughable infatuation with a man who did not really want her,
at least not the way she wanted him.

She was a liar, and she knew it.

Infatuation was long behind her. She was in love the way
it happened in the books disappointed women clutched on
trams. Helmut was wonderful and perfect, and he would never
surprise her in ways good or bad. Evan was . . . Evan. He
would likely go to his grave poor as a student, and he might
never find an adequate parking place for his heart, and he
would always be half a step ahead of her. It was not even the
sex. Or not only the sex. Even after the lovemaking was over,
she dwelt on him as she had never done with another man,
and she wanted to be with him, to touch him innocently, to
breathe the air he breathed. She thought about him now as the
non-taxi turned into an alley, then angled between a pair of
black metal gates that opened automatically at their approach.

No one came out of the house to meet her, but that was
routine. With the taxi waiting, engine dead, she followed the
path between the late-summer roses and only just noticed the
guards stalking back in the trees.

The door opened before she could press the buzzer, and a
familiar face smiled at her.

"Fraülein Seghers," the man said, "how lovely to see you
again."

"Don't be an ass, Oskar," Heddy told him. They had been

lovers years before, when they were both assigned to the embassy in Budapest. The affair had left them unimpressed with one another. "What's this all about?"

"Come in. Sit down. You'll find out." He led her into the sitting room. She had been to the house frequently for instructions or discussions, but this time there was a surprise waiting.

Amid the expensive, unimaginative decor, sitting just below an institutional painting Evan would have teased her about, her boss waited.

Her real boss.

The *big* boss.

"Herr Minister," she said, losing her equilibrium for a moment. "Excuse me, I . . ."

"Nothing to excuse, nothing at all." The man smiled as if posing for a magazine cover. "Please, Fraülein Seghers. Sit down with me for a few minutes. Then we'll have you on your way to those insufferable colleagues of yours at the Foreign Ministry."

Heddy took a seat, wishing she had paused in the airport to comb her hair and straighten her clothing. She did not know what this was about, suspected several possibilities, and knew with certainty only that it was important. The minister had better things to do than welcome back a mid-level operative on a Sunday afternoon.

The BND was, of course, delighted at the prospect of her marrying Helmut Hartling. No better cover could have been designed, it was a gift from God. Perhaps, she thought, that's what this is about. The thought that the service might interfere in her personal life flushed her with a variety of anger she would not have felt a year before.

"So," Heddy began, "the recall wasn't—"

"Was *not* a routine matter." The minister finished the thought for her. "Hardly. You're not just checking in with us this time. No, no. I arranged for your recall personally. Tricky business. Don't want to compromise your identity now. Certainly not now." He signaled faintly with his hand, as though brushing away invisible crumbs, and Oskar left the room, gently closing the French doors on his way out.

Heddy looked at the man. She had met him twice, once for a handshake, a second time during an award ceremony to which the press had not been invited. He was well and conservatively dressed, and Heddy, who knew a great deal about how men armored themselves, would have bet that the suit was from Zechbauer, the shirt a van Laack, and the tie something French upon which his wife had insisted. It was the uniform of the class to which she now belonged. Helmut, on the other hand, had his suits made in London and his shirts done, by the dozen, in Hong Kong. The cotton in the shirts was so fine that it could not be starched and, instead, Helmut changed them two, sometimes three, times a day. That was the world into which she had been invited.

"Now, Fraülein Seghers . . . this *is* a matter of some complexity—and of not a little delicacy. This matter of the kidnapped girl, the American senator's daughter. Miserable business. Bonn wishes to do everything possible to help return her to her father, of course. Your . . . friend, the ambassador, has received his instructions. A very good man. You know that, of course. But he is, in the end, a diplomat. And I think you'll agree that diplomats are, by definition, limited. I do not mean that in any personal sense, of course."

The minister corrected his near-perfect posture. On the table before him stood a small, green, half-emptied bottle of mineral water and a glass. He looked at the arrangement, then looked away, not bothering to ask Heddy if she might like something to drink herself. Helmut, she thought, would never have committed such an oversight, not even if he were Chancellor and she a charwoman. But she and the minister came from similar backgrounds. She understood.

"Now . . ." the minister continued, ". . . if it were only a matter of the girl, it would be rather a simpler affair. But the case is interconnected with other matters. The pipeline, of course. But also the matter of relations with Iran." He edged closer, breaking the plane of his posture. You could almost hear his clothing crack. "We would like to see the girl returned to her father. Of course. But there are various ways in which she could be returned." He sighed. "First . . . we believe that the kidnappers may have an affiliation with elements in Iran. Probably informal. Not sanctioned at the highest levels. But such a distinction hardly matters, in the eyes of our American friends. Washington cannot get over its little spat with Teheran, and many on the other side of the Atlantic would like to prolong the feud for political reasons. I will not elaborate on their Jewish lobby."

He leaned closer still and Heddy felt as though he had been circling her. "But to the point. If the kidnappers are, indeed, unmasked as Iranians or as tethered to Iran by even the finest of threads, we are likely to face a great deal more nonsense from Washington. We will hear renewed demands for a European economic boycott of Iran. Which is utterly unacceptable, of course. Impossible for German business. But you know that. We do not want to be forced to choose between doing business with the States and doing business with Iran. Not a real choice at all. No sense of fairness from Washington these days. Remarkable naïveté about the world—although the Chancellor enjoys his White House dinners. But that is irrelevant. The thing is that the Americans have the capacity to do a great deal of thoughtless harm to us all."

The minister took a drink of his mineral water and failed again to offer anything to Heddy. Below two black patches of briers, his eyes stared at you without seeing anything beyond that which affected him personally. "Second," he said, raising two fingers, "the Russians are up to something. A people with a stepchild culture and bloody ambitions. Only hours after the girl was kidnapped, communications between the Russian mission in Baku and Moscow lit up. Frankly, we're reduced to reading the externals on most of the traffic . . . but the increased volume cannot be a coincidence. My best analyst is convinced they're up to something. Exactly what that might be, we're unsure . . . but they do rather have an interest in the region. I would offer the hypothesis that our Russian friends may want to find the girl first. Either to deliver her to her father for goodwill and to make the point that Azerbaijan remains too turbulent a site for the main pipeline, as compared to the blissful quietude of southern Russia. Chechnya notwithstanding." He tightened his focus on her, a doctor inspecting a patient. "Or . . . to kill her on the sly and make the same point about pipeline routes. Somewhat reinforced."

He put his hands on his knees as if he might rise, but made no further motion. Afternoon sunlight buttered the room through sheer curtains. "Our interests are powerfully engaged in this entire *Schweinerei*. While we do not oppose multiple pipeline routes, we must be absolutely certain that at least one major route exits the Caucasus through Turkey. It's a matter of stability. And economics. Azerbaijan for the first leg, probably Georgia after that—although I would not rule out Armenia over the long haul. But egress *must* be through Turkey. Unfortunately, with the present human rights fuss, Bonn cannot appear too heavy-handed in our support for Ankara. Do you understand me, Fraülein Seghers?"

The policy issues were obvious. They had not needed to call her all the way back to Bonn for this. But the real business was coming up now. She felt it. The way you sensed someone at your door with bad news.

"What do you want me to do?" she asked.

The minister changed his face to hint at a smile. Then he reached down beside his chair and produced a thick attaché case. He eased it over against her shoe.

"There are one million U.S. dollars inside. You will call on our 'friend' General Hamedov immediately upon your return to Baku. You will instruct him that his German friends would like him to do his best to ensure that, one, the kidnappers, when they are found, have no connection to Iran. I would suggest, rather, that they turn out to be Russian bandits. *Dead* Russian bandits. Two, it would be best if the girl were found by loyal Azeri forces, not Russians. But Hamedov would realize that. The question is this: To what extent is our friend the general in collusion with the Russians these days?"

"Hamedov's in collusion with everybody."

The minister nodded. "Yes, well . . . you will also tell General Hamedov that, should he deliver what is required, you will present him with an additional four million dollars—or it can be deposited in Luxembourg for him. I suspect he'll find that a competitive amount."

"That's it?" Heddy asked.

The minister offered her another pretend smile. "Well, not quite. Relax, Fraülein Seghers. Please. Would you like a mineral water? Something else?"

"No. Thank you, Herr Minister."

"Now, you have a close friend, I believe. Lieutenant Colonel Burton, of the United States Embassy. Do you not?"

Nameless things were moving inside Heddy, and she surprised herself by thinking: Just tell me to walk away from him. And I'll walk away from you. Right out that door.

But the minister surprised her. "A stroke of good fortune, really. Normally, we don't pry into private lives. Not unnecessarily. Nothing beyond the routine background checks. But this man Burton. He's notoriously well-connected. And, as the Americans say, he's 'got the ball' on this matter. I would be disappointed if a colleague with your potential failed to capitalize on such a relationship." The minister waved a hand. "I'm familiar with your file. Two professional lives, both well managed. You'll be an ambassador in no time. In a very good embassy. You're the stuff of the future, you know."

"What are you asking me to do?" Heddy demanded. But her voice was not as strong as she imagined it would be.

"Direct. I like that," the minister lied. She saw that he lied and that he did not care that she knew it. "You will make certain, to the best of your considerable abilities, that Lieutenant Colonel Burton does *not* free the girl. At least not in a manner that might . . . embarrass the policy of your government."

"But I can't control his actions, we don't—"

"Yes. I understand that you and he have come to something of a separation agreement. Undoubtedly better for you in the long run. Mustn't get caught acting in too many plays at once. But, just for now, I think it's best that you keep this relationship going." He looked at her with a hardness that was a revelation. "Whatever you must do. Oh, we understand that you cannot control his actions. Not all of them. But . . . you may be able to influence them. As a minimum, you will keep us informed of his activities."

"It isn't that kind of relationship," Heddy said honestly. "He doesn't talk about things like that, he—"

"Make it that kind of relationship," the minister said flatly. "He's playing a very dangerous game and we just want to be certain he doesn't hurt himself. Frightful things happen in that part of the world." Then the minister put on his horrid smile again. "Oskar," he called. "Oskar." Barking the way his innkeeper grandfather might have done. "I believe you know Oskar Schiele," the minister said. "He's my personal assistant now."

Her ex-lover appeared behind the French doors, then opened them. The swinging glass caught a blaze of sunlight.

"Herr Minister?"

"Bring us that little gift. From the refrigerator."

"Yes, Herr Minister."

"I understand your . . . friend . . . has gone down to see Galibani," the minister said, turning back to Heddy. "You see, for all their blather about rectitude, the Americans are perfectly willing to deal with the devil when it suits them. Galibani . . . let me offer our friend Hamedov one further alternative. Were Galibani to prove responsible for the kidnapping . . . were he to prove responsible and dead . . . Bonn would not be disappointed." His mouth twisted like a rind in a sour cocktail. "Constitutionally, there's little we can do against him. Without

Azeri cooperation. Even with it, in fact. But I think you'll agree that Galibani would not be missed."

Oskar returned with a small shopping bag folded over on itself. He placed it on the table in front of the minister and exited again. Slowly, as if waking, the top of the bag rose up.

The logo was from Leonidas, the Belgian chocolate firm. From the shop in Cologne.

"You'll be flying back first thing in the morning," the minister said, "and we wanted to make sure you returned bearing gifts. I believe Lieutenant Colonel Burton asked for these? Awfully expensive, you know. There's a full kilogram there."

Heddy knew she had lost control of her face. As surely as she had lost control of her life. The minister continued to smile his predator's smile, utterly unembarrassed. Finally, Heddy said:

"You . . . you listened . . . my apartment . . ."

The minister nodded. "Yes, Fraülein Seghers. And I am not inconsiderate of your embarrassment. I would only ask you to think about why I would reveal such a thing to you. By the way . . . Oskar will deliver an additional gift to Ambassador Hartling's villa for you to take along. A few recent jazz recordings. Lieutenant Colonel Burton doesn't have them yet, and he will be pleased. You'll want to show your devotion. It's the small touches, you know."

"You bastard," Heddy said in a little girl's voice. She felt near tears, but refused to be broken that far. She thought of a thousand matters of practical shame. Of all the stolen secrets of her life.

"You will excuse me," the minister said. "I have a lawn party ahead of me. Dreary embassy affair, but it's my excuse for being in town on a Sunday. And you *must* gather yourself together. For your little exchange with your colleagues at the Foreign Ministry. I'm sure they'll want to know every little thing about events in Baku. And they'll be awfully bad-tempered about giving up the best of their weekends."

He rose to leave, trying to escape while Heddy sat in confusion. But she was, in the end, clear-thinking. She flung the final question at him before he passed the French doors.

"*Wait,*" she said. "You didn't . . . what about the girl? She'd know who took her. How could we pretend it was Russians if it was somebody else? She'd tell—"

The minister's overgrown eyebrows did not even move. "You're a clever woman," he said. "Bound to succeed."

The dancers smiled like hopeful bankrupts. With the remains of the feast congealing, Galibani barked at the musicians to play faster. They bowed their battered instruments with the urgency of Boy Scouts using sticks to make fire. The dancers looked upward, grins immobile, the musicians looked down with the timeless caution of peasants under scrutiny, and Galibani looked at them all in random succession, bashing a soft-drink-sized bottle of vodka on the table, now to mark time, now to demand attention. His gunmen chewed on, puffing up their bellies, and their chieftain spoke drunken Russian to his guests, forgetting for now that Burton spoke Turkish and was not down from Moscow and the old, squeezing apparatus of state.

The banquet was a cartoon of better days when hospitality had been heartfelt and this same music had stirred the heart. It was all dying now, the dance steps incompletely learned and untidy, the music a lingering habit, the hospitality bad theater, and not all of the delirious multiculturalists and anthropologists on earth could save it. The satellite dish was conquering the world, and Burton accepted it as the way of things.

He barely sipped his drink, impressed as ever by the ability of the dead Soviet Union's orphans to hammer themselves with shots of anything from brandy to aftershave. By his side, Spoon followed his lead, toasting delicately, accepting the condescension of the roomful of hard-drinking males. But it was a long evening, and Burton still managed to ingest enough wine and sweet champagne and brandy and vodka to feel the effects.

Finally, the dancers left and the musicians dwindled in number. A bass sang with more volume than skill, and Galibani led his clansmen in applause. In a tiny time-warp, the bass followed up on his success by bellowing "Moscow Nights," as he had doubtless done for decades of Party officials, and Burton clapped fiercely out of pity, only to be rewarded with a Russian-language version of "Getting Sentimental Over You." Then Galibani rose. He was steady on his legs, but his body seemed reluctant to do anything beyond standing still. He looked at Burton with fat tears in his eyes.

"The old times are passing," he said, returning to his own language. "And what can a man do? Our fathers were giants . . . our grandfathers kings . . . and who are we? The old ways were the good ways."

Then the chieftain grumped in dialect and Burton could not follow it. But two of the retainers moved very quickly.

"I show you something," Galibani announced in a burst of jailbird Russian. "Now is time for duel. We will see who is best."

Burton had no idea what to expect. And he did not feel in prime dueling condition. But he was not about to back down from anything short of pistols. He wondered quickly if Galibani intended to frighten him, hurt him just a little, to make a point.

He plotted the trade-offs. The clansmen were all far drunker, but that meant they would not feel a lot of pain. And they would not want to lose standing in front of old Haji the G. On the other hand, Burton knew he could take care of himself—probably better than Galibani expected—and he damned well intended to hurt anybody who faced him.

Rising to his feet, with the gravity of the liquor insisting he sit back down, Burton offered the chieftain a resolute face.

But Galibani had something different in mind. He dropped a slaughterhouse arm over Burton's shoulders, offering his guest the smell of his breath, and guided him from behind the table, with gunmen jumping out of their path. The chieftain swayed as though his mansion were a ship in rolling seas and Burton went with the rhythm, almost breaking into laughter at the mental image of a line of Talysh hoodlums doing a stadium wave. After squeezing through a threshold curtained with a cheap, brilliant weaving, they entered a domain where East and West collided.

It seemed to be a combination office, reception hall, and entertainment center. European-style chairs stood like disoriented survivors among heaped rugs and stuffed cushions. A desk carved with all the dignity of old Persia supported a plastic lamp that might have been won at a carnival. But the undisputed focal point of the room was a huge black rear-projection television surrounded by a suite of VCRs, amplifiers, and speakers.

"Now we will see who is best," Galibani howled. "Now we will judge!"

His retainers, with Spoon distinctly upright in their midst, slunk into the room like eunuchs in service to an unpredictable sultan.

"We will solve this problem!" the chieftain continued. "Who is best? Who is most beautiful? Sharon Stone or Kim Basinger?"

And that was exactly what they did. The double feature went by swiftly, though, since Galibani had no interest in the relative merits of Mickey Rourke or Michael Douglas. The chieftain sat on a plastic chair, close enough to the screen to cause severe eyestrain, remote control a magic wand in his big paw. He fast-forwarded through the plot development, such as it was, slowing for lingerie and freezing time for nudity.

"I think Sharon Stone is too beautiful," Galibani said at a strategic point. "She is like Queen Tamara, hurling men to their deaths from the towers of her castle. Many men would fear her." The chieftain's tone made it very clear that he would not. In the near dark, the eyes of his warriors shone as they gasped with horror and desire.

Burton knew that they would have killed any of their female relatives who even hinted at such behavior, but it also struck him that Sharon Stone sent exactly the message most of the men in the world wanted to hear: that women were insatiable demons who needed to be used, mastered, contained, but certainly not respected. The great thing about Sharon Stone and company to the guys of the planet was that you did not have to bother with conversation or emotions or anything else that diverted you from the point. Madonna had been a genius at it. The U.S. military was a feeble thing compared to America's world-conquering blondes. This was psychological warfare at its best: hilarious, irresistible to the targets, and irreparably destructive.

As the last video rewound, an aura of post-coital sorrow filled the room.

"How can a man decide?" Galibani sighed, his voice laden with tragic poetry. "It is beyond a man to judge such things . . ."

Burton felt filthy sick of it all. Thirsty for water, ready for bed. It was not even funny anymore. It struck him, suddenly and very hard, that he had wasted a day and a night, that there was a very good chance Galibani was just fishing for bennies, and, meanwhile, Kelly Trost was enduring God only knew what somewhere in the basement of Shitsville. If she were still alive. He had an alcohol-weighted sense of failure, of having handled things badly, of having made poor decisions. And he had found the jerking film scenes depressing. He felt as though he had gotten dirty through sheer carelessness.

There was one more surprise waiting for him. In his room. A young woman with a narrow, almost pretty face and a beautiful profile sat on his bed in the lamplight. She jumped when he entered, but after a doubtful moment, a look of unmistakable relief passed over her face and she smiled to show a gold tooth.

She spoke no Russian, no Turkish. Only the local dialect that had shaped itself to exclude outsiders. When he made no move to embrace her, she seemed to lose confidence and quickly turned away to undo her garments. As though preparing for an inevitable punishment. Burton put his hands on her then, but only to stop her. He had heard about the custom, which was still widely practiced over in the highlands on the Iranian side, where the feudal landholders weathered every storm. The woman would be a young wife from the lowest fringe of the clan, summoned by the chieftain to satisfy his guest. The situation was one of those oddities that make humanity so difficult to fix into categories. Had Burton approached this woman by day, without introduction, offering her the least untoward gesture or word, her husband would have killed him or died trying. And his brothers and cousins would have carried on the vendetta. But the will of the chief was like the hand of God. This did not count as infidelity, did not count at all. It would be forgotten, hidden away, buried, and life would go on.

Burton wished they shared a common language. He would have tried to explain that he found her very attractive, but that he would not touch her on principle. He would have lied that he had a wife with whom he was wildly in love. He would have stumbled but tried to patch together some human decency with which to cover the situation. In the end, he just pointed to the bed, stopped her again from undressing, and let her lie down. Still dressed himself, he lay down beside her, staring at the ceiling. He could not send her away, because that would have shamed everyone involved. So the night was a thing to be gotten through, like a bad run of maneuvers.

After he put out the light, she touched his arm once, and he found her hand, squeezed it, then let it go again. He wondered what was in her head, whether she thought him impotent or herself insufficiently desirable. Not competitive with the world from which he came. He wished again that he had words for her, realizing how much communication meant to him and how far he was from the world of female caricatures that drained the leisure dollars of the males of a shrinking planet.

He would, in fact, have liked to make love to her. Out of raw desire. But he would not. The wives of other men, even of enemies, were not to be touched. And he damned well was not going to accept such a gift from the neighborhood bully, a heroin-pushing murderer with bad taste in movies.

But he could not sleep for a long time, and he listened to the other human being beside him as her breathing settled from fear into doubt into slumber. She smelled like heavy flowers and he would have liked to embrace her, to hold her, just that much, but he did not trust himself to stop. So he drowsed in disappointment at himself and the day, gnawed by a sense of duty undone, of events badly managed. Then bigger issues snaked around him, questions about his life. For years he had enjoyed this world, its exotic confusions and the surprises that waited just over the next hill. But he wondered now if that had not been his version of pornography, if he had not been a voyeur of the misery of others.

He thought again of Kelly Trost, not quite remembering the details of her face, and then he thought of the rape he had watched through binoculars and of the difficulty of living an honorable life without just quitting the human race. No wonder the saints ran for the desert.

Finally, Burton slept. He woke once from an imageless nightmare to a faint, imagined scream in English, a cry of, "*Help me.*" It made him start, and the woman beside him moaned once without waking and settled her arm over a stranger as she might have done over her beloved. The dream sound had been fiercely vivid, and Burton felt disoriented for long moments as his wakefulness fenced with the silence of the big, dead house. But the call did not come again, it had been only a phantom from the subconscious, and soon he slept again, deeply and truly this time.

Kelly heard music. Buffered by floors and walls, the sound was faint but electrifying. Music. It astonished her that anyone in the world could be making music at such a time. Her throat tensed and the gag over her mouth brought on a renewed fear of choking. Distant, yet notably foreign, the music was of a sort she recently might have forced herself to enjoy, committed to the equitable treatment of other cultures. Now the scales were snakes.

The music drove her down into despair. Without really thinking about it, she had imagined that even for her captors her fate must be the most important thing in the world. Now they were listening to music. Maybe even having a party. The muted clangs and thumps riding the house beams down to her prison were devastating. She struggled to rise, and failed.

She hated vulnerability in herself, had built her strength out of a refusal of weakness. As much as anything, she thought, it had been a fight against her father. And his overwhelming, unpredictable attentions. As an adult, she had believed herself free of the weaknesses that limited others, picturing herself as a toughened veteran. Now the impact of music, of a voice barking incomprehensible words at a melody, broke her down.

He had always made her fight. She dated the discovery of her Self from the swim-team tryouts when she had been in the ninth grade, a scrawny, nervous girl, her adolescent gawkiness worsened indescribably by a swimming cap and goggles. She had been padding from the locker room toward the pool when she overheard her father's voice from the coach's office, a voice that even a flat-chested, flat-bottomed kid could recognize as a menace to women everywhere, nudging the coach artfully, drawing a promise that never quite got into words, that his Kelly would make the team.

It had been the angriest moment of her life. Until that afternoon, she had never imagined that she could feel such fury. Her swimming had been her own, something she did all by herself, and now her father was ruining it, taking even that away. She marched out to the pool in a rage and swam the second-fastest breaststroke in the history of the school. By the end of the season, she had broken three school records. And her father had been daddy-proud of her. Yet she later wondered if he had not been disappointed by her independence. There had been something about him that just made her want to curl back her lips and show her teeth.

Of course, ninth grade had been a bad year. In lots of ways. And her father had not yet managed to fit himself back into her life with any steadiness at that point. But it had been a mark of real progress when he stopped calling her his "little filly" and nicknamed her "the barracuda."

He had a way of putting fear in you, though. Later, at university, she had dreamed of making the Olympic team, but had been mature and clear-headed enough to realize in time that she was not that good. She had, however, made the appalling mistake of mentioning her ambition to her father during one of the heart-to-hearts he contrived, then lived in terror that he would try to pull strings on that, too.

She supposed you could only hate people so much when you really loved them deep down inside and wanted them all to yourself. So many things had clarified with the years, and she had lately come to see that she had not been blameless. If the old resentments and jealousies still clung to her bones, they had less and less power over her now. Her father really had become her friend, if one who needed watching. With the music tormenting her, Kelly tried to guess the time and calculate the difference between her part of the world and Washington, imagining what her father might be doing and hoping almost maternally that he was not too worried about her.

Odd, she would have been shrieking grateful had he smashed through the door personally to rescue her. This one time she was ready for any help he could bring. But she also saw him as older than she had allowed, his shoulders thinned, and she saw his weaknesses and loneliness with disarming clarity, and she did not want to cause him any grief. She wanted him to be happy, and not too disappointed in her.

Eventually, the music stopped, and she lay in the darkness with her fears and the bug-bristle of the ropes on her wrists and ankles. The old house had a life of its own, creaking above her head, and she imagined she could hear things moving over the floor. A humiliating wave of sickness swept over her again, ruining what little comfort her body had salvaged from her predicament. In another flight from lucidity, she imagined that she must not fall asleep, because if she did, she would never wake up. She fought sleep, or believed she did, as she had fought so many things in her life. But sleep won, a gigantic father.

She awakened to the sound of an opening door, to darkness, quick footsteps, and hands upon her.

In the evening, Heddy took a real taxi from her fiancé's villa up to Cologne. The cost was horrendous, but she paid it as a form of penance. She got out by the main train station, which was quiet now, ornamented only by a few bottle-sharing derelicts and an impossibly skinny boy with spikes of green hair. The clouds had reached the city from the west, dulling the last light. She walked, low heels clacking on the sidewalk. Beginning at the resurrected cathedral, where Burton had kissed her profanely on one of their shared vacations, she retraced the routes they had taken. With the hollowness inside her.

Heading for the Rhine, she passed the art museum that had been boxed together at the peak of the postwar will to ugliness, and a light rain began. She had no umbrella, did not care, and just flipped up the collar of her summer jacket. Ahead of her, the Rhine chopped gray and it felt as though the autumn had arrived in a matter of hours.

The museum was one of their important shrines. Burton had been as excited as a child, leading her toward a Dutch landscape painting she had passed a dozen times without noticing. At first, she could not fathom his enthusiasm, but he talked on, far more rapidly than was his habit, and finally she got it, got him, understood why she wanted him so much. His words had not been scholarly, and his eyes had plunged back and forth between her and the painting as if he were afraid she would run away. He held out his hand toward the painting as if lifting a curtain so that she could see, and he was so open and unguarded that it pierced her and she wished she could be like that, too, to join him in his tumult of joy over a minor painting on a rainy day. She wished she could see the way he saw.

That was the thing about him—he truly knew how to see. He looked at things without the prejudice of sophistication, taking them on their own terms. Briefly, she had seen, too. Burton loaned her the eyes of the artist, some secondary figure who could not bear that the world should forget the way those green boughs rustled on an unimportant afternoon. Captured in oils, a white-capped girl went about her chores to the amusement of a dawdling cavalier. One shaft of sunlight struck the hilt of his sword. In a farmhouse window, an old woman swept, and the spires of a town lured the eye into the distance.

It was all common and unheroic and beautiful beyond measure when you took the time to see what the artist had seen. For a moment, Heddy had felt the weight of the clouds pressing down on the dark trees, the cool of their shadows and the damp air, and the intensity of the light. And it frightened her and angered her a little to think that the man beside her might see the world with such intensity every day, while she saw nothing at all.

Then they had a late lunch with a bottle of white wine in the trattoria of the moment, and they walked by the river where the old town had been reconstructed after the bombing, and he felt her body with the enthusiasm of a teenage boy. They could not wait to go back to their borrowed apartment in Bonn, so they took an exorbitant room in the Maritim and made love till it hurt, and she still did not want it to stop, then they were lying beside one another with the drapes opened and the brown spires of the cathedral guarding the city's rooftops from all the devils in the world.

Wet hair clinging to her face, Heddy walked beside the river. White tour boats punched into the waves and a lone coal barge rode low in the water, violating the dictated rest of Sunday evening. Turning back into the alleys, with their shut pubs and waste bins, she could not think of anything but the man she loved, and the rain made it better and worse, and she wanted to kiss him now in one of the empty doorways. She walked past their trattoria, shut now, where they had eaten and touched each other under the tablecloth, and on past a weary trolley and awful *Gründerzeit* statuary and the cars sizzling over the wet bridge. Huge, impersonal, gorgeous with memories, the Maritim glowed, a beacon for businessmen flying in for Monday morning meetings. Across a sliced-through park, an old beer hall, the *Malzmühle*, waited darkly for the next day's customers. She remembered Burton laughing against an old wooden bench, delighted at the Rhenish peasant food, "Heaven and Earth," downing finger glasses of beer, and it seemed he was always laughing, her laughing cavalier, except she knew there was a restlessness in him that would have turned into unhappiness if he ever held still, and more than anything else in the world, she wanted him to hold still.

Tasting the rain, she almost smiled, thinking of the time she came back to her flat in Baku to find him waiting for her, sitting back on the bed clad only in a T-shirt, listening to cranky jazz and playing an imaginary saxophone. He had grinned, unembarrassed to be discovered so, and the realization of how different he was from her and her look-alike world almost made her weep.

Helmut sat upright and listened to string quartets.

Ravished by memory, Heddy saw herself as flat and very German and tepidly damned. She loved Burton, accepted it, and this was all a self-indulgent farewell. Because she knew she would not choose him. She would do what was asked of her, and marry Helmut, and have a good, successful life, because that was the way things really happened, and there were more important things in life than mediocre Dutch landscapes.

CHAPTER

■ ■ ■

Trost's sense of outrage began to ease as he paced the Sunday afternoon traffic along the George Washington Parkway. His home phone number seemed to be the stuff of rest-room graffiti now and one of the last of the many callers who had choked his day had been a witch from Justice who warned him not to give the opposition party an opening on "all this" that would let them put a negative spin on the Administration's anti-terrorist posture.

With his anger dwindling into sorrow, Trost passed a minivan driven by a woman whose caloric intake could have fed an entire Third World country. He sighed at the loss of elegance in the world. Laura, who had been more of a comfort than he expected in the night, deserved greater attention than he paid her. She was one of the last of those splendid women who understood that the world would never behave as neatly as the professors and ideologues would have it. That was the problem with the kids sulking in the White House—they remained astonished that the world would not sit up and beg at their command. Even the mayor blew them off.

The river glinted down through the trees and he pictured Laura reclining, with her ginger hair and white skin and smoked voice, her grammar sound even in passion. Laura was the kind of woman he had hoped Kelly might become. Not the sexual part so much, although he liked to think he was a realist about such things. But he wanted his daughter to have the ability to speak in complete sentences, to enter and leave a room with dignity, to take the world seriously but without absurd expectations. He wanted his daughter to be a woman who could laugh at mankind's shortcomings without meanness and who did not view every male as an apprentice rapist.

Kelly's generation seemed determined to remain sullen undergraduates, deniers of beauty, joyless. The young people who came to the Hill to work as interns or apprentices seemed addicted to drabness, hooked on a mock intensity that concealed their ignorance about the wants and needs of real human beings. They could not laugh without thinking about it first, and even going to the grocery store was a crusade. He had been helpless to stop Kelly from being a part of her time, and he had even been glad of some of it, proud, if a bit unnerved, as she won swimming championships, then launched herself to fix the world. Now she was missing, gobbled up by the revolting shred of the planet she had assumed she could repair, and not a damned person in Washington had a clue about what had really happened to her, or where she was, or even if she was still alive.

Well, maybe one person had a clue. Maybe. If he wasn't just another D.C. bullshit artist. Trost pulled onto the ramp that led to the Beltway, heading north across the bridge. Bob Felsher had called him just after the woman from Justice. Trost had answered belligerently and it took him a moment to place Felsher. Even after the embarrassing scene of the night before. Felsher asked him—almost begged him—to come out to his home, insisting he had someone the senator needed to meet, someone who could help find his daughter, but who was best met on neutral ground.

Anxious but wary, Trost told the man he would call him back. Then he phoned a fellow senator who had oversight for energy matters, asking him if Felsher was a known quantity.

"Bob Felsher?" the phone voice asked after the mandatory remarks of sympathy. "Hell, he's all right. His onboard computer's a little slow. Avoid lunch. Set it up so you can break away right quick. Fella might just be the most boring human being ever washed up in this town." The other senator chuckled. "Tell you the truth, he's hard to figure, Mitch. Not the sort of shark who usually swims on K Street. You remember those old Fuller Brush boys selling door-to-door? They have 'em up your way? Wouldn't make Felsher for Big Oil at all, if you didn't know. You be nice to him, though, hear? Oak Leaf Oil crowd are heap big contributors."

"Can I trust him? Is he dependable?"

Trost's colleague laughed. "Well, the contributions come on time. I'd figure he's about as dependable as they come around here."

"Cold comfort."

"Really sorry about Kelly, hear? Anything I can do, Mitch . . . anything at all . . ."

Trost turned off on the exit for Potomac and in less than a minute the suburbs resolved themselves into screw-you wealth.

As a teen, Kelly had come out to Potomac to ride with a girlfriend who later died of a drug overdose at Vassar. He wondered if Kelly had ever fallen into any of the drug stuff, and decided probably not. Her swimming was too important to her. He had been proud that she had not failed as immediately as had so many of her privileged peers, proud that she possessed the discipline and energy to survive.

He wished he could just speak to her on the telephone, hear her living voice.

Felsher lived down a magazine-cover lane where horses bent their necks to the grass of long swales. His home was not one of the most vulgar, but the orange brick was bad. There were two cars in the crescent driveway, a Lexus and a plump Buick with diplomatic plates.

The oilman shot out of the front door as though he had been listening for the sound of Trost's car.

"Good to see you, Senator, good to see you again," Felsher said. Smiling. Then he decided that the smile was inappropriate. He straightened his face and clasped his hands together in a way that reminded Trost of an undertaker. It was a pattern Trost already recognized in the man: the impulse to smile followed by the self-critique. He struck Trost as the sort who read self-help books. "Come on in. Please. Won't take much of your time."

The oilman led the way. Upon entering the house, Trost decided that Felsher had bought it, not built it. Rooms with good woodwork held furnishings that reminded Trost of a split-level from the sixties or seventies: plaid couches with wooden arms that aped the sheen of plastic, prints of Paris of the sort you might see at a yard sale, a stranded coffee table with little drawers.

Trost almost collided with a gray woman bearing a tray of decorated crackers gone missing from a bridge club. At first, the senator thought the woman was a servant, but Felsher introduced her as his wife just before she darted into the room ahead and reappeared immediately without the tray.

"I just don't know what I'm going to do," she said, then disappeared.

Pausing just inside a library with a couple of books and dozens of statuettes of Teutonic children with heads too big for their bodies, Felsher said: "Senator, I'd like you to meet Major General Kulikov, Defense Attaché down at the Russian embassy. General Kulikov, this just may be our greatest living senator, Mitchell Trost."

"I am honored," the Russian said. "It is a very great honor for me."

"Well, let's all sit," Felsher told them. "Let's just sit right down. Help yourself to the snacks."

Trost knew he should be thinking hard. But he was tired
of thinking. And he supposed it was all right to meet with a
Russian now. Goddamned Drew MacCauley would probably
love it.

"General Kulikov here has some news for you," Felsher
said. "Now . . . I don't want to get you all excited. But there's
something there. General?"

The Russian was a lean man with the posture of a cadet,
very much unlike the Russian generals of Trost's imagination.
He wore blue slacks in a faintly chemical shade and his shirt,
not exactly wrong, looked like a bad choice from a good store.
The general had menthol-blue eyes and the red skin of an
outdoorsman, not of a drunk.

"Senator," the Russian began, intoning each syllable with
classroom seriousness, "the Government of Russia is . . . sensitive to your, shall we say, situation. It is a terrible thing, I
think. These southern people . . ."

The phrase made Trost flash on Laura, who was High
Virginia.

". . . these southern people are not so civilized." The Russian's lips mustered a barracks smile. "I know the Soviet pe-
riod has contained"—he pronounced the word with three
syllables—"many bad things. But I think you do not know
how we have been keeping the peace in these places in the
south." He cocked his head as if taking a salute.
"Azerbaijan . . . there was never such a country. It was only
a place where no one wished to go. Now there is freedom that
is only an illusion, and a government that only pretends to be
a government. How is it that your unfortunate daughter must
go there?"

Yes, Trost thought, how the fuck is it? Get to the point,
man.

"You see," the attaché continued, "we do not think this
government will ever be able to take control. They sit in Baku
and make themselves rich. While there is anarchy everywhere.

The oil is not safe. No pipeline will be safe. Your daughter is not safe . . ."

Felsher was quick enough to catch Trost's mood. He interrupted in a Sunday-school voice: "General Kulikov, I know the senator is anxious to hear about his daughter."

The general nodded. "Yes. Of course. But I have to make the background." He looked at Trost with arctic eyes. "We believe we know who has taken your daughter. They are Islamic terrorists. We are going to rescue her for you."

Over breakfast, Burton summarized his case. Severely hungover, Galibani had the look of a baited bear, reaching out a paw to cram his mouth with goat cheese or olives—which he ate in multiples, spitting the pits on the floor—or dripping honey from a rip of bread. The chieftain had not washed or shaved. Feeling healthy and vivid despite poor sleep, Burton chose his words carefully:

"The United States . . . would be enormously grateful for your help in recovering Senator Trost's daughter. On the other hand, I can promise you that anyone who might harm her . . . will be caught and punished. Americans have long memories," Burton lied. "But we help those who help us."

Galibani snorted and crumbs of cheese fell from his mustache. "The Shah of Iran helped America. Now his son is a beggar without a home."

Beautifully on cue, Galibani's own son trotted into the room, followed by the hunchbacked retainer, a man whose face reflected all the misfortunes of the world. The boy plowed into his seated father's flank, drawing the first smile of the day from the chieftain.

"I want to make it very clear," Burton continued, "that the United States will be merciless in the pursuit of the kidnappers. Especially if the girl is hurt in any way."

Galibani lost his smile. "Why tell me that? I know nothing about the girl. I only want to help my friends. But America pushes away my hand."

Burton met the man's bloodshot eyes head-on. "America . . . wants Kelly Trost back."

But the chieftain had retreated into posturing. "We all want this girl back . . . nothing but trouble . . . the times we live in . . ."

The last image Burton had of Galibani was of a bulky figure waving goodbye as if giving a fascist salute and balancing a pudgy boy on his left arm.

Spoon did not say much on the leg down to Lenkoran, and Burton was not in a talking mood, either. At the edge of a settlement, a crowd of somber men milled around a broken-down bus and kerchiefed women fingered their lips behind the vehicle's smeared windows. Where the road followed a ridgeline, Burton noticed four helicopters off to the northwest, too far out for the rotor noise to be heard. They looked like HIPs, the snubby workhorses of the former Soviet empire, but the distance left Burton uncertain. God only knew what they were up to, or even to whom they belonged. The region was spiked with armies and ethnic militias and overequipped bandits, all of whom possessed as much of the surplus of the collapsed Soviet military as they had been able to steal or bribe away.

Spoon braked for a goat in the middle of the road, a problem more pressing than helicopters, and Burton had to dismount to cajole the animal back into its field.

The landscape greened and the vistas narrowed. The air thickened with each downward curve. Soon they were on the flat coast, with the sun smacking tin roofs and their shirts soaking with sweat despite the open windows.

With Lenkoran a smudge in the sky behind them, the rules changed. As if they had passed out of prison gates. Spoon said, "Sir, you got to tell me. Was there a woman waiting there in your room last night?"

"Yep."

"And?"

"And what?"

"You know."

"No."

"Oh."

"You?"

"*Me?*"

"I take it there was a woman in your room, too," Burton said.

"Oh, yeah."

"Do I even want to hear about this?"

"Sure. I mean, I didn't do anything, either." Spoon shook his head as though clearing away the last sleepiness. "No way. I even tried to get her to leave, but she wouldn't go. I don't much like the way they treat women around here. So I slept on the floor. Uncomfortable as hell. I mean, I would have gotten in bed just to sleep. But you know how one thing leads to another. She snored, too. I think she needs her tonsils out."

"You know . . ." Burton said after a few moments, ". . . things that seem fascinating when you're young just seem sick when you get a little older."

"Ain't that the truth. Sleep in the bed with yours?"

"Yeah."

"And you really didn't?"

"Really didn't."

Spoon whistled. It was a peculiar but unmistakable form of tribute. "I thought maybe you'd do it just to find out what it was like. Kind of like research."

"Sorry to disappoint."

"Aw, you don't ever disappoint me, sir. You just surprise me sometimes. I kind of think of you like those Brit officers in the movies on the oldies channel. Like in *Gunga Din.*"

"They weren't officers in *Gunga Din.*"

"You know what I mean."

"Yeah. Thanks, I guess."

They passed a new brick bazaar that retailed the junk produced by cultures that bought their machinery abroad. Burton had stopped on his last trip down the coast, disappointed to find only blond plastic dolls, Turkish-made underwear, re-tooled auto parts, and the cheap machine-made rugs that had destroyed the local tradition of weaving beauty. It was *Homo Shoppingmallus* right out of the swamp.

Spoon stopped at a patch of grubby trees that served as a public convenience. The two men stepped carefully away from the sandy parking space, halting only at the sight of a snake trestled between two bushes. When they were done, they loped back to the jeep, seeking a rhythm that fit the heat.

"All this shit with the girl is getting to me," Spoon said, cranky-voiced. He settled in behind the wheel, although it was Burton's turn to drive. "Even dreamed about her last night. Funny stuff. One of those dreams so real you can't tell the difference for a while. Woke me right up." He paused with his hand on the ignition. "Could've sworn I heard a woman's voice yelling, 'Help me.'"

It was one of those rare moments in his life when Burton actually got gooseflesh. He stared into the turd-mined grove and saw only his own stupidity.

"Christ," he said. "He's got her right there in the house."

"It'll be dangerous, Spoon. This is no bullshit."

The NCO made a John Wayne face. "Hell, that's what we're getting paid for."

"No. It's not what we're getting paid for. This is a real long-shot. Both our asses could end up dead or something in between that might be worse."

Spoon looked at him hard. "Sir, I ain't going back to Baku like some sorry-ass State pussy knowing they got that girl up there." He spit, but they were both so dry-mouthed there was not much to it beyond the gesture. Then the NCO punched the steering wheel. "Just think about us sitting there like two dickheads, eating and drinking and hanging out with the porno king. While that kid's probably thinking the whole world's forgot about her and don't give two shits."

"All right, partner," Burton said.

As they drove, Burton bent to undo a panel under the dashboard with his Swiss Army knife. In an emergency, the panel could be ripped away, but Burton was glad to have something to do that required concentration. He knew he should be constructing a plan, but he really did not have any brilliant inspirations about how two guys on the wrong side of the planet could sneak their way into an armed compound in the clearglass daylight, find the girl, then get her out without enough trouble to make life difficult for a company of Rangers. He suspected he was going to do the first thing that had occurred to him, which was just to drive up to the front gate and lay it all out and demand the return of the girl. Sure as hell couldn't call the local cops, even if they were awake. They'd only phone ahead to Galibani, and the girl would be gone quicker than a Congressman with a cripple's wallet.

His shoulder nudged the gear shift and Burton said, "Sorry." He got the last screw out, dropped the panel, and felt for the taped weapons: two Makarov nine-millimeter pistols with a spare magazine each, just enough firepower to stop a toy poodle if you hit it right between the eyes. But even these were a hanging violation. Kandinsky was a fine ambassador, but he was true State Department in his terror of armaments, and he had forbidden any of his staff to carry arms. Burton, who was a realist with a wide-ranging itinerary, had decided to keep the guns hidden in the vehicle for emergencies.

Clearing Lenkoran for the third time, Spoon took the mountain road as fast as the jeep would go. In the gulch where they had eaten lunch the day before, kids were playing in the stream again. Farther along, the bus was still broken down, its male passengers still milling about the engine compartment. Dark faces turned to follow the jeep. Across steep valleys, sheep glaciered the hillsides.

Everything was normal until they got to Lerik. They passed the fountain with President Aliev's profile in mosaic, then rounded the last spur, and Burton knew something was wrong even before he understood what his eyes were telling him.

The town sat on the hillside as it always had, and above it, the compound with the mansion waited just as they had left it.

But it was not just the way they had left it. And Lerik had changed in a way that sent a chill over the high valley, a change in the air that made no scientific sense but was as real as a punch in the nose.

Halfway down the road, Burton realized what had changed.

There was no sign of life.

No movement.

Even the sheep had been driven out of sight.

As Spoon downshifted, a lone dog erupted from a ditch and stretched its body across a field as if being hunted.

"Stop for a minute," Burton said.

"White man very wise," Spoon told him. But his voice held no real humor. Just cracking a joke on the way to the gallows for form's sake.

Whatever was going on, it was unlikely to be good. They sat in the idling jeep, facing off with the deadened town.

It made no sense. There was no way the town could have been evacuated that quickly. They had been gone less than three hours. The people had to be in there.

"Hey, boss," the NCO said, squinting through the windshield. "Take a gander at the sky up over Galibani's place."

The sky was clear and travel-poster blue. But if you looked hard enough you could see a distortion a bit thicker than haze coming off the hilltop compound. As if campfires had been put out badly.

"Dig in the spurs," Burton said.

There was no way to reach the compound by vehicle without going through the buffer zone of the town. Spooner took the streets and the badly canted corners at about thirty miles an hour, quick enough to outrun most trouble, slow enough to stop fast. Burton primed his pistol, but kept it out of sight behind the door.

"Jeez," Spooner said. "It's like aliens took them."

"They're here," Burton told him. "Hiding under their beds." Above the ruts that passed for a main street, the shop windows had been methodically shuttered and several of the doors wore big steel padlocks. The merchants, who would have been prepping for the local bazaar, had not simply run for cover. They had done their risk-benefit analysis and decided they had time to lock up properly. That meant the problem had been isolated up at the compound, but big enough to threaten a spillover.

At the far edge of the town, where the lane turned sharply uphill toward Galibani's fortress home, Spoon stopped the jeep again and yanked up the emergency brake. He looked at Burton: Final decision?

Burton was thinking.

Trying to think.

Yes.

Definitely smoke.

Shoot-out at the OK Corral, and no doubt about it.

What the hell, though? It certainly had not been a government raid—they would have had to come up the road, and he and Spooner would have passed them on the way down. The only other road was the glorified trail that came from the Iranian side of the border, and the Iranians had always been scrupulous about observing Azerbaijan's sovereignty, fearing embroilment in the Karabakh war, fearing the bad temper of the Russians, fearing their own ethnic Azeri population.

So what the hell was it? Bandit raid? Clan feud? Commandos who worked their way in over the hills? The best way to come would have been by air . . .

Burton crushed his forehead against the dashboard.

"Fuck," he said. "Goddammit. Fuck, fuck fuck . . ."

"What?"

"The goddamned helicopters."

"What helicopters?"

"I *saw* them. Flying the valley trace."

"I didn't see any helicopters," Spoon said. "You didn't say anything."

"Right before we came up on that fucking goat. Jesus, I feel dumb as a rock." He smacked the dashboard with the butt of his pistol.

"Careful with that pork chop, boss."

The last indecision was gone. "Let's move out, partner."

"Up the hill?"

"Up the hill."

It looked as though the checkpoint halfway to the compound had been abandoned. They were almost in the slime when they saw the remains of the two guards who had been on duty. The men had been chopped apart by an auto-cannon.

Spoon slowed, instinctively unwilling to drive over what was left of the bodies, a horse shying at a rattlesnake.

"Go on," Burton said. "It doesn't matter now. *Go.*"

The compound wall had been shot through at several points and the main gate had been blown out. Rockets and Gatling guns, Burton figured. Not exactly a surgical operation. The hilltop smelled as though it had been coated with sulfur.

Who had been holding the intelligence?

What about the girl?

Chunks of masonry and a meat market of corpses blocked the entranceway. The destruction had been localized, but so powerful it had bent or gouged the gunmen's weapons into uselessness. Steady hand on the gat, Burton thought. He imagined the helicopters appearing over the nearest ridge and coming straight in. Thirty seconds to their LZ, all weapons on rock and roll.

Spoon paused again. "Want me to try to drive over all that?"

Burton shook his head, wishing he could think faster. "No. Can't afford a flat now. We might have to get out of here fast."

Spoon edged the vehicle to the side of the trail, unwilling to block invisible traffic. "Shut her down?"

"Yeah. Jesus. Listen, you stay here with the jeep."

The NCO looked at him with a doubtful face. "You don't want to do that, boss. You might need cover in there."

"Right. Yeah. Shit. Let's go."

The two men dismounted. They crouched down automatically, prisoners of their training, but there was no sign of life beyond a few curious birds. Burton led the way, avoiding the human leftovers. There were no wounded. Inside, the courtyard glittered in patches, as though it had been seeded with gold. Shell casings. Hundreds of them.

The wall of the main house had been shot through in two places. One spot had burned a little. A bed hung out in precarious balance, two of its legs dangling in the morning air. It was an old brass bed, a Russian legacy, unlike the lower, simpler beds of the locals.

"Let me go first." Burton pointed across the courtyard. "I'll clear the doorway."

Spoon nodded. Compared to the devastation of the compound, the little Russian pistol looked like a toy in the NCO's hand.

All right. Burton sprinted straight across the courtyard, waiting for bullets. But that was conditioned fear. The compound was dead. You could feel it.

Burton made the cover of the main entrance to the house, hugged the wall, then threw himself inside and went into a defensive crouch, pistol up.

Three dead men lay just beyond his knees, hard on the senses. These had been killed with small arms. Overkilled. Dead had not been good enough. Burton believed he recognized one of the men from the party the night before, but it was hard to tell. Automatic rifles lay by the corpses and Burton picked up the nearest one, checking its action and the load of the magazine. Blood slimed one side of the weapon. It was not yet fully congealed and it smeared his shirt just above the waist. Calmly, Burton put his pistol on safe, stowed it in a cargo pocket of his khakis, then cleaned the rifle with his handkerchief. The blood-grease on his clothing and hands left him queasy, but possession of the weapon made him feel distinctly more secure. Although it had not done much for the dead men.

He moved back outside and waved to Spoon. The NCO jogged across the open space, zigging and zagging as though demonstrating evasion methods to an audience of recruits. When he made it in under the shade with Burton, he said, "Nice smoke-pole you got there, boss. Any more where that one came from? Jeez, you all right?"

"What?"

"You got blood on you."

Burton followed Spoon's eyes downward. The smears at his waist.

"AK was a little messy."

Spoon glanced around. "Well, whoever it was, I guess they weren't weapons collectors. Left the arsenal." He looked at Burton. "Came for the girl, right?"

"Had to be. Too much of a coincidence to be anything else. Although the heroin trade does have its ups and downs."

"I should've said something earlier," Spooner said, voice raw with regret. "About hearing that voice." He sorted through the weapons littered by the bodies.

"Yeah. And I should have said something, too," Burton told him. "We both should've said something. And then we could've been back here in time for all this, to get our own asses waxed." He snorted in general disgust. "Forget it, partner. We're two lucky pilgrims."

"She's not."

Something in the tone of voice got Burton's attention and he looked at his companion. Face too pale, expression slipping out of control. Burton recognized the symptoms. Spoon was hitting one of those emotional walls that paralyze men at the worst possible times.

Burton could not afford to lose him now. The truth was

that he was scared as hell. And he really did not know what to do.

"Come on," he told the NCO, slapping him hard on the shoulder. "We'll earn our beans yet. But right now we need to move fast. Before the locals lynch us."

But they could not move fast. First of all, there were security issues: how to enter a room that might still contain a frightened, trigger-happy survivor, how to avoid booby traps. Then there was the labyrinthine nature of the house: warrens, crannies, corridors, cold cellars. Everything had to be checked.

They began with Galibani's reception room. The big chieftain had made a last barrier of his desk, turning it over as a shield. The pattern of devastation told Burton that the assault team had tossed in a grenade or two before storming the room with weapons on full automatic.

Galibani lay belly down with his face to the side and his lips puckered. He clutched the body of his son, whose head had been shot half away. The hunchback lay in a fetal position at the chieftain's feet. The big TV was a blasted shell and videotapes covered the floor, some partly unspooled, others still in their jackets, an odd mix of glam-porn, action flicks, and Disney films. A bootlegged copy of *Aladdin* lay by the doorway.

After that, they did not speak for a time. They found dead women in the kitchen and pantries, in the bedrooms, and hidden in cupboards that seeped blood. Dead men, some with weapons, one holding a dirty rag, lay in hallways or in a connected barn where several of them appeared to have made a last stand. The cattle and horses had been killed, too.

Finally, at the end of a half-subterranean corridor at the back of the main building, a gunman who looked more like a mujaheddin than a Talysh bandido sat waiting in the gloom of the last doorway.

Burton almost shot him.

But the man was already dead. He sat upright, eyes opened, punched into his chair by a spray of bullets.

Burton got it. Adrenaline did as much for your brain as for your muscles. It was a perfect setup to hold a prisoner.

He led the way down the long hallway, kicking in one door after another, finding only sacks of grain and ancient farm implements except where one door opened out past a manure pile to a meadow. The peaceful green-and-blue world beyond the house came as a shock and Burton turned away from it, eyes suffering from the sudden daylight.

When he came up on the dead guard, flies lifted off the man's face. Burton motioned to the NCO to wait and cover him.

Only one thing mattered now: He did not want to find the girl dead behind the door. Sweating so badly he could smell himself, he hammered the sole of his boot into the wood.

The door had not been latched and he almost fell as it gave way. Recovering his balance, he brought his weapon up, heart thumping.

The room was empty.

Burton gasped as though he had been holding his breath for a long time. No blood on the floor. He looked around again. There was a bed with ropes tied to its crude wooden legs. The mattress was stained. He rushed over to it, trying to read the discolorations. Then he bent close, sniffed, and recoiled.

This was the place. This was where they had kept her. He would have bet his life on it.

Then he noticed the chains fixed to the wall.

"*Spoon*," Burton called. "Get in here."

The NCO ducked his head under the low doorway and looked around, wrinkling his nose.

"Smells like an outhouse."

"The bucket. And the bed's a mess."

"That blood on the bed?"

"No. She was sick."

"No blood?"

"Right."

"So they got her," the NCO said. "Whoever they are."

Relieved and discouraged, the two soldiers who had failed made their way back through the house full of corpses and stepped into the light of day. Larger birds had begun to perch on the compound walls now. Down the hill, a vehicle fired up.

"Time to get moving," Burton said.

But the NCO paused, considering the devastation of the courtyard one last time, thoughts tightening the skin on his face.

"Christ," he said. "Nothing but a goddamned slaughter."

"Welcome to the new world order," Burton told him. Spoon had arrived in-country after the war had stalled and he had not seen anything like this before.

The NCO could not work through it. It was a very bad day for a good man. He put his hand on Burton's forearm, holding onto him, and Burton could feel his companion trembling.

"Who did this? Who in the name of Christ would do a thing like this? Just tell me that. They didn't have to do this."

"Russians," Burton told him calmly. "They're the only ones who kill every living thing."

CHAPTER 9

A party roiled in the mansion beside the house the embassy had assigned to Burton. The mansion belonged to a gangster whose brother was the minister of trade. The gangster's parties were unpredictable and punctuated by gunfire, most of it celebratory, some of it focused. Mornings after, Burton often saw women leaving, Russian tarts from the hooker diaspora, their faces painted into masks, and Azeri girls barefoot on the broken road, high heels in their hands for safekeeping. The Azeris tried to appear defiant but looked ashamed, while the Russian women just seemed as though they were waiting for a hard burp to clear their systems.

Monday night had slipped into Tuesday morning, but Burton heard music as soon as he turned into his street. The gangster's stereo strained with an old Bee Gees recording from the valley of the disco shadow.

Burton garaged the dented Lada he drove in town, securing the wheel with a steel bar, locking the car, cuing a security system, then double-locking the garage. Walking to the house with his attaché case, he heard the meat-and-breath sounds of someone being beaten up just behind the wall of the gangster's property. Burton marched on, convinced that he had trouble enough for one very tired man. But passivity in the face of violence always left him feeling whorish. Selective intervention, he told himself. I am a paragon of fucking foreign policy.

The embassy had been a struggle, with Kandinsky under pressure from Drew MacCauley in Washington to show results and Vandergraaf, the DCM, horrified then argumentative when Burton told the two diplomats about the Russian involvement. Department policy—which meant MacCauley's policy—was that the Russians were good guys. No matter the evidence to the contrary.

Burton did not back down, although he had one very bad moment when he realized he still had the forbidden pistol in his cargo pocket. He wondered if the outline showed. The ambassador said nothing, but might have been postponing comment. It was another needless distraction and it reinforced Burton's desire not to play with guns anymore.

There were greater issues at the moment and it was time to take a stand. No one but the Russians could have conducted the raid on Galibani's compound. Shabby as the Russians had become, no other regional player had the combination of resources necessary to plan and execute a raid like that. And it damned well looked as though the Russians had the girl now.

Unless she had slipped off to pick wildflowers in the nick of time.

The backfield was in motion, too. Just as he and Spoon had reentered civilization—defined by the reach of Baku's cellphone net—they encountered a column of military trucks with bumper markings from one of the president's palace guard regiments. The convoy was loaded with troops and headed south. Meanwhile, no one in the Azeri government would answer a call.

The ambassador had gotten on the phone to the Land of the Big PX while Burton drafted the cable—a job soon complicated by a series of exchanges on his secure line as the Washington desk officers returned from lunch. With the cable done, Burton had gone back into the ambassador's office only to find Kandinsky shoving his eyeglasses up his nose and yelling at Drew MacCauley from half a world's remove.

"I'm *not* going to lie," the ambassador said.

Burton had done his best with the cable, keeping the language sober and precise. But the DCM objected to almost every sentence. The ambassador had to referee and the exchange got mean. They were all blown by sleeplessness and stress, and the DCM knew how to play the fear card. The message Kandinsky finally released was far more cautious than Burton would have liked and it went out as an "Eyes Only" to Drew MacCauley.

Nobody was happy. The ambassador closed the argument by saying:

"Just send the damned thing. We'll do a follow-up tomorrow."

Before he bailed out of the embassy, Burton tried one final round of calls. To his counterpart from the Russian embassy, to General Hamedov, and to a few other local contacts. But the town had gone into quarantine. On his way home, he detoured past the Russian embassy to check for any lighted windows, but the building was darker than local politics. Exhausted and driving very carefully, he made a mental list of offices to crash first thing in the morning. And he fought his growing suspicion that Kelly Trost might not get out of this alive.

The greatest danger now was that the girl would know too much. Her captors might feel themselves boxed in. Especially if they were Russians too dumb to hand her over immediately and take the goodwill profit. Zombied by the late hour, Burton sensed his defenses slipping down. The thought of losing the girl was vivid and sickening, and his visions were slow and dark and stained. He had wanted to end his military career with a small victory for humanity. It had been a selfish desire, of course. Instead, he found himself imagining a dead girl embalmed in the language of diplomacy.

Kelly Trost was at the top of everybody's A-list at the moment. Kill her, and in a month nobody would remember her but her family and a couple of underpaid analysts.

As Burton unlocked his house, automatic-weapons fire bit the night and the party next door surged.

His housekeeper had left on several lights and the quarters had the feel of a sanctuary. Fort Burton, dedicated to the defense of democracy, human rights, and jazz. His body revived just enough to register fundamental wants. The kitchen lay off the entranceway and he fetched a dish of eggplant casserole from the fridge. Plopping down at the kitchen table, he began to eat the food cold, soaking up the congealed oil with staling bread. The dip pouches had come in and his attaché case was full of mail, but he was too shot to even look at the return addresses. He closed his eyes as he chewed and tried not to think about anything, but he had reached the combination of weariness and agitation where the mind goes spinning off, with good and bad ideas tumbling over each other uncontrollably. He craved sleep but suspected it might not come easily.

Why did the Russians want the girl? Was she all right? He still felt shaken by the bloodbath at Galibani's compound. If anything, the spectacle hit harder as a memory, unbuffered by adrenaline.

In the morning. He was going to move mountains in the morning. Beginning with the Russians. The ambassador had agreed to his playing the bad boy and in the morning he intended to make the nastiest scene the Russian embassy had ever had to contain. Serious brinksmanship with the non-workers of the world. Where's my all-American girl, Ivan?

Burton opened his eyes and stared down into the dish of eggplant. It looked like something spilled from the belly of a corpse.

He could not forgive that kind of killing. Not even when it involved a pig like Galibani. There was altogether too much

175

killing in the world, and something had to be done about it. He knew he was a naive ass for thinking like that, but it did not matter anymore. Too much goddamned killing. Blood on the hands of every man, woman, and child. It had to stop.

Burton stood up. A last look at the eggplant only made him queasier. He could not even put it back in the refrigerator. Let the roaches have it. An offering to Saint Francis. Picking up a fresh bottle of mineral water and his attaché case, he slumped into the dining room, headed for the stairs. Beyond his walls, the party music had switched to a clanging, interminable local song in which a female singer gargled with chicken bones.

The air in the dining room had gone off.

Dead flowers in bad water. The stems drooped in a vase in the center of the table. Heddy had given them to him the week before. She was the first woman who had ever given him flowers, and she did it frequently, but the gesture never quite worked. Flowers seemed too delicate for her temperament, a gift drawn from the Book of Stylish Gestures rather than from the heart. He felt enough affection for Heddy to find it painful when she tried and failed. She was the kind of woman who was far better at fucking than flirting, literally too smart for her own good. Heddy would think her way out of any happiness she ever stumbled into.

The flowers stank and the housekeeper should have gotten rid of them.

He slapped his attaché case flat on the table and the commotion of air brought a snow of withered petals.

The unexpected beauty of it stopped him. Fading pink and white and lavender, the petals floated down and settled on the varnished wood. The lamp shed gold dust. A few patches of color still clung to the stems, and the water in the vase oiled the light, and for the first time in his life, Burton understood why a painter would spend his gift on a still life.

The accidental beauty of this world.

Good jazz.

Burton sat down for a moment, captured by the random arrangement of color and light. All his life he had just swept fallen petals into a cupped hand, ferrying them to the trash in a programmed gesture. In four decades on the earth, he had never noticed this miracle of light on dust and varnish, of petals scattered on wood.

He wondered if he would ever learn to see the world around him.

And he wondered how Heddy was doing in Bonn, hoping she would not hurry back. He needed time to break himself of the physical habit of her.

The soldier at the table reached for the pistol in his cargo pocket.

Burton had just realized that he was not alone.

Someone was sitting in a big high-backed chair in the shadows of the next room. The chair was an antique he had bought at a flea market, ugly to the point of beauty, obesely velveted, with a frame of Oriental carvings that might have been done at the command of one of Baku's turn-of-the-century oil titans. The chair faced away from the dining room and there was nothing visible of the intruder beyond a white hand on one of the arms, a paleness in light the color of molasses. A slight movement of the fingers had tugged Burton's eye.

Burton stood up quietly, clutching the pistol he had so recently wished away. He cocked the weapon and the sound cracked like thunder.

His presence was certainly no secret. But he tried to do everything according to his training now, each belated gesture a penance for his inattention. He scanned the flanking shadows, alert to the possibility of still other men in the house, startled that he had not sensed a living presence. He usually had good physical instincts. It was uncanny: The hand on the arm of the chair still lacked the palpable feel of human flesh. It was almost as if the intruder had no substance.

Burton shuddered and moved.

Was it killing time?

Everything seemed to be about killing now.

Was there a gun in the intruder's other hand? Was another weapon trained on his back?

Smelling the death off Galibani's compound, he walked toward the back of the chair, pistol ready. When he had closed to within three paces, he jumped to the side so that he would be out of the line of fire from room to room and shouted:

"Get up. *Now*."

A gray-haired man in a suit rose slowly. Even before he began to turn around, Burton recognized the German ambassador.

"This . . . is very difficult for me," the ambassador said in a voice notably weaker than the one he wielded at receptions. "However, I saw no alternative." He stood in the cast of light from the dining room and his eyes were pink, like canned salmon. Even at a respectable distance, his breath freighted alcohol. "Please do not make difficulties for your housekeeper. I was very insistent." He hinted at a smile. "We Germans can be that way, you know."

"Would you like a drink, Mr. Ambassador?"

When you had no idea what to do, you offered the other guy a drink. Burton dreaded what was coming. He caught himself gesturing with the pistol still in his hand and he put it on safe, then worked it clumsily into his pocket.

The ambassador looked as though he had been mugged by God.

"Perhaps an American whiskey. If it is not too much trouble."

Burton lurched back into the dining room, hoping the housekeeper had possessed the decency to leave at least some of the alcohol unfilched. Burton was not a private drinker and he brought in only what he needed when he had to host a dinner. The liquor cabinet harbored the leftovers, which disappeared at a steady rate without Burton's help. Now it held only a half-empty bottle of Unicum, some fruit liqueur concocted by the cousin of a cousin of a friend, and the dregs of a bottle of Georgian cognac.

"Brandy all right, Mr. Ambassador? It's local, I'm afraid."

"Yes, yes. Thank you very much. And I think, under the circumstances, it is not necessary for you to address me as Mr. Ambassador. Please call me Mr. Hartling."

Burton almost laughed out loud at the perfect Germanness of the man, but he managed to bully his facial muscles into a mask of diplomacy. He poured a double shot of Tbilisi's pride into a snifter.

"Please," Burton said, recrossing the room and extending the brandy, "have a seat. I'm too tired to stand up." He flicked on a table lamp.

The two men sat. The ambassador sipped the brandy, made a sour face, then knocked it back. Holding the empty glass, he gestured and opened his mouth, then could not make the words come. The man looked so beaten that Burton turned his eyes away for as long as he could, watching a moth go dizzy inside the lamp shade.

"This is so very hard," the ambassador said. Then he went quiet again.

Burton disliked and pitied the man. He could foresee the course of the ambassador's marriage to Heddy with nauseating clarity. Heddy's inevitable betrayals. Her cold-blooded attempts at discretion. The discoveries and embarrassments. Disappointment, then sorrow, scribbling over the ambassador's aging face. Accommodation. Repetition. Ice. Vulgar deathbed affection.

"Colonel Burton . . . Hedwig Seghers and I are to be married. I must assume that you know this."

Burton nodded.

"I think," the older man continued, "this is a great opportunity for happiness for Hedwig. I do not mean to be tactless . . . but there is a great deal that I can offer such a woman. So many things. Things that a man in your . . . your line of duty could not . . .'"

"Can't afford her. Got it."

The ambassador set the glass on the floor and raised his hands as if fending off an invisible blow. "Please do not be offended. I only think that . . . that you and I must speak frankly of these things. For Hedwig's sake."

"I'm not offended," Burton said. Wounded by truth, he thought, but not offended. Not yet. "I'm a realist."

"You see?" The man brightened. "That's it. We must be realistic about this. It is best for everyone, I think."

"Next issue?"

"I understand why Hedwig might be attracted to you, of course. I am not naive. As a younger man, you, too, have something to offer. I do not know how to put this very delicately . . ."

"Heddy likes to fuck. I'm reassured that you noticed."

"Well . . . I suppose that's an American way of putting it. I must say, Colonel Burton, I find such remarks—"

"Heddy and I are finished, pal. She's a fine woman and I'm not going to do anything to spoil her party." He looked at the older, smaller man. The ambassador struck him as at least as repulsive as Galibani had been. Civilization, my ass, Burton thought.

"But—"

"She's your girl, Helmut. Show her a good time and she'll do you proud. And now that we're done dividing up Poland, I'm tired." Burton put his hands on his thighs to help himself rise. The weary warrior, he thought, and everybody's chump. He could not imagine how Heddy could believe she might be happy with such a dishrag. Or even marginally content.

The ambassador half rose, gesturing frantically all the while. "Please. Please, let us talk. We have not discussed the most important matter. *Please.*"

Burton wondered if the man was about to offer him money. He had never punched an ambassador before, but it was beginning to seem like the sort of thing a man should do at least once in his life. He sat back down out of pure curiosity.

"Colonel Burton . . . this is a very delicate matter. For both of us. But above all, for Hedwig. I must ask you to release her from any agreements she has made to serve you."

Burton did not understand.

"Please," the ambassador said, "do not make a pretense. I am not a stupid man. I realize you have recruited her for American intelligence."

Burton had no idea what to say. The idea was too loony. Sure, he had poked around with a few pillow-talk questions. But he had never considered recruiting Heddy as a spy.

"I am trained to recognize the patterns, you see," the ambassador went on. "The things she cannot explain. The meetings that I have not approved. I demand that you release her and destroy any papers or evidence. If you do so, I will not make a protest to your government. There will be nothing else. We will forget all this. Most importantly, there will be no harm to Hedwig. I will make certain that no one discovers her secret. For once in your life, behave as a gentleman, Colonel Burton."

Burton stood up. "Listen, motherfucker, I never even *dreamed* of trying to turn Heddy into a goddamned spy. That's the dumbest thing I've ever heard." He unclenched his fists, but it took a triumph of the will. "Now get out of my house so I can get some sleep."

The ambassador, too, got to his feet. He swayed like a rummy in an old cartoon. "You are *not* a gentleman. You have attempted to ruin this excellent woman. I know all that is happening. I know where she goes when she spies for you. You are a typical American liar and a boor."

The door by the kitchen opened and closed. Burton had locked it. Only two other people had keys. And Spoon would not have come in without knocking.

The two men stared at each other, and Burton thought: We earn our fates. He heard the familiar sounds, the brisk footsteps, and Heddy's voice called from the hallway:

"Evan? Are you still awake? Evan?"

She rushed into the light of the dining room, letting a summer raincoat fall away from a green silk teddy with spaghetti straps. White legs drank the lamplight.

Her initial expression was one of horror. But it did not last. As Burton and the ambassador stared, her face shifted through a repertoire of emotions: fear, disappointment, anger . . . hatred . . . calculation. No one said a word as she drew her coat back over her fine shoulders and belted it around her body. She looked less at Burton, more at the ambassador, and her eyes narrowed as if she were aiming a weapon. Burton had a strong sense of her and he could feel her reaching for the words that would wound most deeply. Her posture remained erect, aristocratic, but the invisible Heddy had coiled and reared. When she spoke, her voice was as cold as a casualty list.

"Helmut," she said, "how tasteless of you."

The betrothed couple began to shout at each other, Heddy shrieking as Burton had never imagined she could do, and the ambassador yapping and crying, threatening and pleading at the same time. After a stunned moment, Burton realized he was nothing but furniture and he went back outside, where the party noise covered everything else. He slept in the backseat of his car.

The truth was that thirty-five thousand lives were not that big a deal. The deaths had been unfortunate, of course. And certainly untimely. Inconvenient. But the dead had not been Americans. Nor had they been the educated sort, by and large. Bit players in the pageant of history. Tragic. And all that. But statesmen could not be sob sisters. The Russians had made a mess in Chechnya. Given. It had taken all of Drew Mac-Cauley's skill and, finally, his personal friendship with the President to keep the matter in perspective. But in the end, he had preserved his Russia policy.

Let history judge.

Now this. Kandinsky was trying to sabotage him. No doubt about it. The man had gone native. Classic case of clientitis.

An ambassador who could not see beyond his own forlorn little country. Not a strategist, the man had no future with tomorrow's State Department. Vandergraaf, too, had proved himself a disappointment. Weak. Letting some military clown take over the circus. The Pentagon had never gotten over their irrational hatred of the Russians. The generals were always trying to interfere with policy. Now came this preposterous report about a Russian massacre committed against Azeri citizens. With the Trost girl supposedly in the middle of it. The entire affair was simply too much. All of the Russian-haters and Moscow-baiters would jump on it. The Hill would put on the usual freak show. It would, MacCauley thought, have been better if the girl had simply been killed outright at the beginning. Although it would have been tragic, of course. And he certainly would never have wished for such a thing. But now you had the military making a power grab.

Drew MacCauley could recognize a plot when he smelled one. The military types were trying to exploit the Trost case to turn an influential senator against the Administration's foreign policy. The cynicism of it was appalling.

His secretary rang in. "Miss Rains is here. Do you want me to send her in?"

"No. Not yet. I'll let you know."

He bent over the cable on his desk one more time. At least Arthur Vandergraaf had seen to it that the message had been transmitted as an "Eyes Only." Still, the man should have killed it entirely. Now it was a matter of record. Something would have to be done about it. Unless, of course, the girl popped up.

MacCauley did not know what to do. He did not want to be caught holding back information. But releasing it would bring no end of questions and accusations that might threaten to disrail his Russia policy again. Just when he had gotten everything back on track.

He glanced around his office as though the answer might be hidden as in one of those trick pictures that changed a witch into a beautiful girl when you upended it. Good woodwork, dark furniture, sound art. A proper place in which to shape policy. Humanized by the books overflowing the bookcases and stacked on the floor. The books and papers really were getting out of hand these days and there was a danger of overdoing the effect. Everyone wanted a comment for a dust jacket or a review. Of course, he had little time for that sort of thing now. But he did read the reviews written by others. Few things in life gave him greater pleasure than reading a harsh review of a friend's book.

There was one way to get away clean and avoid policy damage. The girl had to be found. Within forty-eight hours. If not sooner. Before this nonsense about Russian involvement became some sort of media myth. There really was no time to lose. Vandergraaf had warned him that the press were already beginning to show up around the embassy.

MacCauley thought of Senator Trost with growing hatred, as though the man had arranged to have his daughter kidnapped just to frustrate a better man's vision. Trost was nothing but a pompous, womanizing lightweight, one of those partisan rubes who could not but excite the disdain of those more responsible. But if Trost found out about the cable, there would be blood all over the Hill.

It all struck Drew MacCauley as terribly unfair.

Even the President had been a bit weak-kneed lately. The little people were getting to him. With their uninformed views of Russia and history. The man was just so inconstant. He had been that way since their roomie days at university, undependable and physically slovenly. Always leaving little messes for others to clean up, a bloated puppy. The only thing about him on which you could depend was his ambition. And his appalling taste in women. That, certainly. Brilliant, of course. Marvelous sense of theater. MacCauley prided himself on being one of the first to have recognized the man's potential. Despite that clammy, trailer-court brand of Southernness. Really, there was something about all Southerners that just wanted a good editor. What a tragedy if, after his years of effort, his *mission civilatrice*, the man were to be swayed by a poll or a pol to turn his back on an old friend and a chance to save the country of Tolstoy and Tchaikovsky for European civilization.

Sitting behind the great wooden desk on which he had insisted, MacCauley had one of the flashes of genius he cherished in himself: Might there not be a way to play the Tchaikovsky angle to get the gay community excited about greater political support for his Russia policy? The fellow had been queer as a three-ruble bill, had he not? Perhaps official sponsorship of a festival? Or something along those lines? Shame Bernstein was dead. The business crowd could fund it. Definitely worthy of consideration. Have to talk to the cultural types. Once the Trost affair had been put to bed.

It never ceased to astonish MacCauley how much more intelligent he was than anybody else at the Department of State. The President would *have* to make him Secretary in the returned Administration. Simply no choice in the matter.

Of course, that would require Senate confirmation.

He called out to his secretary. "Lydia, get Ambassador Kandinsky back on the phone. Wake him, I don't care. Yes. The secure line. Meantime, send in Rains. And call my wife and Mrs. Graham. Tell them I'll be half an hour late for dinner."

The analyst niced into the room like the little drudge she was. Garbageman's daughter at the country club dance. Where did the department get these people? How had State gone so far off the rails?

"Have a seat, Ms. Rains. Over there, if you would."

She sat down. Dreary and bleary, hair limp at the end of the day, wearing a dress that did not fit properly. Even the President would not have given her a second look, and MacCauley had seen the man look wistfully at barnyard animals.

"Now," MacCauley said, "first things first. Senator Trost has not initiated any further direct contact with you, I take it?"

She shook her head. "No, sir. And—"

"Good. Let me warn you, Ms. Rains—it's Ginny, is it not?

Let me attempt to share rather greater experience with you. People like Trost can*not* be trusted. Oh, they may seem affable and genuine. That's how they get the common man to vote for them. But it's our duty to rise above the personal, to keep the best interests of the department in mind. Don't you think?"

The young woman nodded. But it was a tepid response. God, the young had no passion in them. What kind of life could such a woman have? Where was the fire?

"Now," MacCauley continued, "I'm told you've been performing very well in your supervisory capacity. You have a great future with the department, Ginny. But you have to take care of the department, too. It's part of the trust." He looked at her, annoyed at the inexpressiveness of her face. As a former journalist, he felt he had the ability to read people on sight. But this girl was opaque. Or maybe it was just that there was nothing there to read.

"Here's the thing," he said. "All those rumors. About Russians and killings and their possible possession of the Trost girl?"

"We're still waiting for the cable, sir."

MacCauley smiled. "There won't be any cable. Rather, there *has* been a cable. 'Eyes Only.' For me. Embassy's already getting cold feet about this nonsense, you see. Don't want to be called to account for their tomfoolery. Some military character just slipped his leash. And you see what happens."

"Burton," the young woman said.

"What?"

"Lieutenant Colonel Burton. The mil-rep. I spoke to him on the STU a while ago."

MacCauley made a sporting face. "Yes. That's right. You praised him the other night, if I recall. You did have the senator rather excited. That was . . . unwise, don't you think?" He smiled. "I mean, aren't we the best people to handle this sort of thing?"

"Burton knows the country," she said. "The region. People over there take him seriously."

"Nonsense. Nobody takes the military seriously. Except other military sorts. And they don't count, Ginny. They're just not players. Tell me, though. What did this fellow have to say? When you spoke to him just now?"

She told him. It was everything that was in the cable and more. MacCauley was horrified. Really, the best thing would be to clear all the military people out of all the embassies. They were nothing but trouble. And their wives always talked too much in the receiving lines and never knew how to dress.

"Who else knows about this?"

The young woman thought for a moment, brushing a colorless strand of hair back behind an ear. "Two of my people have bits and pieces. We didn't have time to sort through it all. It's been a madhouse downstairs."

MacCauley sat back. Then he patted his desk. "Know who this desk belonged to, Ginny? Before me? The original owner?"

She looked at him, waiting for the answer.

"Cordell Hull. That's right. A *great* man. And that man knew how to keep a secret. How to shape policy behind the scenes. How to do the right thing. Under the most trying circumstances. Now . . . I want you to go back and talk to those two subordinates of yours. Tell them this business about Russian involvement is nonsense. They are not to speak of it with anyone. Not a word."

"I don't think it's nonsense," the analyst said. Miracle of the talking mouse.

MacCauley sat up. His first instinct was to give her a good dressing-down—she was, after all, nobody, a disposable. But these were dangerous times. He laid his forearms on Cordell Hull's desk—someday, he was certain, people would describe it as the Drew MacCauley desk—and put on what he imagined to be a fatherly expression. Although he was, of course, too young to be her father. Too young, too tall, too everything.

"Ms. Rains, I think I know the Russians. After all, I translated Kosygin's memoirs. I've spent *months* in Moscow. And the President has faith in me. He put me in this position to shepherd in a new era. So, while I respect your opinion, of course, I have to lay down my marker on this one. The Russians are *not* involved in this. Unless it's in a helpful way, of course. And no one in this building is to say a word about any Russian involvement. Not to anyone. Not even to a United States senator." He smiled. "You have a marvelous future ahead of you. But make no mistake—should one word of this nonsense slip out, I'll hold you responsible. Personally responsible. Do you—"

A large gray phone console rang on the credenza behind the desk. MacCauley whirled about in his chair and picked it up.

"Yes. Put him through. Hello? Yes. All right, I'll initiate." He pressed the button to go secure and waited until the warning display settled into approval. "Listen to me, Kandinsky. You have forty-eight hours to find that girl. Alive and well." The firmness in his voice pleased him. One had to be hard at times like this. He looked at his watch as though the distant ambassador might witness the gesture. "Forty-eight hours, and she'd better be wheels up for home. Or you'll be. And get your staff under control, man. No more ridiculous cables about the Russians. Not one more word. *And* I want that military troublemaker out of there tomorrow. Do you understand me?"

Virginia Rains had grown up in a small town in Wisconsin, and for as long as she could remember, she had dreamed of leaving that town and Wisconsin behind. She had gone to Stanford on a partial scholarship, then to Georgetown for her graduate degree. She passed the foreign service officer test and she had already served in three foreign countries, alternating her foreign tours with assignments in Washington. Unmarried and unattended, she believed in her work, enjoyed it as often as not, and could think of nothing else she would prefer to do with her life. So the action she had decided to take was not an easy one.

She believed Burton. Even allowing for the affection she

had felt for him—an emotion he had not even noticed, let alone returned—she was convinced that he was an honest man and that he was reporting what he had witnessed as accurately as he could. And she knew Drew MacCauley was a fool. She had served in Moscow for two years, and she had not just dabbled with the literati and tennis set like MacCauley. Friend of the President or not, the man had given away the freedom of one newly independent state after another, delivering them back to the Russians, and she had seen it and kept her silence and kept her job.

It made her sick to think about it, and there were days when she just wanted to scream from the Capitol steps that everything her country was doing in the former Soviet Union was wrong, wrong, wrong. It was not just about diplomacy, or treaties, or even about oil. It was about people. Tens of millions of human beings who had just escaped from slavery, only to have Drew MacCauley herd them back toward the Russians. She wanted to *do* something, to take a stand. But she told herself she was not important enough to make a difference, that no one would listen, and the only result would be the loss of her job. Imagining the rest of her life without her work, she could not see beyond an immeasurable, gray emptiness.

But the Trost case was the end of the line. She could not play along anymore. Rationally considered, one kidnapped girl should not matter as much as the fate of nations. But there was something so fundamentally wrong about withholding information about her from her own father, whether he was a senator or a shelf stocker in a supermarket, that Ginny Rains could not bear it. Her misery made her smile. Maybe she belonged in Wisconsin, after all. Maybe she didn't have the toughness for Washington, D.C. But maybe it wasn't worth having.

She could still hear Burton's voice on the phone, electronically distorted but still recognizable, saying, "The Russians killed every living thing in that compound, Ginny. Except the girl. And she's gone."

If the Russians did it, the whole world had a right to know. If the Russians had the girl, her father had a right to know. Ginny Rains had spent a total of seven years of her life in Washington, and it struck her that it was time for somebody, however unimportant, to do the right thing.

Burton woke early. In discomfort. The Lada was tough just to sit in. Sleeping in the little car required miracles of geometry. And the mosquitoes had gotten him.

With his back and limbs as stiff as prejudice, he left the garage and dead-walked toward the house. A thin cat looked at him in surprise and fled. The mansion next door was shut up like a coffin, and Burton had the world to himself.

When he paused to stretch, his kidneys reported in. He rubbed his hands over his face and hair, breaking off flakes of scab from his cuts. Life not at a high point. He looked at his watch. Six-thirty. The city had not yet gotten up its noise, and you could actually smell the sea cutting through the stink of oil and lingering exhaust. He closed his eyes, drinking the air. Maybe this would be a better day.

He needed a better day.

Shoulder cranky and his back mean, Burton unlocked the house door. A smarter, braver man would have thrown the Heddy & Helmut Review out into the street and slept in his own bed. As soon as he opened the door, the smell of the dead flowers and bad water hit him. But he ignored them for a moment, heading for the kitchen to make coffee, kidneys bitching.

The eggplant casserole from the night before had become a vibrant, living thing. With his stomach launching an insurrection, he got the mess into a plastic trash bag, then wiped the remaining colonists from the top of the table. He made coffee, using bottled water. While it was brewing, he visited the hallway toilet and went into the dining room.

Terrible stink. And the dead petals on the tabletop looked like dead petals on a tabletop. He could not even begin to recapture the interlude of beauty from the night before. On the other hand, the stench had probably driven his uninvited guests back to at least one of their own beds. The house did not feel as though there was anything else alive in it. Beyond the creatures that had answered the call of the eggplant casserole.

Breathing through his mouth and keeping it shallow, Burton went into the living room and put Miles Davis on the stereo. *In a Silent Way.* Just loud enough to follow him through the house. He picked up the snifter the ambassador had drained the night before, but set it down on the dining room table. The bad water and the flowers were more important. With Miles skulking through the scale like a recon patrol, Burton emptied the water in the toilet, flushed it, and took the stems out to the trash bag he had left living in the kitchen. Slime clung to his fingers.

With the mess shut outside the house, he washed his hands and drank his coffee hot and black, keeping the aroma close to his nose. Refill in hand and Miles playing his trumpet as if sneaking a hand up a woman's dress, Burton headed for the stairs to wash and get human.

But even the stairs were tough. His stiffness was unusually persistent. Not so many years before, it would have passed with the first hit of coffee.

Another reason to hang up the uniform. As hard as he struggled to keep in shape, he was not going to pass many more twenty-year-olds on the two-mile run. Soldiering was for the young. For kids so intoxicated by the vitality of their bodies that they did not need to think. For kids who had no idea what the world was really about.

Near the top of the stairs, he stopped.

Thought he heard something.

The sound did not come again.

He turned down the hallway and saw a good suit that was

not his own slung over his bedroom door. The door was nearly, but not quite, shut.

So much for old-school manners, Burton thought. Wondering how he could get to his closet. He had no interest in seeing Heddy in the arms of her asshole fiancé.

Could have used the guest room. At the very least.

Oh, to hell with them.

Burton decided to postpone all important decisions.

Just take a shower.

Screw them, though. Inconsiderate bastards.

Krauts. Emotional knuckle-draggers. Every one of them.

Burton let himself get noisier. Wanting them to wake up and put on their damned clothes.

He felt angry and mean and his back hurt. But his self-absorption faded when he opened the bathroom door.

Helmut Hartling lolled in the bathtub. He turned his head slowly and looked at Burton through fading eyes. His face was very pale, but the water was pink, and the wrist that hung over the side of the tub was draining blood onto the floor.

CHAPTER

· · ·

When you train to be an attaché or military representative, you attend a course at Bolling Air Force Base, a sliver of civilization between the Potomac and the badlands of Washington, D.C. Most of the classes are held in a massive, remarkably ugly building where the Defense Intelligence Agency hides from the future. Other classes take you to shopping malls so you can practice shaking surveillance or to racetracks so you can learn evasive driving techniques. You go over to Alexandria for lunch in a French restaurant where the proprietress explains how to use a fish knife. All of the relevant Federal agencies describe their excellence to you, and you role-play to prepare for intercultural collisions. You graduate with a basic competence in protocol and paperwork and with enough sense of the country in which you will serve to know which actions to perform with your right hand and which with your left. But at no time during the course do the instructors tell you what to do when you find a foreign ambassador who also happens to be your lover's fiancé bleeding to death in your bathtub.

"*Lass mich sterben,*" the ambassador cried in the voice of a tormented mouse. Burton tied off the man's forearms with T-shirt tourniquets. The ambassador put up a weak struggle that splashed blood and water onto his rescuer. His skin had the silvery whiteness of lard and his limbs had long gone unexercised. Slow-motion tears gathered in the ambassador's eyes and mazed down his cheeks. *"Ach, lass mich sterben."*

"Sterben, my ass," Burton told him. He tied off the second tourniquet with a vengeful jerk, then wiped the blood and water from his face. "You die and I'm going to kill you."

"Es ist alles vorbei . . ."

"Just shut up, asshole."

Burton dashed into the bedroom. The bedclothes had not been disturbed. He picked up the telephone, only to realize he had no idea whom to call.

He considered wrapping the ambassador in a bathrobe and driving him to the Azeri clinic down the hill. But the scandal would be uncontainable. He did not care about his own reputation—in fact, the Azeris he dealt with would give him big macho points—but he could not do it to the ambassador even now. Hurting the ambassador meant hurting Heddy.

He phoned Kandinsky and woke him.

"Sir," Burton said, "I've got some bad news . . ."

Kandinsky agreed to hustle the embassy's resident nurse over to Burton's house as soon as possible. In closing, the ambassador just said, "Jesus, Evan. Is that music? You're playing *music?"*

Miles blowing a wrist-slasher sound track.

Burton went back into the bathroom to make sure the ambassador was still alive and that he had not removed the tourniquets.

The ambassador contented himself with whimpering now. He was still very much alive. *" . . . sterben . . . die Liebe meines Lebens . . ."* Burton began to wonder if the whole business had been a sick bit of theater, timed for effect.

"You," Burton said, "are the most inconsiderate fucking guest of the century." Then he bounded down the stairs to turn off the stereo, with the lower level still stinking from Heddy's flowers.

He tried to call her. But there was no answer at her apartment. He rang the German embassy. The duty officer picked up, but had not seen her yet. *"Ist doch früh,"* he told Burton. *"Ruf mal um zehn Uhr zurück."* The man sounded as though Burton had roused him from an end-of-shift nap.

He needed her help. Above all, the ambassador needed her help. Burton could not imagine where Heddy might be this early in the morning.

General Hamedov's office smelled of backed-up plumbing. The air conditioner had bled rusty water down the wall before dying, and yesterday's cigarette smoke drifted.

"You will find one million American dollars in the bag," Heddy said. "All my people ask is that Mustafa Galibani never . . . that he never export heroin . . . or anything else . . . that he never be in a position to . . . export such things to Germany again."

Unshaven and oddly out of character in the uniform he rarely bothered to wear, Hamedov smiled with a confidence Heddy did not understand. He took the bag, letting his touch linger on her hand, then turned without a word to the safe beside his desk. He knelt, wheezing, and spun the dial. As soon as the door opened, the general thrust the leather bag inside. Then he slammed the safe shut.

Still smiling, he took a seat closer to Heddy than the one he had occupied before. Their knees almost touched and she could smell the past night's adventures on him. Pretending to shift to a more comfortable posture, she drew herself as far away from him as she could manage without changing chairs.

"My dear friend," Hamedov said, "I swear to you that this man Galibani never bothers you again. *Never*." He spoke English as if hacking a carcass with a cleaver. Enjoying himself. "Galibani is a dead man." He seemed on the verge of laughter. "My German friend tells me to kill the man"—he snapped his fingers high in the air—"and he is dead. I do everything for you." He leaned closer.

"I did *not* specify that anyone was to be killed," Heddy insisted, terrified of legality, of headlines, of a failed life. Things were bad enough. When she had left Burton's house, Helmut had shouted after her that she was nothing but an American whore. And Burton had disappeared. "I never asked you to kill anyone. I only—"

Hamedov laughed loudly, theatrically, and his breath hit her like gas released from a corpse. "You German people are so clever . . . so very clever. All things very correct, yes? You say a thing, but you do not say it. Such a diplomat." He tapped her knee, then let his heavy fingers rest on her stocking for a moment before he removed them. He clapped his hands together, still smiling. "But it is all the same. I promise you, Galibani is a dead man." He chuckled as if a ghost had whispered another joke into his ear.

Heddy realized she had gotten something wrong, but she had no idea what it might be. He was laughing at her. She wondered if something had happened while she was away. She had just made it in on the last flight after two close-call transfers, rushing to her apartment for an ill-judged change of clothes, then right to Burton's house. Letting her heart rule.

She told herself that she should have stopped at the embassy first. To check on the latest developments. It was the most basic professionalism.

But then there would have been questions. And holding the money had been a painful, worrisome thing.

She wished she could have talked to Burton. She wished she could have made love with him. She wished she were anyplace else but here. A fly sagged through the air, suffocating in flight.

She knew she had to go on, to finish it. But the business sickened her. The way Hamedov sickened her. With his liquor breath and sweat and his too-tight uniform.

"I think there is something else, my dear friend," Hamedov

said, cheating on the script she had prepared for him. "But you are reluctant to share it with me. Perhaps the people of Germany want someone else killed?"

Heddy jerked as if the general had grasped her with both hands. But he only sat, smiling, looking at her as if she were a specimen.

"*No,*" Heddy said. "It's just . . . about the girl. The American girl. The one who was kidnapped."

"Miss Kelly Trost."

"Yes."

I cannot do this, she thought. I cannot go through with it.

"Of what interest could Miss Trost be to you? I am very interested now."

"There will be more money," Heddy said suddenly. It was as if she had divided into two, one of whom spoke the words, with the other listening and hating it. "We believe in commensurate rewards. Ample rewards. All we want . . . we want what is good for Azerbaijan. Bonn believes it is essential that the kidnappers not turn out to be ethnic Azeris. Or other citizens or residents of Azerbaijan. Nothing can be allowed to soil the image of your country as a stable . . . as a sound place for the oil pipeline. It is . . . in our mutual interest, you see."

"But . . . my dear friend . . . what if these kidnappers, these bandits, are truly from among my people? These days . . ."

"*No.* The kidnappers must be Russians. Perhaps Russian bandits. Or Russian military. But Russians. Only Russians." She looked into his eyes and saw herself reflected as a small, vulnerable animal. "There will be a great deal more money."

Hamedov's smile had disappeared. They were alone in the big room, but he leaned closer, a fellow conspirator now. "The Russians will be very angry, I think. But . . . perhaps the kidnappers are indeed such Russians. Who is to say?" His smile crept back over his lips, a worm curling in the sun. "I do nothing for money, of course. It is my duty as a patriot of my country."

Dear God, Heddy prayed, please let it be over now. I've

done my duty. Just let me go. Praying was something she had not done since girlhood.

But Hamedov was quicker than God. He stood up. Staring out of the filthy windows with his hands clasped at the top of his rump, uniform ready to explode its buttons and seams. He had the profile of a boxer who had long since broken down.

"There is, of course, the problem of the girl," he said.

"I . . . don't see why she should be a problem," Heddy lied.

Hamedov smirked, turning on her with a boneless movement. "All this talking and not saying. You Europeans. You know the girl is a problem. If these bandits who have taken her are not Russians. I think she is not so stupid that she cannot tell the difference. She will tell everyone the truth."

"She'll be happy to be free," Heddy said. It sounded stupid.

Hamedov waved a hand at her in disgust. She sensed that she had managed to shock the man, a thing she had never imagined she might do. He had expected better of her, of her kind.

"You . . . want us to kill the girl for you." He looked down at her. Heddy, who had been preoccupied with her own feelings, noticed that the man's eyes had grown less assured. "If she did not choose the right kidnappers. If she is an inconvenience."

"You don't have to kill her," Heddy said. A whore saying, "I love you."

Hamedov took out a cigarette and did not bother to offer her one. He lit it by dipping his face down into his paws. Amazed, Heddy saw that his hands were shaking.

"How much?" he asked.

"Four million."

"U.S. dollars?"

"Yes."

He nodded. "I'll see what can be done." Then he turned to face her. "But I want you to say it."

"What?"

"Tell me to kill the girl."

"I never said . . ."

He lunged toward her, an attacker, braking his body just in front of her chair.

"*Say it,*" he shouted.

Voice of a madman. Fresh sweat on his temples. Big hands anxious to grasp flesh.

"Kill the girl. If you must."

"*No.* Not 'if you must.' " His anger seemed the most genuine thing she had ever encountered in the man.

"Kill the girl."

"*Say it again.* Once more. So that my ears can believe it."

"Kill the girl. Make it look like the Russians did it. We'll pay you."

Heddy believed she was going to be sick. Her stomach boiled. And she wanted to be alone so that she could cry. She was not a woman who wept, as a rule, but this would make the third time in a matter of days. It was all slipping out of control.

Hamedov turned away from her. He walked until his desk blocked his path, then stood still, bracing himself off the wood. He shook his head over his thoughts.

By way of dismissal, he said, "Remember me to your friend Colonel Burton."

The Russian attaché understood the purpose of the visit. Normally, Sviridov was all heat and friction, fond of keeping visitors waiting. This time he rushed out to the guard station in the embassy lobby to greet Burton. The Russian colonel had the haggard look of a priest just back from Siberia. Up all night, Burton judged, and not at a party. No telltale alkie sweat. Yet Sviridov had not been in his office, either.

The bugger knew he had a beating coming.

Burton waited until they stood in Sviridov's office in the heart of the embassy. The Russian shut the door and Burton let him have it.

"Where is she? Is she all right?"

"Colonel Burton, seat yourself. Please."

"Where's the goddamned girl?"

"What girl?" The Russian had all the self-possession of a choirboy caught shoplifting.

"Don't give me that shit, Mitya. Don't give me *any* shit. Just tell me where you bastards have Kelly Trost. Then tell me she's in good health and anxious to go home to Daddy."

The attaché drew himself up as if he had been insulted at a ball. "I have no idea what you're talking about."

Burton brought his fist down on the man's desk. Junk jumped. "I *saw* the goddamned helicopters," he shouted. "I saw the goddamned *mark*ings. You didn't even bother to cover up the flags and the bort numbers."

It was a lie. The helicopters had been so far away that Burton had not been able to tell for certain if they were HIPs or HINDs. But he was willing to bet the attaché did not have a sufficient level of detail in his possession to call his bluff.

Sviridov raised his hands in horror. Gesturing for quiet. Begging for it. With his hungry wedge of face and nicotine fingers.

"Do not shout. Please . . . the ambassador . . ."

"Fuck your goddamned ambassador. Where's Kelly Trost?"

"Please to sit down. We must talk. We must help each other."

"You talk," Burton said. But he sat down. He noticed that Sviridov had put up a new map since his last visit. A very new map. The folds were still obvious.

It was a map of Baku.

The Russian pulled a chair close to Burton. When he spoke, his voice came in a sentinel's whisper.

"We do not have the girl."

*"Bull*shit. Crap."

The Russian hushed him again. Sviridov had dark circles that looked like old tires. He definitely had not slept much of late. Well, Burton thought, that makes two of us. He had washed himself and shaved in a downstairs sink, leaving Kandinsky and the nurse with the German ambassador. Kandinsky had told him bluntly that he would have to leave the country. Burton had lied to him, breaking his own rules, telling the ambassador that he was close to cracking the code, that he would have Kelly Trost beside him on the flight out. He just needed a little time. Kandinsky shook his head, but his words were more indulgent than his expression:

"Drew MacCauley wants your ass out of here today. I can stretch that into tomorrow. But no more fuck-ups. Please. Just get the girl." The ambassador pushed his glasses higher on the bridge of his nose and turned back toward his lovesick colleague, calling over his shoulder, "The press are all over the place. B-teamers, and they're hungry. Keep away from them, Evan."

Sviridov's eyes looked like twin maps of Mars. "We do not have the girl. I swear it. I admit the raid. But we only wanted to help."

"You killed every living thing in that compound. You killed children. You killed the goddamned goats."

The Russian shook his head. "We didn't want that. It's Chechnya, the legacy. The special troops take no chances anymore. We cannot control them. They did not tell us they would do such a thing."

"Blame it on Cain. Just tell me about the girl. I know you've got her, Mitya."

Sviridov's face changed. There was a rise of confidence, almost rectitude, behind the gray skin and fear. "No. That is a lie. You could not know that. Because we do not have her."

"So she's off picking wildflowers? Give me a break."

The Russian looked down. "I don't know where she is." Then he looked up into Burton's eyes. "Truly. Nobody knows. She was gone when the special troops arrived. All of it . . . it was all for nothing."

"*Chistaya Skazka.*"

"*Nyet. Eta pravda. Absolutnaya pravda.*" The attaché tugged at the thin necktie that matched the color of his military shirt. "We *tried* to get the girl. We thought it would be an opportunity. To demonstrate to you that Azerbaijan cannot govern itself. That only we Russians can bring order. She was to have been a gift. To her father, the senator. To your country."

"Out of the goodness of your hearts."

"No. Because of the pipeline. This is no secret. We believe you are very foolish to build a pipeline here. Russia offers you the only safe route. But you will not listen. We wanted to prove it to you."

Burton slapped his hand down on the desk again. But the blow was not as hard this time. He was trying to think quickly, but his brain was on Slow. "I still think you have her. So don't try to chimp me." The damned thing was that his instincts told him the Russian, who was one nervous puppy, was telling the truth. And he was too tired to sort it all out. Stretching, disgusted, he half turned and the new map caught his eye again. "That's the best map of Baku I've ever seen—got an extra one?"

The attaché whirled about. He looked at the map and the nerves showed again. After a moment, he jumped up and walked toward the back of the office. Then he sat down in a chair that forced Burton to look away from the map.

"We must work together," Sviridov said. "To solve this problem of the girl. I think there is no solution but to work together."

"I'm not accustomed to working closely with people who slaughter women and children in broad daylight," Burton said.

The attaché made a disbelieving face. "Evan, these things happen. You know that. It is a violent world."

"Show me some leg. Tell me something I don't know. First you try giving me a one-hundred-percent lie, now we've got it down to maybe fifty percent. Make my life easier."

The Russian colonel held up imploring hands. "Please. You must believe me. This is all a terrible inconvenience. We do not want any trouble now."

" 'Now?' As opposed to tomorrow? Or yesterday?"

The attaché looked off to the side. "No trouble. These are difficult times. When Russians and Americans argue, these blackasses play us for fools."

Burton stood up. "Until you prove otherwise, I have to assume you've got the girl. And the evidence is on my side, pal." He shook his head in mock pity. "You're going to feel the heat, Mitya. You. Personally. We're going to convince your oil mafia that it's your fault when they lose that pipeline. You'll make new and interesting friends." He watched the Russian's face shift from desperate to terrified, then he marched for the door. "And since you don't have time for 'blackasses,' you can just give me back those Duke Ellington discs I loaned you."

The attaché followed him out into the corridor, calling, "Evan, *please*. We do not have the girl. I tell you honestly." Even when the guards alerted to the turmoil and moved to escort Burton to the exit, Sviridov followed, ordering them not to touch him, to treat him with respect, alternately screaming at his subordinates and begging Burton to be reasonable.

Instead of going directly to the German embassy, Heddy stopped by her apartment. She had sweated through her clothing in Hamedov's office. She wanted to shower again. And to put on something clean and fresh. But she knew there were some things a shower would not wash away.

What have I done? she asked herself. What have I done?

She did not really try to answer the question. Her thoughts careened from Hamedov and the filthy business that connected them now, to Helmut weeping and accusing. She simultaneously feared that she had lost him and could not imagine a life by his side. It had been foolish, childish, to walk out on him like that.

She thought of Burton with fear. Afraid he would somehow find out what she had done, that Hamedov would share their secret. Or sell it. She saw now how completely she had put herself into the Azeri general's hands. And into the hands of the people back in Bonn and Pullach who had turned out to be both more and less than she had ever expected. The worst of it was that they had known exactly what they were doing.

All of her plans were collapsing.

She parked her car half on the sidewalk in front of her building and let a succession of quick vehicles flash by. She touched her face and realized that she had been crying.

"Evan," she said.

Perhaps he would never find out. Perhaps they would still have a little time together. She thought she had reconciled herself to a methodical, well-managed loss of him, but now she felt sicker at the thought of never holding him against her again than she had felt when she promised to pay a man to kill an innocent girl.

She opened the car door to vomit, but her throat remained dry except for a taint of bile. A furious driver swerved to miss her, banging off the opposite curb of the narrow street and pounding his horn as he disappeared. With her head down, she saw boots like the ones Evan sometimes wore, and a voice said in English:

"Miss Seghers, you got to be careful."

It was the sergeant who worked for Evan. Spooner. He looked as though he had bad news.

Burton almost fell asleep waiting for his lunch to be served. It was early, and Charley's was empty except for a table of oil roustabouts in town for the day and three new gringos in safari outfits who could only be journalists. They complained loudly to one another about the hotel accommodations and the inability of the local government officials to speak decent English. The duty waitress wore black jeans that gripped her closer than a pair of tights. She stared a bit too long at the cuts healing on Burton's face, but still tried to flirt on principle. Until she realized that his mind was not occupying the same space as his body.

He *wanted* the Russians to have Kelly Trost. He wanted the

Russians to have her and to give her back in good health. Let them have bragging rights. He just wanted her safe and sound. He could watch the business becoming an obsession to him as if observing a stranger through one-way glass.

Besides, a good ending might give him enough time to pack up his possessions for shipment before he had to leave. That would be the difference between having half of the shipment stolen and losing all of it. His disc library would have to go by mail in the pouches. The Azeris would rip off the stereo, of course, but that was replaceable. In the plus column, they would probably let the antiques and rugs he had collected pass unbothered to America. The locals were only interested in shiny new goods that you could plug in or sell quickly. History was disposable, an enduring Soviet lesson.

An Englishwoman, ferocious and thin, marched in and cursed everybody. She sat down at the table with the journalists and shrieked for a beer, her accent horrid.

Burton wished he had never seen the side of Heddy he had encountered the night before. He could still hear her lashing out at the ambassador, humiliating him with unnerving precision. Did men and women ever really know each other? Beyond a few intimate, slaughtering details?

You're veering off the road, boy. Both hands back on the wheel.

He hoped that the Russians had the girl, alive and well, but he had begun to doubt it. Sviridov had been scared of the wrong questions.

Now what? His stomach burned from coffee and hunger and arguing and worrying and spite. His warping sense of reality reminded him of the way you felt at the end of a major field exercise, when you and every other officer had just spent a week pretending nobody had to sleep in wartime. Not in prime condition to make life-or-death decisions.

All he could think to do was to start his rounds again, knocking on one door after another, begging for scraps of information. With precious little to offer in return. "The goodwill of the United States." Which would not pay for his lunch.

The waitress brought him a burger made of ground mutton, along with green fries and a bottle of watery Euro-ketchup. There would be some advantages to going home. And retirement out-processing would be a leisurely affair. They would probably stick him over at DIA for the last few months, letting him write reports no one would read.

The first bite of food magnified his hunger. He ate with a disregard for manners that would have embarrassed him on any other day. The waitress, conditioned to local customs, watched approvingly.

First visit Hamedov. See what that wheeler-dealer had on the burner. Then . . . maybe drive up over the cape to Sumgait. Talk to the girl's co-workers at the aid project. Just start again from the beginning. Look for the obvious things everybody might have missed.

If he could have done only one thing that counted for all the rest of his life, he would have found Kelly Trost.

A bright red dribble of ketchup fell from the burger, landing where the cell phone bulged out the lower pocket of his khakis.

Burton performed first aid on his trousers, then finished eating and gathered up a fistful of paper napkins, leaving enough money to cover the bill and a tip. On the way out, he paused to talk to the bartender, who had just appeared to wipe down the wood with a wet rag.

"Red Indian, innit?" Eamon asked an invisible companion. "Don't know what the gash see in him." He looked at Burton at last. "Found your Kelly, then?"

Burton shook his head. "I've been down-country. What's the word on the street?"

"Oh, kidnapped by fooking Martians. Fook-all, they know. Not a rumor worth the spit of it." He gestured toward the journalists, who were drinking beer and plotting. "And the daft questions *they* ask. Like I'd be hiding the girl behind the bar, for the love of Christ." He snorted. "Don't even listen to your answers. And you'd think it was a gathering of the clans, for the poorhouse tips. Sitting there since we opened, they've been. Squeezing pennies out their arses one at a time." He tossed the rag into the sink. "Nothing new about your Kelly at all, Evan lad."

Burton caught the inflection, the teaser. It was always a game of thirty questions at Charley's American Bar. "Something else, though?"

Eamon shrugged. "Fuzzies are fixing bayonets over something. Fooking Belfast, innit?"

"I saw some troops headed south last night."

"And you know who was doing a booming business till the wee hours? Old Torgut, the Shylock of Mecca."

Torgut Keyseri was a money-changer. Black-market rates, large amounts only.

"Into dollars?"

"Not fooking rupees."

Burton nodded. When the politics got rough, everybody rushed to change the local currency into dollars. "What kind of rate?"

"Not for shit."

"Thanks."

"Hey, Evan. Know why your Welsh regiments always have English officers?"

"Tell me."

"Colonial troops need white leadership. Hey, you got fooking blood on your knickers."

"Ketchup. Thanks."

Clutching the paper napkins, Burton headed toward the public toilet to clean his trousers as best he could. The johns were the worst part of Charley's, a rich Third World experience built to service the sports hall upstairs. At least there was running water in the sinks.

When you're tired, you make mistakes, he told himself. You spill things. And you can't think.

Baku gone turtle, all pulled into its shell.

Tell me why, Mr. Wizard.

Kelly Trost reverberating? Prop blast from Galibani's death? Another forlorn offensive ready to kick off up in the mountains?

Burton knew he should be grabbing information on all sides, writing cables, following convoys. The truth was he was too tired to drive himself around safely, but needed Spooner at the embassy and could not trust the local national drivers at this point. Just me and my Lada, he thought.

He looked down at the stain on his khakis, disgusted with himself. Didn't even have the rocks to go home and change. He was afraid Kandinsky might have kept the German ambassador hidden in his bed, and that Heddy would be there, and that it would get uglier than a whorehouse in a leper colony.

Alone in the lavatory, he scrubbed at his thigh, turning the napkins into mush, and spoke to an imaginary companion:

"Heddy . . . you could've done better."

He *thought* he was alone.

But he was wrong.

Little Talaat, Azerbaijan's answer to Peter Lorre and the rumor king of the Caucasus appeared in the mirror, a head lower than Burton even with the American bent to work on his soiled trouser leg. Mildly lame, Talaat leaned to favor his good leg.

"I have found you, Burton-*effendi*."

I don't have time for this, Burton thought. Neither the time nor the patience. Not today.

Shortcutting the ceremony, Burton reached for his wallet to give Talaat enough money to get himself a shashlik from one of the street vendors. But the little man closed his hand gently over Burton's wrist. In the hierarchy of local castes and customs, it measured out as an act of extreme urgency and desperation.

"*Please*. You must listen."

"Could we talk later, Talaat-*bey*?"

The smaller man shifted to keep his balance and tightened his grip. It was like having a parrot fasten itself to your arm.

"Please, Burton-*effendi*. You are my great friend, the kindest of men. I must help you. Please. A moment."

Burton straightened. He was being a pig, he decided. Of course he had a minute for the poor old coot: There but for the grace of genetics, nationality, education, and personality go I.

"Speak, my friend. Please. Share your news."

A smiled shone over the little man's face, then faded again. His eyes reminded Burton of the hard little marbles in which his father had tried to interest him when he was a child.

"You are wrong about the Russians, *Bey-effendi*. They do not have the girl. She is here. In Baku."

The guard in the lobby of the Ministry of Internal Affairs would not let Burton pass. He was a boy from the uplands, new to the city and new to his uniform, and Burton could barely connect with his dialect. The boy's uniform was not only new, it was wrong. The regular guards, most of whom knew Burton by sight, wore gray. This boy wore the baggy mustard fatigues of the army and he carried a battered Kalashnikov over his shoulder.

Shake up in the ministry? Somebody relieved? Another assassination attempt? Burton had the sense of too much happening too quickly again. It was almost a constant feeling now.

"Listen," Burton said, speaking slowly and firmly, "I'm here to see General Hamedov. Do you understand?"

The boy looked at him without curiosity. "No pass, no come inside."

"Soldier, I want you to go over to that desk and call General Hamedov's office."

In the background, more young men in mustard began to gather.

"No pass, no come inside."

Burton tried his accreditation card from the Azeri government. The boy examined it, holding it in both hands. Burton did not think he could read it. In a moment, the boy gave it back, his expression embarrassed yet intractable. He said nothing, but stood blocking the way.

"Would you *please* call General Hamedov's office. Tell him Lieutenant Colonel Burton is here to see him. Otherwise, I'm going to walk down that hallway on my own."

Slowly, the boy unshouldered his rifle and pointed it at Burton's stomach. Burton wondered if the boy had ever fired it. He hardly seemed to know how to hold the weapon. But there was no mistaking his determination.

An NCO appeared from a side corridor and demanded to know what Burton wanted. He was smarter and less assured than the private, and Burton saw an opening.

"I'm here to see General Hamedov," he said in his command voice. "Get him on the phone."

The general's name registered. The NCO spoke to the boy as if slapping his face and the rifle barrel lifted away from Burton's torso. Then the NCO marched to the phone and raised the receiver. But he never spoke into it. A moment later, he came back to Burton with a diffident expression.

"The telephone is out of operation. It is unfortunate."

"All right," Burton said. "Call an officer. Any officer." He looked at his watch with exaggerated concern and lied, "I have an appointment with General Hamedov and I'm late."

The NCO nodded and hurried back into his corridor again. Three soldiers had gathered around Burton now. He wished he had cigarettes to offer them. Although Burton did not smoke, he generally carried a pack or two of Marlboros when he was in the field to break the ice with sentries and the like. But he was running a bare-bones operation today.

"So," Burton said in slum Turkish, "you boys been in Baku long?" He glanced around the big, drab lobby.

"Just since last night," one of the boys said. He looked slightly older and more confident, a bit cocky.

Burton nodded. "Long trip?"

The cocky soldier grimaced. "All the way from Gyandzha. Bastards wouldn't even stop to let us take a piss. Ever try pissing out of the back of a truck? Splashes back in all over you."

"Been in the army long?"

A major appeared, his uniform no neater than those of his troops. His facial features were very fine, though, more typical of northern India than of the Caucasus. He rushed toward Burton, fastening his belt as he approached, and his skull seemed too small for the rest of his body.

"My apologies, sir. My apologies. You are here to meet with General Hamedov? The soldiers do not understand. I'm sorry. I thought everyone was already here for the meeting. I didn't know. I would not have been away from my post. Please accept my apologies."

Immediately, Burton began to stride toward the central corridor.

"I'm late," he lied again. He had not even called Hamedov, afraid the general would put him off. Now it sounded as though he had hit an accidental jackpot. "You said everybody else is here?"

"Yes," the officer told him, struggling to match Burton's stride.

Burton had hoped the officer would name names.

"And the meeting's in General Hamedov's office? Just like the general told me?" Liar, liar, pants on fire, Burton told himself.

"Yes, yes. Everyone is there."

"You're from Nakhichevan, right? Your accent?"

"Oh, yes," the major said proudly. "From the same village as General Hamedov. But I am not related."

"Your unit's from Gyandzha, though?"

The major shrugged. "A soldier serves where he is sent."

"Gyandzha's a fascinating place," Burton continued in perhaps his greatest lie thus far. Gyandzha was a grubby industrial city whose top products were unemployment and crime, its glory days centuries past. They climbed toward Hamedov's office. "City of Nizami, of poetry and roses. I suppose the general brought you in so he'd have troops he can trust."

"Yes, yes. These are most terrible times. The general called for us very suddenly. As you can see, my men are not even completely trained. Our battalion had not finished with the recruits. But the rest of the regiment is very good."

"They came, too?" Burton tried to make the question sound as casual as possible. There was not much time. Hamedov's office was only steps away.

"Yes. But they are waiting outside of the city. In case of trouble."

Two guards with automatic weapons stood in front of the outer door to Hamedov's office. Burton, who realized with absolute certainty that he was not wanted in this place at this time, expected his bluff to be called at any moment and to be escorted out of the building with a muzzle in the small of his back.

He wished he had told Spoon or the ambassador where he was going. The cell phone in his pocket was not worth a damn now.

The major snapped at the guards and they jumped aside. One of them even opened the door for Burton.

This major, Burton thought, is going to have an abbreviated career.

Burton almost ran across the outer office. There were no more guards, only an astonished secretary in uniform, and Burton ripped open the inner door before anyone could stop him.

Inside the office, gathered over a map spread across the conference table, Hamedov stood in the midst of the most unlikely grouping of human beings Burton had ever encountered. Sviridov, the Russian attaché was there, bending over the map beside Dick Fleming, Mr. Scumbag Oil. Fahrad Adjami, Iranian merchant-trader extraordinaire, had just turned to a short man Burton did not recognize but who looked as Armenian as a *khachkar*. These were not people who normally had much in common, and in the case of the Armenian—if he really was Armenian—he was risking his life just being in the country, let alone in the headquarters of the secret police.

Burton did not yet understand what he was seeing. But he knew he was not supposed to see it. If he could have done so safely, he would have backed out of the room, shut the door behind him, and run.

Hamedov's face turned the color of a bad sunburn. Fleming, on the other hand, paled. Adjami's face did not change in the least. The Russian attaché looked as though he had been caught with his hand in the cookie jar. And the Armenian appeared baffled.

Burton hoped he did not look *too* frightened.

Hamedov mastered himself. "Ah, Colonel Burton. What an unexpected pleasure. But I'm afraid you have come at a bad time. I have guests."

"Tell me about the girl and I'll go."

Hamedov lifted an eyebrow. "Bad manners do not suit you, Evan."

Burton looked from face to face. They were recovering from their surprise. And they did not mean well by him.

"I was just hoping you'd heard something." Burton tried not to let his voice falter.

Hamedov sensed the fear, though. He smiled. "I'll be in touch. But I think you should go now." He shifted his eyes toward the major and his expression hardened. "Escort our guest from the building. Then return to my office."

It was not a game now. Burton wondered if Hamedov would shoot the major or only torment him. He suspected the major was wondering the same thing. Homeboy or not.

The major understood how badly he had erred. To compensate, he drew his pistol.

"That will not be necessary," Hamedov told him, voice harsher for the self-control you could hear in it. "Colonel Burton will not make any trouble." He turned again. "Will you,

213

Evan? By the way, we are all very concerned about the girl. We are determined to help you."

"I appreciate any help I can get," Burton told him. He held his eyes on Hamedov's as steadily as he could, then turned abruptly to go. He figured if he made it out of the waiting room, he had a fifty percent chance of making it out of the building.

He had gotten a look at the map on the table. Identical to the one that had hung in the Russian attache's office, it covered the city of Baku.

The general was about to stage a coup.

Burton walked down the main corridor, flanked by the two guards from Hamedov's office, with Major Small Head walking behind them. It was the longest walk Burton could remember.

He could not believe Hamedov was going to let him leave with this knowledge. Unless things were so far along the general did not believe Burton or the U.S. ambassador could do anything to alter the course of events.

Even if that were true, Burton knew he had seen too much. The corridor was not overly warm, yet he felt his clothing soaking. The constellation of actors in the office did not make sense to him yet. But he knew he would figure it out. So many other things made sense now. Like the presidential guard sent south the evening before. And the takeover of the ministry by line troops from up country. Hamedov had been clearing the capital of troops loyal to the current administration while the president was out of town. Aliev was in Central Asia at a CIS conference, due back tomorrow.

Tonight was the night.

Thoughts clawed at one another. Even the raid on Galibani's compound could have been part of something larger. Was the kidnapping tied in with the coup somehow? And what was that maggot Fleming's connection? Oil, of course.

But what was the angle? Wasn't he in with Aliev, too? And the Armenians, for Christ's sake. Go figure, Mr. Wizard.

The major stepped on Burton's heel, a petty thing if not an accident, but it made Burton sense anew how badly the major wanted to hurt him. Or, preferably, to kill him. The man was only afraid of making another error. Burton had never seen a man so frightened and furious at the same time as the major had been in Hamedov's presence. The major's footsteps followed close behind now, hot as a stranger's breath on your neck. But the gun never cocked, the fist never landed.

Maybe it was the good old American magic. Maybe Hamedov, for all his bravado, did not want to risk hurting a U.S. officer. Even if there were no friendly witnesses. There was a good chance, of course, he just did not want the others in the room to see the act, not wanting them to have that kind of knowledge about him at their disposal.

The lobby at the end of the hallway seemed impossibly far away. The corridor reeked and Burton wondered if it was the smell of his own fear. After the lobby, there would be a patio to cross, then the street. A corner to turn. Half a block to where he had parked. They could put a bullet into him in his car, of course. But every remove bought a little more safety.

Curious, how you could feel another human being's emotions. You could almost step into them like a pair of trousers. Major Small Head wanted more than anything else to put a bullet in the back of Burton's skull. To beat him to a bloody pulp with the butt of his pistol. Before or after pulling the trigger. To cause the greatest possible harm.

Just before they reached the almost-safety of the lobby, an enormous voice filled the hallway.

"Wait. Hold him there."

It was Hamedov.

Burton tried to turn around. He wanted to face his fate. Not get it in the back like a discarded gangster. But his guards braced him so that he could not move.

The general's footsteps boomed on the old tile. As they

made their long approach, the major stepped in close and whispered into Burton's ear, "If I live, I will find you. I swear I'm going to kill you."

Get in line, Burton thought.

The boots came closer. Burton waited for a fist. Or a bullet.

"Leave him to me," Hamedov's voice commanded.

The guards moved off. Quickly. Followed by the more reluctant major. And Burton turned.

The general had torn open his collar, freeing his big neck. His face was still red. And sweated. But he, too, looked tired. And he did not have a gun in his hand.

The general pulled Burton into a side office, chasing two startled secretaries into the hallway with a curse. He slammed the door shut and immediately began popping his knuckles.

"Evan. Listen to me."

You bet.

"You are an intelligence man. You understand what you have seen. Or you will understand it soon enough. But I do not think you understand Azerbaijan."

Your nickel, Burton thought. His legs felt as rubbery as those of a frightened character in a cartoon. Bravery, he thought, was pretty damned circumstantial.

"Evan . . . my country needs peace. There is no peace. We need peace with the Russians, with the Iranians. And, although it sickens my blood to say it, we need peace with the Armenians. The oil will mean nothing if there is no peace."

"I'm all for peace," Burton said.

"You do not believe me."

"Every man in that room is an enemy of your country. Except maybe Dick Fleming, who's just an all-purpose parasite."

"Enemies change. And men do many things for money."

"Azerbaijan has an elected president. Recognized by the United States."

Hamedov smiled bitterly and shook his head. "You are a very brave man to say that to me. You know I could kill you now. And no one would be able to prove anything. America would forget you."

That's one ugly truth, Burton thought. He tried to picture the man standing before him as the leader of a country. It was disgusting, but not hard. Most of the countries Burton knew firsthand were run by similar men. Worse men, for that matter.

"What do you want me to do?"

Hamedov looked at him. The Azeri was shorter, but bigger in every other way. "Forget what you have seen. For just a little while. Do not go to your ambassador."

"It's my duty. You know that."

"Why? Speak to me like a man, not some military puppet. Tell me that you truly believe your government wants democracy here." He flailed an arm at an imaginary Washington. "*Oil*, Evan. America wants our oil. You are the same as everyone else. And I am going to give you your oil. You saw Fleming in there."

"It's my duty to report to my ambassador."

The general waved dismissively. "Duty . . . is a complex thing. But listen to me, Evan. If reality does not matter to you, how about the girl? Miss Trost? Yes. You see? I say her name and your face changes for me. You would never make an Azeri. You care about this girl and you do not hide it. But, my friend, you are the only one who cares. She has become a burden to so many people. I believe that many people think it would be better if this girl is already dead when she is found."

"That a threat?"

Hamedov smiled as if confronted with a well-intentioned but slow child. "Of course it is a threat. Made with much reluctance. But how else can I deal with you? You are like a holy fool. Listen to me. I will find the girl. It is only a matter of time. You know my eyes are everywhere in this country."

"You didn't see into Galibani's compound."

"How do you know that?" The general smiled. "How do you know that I did not see? The Russians are so clumsy, so stupid. They spoil things. But to the point, Evan. I promise you I will have the girl. And my offer to you is simple. If you go to your ambassador . . . if you make any trouble for me . . . I'll let the others do what they want with her. They're standing in line like Russians for free vodka. I would not have to lift a finger."

"And if I forget what I saw?"

"I will give you the girl. I swear it. I will find her and give her to you. Alive. After everything is finished." His face took on a look of genuine sadness. Or of sadness that looked genuine. "I speak to you as a friend, Evan. Why can't you believe that I wish to be your friend? It would never be my choice to hurt this girl."

"You're bluffing."

"Yes?" Hamedov shook his head as if in deep regret. "How can I prove all this to you? Will you listen to me? I will tell you what I know. The girl was kidnapped by Islamic fundamentalists. By idiots. Lunatics. Amateurs. They knew very little about her, really. And they thought they had a deal with our friend Galibani. But something went wrong. Perhaps your visit scared them, I do not know this. But a young man took the girl away before dawn, while you were still sleeping with the woman Galibani gave you. My people have tracked them as far as a smuggling village on the border with Iran."

"Maybe she's in Iran now. Maybe she's already out of your power."

Hamedov shook his head. "They tried to cross the border. But they had to turn back. The Iranians have two divisions' worth of troops searching the border area for the girl. Two *divisions*, Evan. Everybody wants her. Your daughter of the senator. No, they are still in Azerbaijan. I will find them. And if you behave as my friend, I will give the girl to you and only to you. She is sick, by the way."

It all rang true.

"Can we make a bargain, Evan? Between friends?"

"How would I know . . ."

The general smiled. "You are usually a quick thinker, my

friend. Isn't it clear? I will need to make friends with America. After I have spoiled your 'democracy.' " He laughed out loud. "Do you have any idea how we conducted the last election? This election that you Americans wanted so badly? Do you have any idea? With all your international observers drunk and whoring?" He closed his hand over Burton's bicep. The grip was very strong. "I think it would be good if I showed respect for law and order, if one of my first official actions was to find the girl and release her. Of course, I would lose the goodwill of other interested parties. But it would be worth it for the favor of America."

"That scenario . . ." Burton said, " . . . almost makes it logical for you to be the mastermind behind the kidnapping."

Hamedov chuckled. "You're thinking like a Persian. Conspiracies everywhere. Azerbaijan is a complicated place. But maybe not so competent. I like your theory, though. Now, why don't you go and have a rest. I hear the German ambassador has been removed to his own quarters." He opened the door for Burton, but held him inside with a sudden look Burton could only describe as tormented. "Listen to me, Evan. My friend. I am the *only* one you can trust now."

General Hamedov believed he had Burton maneuvered into powerlessness, which was the best thing for all concerned, including Burton. But the affair saddened him. He genuinely liked Burton and would have preferred dealing with him, making him a partner. But Burton made everything so very difficult.

Burton was a *dzhigit*, a warrior from the old legends, a man of honor and probity and absurd courage. But the age of such men had passed. If, indeed, it had ever existed. If all of the stories and songs had not been a testament of lies.

The American's intrusion into the meeting had been jarring. Even more so to the other men in the room, who had not wanted Burton to leave the building alive. Fleming, especially, had been adamant. Hamedov had been the lone voice against an immediate execution.

But the others had been more right than he had been willing to admit to their faces. His respect and affection for Burton always clouded his judgment. The truth was that Burton was unpredictable. With his fanatical honesty. Americans like Burton reminded Hamedov of the religious fundamentalists across the border in Iran. Unwilling to compromise on even the smallest points, unable to accept the world as it truly was.

The best Hamedov had been able to do was to buy a bit of time for Burton, and it had taken all of his authority. Now it was up to Burton to keep himself alive.

He pitied Burton, too, now, and it made him feel closer to him. They had both suffered betrayal. Burton, who always seemed to have fine women at his command, a man to be envied. See how he had been betrayed! Women had weak souls and could never be trusted. And the German woman was a monster.

She had shocked him with her shamelessness, her thirst for blood, her unconcern in the face of cruelty. She had been nervous, but heartless. How wicked a woman could be!

Still, Hamedov was convinced he could control her. The Germans had gone soft, they needed others to do their killing for them. Fraülein Seghers would never have the strength to pull a trigger herself.

But all of these developments had been troubling, and they were haunted with dangers, some obvious, others flitting at the edge of the imagination. So, after the timetable for the night's actions had been finalized and the meeting adjourned, Hamedov phoned his most important sponsor of all.

"Vandergraaf," the man answered.

When Hamedov identified himself, the diplomat said, "Wait until I shut the door."

Hamedov told him what had happened, leaving out only the details about the girl.

"The conniving bastard," Vandergraaf said. "He'll tell Kandinsky. And that fool will call Washington."

"You said Washington would not be a problem."

"MacCauley won't be a problem. He's absolutely supportive. I mean I haven't bothered him with every little detail. But Drew knows that Azerbaijan needs a healthier relationship with Russia. He's even prepared to tolerate your rubbing elbows with the Iranians, as long as you don't jump into bed with them."

"But other people will make problems?"

"Well . . . the Secretary takes this democracy-and-human-rights business a bit too seriously, perhaps. And the press can twist things."

"There are many journalists here now. Because of Miss Trost."

"Don't worry. I'll help you spin it."

"What?"

"Don't worry about the press."

"You will manage it, then? America will support me?"

"After a few weeks. After the dust settles. MacCauley will take care of everything, once he thinks it through. But we can't have any fuss in advance. You understand?"

Hamedov said nothing for a moment.

"Well?" Vandergraaf said.

"What does this mean? That I made a mistake? Should I make Burton a prisoner for the night? What are you saying to me, Arthur?"

"I'm saying," the diplomat told him, "that there are more important concerns than a lieutenant colonel who cannot be trusted."

"What do you want me to do?" Hamedov hated talking to diplomats, but they were as necessary as women. "Can't you stop Burton from talking to your ambassador?"

"Burton," Vandergraaf said after a moment, "doesn't matter."

"What?"

"Listen to me, Hamedov. *Burton doesn't matter.* He would not be missed. Just take care of it. Do you understand?"

Hamedov understood now.

"And the girl?" he asked the diplomat.

"Stale news. I don't care either way. Just make damned sure nobody can blame you. Now I'm very busy, all right?"

Hamedov was shocked. Was there no end to the perfidy of Westerners? He knew what they said about him, about his countrymen. But were any of his people as bad as this? Did these Westerners have no sense of loyalty at all?

The thought of killing Burton remained repugnant and wasteful to the general. He had hoped that Vandergraaf would defend his fellow countryman, protect him, insist on his inviolability, so that Hamedov could tell his colleagues that his hands were tied, that Burton had to be left alone. But just the reverse had happened. His own lack of foresight, of understanding, angered him now. How else had he misjudged Vandergraaf?

Hamedov decided that he would let Burton be killed only if it proved absolutely necessary. And he saw now that it might be necessary. But there would be no pleasure in it for him.

If he could discover a way to keep Burton alive, he would seize it, he told himself. He would look for a way. Unless Burton wrote his own fate. Which Hamedov, to his genuine sorrow, suspected the American might do. He imagined a terrible confrontation.

It would not be the first time that Hassan Hamedov had been forced to do something that was hateful to him.

The girl was another matter. He had no taste for her death, either, but she was not important. He truly would have liked to present her to Burton, thus to win America's gratitude. But that door appeared to have closed. He needed Vandergraaf's support and would have to do most of what he asked. Hamedov thought bitterly of the man's soft flesh and hard heart. Vandergraaf reminded him of a eunuch from a seraglio.

How had he come to depend most on those he liked least? The general ached to see a better course and could not.

Well, if the girl needed to be killed in the end, she would only be one of many who had died because of their own choices. He could make it look as though the president's people had done it. To hell with the Germans. And their devilish women. The Russians were closer, and far more powerful. So to hell with the Germans and their four million dollars. Four million would be nothing. Who did they think he was? A little gangster? Perhaps they would try to dispose of him next?

They would see. The world would see.

Alone, the general sat back in his chair and looked at nothing. On the edge of greatness, his day had the taste of ashes. The darkness of mankind bewildered him.

CHAPTER

11

Bob Felsher sat over a very early breakfast at the International House Of Pancakes, letting his food grow cold. The food was fine, but the news was unappetizing.

Major General Kulikov of the Russian embassy sat across the table, dressed in clothing Felsher's wife would long since have donated to charity for the tax deduction. Buttons no longer lined up with their buttonholes. The Russian ate furiously as he spoke, and he was unpleasant to watch.

Mouth not empty, the general repeated, "It is a terrible disappointment. The plan was very good, but the girl has gone. Our soldiers searched most carefully, they are very good professionals of special operations." He lifted a forkful of pancakes the size of a small loaf. The food dripped as the general brought his mouth to it. "Still we cannot find her. Now there are disagreements. But I think everything will be all right." He looked at Felsher with the eyes of a petty criminal hauled into court.

Felsher still had some difficulty following the general's English. All in all, the oilman did not like dealing with foreigners

224

or blacks. He liked clarity and despised evasiveness. Now he struggled to hear each pancake-filtered word.

"We will find this girl," Kulikov continued. "Hamedov will find her for us. Although I think we must always be careful with this man. But maybe we will find her, too." He took a deep breath, as though the pace of his eating had deprived him of oxygen, and Felsher marked that the man's eyes were far less confident than his words. "Everything will be all right."

The waitress stopped by with a coffeepot in each hand, one with a green collar, the other orange. She held them out in front of her like a gunfighter's pistols.

"Top you boys off?"

The general nodded vigorously. Felsher had barely touched his own coffee.

"Well," Felsher said when the waitress had moved on, "it had better get all right fast." He glanced around, then bent across the table. "The rescue was supposed to be the trigger for Hamedov to move. Restore law and order to that place over there. Prevent anarchy. Now what's he going to use for an excuse?"

The general rambled for a bit about oppressive government and the refugee situation, but that was all crap and they both knew it. Felsher looked down at his plate in sorrow: a plump omelette, with ketchuped hash browns and a double order of bacon. A terrible waste. Normally, he possessed a manly appetite, and he appreciated the value of a solid American meal at IHOP. But he could not bring himself to lift his fork today.

"*Listen* to me," Felsher said in a voice reserved for subordinates. "First thing, it's your responsibility to find the girl. That's the deal. *Get the girl back under our control.* You people were supposed to take care of all that." He examined the general. The man looked defeated. A bad sign. And damned premature, if you had any fighting spirit. He had never imagined that the Russians would turn out to be quitters. "You're not trying to back out on us, are you?"

The general almost spit out his food. "*No, no*. No. We are doing everything. *Everything*. This girl simply cannot be found. There have been errors. We are better to do everything ourselves. These fundamentalists are not predictable, we should not have allowed—"

"Find her."

"Yes, yes. But it can take time, I think."

"Can Hamedov postpone the coup?"

The general looked tormented. "It would be most difficult. There are the troops, the movements. I think he has made many promises. People must not lose faith in him. And the president returns tomorrow. Perhaps then we must wait many months." He looked solemnly at his watch, a tinny affair that might have been bought from a street vendor. "The night is very soon in Baku. I think it is too late to stop."

"Well, it damned well won't look very good if Kelly Trost turns up dead *after* the coup, now will it?" Felsher did not like to use profane language, but he was uncharacteristically upset. The general had put him on the spot. Dick Fleming should have called in the news first. It was grating to learn about the failure of the raid from the Russian, akin to being audited by some wet-behind-the-ears terrorist from the IRS.

He needed time to think, to shift resources, alter tactics.

The general slowed the pace of his eating. Not that there was much left on his plate. "Perhaps . . . I think perhaps we can make this coup without the girl. I think we do not need her."

Felsher rolled his eyes. "Nickie boy, we've been over all this. I explained to you that we need Senator Trost's support on the Hill. That's the whole point. The only way we're going to get any post-coup Congressional movement on those treaties is for us to round up the support of every Congressman who doesn't have a clue where Azerbaijan is or what all this is about. And that's most of the members, by the way." He made a fist as a gesture of strength. "Mitch Trost can rally 'em. We need him mad as . . . mad as a hornet at the Aliev government.

We want the U.S. Congress to *wel*come the change of regimes. Otherwise, we'll get both barrels from the democracy-and-human-rights crowd. We need folks to see Hamedov as a savior, the restorer of law and order. You have syrup on your shirt. By the pocket there."

The general looked down in regret.

"Don't go getting all soft on me, either," Felsher said. "I thought you boys were supposed to be tough." He glanced around the room again. Bleary truckers, laborers, old men who could not sleep. The waitress was busy and far away. "You just get the girl under control. Or the money doesn't flow. And I'm talking about your personal gratuity, too, Nick."

The general seemed like a man who had reached the sloppy stage of a drunk. He nodded, then nodded again, but his eyes only wandered over the ravaged landscape of his plate.

"I think that the person I do not understand the most," he told Felsher, "is Hamedov. Perhaps I have been an officer too long. But I do not understand how a man can betray his country in such a way. The pipeline, the oil . . . that is their only future. For Hamedov to give that up . . . to give it to *us* . . . this is very hard for me to understand."

Felsher smiled. He was on firmer ground now. "Nick, I figure this whole business . . . the oil, the pipeline, the user fees . . . it's going to be worth maybe eighty, maybe a hundred billion in the next ten to fifteen years. That kind of money buys a whole lot of Hamedovs."

The Russian's eyes moved to Felsher's still-laden plate.

"Anyway," the oilman continued, "Hamedov's type is international. This town's full of them. I met the guy when I went over there—and I'm here to tell you, you can't get a breakfast like this in that city. But Hamedov . . . that fella just wants power. He wants to be the boss. Likes the money well enough. But mostly he just wants to be the big chief."

The Russian nodded. But he still looked melancholy. Felsher wanted the man energized.

"I think you are very clever people," the general said. "Perhaps we should not trust you. I still do not understand why you want the pipeline to go through my country instead of Azerbaijan. Everyone thinks it is the other way around."

Yes, Felsher thought. Indeed, they do. "Nick," he said, feeling his appetite just beginning to return, "everybody in the world is in on that southern-route deal. A.I.O.C., all the big energy players, everybody but the Salvation Army. But Oak Leaf Oil is the *only* company that has a deal signed for a new pipeline that comes out through Russia. Thanks to your prime minister, who happens to have an excellent business head on his shoulders. Build the pipeline along the southern route, and we'd have to share." He wondered if they could reheat his platter. Hated to waste anything. "And Oak Leaf Oil doesn't like to share."

He let the general absorb that much, then leaned closer. "Listen here, Nick. You've put me in a bad position. Letting the girl slip away like that. With Hamedov making his move tonight."

"We will find the girl."

"Right. I *know* you will. But . . . do you see the position we're in now?"

The Russian stared at him, punch-drunk with failure.

"We have no choice now," Felsher told the man. "Can't afford any embarrassments. We've got to make sure that the failure to find Kelly Trost is laid at the feet of the current government, not Hamedov's. She can't suddenly turn up. It's too late."

"But . . . you want me to find her, yes?"

"Find her. Get her under control. Discreetly, Nick. Then make her disappear again. Forever."

The general seemed bewildered. "But Hamedov could still deliver her . . .'"

Felsher held up his hand like a traffic policeman. "Too late. Too complicated now. Whole thing's dragged on too long. And we don't know how much the girl knows at this point. It was supposed to be a quickie, Nick. But you boys dropped the ball."

The Russian looked at him in wonder. "But . . . you can't want . . .'"

"I think I've made myself clear. It's all too messy already. We have no choice. This problem has to go away. For keeps."

"But . . . if anyone finds out . . .'"

"It's your job to make sure they don't." Felsher sat back. "Well, I suppose that takes care of things, wouldn't you say?" He signaled to the waitress for the bill. He had decided to get rid of the Russian, then come back and splurge on a relaxed breakfast by himself. He did not like the way things had gone, but they could be managed. You just had to retain your clarity of purpose.

Two tables over, a man unfolded the front section of the *Washington Times* and a headline caught Felsher's eye. Before the waitress could make her way across the room, his appetite had disappeared again.

Mitch Trost returned from his morning run and found the press gathered in front of his house. The street had been dark and empty of everything except parked cars and cats when he left. Now over a dozen figures crowded his front steps in the gray light, with at least one television camera and a still-dark bank of lights set up in ambush.

They did not know his patterns and the reporters remained so focused on his front door that none of them noticed him until he was two houses away. Then the rush began, the barked questions.

"Senator, do you have any comment for our listeners?"

"Were you briefed in advance on the raid?"

"*Was* it a massacre, Senator? What about the women and children?"

"Any further word on your daughter?"

"Are the Russians coordinating their actions with the United States Government?"

"Senator, did your office leak the report?"

Trost had no idea what they were talking about. But the words "massacre" and "daughter" made his chest hurt and brought a fresh wave of sweat to his forehead. The mention of Russians set off a different series of alarms.

He could not respond. He had no information, he was unprepared, and he felt himself reaching the verge of panic. He struggled to bring years of practice and discipline to bear, composing a frightened father in running shorts into a senior United States senator. It was a fragile construction, and he did not think he could maintain it for very long.

"Ladies and gentlemen, I will have a statement for you later this morning. Thank you for your concern."

He had to elbow the CNN rep out of the way to unlock his front door and get inside. And he noted that someone had stolen his newspaper from his stoop.

The coffee smell held no charm. He rushed to the phone to call his chief of staff, but Ruby had been quicker. There was a message on his answering machine, ordering him—as only she was allowed to do—to ring her on her car phone or, if that did not answer, at work. She was on her way to the office and her voice sounded angry. Ruby, his protectress. God bless her.

He caught his chief of staff as she was driving up 395. She told him about the newspaper article. A leak from State. MacCauley had been holding back information.

"That bastard," Trost said.

"Seems like a fair summation," Ruby said.

"But the article says that Kelly's all right?"

"Well, it says there was no indication she'd been injured. Though the Army officer they cite thinks she may be sick."

"Get me that shit MacCauley."

"I've tried to raise him," Ruby told him in a voice that scorned the other man, this city, the world, "but his wife says he's already out the door."

"I'll call the White House. They'll find MacCauley. Listen,

Ruby, fax me that article as soon as you hit the office. I've got a herd of reporters at the front door and I need to know at least as much as they do. Then call the travel office. I want a seat on the first flight over there." He stared at an ugly ghost of himself. "That's what I should've done in the first place, Ruby. I've done it all wrong." He felt himself on the verge of tears. "I need to be near Kelly."

His chief of staff cursed at a fellow commuter, then said, "Really think that's wise?"

"I'm tired of wise. I'm going to go find my daughter."

"Well," Ruby said, reading his tone and resigning herself to the decision, "I suppose we'll have to get you a visa, that sort of thing. You might need shots."

"Screw the shots. And get the State people jumping on the visa business. Rip their heads off. They thrive on pain. Just let anybody try to keep me out of that country. When I get off that damned plane, they'd better have the U.S. ambassador standing there sprinkling ashes on his head and the president or whatever they have over there down on his knees. Pull out all the stops." He thought for a moment. "I'll be in the office in an hour. No, make that an hour and a half. I'll need to throw some clothes in a bag. Stack up anything you've got for immediate signature. And send Laura flowers twice a week. I'm going to stay over there till they give Kelly back."

He hung up and listened to the sounds from his street. Vehicles shifted. Two shouters went at it over the positioning of a van. He hated all reporters at that moment, wondering how he could use them to his advantage. It was important, of course, to take a long-term view, not to say anything he would regret later. MacCauley, damn him, was a personal friend of the President's.

Getting MacCauley would have to be a matter of art, not impulse.

Trost went into his bathroom and shut the door. But the circus noise followed him. The only way to escape the press was to turn on the news.

His bathroom radio was preset to NPR, smarmy and barmy, leftie propaganda for America's mornings and absolutely indispensable. Blessedly, there was nothing about his daughter. He did not feel he could bear any more news at the moment. All that mattered was that someone had told State they believed she was still alive.

He wanted to hold onto that.

"Yes, Senator," Drew MacCauley answered. "*No*. Absolutely not. We were only waiting for verification. I didn't want to alarm you unduly. It seemed premature. No. Absolutely not."

The voice in the receiver was exactly the sort MacCauley despised: accent inflated above the social origins. Trost was nothing but a state university grad. And a football player, for God's sake. With a tack-on degree from some hick law school. It was criminal to allow men like that to interfere in policy matters they could never fathom.

"The message only reached my desk late yesterday, Senator. I still cannot attest to its credibility. The cable isn't really an eyewitness report at all. No. Just some military type who claims he happened on the scene after the fact. I, for one, emphatically do *not* believe the Russians would have perpetrated such an act. Although they are, of course, fully committed to locating your daughter, to the extent it lies within their power. I have received personal assurances from the responsible deputy prime minister, a man I consider a friend."

The voice on the other end of the line insulted him again.

"Really, Senator . . . I do not believe that would be a constructive action. I can tell you from experience, it's usually easier to maintain one's objectivity from a distance. By going over there you'd only—"

"Work out the fucking visa," Trost said. "Tell them I'm on my way."

He hung up.

For several minutes Drew MacCauley simply sat behind his

desk, feeling immensely wronged. He could not believe the Founding Fathers had intended democracy to come to this. The government they had envisioned had been an affair of gentlemen, where learning and experience, to say nothing of breeding, were assigned proper value. With Jackson, it had all begun to slide downhill. Nowadays any rube with a little money and a decent haircut could end up in Washington. Men like Trost, with their populist pretensions and slovenly womanizing. Of course, the President was not without fault in either of those departments. But he at least had the sense to appoint men of quality to key positions.

Stirred by his musings, MacCauley called down to summon an assistant secretary who had gone to his prep school a few years ahead of him. Two minutes later, a thin face appeared around the door, followed by thin shoulders, thin hips, and, finally, gray trousers that might have enclosed broomsticks.

"Come on in, Tick. And shut the door. Sit down."

Tick said nothing. He knew better. MacCauley indulged his sense of being horribly wronged for a few more delicious moments, then said:

"I need you to do something for the department, Tick. I know who leaked the document. I have absolutely no doubt about it. Bitch named Rains. An analyst. First name's Virginia. Drab little creature."

"Don't believe I know her, Drew."

"You wouldn't, Tick. She's one of the little people. On the FSU side of the house. Handles the Trans-Caucasus, that sort of thing. Virginia Rains. Goes by 'Ginny.' I mean, good Lord. She's still got one foot in the trailer court." MacCauley touched at his immaculately shaven chin. "I want her arrested. Breach of security and all that. Plenty of evidence. Have them cuff her at her desk and march her out. Make sure all her peers see it. Generate a lot of paper on it."

Tick looked doubtful. "Really, Drew. I can't see us prosecuting this one. Trost would rally the tribes. We'd have Congressmen coming over the walls of the legation."

MacCauley smiled and waved his hand as if shooing a fly. "We're not going to prosecute her. I'll explain to Trost that the arrest was a mistake, a matter of overzealousness on the part of the security boys. I'll send him a personal letter of apology." His smile faded into a New England winter. "Just make damned sure there's a record of her arrest. She's not an FSO, I've checked. We'll boot her. And she'll never work in government again. The FBI won't clear her, and nobody else will, either. Without a clearance, she'll be teaching government at some community college."

Tick shook his head. "Drew, I'd never want to be on your enemies list."

"One other thing," MacCauley said. "Trost is determined to go over to Azerbaijan and make a fool of himself." He held up a hand like a policeman at an intersection. "I know, I know. But he's made up his mind. So make it look as though we're moving heaven and earth for him. I have reason to believe the Baku airport will be closed to all traffic before his plane ever touches down. And letting our favorite senator cool his heels for a few days in Istanbul or Moscow might not be a bad thing at the moment." He smiled the way he did whenever he won at tennis, which was most of the time. "Damage control, Tick, damage control. Get to work."

When his disciple had gone, Drew MacCauley buzzed his secretary and told her, "Lydia, get Arthur Vandergraaf on the phone."

Trost's colleagues clogged his office to offer their sympathy and support. Some were sincere, others only dutiful, and a third group was alarmed upon hearing he intended to leave town when bills they had sponsored were coming up for a vote. With Congress long overdue for its summer recess, everyone was tired, tempers were short, and civility was strained. But politics had the constancy of alcoholism.

"I'll support you on the Farm Bill," Trost told a senior senator from the other side of the aisle, "although I still think you're going the wrong way, John. I'll bring our freshmen on board. But I want you to swear on your immortal soul you'll never back Drew MacCauley for SecState if the President's reelected."

Ruby had him flying out of National at eleven-twenty, with connections in JFK, Heathrow, and Istanbul. Even though the airline carrying him on the first two legs had called back to offer an unsolicited first-class upgrade, it was going to be a brutal trip, lost luggage guaranteed. But Trost refused to break for an overnight along the way. At a level below language, he had convinced himself that Kelly's fate depended upon his presence on the scene and that, somehow, his arrival would trigger her release.

He refused to imagine losing her. The whole business disturbed him to the point of physical illness and he had the worst case of heartburn he could remember. Ruby had a junior staffer fetch him breakfast, but all he could manage to eat was half a banana. He drank coffee, though. So much that it burned out of his kidneys. He gobbled Tums from his desk, then drowned them with more coffee. The cramping in his torso did not go away.

The President called, solicitous but unmistakably impatient to punch the ticket and move on. His testimony had just been subpoenaed by a special prosecutor and he clearly had other things on his mind. He offered to send a White House limo to take Trost to the airport, but the senator did not want that now. He left the office with his garment bag, an attaché case, and Ruby Kinkiewicz by his side.

Driving over the bridge in Ruby's Buick, he remembered to call Laura. She had wanted to come over and stay the night again, and now he was sorry he had eased away from her. She was one of the good ones. Just maybe the best. But her voice seemed distant on the phone, even though her words were supportive. He wrote it off to the wireless connection, unwilling to think anymore.

National was a Darwinian struggle of cabs and shuttle pas-

sengers. He had Ruby drop him off in front of the old terminal
building. A staffer had phoned ahead to clear him, but he still
had to go through the rigamarole required for an international
connection and he was running late. He hurried through the
crowd with his garment bag flapping and announcements
threatening tardy passengers.

He was almost at the airline desk when his chest exploded.

An instant later, his torso seemed to collapse. The pain
translated into streaks of silver, slashes on the near horizon,
making the world look like a slashed photograph. He could
not control his body, his balance. His mouth opened and it felt
as though the contents of his chest would burst from his throat.
There was something living and terrible in him, something
foreign.

"Oh, my God," he said.

Then he was falling, clutching his chest, and he sensed people gathering around him the way you sense objects under
flowing water.

"*Doctor*," someone cried, and Trost wanted to say, "Yes,
please," but could not speak yet.

"Isn't he somebody famous?"

"Call a doctor."

"Stand back."

"Don't touch him, Marty, he can sue."

"Stay *back*, everybody."

"Kelly," Trost said. A moment before, she had been right
there beside him. Now he had no idea where she had gone.

Machinery chimed and beeped, and dull figures shifted.
His body jerked, fighting the pain. A dark face bent over him
and hands tugged at his clothing. Trost could not understand
how he had gotten back to the Mahantongo Street house. He
was supposed to be somewhere else, but he could not remember where.

There seemed to be a terrible fuss about something. His
chest hurt indescribably.

"It hurts," Trost said. "It hurts so bad."

"Don't you worry, mister. Everything's going to be all right."

"*Kelly*," he cried suddenly. "*Where's Kelly?*"

Kelly knew she was in Baku by the stench. Oil and salt water, with a coating of traffic fumes. She had smelled it in the seconds that took her from the back of the truck into the old house with the locker-room stink.

Baku.

She could only imagine one reason why her captor would have brought her to Baku. He was going to release her. They had made a deal without telling her. She would be free very soon now. There could be no other explanation.

"You must walk," her captor told her. His name was Abbas and he was an inexplicable mixture of solicitude and viciousness. "The stairs are too narrow. There is no carrying."

She stepped carefully, haunted by dizziness. She still had her hiking boots, but her socks were gone, along with her ruined clothing. In the last village they had given her a pair of pantaloons so baggy they tripped her if she did not go carefully. She laid both hands on the shoulders of the young man in front of her, hating to touch him, and sank into the shadows.

The basement had no windows. It smelled of bad earth and motor oil. A single weak light showed brickwork foundations that did not match, as though buildings had been replacing one another on the same site for centuries.

"Please," she said, "I have to sit down." The medicine Abbas had gotten for her had stopped her diarrhea and the chills came on less frequently. But her weakness had turned into a lassitude that wanted nothing more than a bed to lie on. She could eat bread and drink water. Once, Abbas had given her a warm bottle of Pepsi and that had been lovely. When she tried to drink juice, it ravaged her insides again.

The man who had met the truck was small and unshaven, with enormous shoulders. He produced a chair with half the rungs out of the back but did not relinquish it immediately. Instead, he looked her over with incendiary eyes and a flicker of gold teeth. His bared forearms showed green tattoos. He said something that Kelly could not begin to understand, but Abbas replied quickly and harshly, and the short man put down the chair and backed away. Kelly sat down gratefully, conditioned to the smallest joys.

She had been living a serial nightmare and she had learned to measure her respites by degree. Sitting in the sour air of this cellar, with the contents of her skull spinning as if she had overdone a party weekend, she felt almost luxurious.

Abbas had awakened her before dawn a day, a lifetime, before. When he removed her gag, she had shouted in fear and peed herself. She believed he was going to rape her, that the end had come. But he had only closed his hand over her mouth, speaking to her softly while the older man with the rifle kept watch. He told her they had to leave for her sake, that she was no longer safe in that place, and he unbound her and helped her dress, bending to lace on the boots he had brought back to her. Then he led her out into the moonlight, past a dog with its throat slit.

She walked as far as she could. The fresh air was so wonderful she did not mind the cold of the mountain night, and she imagined herself to be strong and healthy again. Yet she slowed without realizing it, and he hurried her as best he could, warning her in a whisper, "You must not speak. This man wishes to hurt you. You must not speak. He must not know we are going."

Then she fell down and could not get up and she remembered the time she had seen a horse like that and her mother's new husband had come out of the barn with a pistol and shot it in the head.

"Don't shoot me," she said. "Please."

"You must not speak. I will carry you."

And he did carry her, the way firemen carried smoke victims or hunters carried deer in old paintings. He was not a big man, not terribly strong, and they had to stop often. She could smell him sweating and she imagined that he smelled afraid. When it began to grow light, he crawled through the high grass, dragging her along, and she did not care about anything anymore.

Then they were in a house lit only by an old-fashioned lamp, and everyone talked in hushed voices until they had tucked her into the backseat of a small car, covering her with quilts and rags, and Abbas warned her again that she must be quiet.

They coasted down a hill, gliding to a stop, then Abbas and the driver pushed the car until it began to coast again. Finally, as it slowed a second time, the driver fired the ignition and they raced off along a bad road.

"You must sit up," Abbas told her unexpectedly. "Look at the world. See how beautiful Allah has made it. But you will hide again when I tell you. Or I will shoot you with a gun."

She sat up. Then they stopped in a ravine to let her empty herself, and she looked up and saw that the ravine was part of a deep, red gorge that looked like the wild country of southern Utah.

On her own, she could not walk all the way back to the car. Abbas came to help her, touching her with a gentleness more repulsive than violence.

They drove through time she could not measure, wobbling up dirt roads and over ridges that opened onto vistas of mountainsides sheer as buttes and narrow glades along the valley floors. Abbas asked intermittently if she needed to stop.

"Soon you will not be sick," he said. "There will be medicine."

The car finally fought its way up a track on which Kelly would not have risked a jeep. In the fold of a hillside, hidden and unexpected, a gray village appeared. It looked like a poor pueblo. Children gathered in delight at the intrusion.

The driver treated the kids harshly, scolding them and slapping out at random. They retreated, but not far. Abbas pulled

Kelly from the rear seat and helped her into a small square house.

The language sounded very different now, without the Turkish gutturals she had begun to recognize. An old woman clucked and shuddered at her, but helped her stretch herself on a sort of bedroll on the floor. There was an open hearth and the smell of green tea and milk. In minutes a small crowd of men, all of them bearded, coalesced in front of the fireplace, squatting on their haunches and speaking with their hands as well as their voices. Every one of them seemed agitated, some of them afraid.

She slept then and when Abbas woke her, she could not say if it had been a matter of hours or of days. He had a bottle of brown liquid labeled in a script she could not read. He told her it was medicine and he fed it to her with a wooden spoon.

It tasted the way she imagined stagnant water must taste and she lost the first spoonful. But Abbas patiently cradled her head and tried again.

"You must eat the medicine," he told her. "This is a bad sickness."

"Please let me go home. I want to go home."

"You must eat the medicine."

She felt so weak. She wanted to fight, but knew she could not. She could not even move on her own now. It was terrible for everything to end this way. She had always felt so strong, so capable.

With the medicine done, he let the old woman give her tea and some bread dipped in acrid milk. She could manage only a few swallows. Yet she felt incredibly soothed when she lay down again. Another male voice argued with Abbas beyond the range of her vision, but Abbas had the last word. Then he came close again, and she saw him intermittently, squatting on his heels, floating above her. He spoke to her in a changed voice, almost a chant, and she sensed that he was reading something to her.

Another male voice interrupted the recital and Abbas went

away. Kelly hoped they would all let her sleep now. She only wanted to sleep, and it surprised her a little that she could not get completely into unconsciousness.

"Help me," she said. "I have to go to the bathroom."

She tried to rise on her own and the old woman came. Sisterly solidarity: She understood. Everyone was alike, after all, weren't they? In the basic things?

No. They were not. She saw that now. She was a long way from the people who were like her. A sense of having strayed came over her, of a mistake perhaps irremediable.

Kelly was too sick to feel shame any longer and she let the old woman hold her as she squatted in an outbuilding.

She wanted to be clean again. She wondered if she would ever be clean again.

When they reentered the hut, it was magically crowded with men, and Abbas turned to her. He was angry.

"This is a bad place," he told her. "The men have no courage. Bad things have happened. Everyone is afraid. We must leave here now."

And they left, driving again over terrible roads in darkness. When the quality of the road suddenly improved, Abbas made her hide under the rags and bedding again.

"Bad people look for you," he said.

She could not tell what was true anymore. But it was all right as long as she could lie undisturbed. Then they pulled into a courtyard and Abbas made her take the medicine again, telling her afterward, "You must drink. It is very important. I think you do not want to die."

Die? It seemed abstract, by no means impossible, yet not quite real.

She remembered them shooting her driver, but the image had no more immediacy than the recollection of a scene in a movie.

Yes, yes. They killed people. People died. She was a witness. But she could not possibly die. Not really.

She could not get at the reality of death even now.

Then they made a nest for her in the back of a cargo truck, giving her bread and cheese and water, along with a basin for her slops.

"You must be very quiet," Abbas told her. "It is a long journey and there is evil along the road."

They stacked crates of melons around her, barricading her in, packing the truck so the cases would not slide and crush her. In the end, the fumes from the truck were worse than the thought of toppling crates.

She slept intermittently, but knew they had driven a long way. In a dream of her father, everything was hyper-real, cool, frank, and she knew that he would be terribly sad when she died. To the best of her knowledge, the truck never stopped. Until city sounds rose around them, engines, car horns, brakes, voices. The truck backed up and they shifted the crates to free her. Abbas lifted her to the ground with grisly tenderness, and she realized that she did feel better, a little better, and then she smelled Baku's radiant stench of oil and salt air.

The basement was just another prison, of course. Maybe worse in some respects. It had the atmosphere of a rat lodge, and the caretaker looked like a murderer or worse. But it was in Baku.

She was almost home.

Her father had fixed everything. She was sure of it. The thought no longer shamed her or made her feel inadequate. She just wanted the ordeal to be over. The medicine had made her strong enough to be absolutely certain that she wanted to live. She prayed silently, although prayer was not her habit, promising God that she would never be cruel or impatient with others again if He let her live. She even thought of old boyfriends, not missing them but ashamed of her heartlessness toward them. They had each seemed so inadequate, and now she saw that their failings were only human. She had always been too hard, too demanding. A bitch. And she wanted God to let her swim again. She wanted to feel the water streaming over her body.

"Please," she said weakly, speaking to anyone who would listen, "I have to lie down."

"There is no bed," Abbas told her. "Soon there will be a bed. You must not lie on the floor. It is dirty here."

It did not matter if it was dirty. She was dirty. Filthy. She ached to lie down. But Abbas only forced more of the medicine upon her.

"Will I go home soon?" she asked dreamily.

It was the only question her captor would not answer.

Abbas Melli finished his prayer and rolled up his mat. Then he sat down against the wall, wondering what to do.

He had allowed himself to be talked into the kidnapping, and he remembered with derision how he and his fellow conspirators had sat together over tea, outdoing one another with extravagant visions of the success they would enjoy when their plan became reality. No one had raised a critical voice, and he had suffocated his own doubts under the weight of belief, burning away his questions in the fire of enthusiasm. They had only to act, and Allah would act through them.

They had convinced themselves that the world would shudder, immediately, at the power of their action. It would be an irresistible blow to the Great Satan America. Abbas had never been to America, and he had never spoken to an American before encountering the girl, Kelly, but he shared the conviction of his collaborators that he understood America and the evil it dispensed among Believers. He understood America because he had seen the satellite television broadcasts, the women exposed and whorish, the men oblivious, greedy, and godless. America was, indeed, a satanic place, degenerate beyond description, alcoholic, drug-ridden, voluptuous, and spoiled. Yet it exuded a secret power Abbas could not reconcile with its immorality. He could not understand how this country that was little more than an enormous brothel could remain so powerful. And he had no doubt that America was powerful.

America was responsible for all the ills of his people, of

the region, of the world. When a job was lost or a child sickened, when a policeman bullied or a bureaucrat demanded bribes, when riches failed to accrue or a woman behaved disgracefully, America was behind it, manipulating the fates of oppressed millions. America conspired with the Jews to destroy the world of Islam. He had never touched America, but America had touched him.

The girl had been a symbol of America, and her father, whom they had not drawn in any detail, became a towering monster who could brake America's wickedness with a word. Formulating their demands had been a joyous, if solemn, affair, and they had all believed in the inevitability of their acceptance, adding still more demands to ensure they would not be cheated by asking too little. The girl herself had been cast as a handmaiden of Satan, deceiving the people with her charity, deserving of the severest chastisement.

Now the girl was all too human, and her father had not been heard from, and there was death in the land.

Abbas had taken her from Galibani's compound after realizing that the chieftain considered the girl's captors prisoners in their own right. And Abbas had seen the look in Galibani's eyes when the old chieftain witnessed the girl's shame. Then he had killed the old woman for nothing. There had been too much evil in the air.

Still, it had been a shock beyond measure to learn of what had happened at Galibani's compound after their escape. He had believed it must be the Americans, but the local people insisted that the Russians had done it. Of course, the Russians and the Americans plotted together, they were both enemies of the Faithful. But Abbas had the soundness of instinct to know that great things had gone wrong. Then he received word in the village that the Iranians had sealed the border with thousands of troops, closing the smuggling trails through the mountains. He and his comrades had expected the Iranians to rise in their support. But the Iranians, too, were looking for the girl. Then the village men, cowards all and faithless, had driven them from his aunt's house. Abbas had been ashamed for Islam, which obliged men to shelter and protect the sick. And the girl had been sick enough to worry him.

His attitude toward her had shifted helplessly. He had been prepared to scorn her, to deliver the torments her kind deserved. Yet he found that he could not hurt her without regret, nor could he bear for others to hurt her or witness her disgrace. Although he still believed that he was prepared to kill her if necessary, he had become her protector in the interim, casting it as a matter of honor, of the charity of the Faithful before the weak. His visions of her cleansed and wrapped in beauty became more frequent. He imagined her freed, returning to him of her own will, running to him, begging humbly to share his life, to re-create herself in the cool shadow of his love and protection. When he touched her, even in her soiled condition, it burned his hands with desire.

He knew that American women had many lovers, that they were deceitful. But perhaps she was an exception. Perhaps she was not like the shameless women of the television broadcasts. She had tried no feminine strategies, had evidenced no lust. Perhaps the daughters of the powerful were sequestered in America, held to a higher standard of morality. It was even possible, he considered, that she was a virgin.

His host entered the room, raising a tattooed arm.

"God is great."

"Truly, God is great."

Abbas had expected to be met by his circle of co-conspirators upon his return to Baku, by the warriors of the Faith, but only this man, who had long been imprisoned for theft, had been waiting at the designated house. All the others had an excuse for their absence, as well as a reason why he should not call them again.

He saw now that they had passed ever more of the responsibility onto his back from the beginning, winning him with flattery: "Abbas, you are the man for this. Abbas, no one has your courage, your talents . . ."

"Abbas," the ex-convict said, "That Russian *suka* next door saw the girl when we brought her in. I say we either move her or kill her now."

Abbas looked at him coldly. "No. Kill the Russian."

The ex-convict, whose name was Ali, thought about that. "She's all right. Her husband's away a lot. You know?"

Abbas found the thought repugnant. This man was supposed to be a mujaheddin, a warrior of Allah.

"Kill her. You said she's a Russian. There is nothing lower."

"Why not kill the American? Get it over with."

"She has too much value. She is a treasure for the Cause of the Righteous."

Ali laughed and gold teeth glinted. "There are some stolen goods you just can't sell, brother. Everybody's looking for that twat downstairs. They're crawling all over this city after her. All over the country. Why don't you just go find a safe place for yourself and leave the girl to me? I'll take care of everything."

"Our protector will take care of things."

The ex-convict laughed again. He had the voice of a man who gladly hurts everything smaller. "Your 'protector.' I don't believe those lies anymore. You don't have a protector. You've all been lying. You're amateurs. It shows what a fool I am for believing you."

"What you've done has been done for the glory of Allah, for the Will of the Prophet. For the people hungry for truth . . ."

Ali shook his head. "You're a fool."

"We will be shown the way."

"To a bullet in the back of the head." Ali snorted. "Where are all your friends? Where are your 'brothers' now? You and your 'protector.' You all lied to me." He spit on the floor. "I should kill *you*. Just to make myself feel better."

"Kill the Russian, if you think she saw anything. And have faith. Allah brings difficulties only so that—"

"Got any money?"

"There will be money. There will be everything. Our protector is only waiting for the proper moment."

"And I'll take my next shit in China. 'Our protector.' Who is he, then? You can't even give me a name."

Abbas Melli could have given him a name. But it would have been a sign of weakness, and it might have spoiled things. Ali was unpredictable, a man who was good for spying and killing, although he was not to be trusted. Not with the girl, not with the identity of their protector.

And the truth was that Abbas had begun to have his own doubts about their protector. He wavered from moment to moment, determined to call the man and alert him that the girl was in Baku, but hesitating, afraid of losing her, of betrayal, of the way of things among men. In the end, he knew, he would have no choice. Yet it was bitter, and he delayed. He told himself that he did not care for his own life, but that he did not want anything dishonorable to happen to the girl.

Thus far, General Hamedov had not lived up to any of his promises.

Drew MacCauley was on the phone with Arthur Vandergraaf for the third time that day when his secretary slipped into the office. Lydia had an excellent sense of protocol and priorities, so MacCauley realized this must be important. He placed his hand over the receiver and his secretary said:

"Senator Trost just had a heart attack. They think it's a heart attack. Over at National Airport. It's on the radio."

"Dead?"

"No, sir. I mean, the report said they rushed him to a hospital. They didn't give many details. But they're treating it as a headliner. Tying it in with the story on his daughter. I thought you'd want to know."

"But it *is* serious?"

She looked at him with a bureaucrat's cautious eyes. "I expect so."

"It's a great blow to our country. Keep me posted. Thank you, Lydia."

She left the room, closing the door gently behind her. Mac-Cauley paused for a moment before resuming his conversation with the DCM in Baku.

It pleased him to take a providential view of the world. He had been raised well, inculcated with a profound sense of justice, and he believed that, in the end, people got what they deserved.

One had to feel sorry for the poor bugger, of course.

CHAPTER
■ ■ ■

If you want to avoid Azerbaijan's new elite or its representatives, the best hides are cultural or historic sites. The national carpet museum has another advantage, too: It is not air-conditioned. By midmorning, the August heat gets a plague grip on rooms sealed against the world and the dense wool of the piled and hanging carpets contaminates your movements, squeezing the sweat out of you like a fever. Your eyes burn and your watch chews into the flesh of your wrist. Colors deepen in the gloom. Your stomach sours, and you become sensitive to each slight noise. You are alone in the vast halls, but the air presses in on you like a crowd of ghosts. The place smells. It is a treasure house got up as a tomb.

Waiting for Spoon, Burton was the only visitor.

Half a dozen mustached women in white blouses crowded by an electric fan near the entrance, eating bread and tomatoes. Recipients of bottom-level patronage jobs, they cared nothing for the glories in their charge and resented Burton's appearance, since it meant that one of them would need to rise occasionally to walk down the long corridors to ensure that their guest was not stuffing one of the enormous Shirvans under his shirt. It also meant they would not be able to close early.

He preferred the place in gentler weather, but even now, melting with sweat and waiting for the thunder of tanks in the streets, he found himself calmed by the grandeur of the antique Karabaghs and Kazakhs, the Tabrizes, Gyandzhas, and then the Perepedils, Seichurs, and Chichis of Quba. He had learned to read the rugs. Their geometries were as resolute as faith, and every bit as complex and deceptive. You had to struggle to master the identities of clans and remote valleys, to love the exuberance tempered by the discipline of tradition and the color harmony that was so jarring at first, like music in an exotic scale. Burton cherished the great carpets and humbler rugs as the poetry of the mute and the memoirs of illiterates, their histories far truer than the scribblings of the khan's courtiers. The museum usually gave him the sense that he was learning more than he could put into words, and he was endlessly surprised that it had not been looted. Men willing to sell their country were, in his experience, not shy about hawking its antiquities.

The sense of refuge that drew him to the museum was absent this time. Burton was humbled by his foolishness, disgusted by his blindness. It had shaken him when he suddenly put together the German ambassador's ravings. And his slowness to interpret Hamedov's coup preparations had been professionally inexcusable. Even now there were too many pieces left that did not fit together and he ached to think clearly.

The oil people had what they wanted from Aliev. So why had Dick Fleming, Mr. Sleazebag Petroleum, been in Hamedov's office with the others? If Hamedov was in cahoots with the Russians, what would the Iranians get out of it? Was Heddy tied into all this somehow? If so, whose side was she on? For that matter, whose side was anybody really on?

He no longer believed the kidnapping could be a separate issue.

But who had the girl?

He remembered little Talaat's urgency. Insight from the Twilight Zone, shared in the public pisser. "She's here. In Baku." Well, the way things were going, poor Talaat had as much chance of being right as anybody else. Kelly Trost could very well be in Baku. Or in Beirut, for that matter.

Footsteps slapped the old parquet flooring and Burton turned, expecting Spoon. But it was a young woman with an expression as resentful as that of a queen forced to scrub pots. Without acknowledging his presence—the sole cause of her journey—she lazed past him, trailing a scent of body odor and garlic. She had the calves of someone who had grown up working on the land and she did not shave them.

His minder posted herself on a chair in the dusk at the end of the corridor and crossed her legs and arms.

Spoon came up next, walking fast and sweating faster.

"Jeez," he said, "this an endurance test or something?" He looked around to make sure they were alone and marked the girl three archways down. "What's up, boss?"

"Ambassador doing okay?"

The question confused Spoon for a moment, then he realized which ambassador Burton meant. "Yeah. Big song and dance, though. Would've taken him six months to bleed to death, the way he cut himself." He looked at Burton with clumsy caution. "I guess he's pretty serious about hanging onto Heddy?"

"Love is strange," Burton told him. The words sang with a bitterness that would have done Nina Simone proud. "Two of them are made for each other." Then he shifted his anger back to himself and said, "Listen. I've been a horse's ass." He spit dryness. "I can't be*lieve* how stupid I've been. Heddy's BND. German intelligence. I fell for the honey trap. Oldest one in the book."

Spoon was a very well-centered man. "Sure about that, boss?"

"As sure as I need to be. Helmut Mega-kraut was giving me sixteen kinds of crap about me recruiting her for A*mer*ican intelligence. Going on about unexplained absences and how he was trained to detect a spy's patterns." Burton jerked his head as though he had tasted something unexpectedly bitter. The room, full of ancient Moghans and Akstafas, had become a mortuary. "Old Helmut was smarter than I was. By a country mile. He just guessed the wrong employer."

"You tell her anything that mattered?"

Burton had thought about that aspect of the problem long and hard. "Don't think so. Nothing I remember. But she saw my patterns, knew where I was going. More or less. Anyway, Heddy's sharp. You'd never catch her going through your briefcase."

"Maybe you weren't her target. Maybe she really likes you. Maybe you were R and R."

"Spies are always on, Spoon."

" 'Spies like us,' huh?"

Burton snorted. "We're bush leaguers. She's a pro."

Spoon thought about it as they drifted past dusty layers of rugs. "And?"

"Not sure. But things are starting to fit together. I don't have it yet. I believe in improvisation, but I'm suspicious of accident."

"Well, it's a crying shame, if it's true." Spoon looked away and Burton could feel the man's disappointment.

"Forget it. Heddy's a side issue. Here's the big one." Their watcher had not moved from her distant chair and there was no one else in sight, but Burton moved closer to the NCO. "Hamedov's ready to launch a coup. Maybe tonight, maybe tomorrow. Maybe in five minutes. With a cast of thousands." He looked hard into the other man's eyes. "Spoon, I walked right in on them. Just stumbled into it. There they all were. Right in Hamedov's office, smoking and joking over a map of Baku. Our pal Sviridov. Fahrad Adjami—not sure you know him, he's an Iranian operative. Along with some fireplug who looked Armenian as Fresno. And Dick Fleming, whose part in all this I still don't get."

"Not just the usual suspects."

"Here's the kicker. These guys actually let me walk out of there. Then brother Hamedov comes stomping down the hallway after me. Doesn't even try his usual bullshit. 'Coups? Sure we got coups. What flavor?' And then it's 'Azerbaijan needs peace with its neighbors,' and he starts telling me how this coup is going to be a good thing for the welfare class and the Dow Jones at the same time."

"You called the ambassador?"

"That's why you're here. Punch line came when Hamedov told me he'd kill the Trost girl if I blow the whistle."

"He has her?"

"Not yet. At least I don't think so. But he's hell-bent and determined to get her."

Spoon whistled. "He's the boy to do it. So what now, boss?"

"Got to tell Kandinsky. I know it's cold, but the coup's bigger than the girl now."

Spooner made a disgusted, agreeing face.

"Maybe we can have it both ways," Burton went on. "I didn't want to call the ambassador on an open line or the cellular. Figure everybody in the neighborhood's listening. I want you to go to him. Lay it out. And stay away from Vandergraaf. I'd sooner trust Hamedov. I need you to move out on this, Spoon. Boots and saddles."

Spooner looked at him doubtfully, sweat glassing his face. "What're *you* going to do, boss? Strikes me Hamedov might be reconsidering his generosity right about now. You ought to come into the embassy. Until the dust settles."

Burton understood exactly what Spooner was saying.

"Can't. Once I'm inside those gates, the Azeris will never let me out again. Neither could Kandinsky, for that matter. I'm on everybody's shit list. Mr. PNG."

"So what are you going to do?" There was a measure of affection and concern in the simple question that summed up all that was good about being a soldier among soldiers.

"Find that girl," Burton told his friend. "The rest of you deal with the coup. I'm going to get Kelly Trost."

Spooner shook his head. "Goddamned officers," he said. "Always got to be hot dogs." Then he yanked Burton into the shadows, out of the line of sight of their minder.

The NCO produced a nine-millimeter pistol and thrust it toward Burton.

"Thought you might need this. You left it up at the house."

Burton shook his head and stepped back into the moted light.

"I carry that thing and I'm dead."

Footsteps clapped toward them. Their disappearance had confirmed all of their watchdog's suspicions. Spooner tucked the gun away.

"Just thought you'd want a fighting chance, boss."

Burton tried to smile.

"Where is he now?" the ambassador asked. He looked tired and his glasses had been taped together where an earpiece joined the frame. He had admitted Spooner alone to the air-conditioned clarity of his office, closing the door in the DCM's face.

"Don't know, sir. And that's the God's honest truth."

"Why didn't he call me personally?"

"He's afraid your line's tapped," Spooner said. "And they have the tech to listen in on the cell. He didn't want to put the girl at risk. Or to put you on the spot."

Kandinsky peered out through his window blinds at the dying day. "We're all on the spot, Sergeant. We're on more spots than I can count."

"Yes, sir."

"He should've come in. If he's in danger."

"Yes, sir."

Kandinsky turned and looked at him. "Think he will?"

"No, sir."

"What's he going to do?"

"He'll find the girl. Or die trying." Spooner instantly regretted his choice of words.

"That's exactly what I'm afraid of."

The embassy had a tiny staff. Fourteen gringos. A few dozen local hires. The Americans lived in great intimacy, despite the wide range between their ranks, and Kandinsky had always been as good a guy as Spooner could ask an ambassador to be. Yet the NCO remained a bit in awe of him—and inextinguishably distrustful of any civilian when the chips were down. Spooner tried to choose his words carefully, but ended up speaking from the heart.

"Sir, begging your pardon, but if anybody's going to get that girl out of here alive and kicking, he's the man. He's got his heart in this one, sir. It almost hurts to see him."

Kandinsky stared down at his desk. "Speaking of hearts, I just had a call from Washington. Senator Trost appears to have had a heart attack."

Spooner frowned. "Hard-luck family."

The ambassador touched at the ball of tape on his glasses. "Damn it, I just don't want to see any of my people hurt. I don't know what you think of us 'cookie-pushers,' Sergeant, but I happen to care what happens to your boss. I'm responsible for him, and I take that seriously." He rubbed his upper arm as if he had just been given a shot. "And I *like* him." He offered Spooner an almost-smile. "Hard not to. I truly do not want to see that man wasted on a hopeless task."

"Me neither, sir. But you got to understand him, like. He's got a sense of mission that'd put John the Baptist to shame. Stuff eats at him." Spooner wished he could remember one of those quotes officers always had plastered on their office walls, but maxims had never moved him as much as the acts of good men. He just said, "You get to know a guy when you're road-dogging with him. Me, I'd follow Lieutenant Colonel Evan Burton to the ends of the earth. And then some. And if that girl doesn't come skipping back to Daddy, he'll carry it with him to the end of his days."

Kandinsky sat down wearily. "I know. I probably understand him better than you think. But this is bigger than individual considerations." He looked up. "If he contacts you again, I want you to tell him to come in."

"I already told him."

"Tell him again. Tell him it's an order. From me."

Spooner glanced down at the carpet. "He won't listen, sir. With all due respect." He expected Kandinsky to get temperamental at that point, but the ambassador only nodded to himself and tapped his fingers on the desktop.

"I suppose I've got some decisions to make." He pushed his glasses back up the bridge of his nose. "Anything else?"

"Coming back, I detoured past the parliament and the president's joint. Everything's still quiet. Maybe too quiet."

"Hamedov's picked the perfect time. Aliev's out in Alma Aty. Scheduled back tomorrow, though. So I guess that narrows the coup window." He looked into the blinds, as though he could see the city through their metal. "I'd bet on tonight. Hamedov's going to be too nervous to wait until morning. That's cutting it too close."

"Yes, sir. Sir, maybe you could just call President Aliev, warn him. He seems like a tough old bird. This is the third coup attempt, right?"

Kandinsky shook his head. "No. I'm sure Hamedov's got ears positioned all around the president. It wouldn't be a secret for more than five minutes. We'd just trigger the very thing we want to prevent. And this doesn't sound like the other coup escapades. They were just thug jobs. Hamedov's a serious player."

Spooner was not accustomed to giving advice to ambassadors, but he wanted to be helpful. "Well . . . maybe you could just call Washington."

"Pass the buck? That what your boss would do?" Kandinsky's mouth looked like a twist of lemon. "Anyway, Drew MacCauley wouldn't lift a finger. Not if the Russians are in on it. Moscow can do no wrong in old Drew's eyes. And he's never been particularly happy with Aliev's independent-mindedness."

"Yes, sir."

To Spooner's amazement, the ambassador began to chuckle. "Well, I'll figure something out. At least I don't have to take my further career into consideration. You can go now, Sergeant. And thanks."

"Yes, sir."

Spooner went out into the antechamber. Just past the ambassador's secretary, in a side office, the DCM was pretending to work. Spooner could read the man like a comic book.

"Sergeant," Vandergraaf called. "Come in here for a minute."

Spooner did as he had been told.

"Shut the door. Sit down."

Spooner shut the door. But he did not sit down.

"Now, why don't you just tell me what that boss of yours is up to?"

The man filled his chair like a big bag of liquid. The office walls were covered with signed photos of every almost-famous person the DCM had ever met.

"You mean the ambassador, sir?"

"You know who I mean."

"We all work for the ambassador, don't we, sir?"

The big man darkened and opened his mouth. Then he caught himself and put on a smile that would have scared Spooner off a used-car lot.

"I'm just trying to do my job," the DCM said. "Help out the ambassador. He's under a lot of stress. Why don't you just fill me in on what you've told him?"

Spooner considered the man with disdain. When he spoke again, his words were carefully chosen and his voice was controlled:

"With all due respect, sir . . . I always think of you as a great big sack of shit."

Spooner turned and walked out, hurrying upstairs to the

office in case Burton called. He figured they were all on the way out and he had enjoyed the look on Vandergraaf's face immensely, and, what the hell, it was worth it. He could always go back home and drive truck for his brother. Pay was better. But he did have one thing nagging at him.

He continued to believe in Heddy and he had not told the ambassador what Burton had said about her. After all, Burton had not charged him to share that part with anybody. And Spooner still imagined that someday, somehow, Burton and Heddy might end up together.

He hoped he had done the right thing.

"Nobody knows," Heddy lied. "Everything's going to be fine."

Wrists bandaged, Helmut held weakly to her hand.

"You see how much I love you?" he said, not without self-satisfaction. He looked gray. Everything about him was gray. The ambassadorial residence was done in pastels so light they might as well have been gray. Helmut had a collection of modern sculpture she once would have admired out of fear of appearing ignorant. Before Burton had taught her that it was all right to laugh at bad art.

"Yes," she agreed. "I've been awful. I'm so sorry, Helmut."

"Don't ever leave me, my love."

"Never. I'll make it all up to you."

He smiled. His sophistication had been stripped away and he looked as mooning and naive as Emil Jannings in one of his pity-me roles.

"We'll be so happy," he said.

"Immensely happy."

"Stay with me a bit longer."

"Yes, darling."

But she was already impatient and trying desperately not to show it. Everyone had made a fool of her. First Helmut with his inexcusable theatrics, then, more seriously, Hamedov. The bastard had been laughing at her all along. He had known that Galibani was already dead. Everyone had known. Except her. She had been tramping about when she should have been at work. As a result, she had handed that pig a million dollars for nothing.

She had already prepared her excuses. After all, the minister himself had told her to give the money to Hamedov. But she knew that she would, at a minimum, look incompetent. Helmut was more important to her now than he had ever been. Helmut, the villa in Bad Godesberg, the family mansion in Hamburg . . .

"I love you," Helmut whimpered.

"Yes, dear. I love you, too. Try to rest."

It embarrassed her beyond measure to remember the scene with Burton and Helmut. She had always been so good at keeping things compartmentalized. Then she had gone and spoiled it all. She had become incautious, letting her body drive instead of her head. That was never going to happen again.

She wondered where Burton had gone. No one seemed to know. If he had a lead on the girl, she had to know. Her last chance to rescue her career was to find the girl before Burton did, to deliver her to Hamedov and let him do what had to be done.

Of course, it was possible that Hamedov already had the girl. Or that she was already dead—that would be better still. Then it would only be a matter of shaping the evidence to suit Pullach. And the blood would not be on her hands. It was certainly possible, she thought eagerly. The girl could very well be dead. It was almost the likeliest scenario. And Hamedov had led her on about Galibani. He could very well be holding back information about the girl's death.

"Darling," she said, "I have to go out for a bit. Embassy business, you know."

His weak grip tightened faintly. "Don't leave me."

"I'll never leave you again. Not that way. But I *must* do a few things at the embassy. And I have to check on my apartment. You know how this town is."

He looked up at her with colorless eyes. "You won't see *him*, will you? Tell me you won't see him."

"Never again, my love. I swear it. You're all I want."

"He's not a gentleman."

"No, darling."

"He's terribly lower-class . . ."

"Yes, dear."

"I still don't understand how you could—"

She laid her finger over his lips. They had the feel of uncooked meat. "You're not to get yourself excited. That's all in the past. You promised me."

He nodded, closing his eyes.

She slid out from under his grasp, saying, "I'm just going to draw the curtains." Turning on a table lamp that would not strike the eyes of her betrothed, she moved to the window. Outside, the city lay at peace in the summer twilight.

"What time is it?" Helmut asked.

"Almost time for your dinner."

"Will you stay and feed me? I'm not well."

She crossed the room again and looked down at him, reconciling herself to the rest of her life. "I absolutely *must* go, dear. The nurse will help you."

"I don't want the nurse to help me."

She sat down by his bedside again and took his hand as if daintily retrieving an item from the garbage.

"I'll tell you what," she said. "Save your dessert. And I'll come back. We'll eat it together. Won't that be romantic?"

"I'm tired," he said. "I might fall asleep."

She stood up to leave.

"Be careful," Helmut said. "I couldn't bear to lose you."

She smiled, wondering if this was how actresses felt onstage. In dreadful roles. "Of course, darling. You have absolutely nothing to worry about."

* * *

General Hamedov sat at his desk, waiting for the first reports. He was disgusted with himself, which was an unusual state of affairs. He realized now that he should not have let Burton slip away. But he had wanted so badly to come to terms with the man. Burton was the only one of them all who had kept his promises, who had never lied to him. It would have been a fine thing to have him as a business partner, although you would have had to keep a second set of books.

Now he would have to find Burton. He had no choice in it. Find him, and decide what to do with him. Hamedov truly wished the American had not barged into his office during the meeting. Now he knew too much. Much too much. Fleming—a miserable man with no soul—had been right. Burton had to be accounted for.

It was the others who deserved to die. And they would live. The thought of the German woman, of her perfidy, enraged the general. The Westerners were idiots to let their women run out of control like that, to entrust them with responsibilities of that order. And she would go unpunished. He would even help her. The prospect disgusted him. He ached to find a way to humiliate her. Without sacrificing the money she had promised.

By tomorrow, of course, he would be running the country. But it was never a bad thing to have an extra few million dollars tucked away. Hamedov recognized that those who rose by a coup could fall by a coup. To that end, he had every intention of sparing the president's life, even of granting him a generous pension in exile.

But the German woman was a monster, a betrayer. Her dishonesty toward Burton angered him. If a woman could betray such a man, whom would she not betray? To Hamedov, Hedwig Seghers had become the summation of all women, of their cruelties and infernal weaknesses. He reviewed the behavior of the German ambassador, marveling at the weak-loined decline of the Europeans. How had such men ever come to such power?

One of the phones on his desk rang and Hamedov grabbed it, expecting a progress report from the first unit that had been ordered to move. Instead, he received a marvelous surprise.

"God is great," the voice said. "Is this General Hamedov?"

"Truly, God is great." Hamedov finished the formula. "Abbas?"

"Yes."

"Where are you, my brother?"

The voice hesitated just for a moment, then said, "Here. In Baku."

"You have the girl?"

Again, there was a ghost of hesitation before the answer came. "Yes."

"And she's alive? She's well?"

"She has been sick. I have given her medicine. I believe she will be healthy again."

"Where are you?"

"Perhaps we could meet at a quiet place?"

"No, no. These are dangerous times, my brother," Hamedov said. "I will come to you. You will have my full protection."

"We must do something. Everyone is looking for the girl. I did not wish to bring her here. But the Iranians closed the border. I didn't know what else to do."

Hamedov smiled to himself. "You did the right thing. Tell me your address."

"We must strike a blow against the Great Satan America," the young, weary voice said. "They must pay for the girl's return."

"They're ready to pay," Hamedov assured him. "I've been in secret communication. America has promised to abandon Israel. And to expel all of its Jews." He thought for a moment, trying to remember more of the nonsensical demands these idiots of religion had swept together. "The President of the United States will apologize to Iran. America will accept Islamic missionaries."

"Their president must apologize before we give back the girl."

"Of course, of course. Everything is being arranged. You're a great hero, a true son of the Prophet. Your deed will be remembered for centuries." The general paused. "Now, what's your address?"

"No harm must come to the girl."

"Of course not."

"We will give her back when the time is right."

"We will choose the time between us. Just you and me," Hamedov told him. He recalled the boy's sheep's eyes and stumbling ideas. One lesson the general had carried over from the Soviet days was that idealists made wonderful tools. "Now I am very busy. Great things are happening. The non-Believers will tremble in wonder. Give me your address."

The young man gave it, halting between words and syllables as if on the verge of changing his mind. Hamedov knew the area. It was a derelict neighborhood, not far from the oil flats, where any possible witnesses would be expendable.

"Good, good. This is a great deed. I will be with you shortly." Hamedov looked at his watch. It was a bad time to leave the office. But he would take his radios and cell phone with him.

"You will come alone," Abbas said. It was half a command, half a question.

"With only a bodyguard," Hamedov assured him. "These are very dangerous times."

After he hung up, the general sat back and closed his eyes. He believed in fortune, and fortune appeared to believe in him. Just before he rose to strap on his pistol belt, he saw his way through another problem as well.

The German woman might get what she wanted. But she was going to earn it. And all of the foreigners were going to learn a lesson.

* * *

Burton used back streets to get to the outskirts of the city. He did not detect anyone trailing him, but knew that, at best, it was only a matter of time. He parked by a district market that had closed for the day, letting the twilight thicken as children kicked a soccer ball over the garbage. When it seemed dark enough to risk it, he headed for Razim's home, hoping to catch Baku's number one fixer before the Azeri headed off to Charley's and the other restaurants and bars that served as his offices.

Schooled in matters of technology by the Russians, the Azeris were convinced that driving with the headlights on exhausted your car's battery. For the first time, Burton was grateful for the lunacy. He rolled through the fresh darkness, with cars rushing blindly past in the terrifying custom of the country, and he laughed suddenly at himself, thinking that he'd been driving with his mental lights off for quite a while.

The gates were open at Razim's compound and Burton pulled in, maneuvering his car so that it was hidden from the road. He noticed a sliver of face disappearing behind a drapery as he got out.

A woman intercepted him at the door. Razim's wife, to whom he had been introduced the one time he had been a guest in the house. Pudgy and nondescript, she had served them wonderful food, peering around a corner to see if the men were enjoying it as they ate by themselves.

"He is not at home," she said in Azeri. "He has gone away."

But Burton had not made it halfway back to his car before he heard an angry male voice from inside. Seconds later, Razim rushed out to overtake him.

"Evan-*bey*! Please. My wife understands nothing. She is only afraid because of the rumors."

Burton smiled, playing it aw-shucks.

"So, my friend," Razim said. He was huffing from the short run across the courtyard. "You have come about the coup?"

"About the girl, actually."

Razim looked disappointed. "You are not interested in the coup?"

"I'm interested, all right. But the girl's still number one."

Razim looked over his shoulder toward the highway. "Come inside. There are ears in the wind."

Burton followed him into a house noisy with invisible children. The furnishings mixed a gaudy Westernness with *sumaq* cushions on the floor and brown family photographs of the sort of tribesmen who had been somberly delighted to kill Persians, Turks, Russians, or anyone else who strayed into their neighborhood.

They sat and Razim shouted for tea. He smiled to show a host's pleasure, but the smile was unsteady and the rest of his face lacked its usual confidence. Then the smile disappeared entirely and Razim lowered his eyes.

"I am sorry, Burton-*effendi*. I did not know that the matter of Galibani would end so terribly. I should never have sent you there. But I could not know these things. And now I must report that I have no further informations about the girl. There are only rumors unworthy of your ears. She has gone to Teheran, or to Chechnya. Then she is dead. And alive again." He lifted his luminous brown eyes to Burton. "Who can say, in times such as these?"

"No other rumors?"

"Only that her kidnapping is a plot by the CIA. To excuse an American invasion to seize our oil."

"Unlikely."

"History laughs at us all, Evan-*bey*. Who knows what folly tomorrow brings?"

Burton looked at the garish machine-made rug, a mocking imitation of the glories in the museum. The Soviets had killed the art of rug-making. Along with the rug-makers.

"Okay. How about the coup?"

"Everyone knows. But they know nothing. They say President Aliev has secretly returned. Or that he has fled to Istanbul. It is always the fear talking."

"Can Hamedov pull it off?"

"Who can say? He's a powerful man. But perhaps he plots too much and thinks too little." Razim touched Burton on the forearm. "Hamedov is a strange man. He is very ambitious. But he is not without conscience. He has done much for the refugees." Burton's host smiled. "At God's will, he is like everyone else in Azerbaijan. Loyal to his clan, to his own people. The country, the state . . . these things are toys. A man takes care of his own kind. Perhaps of his friends as well. But in the end, only the blood matters." Razim's smile broadened. "You know Hamedov and Aliev are related? Distantly. They will feud now. But we will live to see them embrace each other and turn against someone else."

"It does," Burton said, "make it a little hard to do business."

"Unless you have the blood ties."

Burton considered. "You're not related to Hamedov . . . or to Aliev, are you?"

Razim laughed. His wife rushed in with a tray bearing a teapot, tulip glasses, and a silver bowl piled with sugar cubes. "Oh, no," he said. "My people are from the high mountains. I am related to none of these men. But I try to be useful to all." He handed Burton a glass of tea and took up his own. "I think Hamedov is only angry because he has not been made prime minister. These things can be settled."

"You don't think the coup is for real?"

Razim looked at him in surprise. "Oh, it is very real. People will die. Perhaps Hamedov will win and favor a different corporation. Or the Russians. Or the Iranians. I cannot say. But the stars will continue in their courses."

"Diplomacy," Burton said, "operates on a shorter timetable." The tea only reminded him of how thirsty he was.

" 'Diplomacy'! What a fine word for the barter of human souls! But tell me, Evan-*bey*. What can I do to help *you*?"

Burton realized that Razim was telling him that his time was not unlimited.

"I need a different car. Hamedov's not happy with me at the moment. I need a vehicle the authorities won't connect with me."

"But, my friend . . . all of the roads from Baku have been blocked by the military. Since this afternoon."

That was news to Burton. But it did not matter. "I don't want to get out of town. I just want to be able to move around the city."

"But they will recognize you."

"Eventually. I just want to buy a few hours." He met his host's eyes. "I've got to find that girl."

Razim nodded, shrugged. "A car is easy. Take one of mine. Come with me."

Burton followed him back across the courtyard to a garage. Razim pulled on a light and the weak glow showed a room inky with grease and crammed with tools, parts, and crates. The little Zhiguli seemed like a toy amid the clutter.

Razim lifted a box from the top of a stack, struggling a bit until Burton helped him. The next container down held an assortment of license plates, all of them suitably rusty.

"I think perhaps we will take away my plates. You will forgive me if I do not choose to anger General Hamedov unnecessarily."

"I appreciate this, Razim-*bey*."

The Azeri waved away his thanks. "It's nothing. I wish I could do more. I wish you luck with this girl, who has come here with good in her heart."

While Razim worked on replacing the plates, Burton walked back to his own car and fetched his necessities. Standing in the shadows, he punched the office number into his cell phone.

Spoon answered immediately.

"The fireplace," Burton said. "Thirty mikes, no riders. Bring sugar."

Ateshgah in thirty minutes. Alone. With the operating money from the office safe.

"Good copy," Spoon said. *"Vaya con Dios."*

Razim appeared beside him and held out the car keys. Burton had not heard the man approach, and as he drove off into the night, he could only wonder whether the Azeri would prove to be a true friend, or if he had been helpful only in order to get Burton off his hands and betray him.

Sergeant Spooner counted out the two thousand, one hundred and eighteen dollars cash from the envelope at the back of the safe. Then he wrote out a receipt, locked the safe again, and put the money in his map case, along with a flashlight and a cellular phone. He had been to Ateshgah once, scouting linkup sites with Burton, and the place had given him the creeps. No lights, plenty of ghosts. Outside in the hallway, he listened until he was certain the stairwell was empty, then he went down the steps two at a time and dashed out past the local-national desk guard just in time to hear the growl of big engines coming up the street.

He ran across the embassy yard toward the gatehouse. Before he reached it he saw a flare of headlights mounted high and the shadow of a turret moving above the gate.

Armored personnel carrier, BTR-series.

No tanks, though. None of the heavy grumbling or the sound of tracks chewing up curbs and road surface. But it sounded like there were plenty of troop carriers.

In the gatehouse, the local hires babbled at him in panic and even the Azeri duty cop appeared surprised at the turn of events. Outside, headlights crossed and vehicles shifted. Voices barked and complained, and uniforms dashed in and out of pools of light.

They were sealing off the embassy.

Spooner ran for it, determined to get away and link up with Burton, but he immediately came up against a wall of steel vehicles and soldiers, several of whom were quick to point their rifles in his direction.

He stopped.

These were army troops, not the usual glorified cops. At least a company of them. The big eight-wheeled vehicles jammed the street, blocking intersections and smashing awkwardly into parked cars. Turrets with heavy machine guns rotated as if sniffing for targets, and soldiers who were not much more than children sat on the high decks with baffled faces. In the roadway, one of the carriers crunched the fender of another.

An officer approached him, shouting in Azeri.

"English?" Spooner asked. "What the hell do you think you're doing? You speak English?"

Another officer popped up by Spooner's side.

"You must go back inside. We have come to protect you."

Spooner turned on him. "From what? We don't need any protecting."

The officer planted his feet farther apart. "We must protect you. There are difficulties in the city."

"My ass," Spooner said. "You're the goddamned difficulties."

"By order of General Hamedov."

"Just get out of my way."

He felt a restraining hand on his arm and almost threw a punch.

It was Kandinsky. "Let me deal with this," he said.

The ambassador's exchange with the Azeris seemed to start off cordially enough, although Spooner did not understand the local lingo beyond the phrases required to get a meal. But within a minute, Kandinsky was shouting, his voice going high-pitched and sounding sadly ineffectual. Spooner did not believe that sort of tone was going to persuade the boys with the guns.

The ambassador surprised him, though. When one of the officers unholstered his pistol and pointed it at the ambassador, Kandinsky slapped it away.

The ambassador turned to Spooner.

"These bastards aren't going to stop me from doing my

job," he told the NCO. "I'll walk to Hamedov's office if I have to." He pulled off his wedding ring. "Here, take this. If they shoot me, give it to my wife. Tell her I love her more than I could ever put into words."

"Sir, what—"

The ambassador turned away. He slapped at another rifle and began to walk down the hill toward the heart of the city.

Rifles came up. A machine-gun turret swiveled to follow him. All of the extraneous noise stopped and you could hear the tapping of the ambassador's shoes on the broken pavement.

Spooner lunged to follow him, to protect him. But one of the officers shoved a pistol into his chest so hard it hurt.

They did not shoot the ambassador, though. Kandinsky bobbed between two big vehicles, pushing back his glasses, and a carrier blew dark smoke as if to salute him. Then he disappeared behind the glare of headlights into the night beyond, strutting off to take on an army, a coup, a country.

Someone else stood beside Spooner now. It was the DCM. He, too, spoke to the officers in their own language, but his tone was very different. One of the officers saluted him.

Vandergraaf turned to Spooner. The man's heavy face was as wet as if he had just stepped out of the shower.

"I'm in charge now," he told Spooner. "Go back inside the embassy. And don't bother trying to contact any of your fellow troublemakers. All communications are down."

"And what if I don't go in?"

The DCM showed the remains of his dinner between his teeth. "I've told these boys they can shoot you."

Burton maneuvered the old Zhiguli up the street with the headlights off, unable to see the potholes and rain furrows until each had taken its turn trying to swallow the tiny car. The neighborhood was not a good one and people shut themselves in after dark. Normally, you could sense the life waiting to pick back up in the morning. But no light seeped through the shuttered windows tonight. Fear clotted beyond the noise of his engine. Once, an old woman croned in front of him, dark clothes flapping and drawing a wail from the brakes. Otherwise, the slum might as well have been dead.

He drove slowly past the high walls of the shrine, ensuring that the caretaker had locked up tight. Parking the car in a feeder alley a block farther along, he backed in so he could pull out into the street quickly, although the road was so bad that nobody was going to do a Hollywood chase scene.

He got out quietly and a cat hissed at him. Ateshgah was a good linkup point. The locals were convinced it was haunted and he had surveilled it long enough to know the cops gave it a miss.

Centuries before Baku sprawled into industrial spoilage, the oil and gas deposits at Ateshgah had been so rich they burst from the earth, catching fire. The inexhaustible flames, where the Apsheron ridge begins to poke into the belly of the sea, became a place of pilgrimage for Zoroastrian fire worshippers and inchoate mystics. Even after Islam tightened up the local manners, holy men arrived on foot from India, braving the bandit mountains and snake deserts to kiss the earth of Ateshgah and starve themselves to death in God's honor.

Now the shrine was a goofily restored tourist site without tourists, watched over by a caretaker who provided misinformation for tips. To please Indira Gandhi, the Soviets had installed an artificial "eternal" flame to replace those that had been suffocated by development, and a few of the rebuilt rooms held mannequins of the sort that frightened children unintentionally.

By the time Gorky came to Baku to write so clumsily and movingly about the oil proletariat, the ridge had attracted roughnecks and job-seekers, displaced villagers and cripples who could no longer work on the rigs that spiked up on all sides. Now the ruckus of the boom years had long since settled into a mash of permanent shacks with walled vegetable gardens and wells that pulled up water spiced with petroleum and the runoff of outhouses. Families lived there, poorly but more happily than in the hi-rise barracks of the Soviet twilight, and during the day kids with mild chemical poisoning thumped each other in the dirt street. At night, the ridge belonged to ghosts and the likes of Evan Burton.

Burton squatted down with his back to the compound wall where it recessed into deep shadows. Where he could see without being seen. And he heard an unmistakable rumbling in the distance.

Tanks.

Coming down the airport boulevard, if the acoustics could be trusted. Probably moving in over the western ridge, too, from the base out at Pirekeshkyul.

This was it.

The coup.

His first impulse was to run back to his car and head for the embassy, to help Kandinsky. But he recognized the foolishness of that immediately. The embassy would be nothing but a prison for the duration. It was the last place he needed to be. He needed to be on the move, with his eyes wide open.

He took out his cell phone and dialed the ambassador's office. But there was a problem with the atmospherics.

Or the Azeris had gained the ability to jam cellular comms.

Russians could be helping out on that, Burton realized. Goddamned Sviridov and his crowd.

He imagined he heard a pickup on the other end, although the static was so bad he could not be certain. He spoke into the device in a controlled tone, not wanting to make any more noise than necessary, hoping Kandinsky was listening.

"This is Burton. Tanks coming down the airport boulevard. Sounds like at least a battalion. I say again: approximately a battalion of tanks entering the city on the airport road. Station, do you copy?"

Static. Zooming sounds from a cheap sci-fi flick. He folded up the phone and put it back in his cargo pocket.

A stream of tracers climbed the sky, then faded. The range was so great that there was no subsequent report.

Out by the airport, he judged.

Were they fighting for the terminal?

He stood up, then made himself squat down again. He realized that Spoon might not be able to get through to him now and he had no idea what to do next. Even if Kelly Trost were in the next house down, he had no way of knowing it. He had a sense of great things happening without him, of helplessness and failed duty.

He let his head drop down. Even if they did not intend to kill the girl, she could easily become a casualty if the coup turned bloody. If the wrong side started losing. Or if one man with a gun lost his temper.

"Hold on," Burton whispered to her. "I'm coming."

But that was bullshit.

He had become an embarrassment to himself.

Burton looked at his watch. It had been almost an hour since he called Spoon from Razim's. The military probably had the main thoroughfares blocked. If they were letting any traffic move at all.

Knowing the Azeris, of course, they probably had not worked out the details of their military traffic management, let alone control of the civilian side.

Then he caught himself. The fact was that he did *not* know the Azeris. Not when it counted.

He waited another fifteen minutes. Twice he heard small-arms fire a kilometer or so away. Shoot-outs at highway check-points, he figured. The movement of vehicles came freight-train steady now, but there were still no large-caliber exchanges, none of the sudden flashes of light followed by thumping that marked a clash of heavy metal.

Two red flares shot up, triggering more lightweight shooting.

Upping the ante, though. There was definitely trouble out at the airport, the city's lifeline to the world.

He took out his cell phone and punched up Spoon's number. But the distortion had grown even worse.

It was jamming. No mistaking it now.

Kandinsky needed him out on the ground, gathering information. Working the troop units. Events like this were prime time for attachés and mil-reps. Ambassadors needed experts who could sort out what they were really seeing behind the spectacle. Burton decided to give Spoon ten more minutes, then to put the girl on hold and head downtown to do the job he was being paid to do.

He thought he heard a vehicle closer in. But the huge groaning of engines in the background made it hard for him to be certain.

No.

Definitely local traffic.

And closing.

Spoon?

Burton's eyes had become accustomed to the dark and soon he picked out a little box jouncing up the road, lights off. It looked like the office jeep.

The vehicle pulled up and stopped in the middle of the street.

Burton's internal alarm kicked in: unlike Spoon to be so obvious.

Someone got out. Then it all went wrong very quickly. Three other men emerged as well. Their silhouettes showed that they were carrying automatic rifles.

More vehicles came up the road behind them, moving in a fast little convoy. Burton made out at least one truck, its canvas flapping like dark wings. Even now, the sloppiness of it offended the soldier in him.

They had not spotted him yet, but the tallest figure, the only one without a rifle, called out:

"Colonel Burton. We have come to provide for your safety."

CHAPTER

. . .

Evan Burton was tough.

One of his "protectors" clicked on a flashlight and Burton launched himself up through the shadows as if slam-dunking a basketball. His fingers barely grasped the top of the compound wall. With more lights snapping on and a swarm of vehicles arriving, the night dazzled. But Burton had chosen his position well. He remained in the shadows just long enough to claw his way onto the top of the wall, skinning fingers, elbows, and knees, even scraping his face open again. He scrambled over the parapet, chased by a searching beam.

Lights flooded the top of the wall as he dropped out of sight. He flattened himself on the gangway behind the mock battlements and started crawling fast, headed toward the steps that led down into the courtyard. Above the idling engines, voices threatened and accused him. But no one fired a shot.

That meant they had been told to bring him in alive.

The interior of the compound was the size of a basketball court. A gas flame flickered under a stone pavilion in the center, flirting with the night. When he reached the steps, Burton got up into a crouch and ran downward, taking the last half-dozen stairs in a jump. He covered the open space as quickly as possible, heading for the parallel steps that mounted the rear wall. The compound was going to cost his pursuers time and manpower. If he could make it over the back wall before they saw him go, they would have to leave behind enough men to check every room built into the walls.

He made it to the rear parapet, listening to the shouting behind him but unwilling to take even a second to look back. He crawled up onto the ledge and stared down into black soup. Unable to see what waited below, he pushed himself off into the darkness, holding his knees together and making springs of his legs the way he had been taught at Fort Benning two decades before.

Something broke his fall, then snapped away under his weight. The obstacle pitched him off balance. His legs came apart and he hit with his toes, then with his knees, body crashing down. The earth met him with so much force he lost the oxygen in his lungs. But there was none of the bodily confusion that went with breaks and sprains. There was a blessed, stinking softness under most of his body.

Garbage.

He quick-checked his limbs, then jumped to his feet. He and Spoon had scouted the area for escape routes, but they had made the classic error of inspecting the ground by daylight. Now, with the neighborhood black around him, he could only stumble toward the dirt track he thought he remembered, hoping he had his bearings.

Behind him and on both sides, the night grew busier by the moment. Anxious, yelled commands told him how his pursuers were progressing. He had failed to focus them entirely on the compound. The noise of their vehicles hunted through nearby alleys. One after another, the vehicles turned on their headlights, helping him track their locations. They were working around on his flanks.

From the compound, voices rose in spikes of anger.

To his left, a flare lit the night.

It struck him that something big had changed, but it took him several long moments of running prayer-footed through the darkness to sort it out. In the distance, the world had calmed. He heard no faraway shooting now, and the rumble of the convoys out on the boulevards had settled into the drone of vehicles idling. It could have meant a number of things. Perhaps the coup had already succeeded. Or things might have bogged down. Maybe it was a pause for negotiations. In any case, the less shooting the better, he decided.

He found the alley he wanted, his eyes relearning the night after the glare of the headlights and the mistake of looking at the flame in the courtyard. Trotting along fence lines and keeping himself low, he tried to gain as much distance as he could before the pursuit vehicles nosed their way through the maze of alleys and ravines. He headed back toward the heart of the city.

A dog went off, howling and growling as though Burton had taken a stick to the child of the house.

His luck to end up as a fugitive in the only Islamic country where people kept dogs.

He veered off where a branch of the alley sloped down through a shambles of low walls and huts. Making good progress. There was a ravine half a kilometer down the slope that separated the ridge settlement from the rest of the city. It was so rugged a jeep could barely negotiate in daylight. Once he was in it, they would have to follow on foot. And Burton was convinced he could outrun the entire Azeri army, whose uniform was incomplete without a cigarette jabbed between the lips.

He almost made it, stumbling and struggling to keep his balance, newly aware of a cold wetness running down one calf where his flesh had taken on the feel of a numb burn. He figured he must have torn his leg when he jumped. It had not even registered at the time. Too much adrenaline. His body was not paying attention to anything less than a mortal threat. But the leg wound was not good news.

He could just make out the deeper darkness at the end of a lane where the landscape dropped away: the ravine.

A swerve of headlights threw a barrier of light across his path.

Throwing himself to the ground, he crawled into a ditch. Slime soaked his legs and one arm. The jeep was definitely headed his way, the sound and the thrust of headlights growing in intensity. He heard running footsteps behind him.

The ravine was so damned close. It was a steep seasonal wash, with rusty barrels and derelict cars punctuating the scrub growth at the bottom. He knew it connected with several paved streets on the far side. Once across, he could hot-wire a car and bury himself in the city before the Azeris could make the long detour back to the airport road to follow him.

Headlights stabbed in from his other flank.

They were coordinating by radio. Had to be. Which meant that not all frequencies were being jammed. Or that the jamming had been active for only a certain window of events.

Scrambling through the slop of the ditch to a dry ledge, he pulled the cell phone from his pocket, hoping his fall had not broken it. It was greasy wet. He snapped up the antenna and stumble-fingered the buttons in the darkness, working from memory. Calling the office answering machine.

He pressed the phone tightly against his ear and cheek.

Wild static.

He spoke anyway. Then the phone died.

Goodbye to the communications revolution.

He tossed the phone into the ditch and low-crawled over to the nearest wall. His world had become an anthill of soldiers and vehicles, the voices and engines and headlights cordoning him off. He stood up, cut leg really beginning to hurt now and stiffening a bit. He flipped himself over the wall.

Soft landing. A garden. He moved quickly, but placed his feet as carefully as he could. Outhouse, rich with human smells. Then, unexpectedly, a plantation of roses, fully ripe, nearly drowning him in their perfume. A thorn tugged at his trousers.

It sounded as though there were at least a dozen vehicles after him and a full company of soldiers. He understood that fear exaggerated things. But even if you divided by five, the numbers were not on his side. He worked his way into the road-less heart of a cluster of family compounds, certain the residents were aware of him as he passed, some of them no doubt watching the show from darkened windows. But they were not a worry. The average Azeri citizen had learned to stay out of government business.

The flow of headlights circled the darkness through which he moved, unable to penetrate the confusion of walls and fences and shacks. Down the slope, his pursuers had positioned several vehicles along the edge of the ravine. Their criss-crossed headlights formed a no-man's-land. But Burton still believed he had a chance. If he moved skillfully, he could be through the light before they could stop him. Then he would be in the ravine and the game would start over again.

Unless they decided to shoot, after all.

He crouched through yards and gardens, past old farm im-plements and the skeleton of an ancient oil rig, the ground around it sucking at his boots. There was a stretch of almost-darkness ahead of him where the Azeris had not been able to maneuver their vehicles over the rugged terrain. If they had failed to move up troops to cover the dead space, it would be a good place to cross.

He almost made it to the safety zone. Then, with one com-pound left to cross, he heard the timeless voice of an NCO hurrying troops along.

Burton balled himself up in the weeds, hoping they would pass him by. There were several figures bunched together, al-ready on top of him.

Only one flashlight cut the night. That made him smile, despite everything. The Azeris would never give line troops anything so valuable as a personal flashlight. The light in each squad would be in the hands of the leader, and had it been an ambush, Burton would have known exactly whom to kill first.

The soldiers were noisy, sloppy, lacking in method and thoroughness. One of them spoke nearby. The voice was young and afraid. Probably had not been briefed, Burton realized. The nearest voice of authority just told him and his mates to go find that guy somewhere down there. The kid probably imagined a steely-eyed killer lurking in the darkness, waiting to cut his throat.

Scared kids.

Scared kids with guns.

Wonderfully, the squad moved on, kicking at scraps and complaining. As soon as he judged it worth the risk, Burton rose again and rolled over the wall of the last compound before the ravine.

Sudden noise sent fright through him like a bullet. For a half second Burton felt the most paralyzing fear of his life, with no idea what was happening. He identified the sounds just as a small living thing veered against his leg and fled, cackling.

He had landed in a chicken pen.

The first flashlight caught him. Shouting picked up. Thrill of the hunt. Then there were more flashlights as other search teams rushed toward him, more voices, and hurried, nervous commands in Azeri.

"Don't move. Halt. Don't move."

Burton considered making a last run for it, but someone sent a streak of bullets over his head. He ducked. And the first hands got to him.

A moment later, lights were bobbing on all sides, stinging his eyes. His captors had a firm grip on him. A number of firm grips. He could smell their dirty uniforms, their breath. Something hard and cold jammed up under his chin, snapping his neck back, then easing slightly. In the shifting light, a familiar face flashed before him. He could not quite place it. Then the officer spoke and Burton's memory cleared.

It was the major he had embarrassed that afternoon. Major Small Head, the officer at the interior ministry whom he had conned into escorting him to Hamedov's office. The lights danced and struck Burton's eyes again and he lost the man's face. But the voice was enough:

"*Please*, Colonel Burton," the major said. "I *beg* you. Encourage me to kill you."

"Is he going to live?"

Ruby Kinkiewicz turned on him as if he had touched her in an ungentlemanly way. When she saw who it was, her expression changed from surprise to consternation. Her makeup was spoiled, her eyes salmon. With that lurid red hair, she always reminded him of Belle Watling in *Gone With the Wind*, a film that never failed to nudge him to tears.

"You shouldn't be here," she said sharply. But he could sense that her bravado was as brittle as overcooked bacon.

Two male nurses rolled a gurney past the waiting room. From a shroud of bedclothes, a crone's face looked up at the fluorescent lights, lips trembling.

"A concerned citizen has a right to know." He had control of his voice, but no matter how hard he tried, he could not soften his expression. There was too much at stake now. "Just tell me how he's doing."

The woman shrugged and turned away to show her middle-aged profile.

He took her by the forearm. She made a halfhearted attempt to pull away, but he held on. He had a sense of exactly how much was due him. He watched her eyes shift back and forth as she wondered whether any members of the hospital staff were watching. Or any reporters. She was an easy woman to read.

"My God," she said. "You shouldn't have come here.

Somebody might make a connection." But her voice had sunk to resignation.

"Is he going to live? I have to know."

The woman gave a little snort. "Trot a blonde past his bed. If he doesn't grab her butt, he's dead."

He began to grow impatient.

"What are the doctors saying, Ruby?"

She would not meet his eyes. That was bad. He did not want a fit of guilt followed by idiotic bedside confessions.

"Listen," he said, "no matter what happens, you're taken care of. You'll have nothing to worry about."

She laughed with a sound like a can crushed in a fist. "Right."

"I'm a man of my word. Always have been. No matter what happens here today, we're going to take care of you." The truth was, of course, that he was already figuring how he could pare down the cost of his promises to her should Trost die. Without Senator Mitch Trost, she was as much use to him as a dirty towel. "But we have to keep this on an even keel, on a business level. Let's just keep right on working together, Ruby."

She looked at him at last. "You must be shitting in your shoes."

He was not offended. On the contrary, he was glad to hear the familiar cockiness return to her voice. "Just tell me what the doctors are saying and I'll be on my way. I don't like being here any more than you like having me here."

She shook her head and the look on her face summed up a mistaken lifetime.

"He's going to live, damn it."

He closed his eyes for a moment. "Thank God."

Ruby began to cry. "Oh, damn you, you sonofabitch. Just damn you all to hell." She covered her face with a hand. "And damn me, too."

Not one to waste time, Bob Felsher hurried down the hospital corridor.

*   *   *

They were going to free her. Kelly knew it. Abbas had changed, his nervousness muted into something like sorrow. He came down into the basement twice to stare at her, the second time leaving her with the promise that "everything is good."

She heard him arguing with the roughneck upstairs, but the tattooed man did not appear in the basement again.

It was almost over. She was going to be free. She felt much better physically and had been able to eat the bread and cheese Abbas brought her. It was as if her life had been handed back to her when she was least expecting it. She wanted to swim, to see her father, to be clean again. She wanted to go home for the autumn, to read George Eliot, maybe to go back for her master's earlier than planned. She wanted to eat a real hamburger for lunch with Ruby Kinkiewicz and hear all the latest gossip from her dad's office.

Abbas came back down the stairs, shoes thunking. There was something different about him.

He had washed himself and trimmed his beard. His shirt was clean and white and buttoned to the neck. The sleeves were too short and his wrists showed tufts of black hair. He had seemed frighteningly strong when manhandling her and it was startling to find that his wrists were slender almost to delicacy. It troubled her, in a way she could not explain, to think that he was really just a boy her age, better suited to books than to the things he had done.

He hasn't really hurt me, she told herself. But it was like trying to reason yourself into not being afraid of snakes. His nearness repulsed her as he drew up a broken chair and dusted its seat with his hand. He was fastidious the way she had imagined the worst Nazis to be in the course she had taken on "The Holocaust: Text and Gender."

He scraped his hands together in a cleansing gesture.

"We will talk," he said.

Kelly warned herself to be careful, not to say anything that might anger him now. She was going to be free again and she did not want any foolishness to spoil it. Do not be confrontational, she told herself. Be verbally submissive.

His dark eyes fixed on her until her belly curdled.

"I think," he said, "that you are not a bad person."

"Thank you," she whispered.

"I think . . . you have understanding for what I have done. How all of this"—he waved his hand toward the basement wall—"has been for the good of the people."

"Yes," she said. "Of course."

He drew closer, almost smiling. He seemed incapable of a full smile. He reminded her of the serious, dateless boys on campus who studied engineering.

"Perhaps . . . you have liked me," he said. "It is understandable."

Kelly alerted.

He waited for her response. When she continued to disappoint him, he fidgeted and shifted his chair. "It is normal. A man and a woman. I do not think badly of you."

"I . . . I've been ill. It's not . . ." She wondered if she had said anything foolish in a delirium or in her sleep. That, or the man was beyond lunatic.

Suddenly, his expression grew radiant. There was no other word for it.

"My religion is very beautiful, you see. I am reading the Koran to you all the time you are sick. It helps to fight the evil. It is better than a medicine. You must learn more about Islam."

"Yes," Kelly assured him. "I have a lot to learn."

That pleased him. "Yes," he said eagerly. "There is very much to learn. It would be my duty to teach you. And the greatest of pleasures."

"But . . . there isn't . . . there won't be time."

Thoughts came down over his face like a veil. A dark veil.

"Allah in his mercy gives us little time on this earth. But do not worry. I will contact you. I will find a way. You must not fear. We will see each other again."

The unexpected thought filled her with venom and she closed her eyes. She had assumed that there would be a clear end, that she would be released and it would all be over. The notion of ever seeing this man again made her want to shriek in horror and strike with her fists.

"Yes," he said. "Close your eyes and think of these things."

His lips touched her forehead and she recoiled, opening her eyes. She almost screamed but caught herself.

Abbas stepped back awkwardly, knocking over his chair.

"I am sorry," he said. He would not even look at her. "Please. I should not have done this. It is too soon. You are frightened."

With the suddenness of revelation, Kelly realized that he had it exactly wrong. *He* was the one who was frightened. It amazed her.

He really was like a little boy. One who lived in a fantasy world. A *dark* fantasy world.

A vehicle with a cancered exhaust pulled up beyond the ceiling and the walls. Abbas straightened and looked back up the steps. As if things were going too fast for him now, as if whoever had arrived might already be inside the house, moving too quickly to be stopped. He turned toward her a last time. Kelly looked down to avoid his eyes and saw that his hands were trembling.

"It will be good now," he said. "I see that you love me."

Hamedov did not go inside the house immediately. A radio message stopped him.

They had Burton.

The general took the microphone from the aide in the backseat of the command car, turning half around as if seeing the radio set might help him communicate.

"The target is uninjured?" he asked.

"A slight injury to the leg. Nothing. He is quiet. Over."

"There must be no harm to him. You will bring him to my location." Hamedov released the key and passed the mike back to his subordinate. "Tell the fool how to get here. Tell him to hurry."

His aide held the microphone at bay. The outstation queried, "Require your location," but both men ignored it for the moment. "Get the German woman," Hamedov continued. "Find her quickly. Tell her I have the thing she wants. Take her to headquarters and keep her there until I call. Treat her with the greatest courtesy."

"Yes, Comrade General."

Hamedov cocked an eyebrow. "We're not 'comrades' anymore. You keep forgetting." Then he chuckled. "Of course, we may not want to get *too* far out of practice."

The general stepped out of the vehicle, awkward in the tightness of his uniform. Bodyguards from the trail vehicle had already deployed to secure the alley. An officer and two men stood ready to accompany their chieftain into the building.

"No shooting," Hamedov said, "until I tell you." Then he walked fearlessly to the door, knocked, and went in without waiting for a response.

Two men waited inside. One was not much more than a boy, with the trim beard and cow eyes of the religious. The other was a thug with jailbird tattoos.

"Where is she?" Hamedov asked.

The religious boy—the one with whom he had spoken on the telephone—opened his mouth to answer, but the thug was quicker.

"There's two parts to this deal," he said, stepping forward. "We're not just going to—"

With a grace no one would have expected from him, Hamedov snapped his pistol from his holster and shot the man in the middle of the face. The sound was very loud in the bare room and it was still ringing when the dead man hit the floor.

Hamedov holstered his pistol and looked at the religious boy. He was quivering. In a calm voice, Hamedov repeated his question.

"Where's the girl?"

"She's . . ." The boy could barely speak. He had made his hands into fists, but Hamedov knew it was only to stop them from shaking. "She's in the cellar. Down there. In the cellar."

"Show me."

The boy was unsteady on his feet. He reminded Hamedov of a fragile glass ornament in the middle of an earthquake. He had likely imagined himself as a lion. Roaring and striking a blow for his idiot cause.

The general followed the boy downstairs, going ahead of his bodyguards to show them that he was unafraid. The girl was waiting as promised, immediately recognizable, if somewhat the worse for her adventures. Her expression was almost comical, her eyes yearning for freedom but unable to judge the meaning of the shot, the appearance of such visitors. Well, he thought, this young woman was about to receive a priceless lesson in human nature. The prospect amused him.

"You must promise me," the boy said weakly, "that you will not hurt her."

Hamedov glanced around the cement hole to be certain there were no more thugs lurking, then he unholstered his pistol again and shot the boy in the side of the head. Abbas's face stretched for an instant and his opposite temple erupted. The mess struck the girl and she screamed against the terrible ringing of the shot.

The boy fell open-eyed. He was dead, but his body jerked in stubborn torment, legs kicking.

The girl screamed on and rocked the chair to which she was bound until it fell over sidewards, bringing her face close to that of the dead boy. She screamed and twitched, struggling to move away as her hair soaked up his blood.

Hamedov set her upright again, repelled by her stink. He took out his handkerchief and strained some of the blood from her blondness. She had stopped screaming to whimper convulsively.

"Don't hurt me," she said suddenly. The shots had almost

deafened Hamedov and he could barely understand her words. *"Please* don't hurt me. *Please.* I'll do anything."

"Nobody will hurt you," he said. "You are safe now. You have been rescued. These are very bad people who have bothered you, very dangerous."

"Please don't hurt me."

"Soon you will be with your own people."

But he made no move to untie her. Instead, he snapped an order at his bodyguards to remove the corpses from the house. Then he turned back to the stairs.

He had sensed what would happen next. His line of work had taught him a great deal about mankind. So he did not even flinch when the girl screamed as if undergoing the worst torture, begging him:

"Let me *go.* Let me *go.* Let me *go.*"

He turned from the bottom step and gave her a look that broke her voice.

"Yes, Miss Trost," Hamedov said, smiling gently. "Of course we will let you go. But first you will meet some new friends. They have been searching for you, too. We have important matters to settle together." World-weary, he shook his head. "In the meantime, it is my duty to protect you in this dangerous city."

With the embassy still surrounded, Spooner posted himself on the rooftop terrace. He struggled to track the progress of the coup by following the arcs of tracers and flares and the ebb and flow of armored-vehicle noise. He tried to interpret everything as he imagined Burton would have done, scribbling notes he could shape into a classified fax that would hit Washington in plenty of time for the graveyard-shift analysts to work it into the morning briefings for the brass. The class fax was the only means of circumventing the DCM's control of the cable traffic, and Spooner was keeping his fingers crossed that the comms interference would stop.

He had tried to phone the watch officer back in the Pentagon, but had not been able to get a call through. So he had given up for the time being, heading up to the roof to gather more information. He held his position dutifully, as he believed Burton would have done, careless of the stray bullets that twice chipped the masonry on the building's facade. His pocket notebook filled up with scrawled time checks and diagrams sketched in the inadequate light. He ached not to let Burton down.

It was only when he ducked back into the attaché's office to get more paper that he noticed the light on the answering machine.

The message was from Burton. It was two hours old.

Stunned, he played Burton's words a second time. As they filtered through the jamming, the effect was of an antique-radio broadcast. The small, broken voice devastated Spooner. He had not been there when Burton needed him. During crises, somebody always had to stand by the comms. It was a rule so basic, every corporal knew it.

If anything happened to Burton . . .

He jumped down the stairs and ran for the DCM's office, regretting his earlier insolence immeasurably. With the ambassador gone, Vandergraaf was in charge.

The DCM's door was locked and the light was out. Spooner slumped against the wall, disoriented and sick at himself, listening dully to the hubbub of guards and staffers downstairs in the lobby, where they had taken refuge. It took him several minutes to notice the wedge of light under the door to the ambassador's office.

Spooner ran to the door and knocked hard.

"I'm busy," Arthur Vandergraaf called out, as though he had been disturbed in the middle of a hectic but typical workday.

Spooner pushed the door open. The DCM looked up in surprise that shaped into anger.

"Who do you think you are?"

"Excuse me, sir. Colonel Burton's in trouble. He's—"

"You bet your ass he's in trouble. He's facing a court-martial."

"No. I mean, the Azeris have him. There was a message. Hamedov's people were closing in on him. That was two hours ago."

Vandergraaf smiled unaccountably. Then the venom surged back. "I thought your boss was so good at taking care of everything. Are we talking about the courageous, infallible Burton?" The DCM's eyes were cold and confident. "Get out of here."

"Sir . . . *please*. I'm sorry about my conduct earlier . . . what I said. But we have to—"

"*I* don't have to do anything. And I don't have time for this nonsense." The big man dropped his pen on the desk and sat back in the ambassador's chair. "Sergeant, you're going to be very lucky if you don't end up being court-martialed beside your boss. Who has, by the way, been declared *persona non grata* by our host government. If, indeed, the Azeris have done anything with *Lieutenant* Colonel Burton, they've probably just taken him into protective custody prior to his deportation. Now stop bothering me."

Spooner had reached the end of his suck-up potential. He imagined Burton being tortured or killed, and it made him want to drag the DCM across the desk and hammer the shit out of him.

"If anything happens to him, you're going to regret it."

The DCM rolled his eyes and his mouth puckered. "No doubt. Our consciences shall leave us no peace. We shall weep. Now you listen to *me*, buster. Ambassador Kandinsky is missing and I'm in charge of this embassy. I'm ordering you to return to your office and remain there until further notice." He glanced down at the document he had been correcting, then looked back up with an expression that would have better suited a secret policeman. "And you are expressly ordered *not* to attempt any communications with Washington. In the ambassador's absence, I will personally approve all messages, to include phone calls. If you so much as face west and breathe, you'll spend your retirement in Leavenworth Prison." Vandergraaf grimaced as though he had stepped in dogshit. "Along with your boss."

With Burton's little thug of a sergeant gone, Arthur Vandergraaf put the final touches to the cable he had been preparing for Drew MacCauley and the rest of Washington. His stomach stung him. He ascribed the sudden acidity to perfectly normal anxiety, given the circumstances and the hour, but he soon had to lift himself from Kandinsky's chair and return to his office to get his jar of tablets, cursing the smaller men with whom he had been afflicted at every step.

Seated again, he scanned his dispatch. He intended it to go down in diplomatic history as a masterpiece of concision and a monument to the ability of a skilled foreign service officer to shape policy in a crisis.

It was good. Really. The sort of thing historians quoted in full.

His wife would be proud of him. And they would get their top embassy. "Ambassador and Mrs. Arthur G. Vandergraaf."

Certain of his future, he read the final paragraph of the message aloud to an invisible audience:

"As of this writing, peace is returning to Baku. The anticorruption forces that have moved to restore Azeri democracy are in control. General Hassan Hamedov, a patriot of impeccable credentials, has been installed as interim president by a popular council. A confrontation with Moscow over energy issues has been averted. It is the considered view of this station that the evolution of events favors the interests and policy of the United States. Our sole outstanding concern is for the safety of any American citizens who may, in the course of this restorative action, have fallen into the hands of criminal elements tied to the outgoing regime. Embassy actively engaged."

On foot, Kandinsky hurried from one government ministry to the next, rebuffed at each, here by locked doors and darkness, there by confused boys in uniform whose officers knew nothing beyond the narrow parameters of their orders. One lieutenant speculated about an Armenian invasion, while a captain whispered darkly about mafias and Russians before strutting back to his jeep, which had a flat tire. Tanks and troop carriers grumbled by with a peculiar feeling of aimlessness, and while occasional shots teased in the distance, the only violence the ambassador observed was the looting by teenagers and policemen of a shop that sold Western electronics.

The cats had deserted the streets, but a dark carnival of people had come to the main square. The curious gathered around the most vocal members of the crowd, packs swelling and shrinking as young toughs and grandmothers hunted the tastiest rumors. A pretty girl of university age wept, while a woman who looked like Nikita Khrushchev in a fright wig pushed a cart past her, shrieking, "*Morozhenoye! Morozhenoye!*"

Kandinsky had just decided to leg it back up the hill to the presidential offices again to see if anybody with a shred of authority had appeared, when he caught sight of Heddy Seghers standing on the curb on the other side of the central fountain. Her blond bob was as bright as a lightbulb. Impulsively, he veered toward her, concerned for her safety, hoping she might have news. He broke into a trot and was about to call out her name when two military vehicles pulled up in front of her.

After an instant's confusion, Heddy tried to run. But she was not dealing with dumb-eyed draftees. Quick men with officers' shoulder boards leapt from the cars and grabbed her, shoving her into a backseat in seconds. The last Kandinsky saw of her was a kick of legs. The vehicles rasped up a side street and disappeared from sight.

What was that about? There were so many layers of reality and intrigue in the city that any pause to think about it almost crushed him under feelings of failure. He had not been much of an ambassador, had not even kept his finger on the pulse of his own embassy, let alone on that of the country to which he had been accredited.

But you could not undo what was done. Kandinsky was determined to focus on the problem at hand. To earn his pay at least for this one night of his career. The first step was to figure out exactly who was pulling the strings. Step two would be to hammer the bastards with fear of the United States while building a front in the diplomatic community to face down any attempt to unseat the elected president.

Azerbaijan was not going to turn its back on democracy—however imperfect that democracy might be—on his watch.

As long as he kept moving, he felt exhilarated. The smell of tank exhaust and the stabbing of searchlights, the anxiety in the faces and the sound track of small arms, all of it was as exciting as anything he could remember. He had a sense of history unfolding on every side and the awareness that he could shape that history for the better if he did his job well.

It was, after all, his moment.

But it was a moment in danger of slipping away. For all of the energy he had expended, he had accomplished nothing. Beyond moving his feet from place to place, he frankly did not know what to do. He just needed a place to start, a hand-hold where he could begin to grip events and shape them to the good. Just one opening . . .

As he picked his way through a crowd listening to a speaker rage about anonymous perfidy, Kandinsky found himself face-to-face with a gift.

A dozen journalists had converged on a young man who spoke some English. Training video cameras and microphones on him, they shouted questions in a competition of American, Brit, and Euro accents, demanding to know who was behind the coup and the opinion of the Azeri public about the night's events. Struggling for words, the young man looked half terrified and half flattered by the attention. Then one of the journalists, a man to whom the ambassador had granted ten minutes the day before and who had all but accused him of incompe-

293

tence for not solving the Trost kidnapping, spotted Kandinsky. They locked eyes and the journalist began to move.

"Mr. Ambassador . . . Mr. Ambassador . . ."

"*Wer ist er denn?*"

"*Der Botschafter, hat er gesagt.*"

"That's him. That's the American ambassador."

"*C'est vrai?*"

"The skinny guy with the glasses."

Kandinsky held up his hands in mock surrender. Before he could address the first question, a second, larger crowd began to form behind the journalists.

"*Shto zhe takoy! On nikogda nye vigladit kak posol . . . on sovsyem normalni chelovyek . . .*"

"AP, Mr. Ambassador—can you tell us who's behind this coup?"

A woman who looked like an off-Broadway Salomé elbowed her way forward and barked, "CNN—get the fuck out of my way—Mr. Ambassador, will the United States send troops?"

"BBC World Service, Mr. Ambassador. Might all this fuss lead to the cancellation of the chess mastership scheduled for—"

"Ladies and gentlemen, *please*," Kandinsky said.

"Trost girl involved?"

"Have you witnessed any war crimes tonight, Mr. Ambassador?" a buck-toothed boy demanded.

"*Deutsche Welle, Herr Botschafter* . . . would you ascribe this coup to the failure of American decision-makers to listen to the advice of their more experienced European allies? What was the role of the CIA?"

"*Skazali, shto on shpion . . .*"

"*Eto govno. On igrayet schak . . .*"

A burst of automatic-weapons fire down the block sent the locals scattering and the press hit the ground. A camera lens chewed into the concrete just in front of Kandinsky's toes, and a moment later, he and the headhuntress from CNN were the only members of the crowd still on their feet.

"Amateurs," she said disgustedly. Then she turned to her crew. "Jack, would you get the fuck up and give me that god-damned microphone."

"Here's the story," Kandinsky began.

Backed by six bodyguards with automatic rifles, Hamedov sat across the table from three longtime colleagues, each of whom had been allowed one bodyguard with a handgun.

"Not good enough," Hamedov told them. "Either the president appoints me premier and gives me the oil portfolio, or he's not president anymore."

"Hassan Pasha," a man with a bedraggled tie said, "the premiership is yours. He will not argue that for a moment." The man's eyes looked from one flank of Hamedov's body-guards to the other. "You have earned it by your services to the republic. But the oil ministry . . . you must understand . . . a family matter . . ."

Hamedov slammed down his fist. The two envoys in civil-ian clothes jumped, but the third, who wore the uniform of a general in the Azeri air force—which had more flag officers than aircraft—only smiled and glanced at the ceiling. He and Hamedov had come to a personal understanding weeks before.

"Oil is money. Money is power. Does the president think Hassan Hamedov is a fool?" Hamedov spit on his own carpet. "Why do I bother to refer to him as 'president' any longer?"

"Hassan Pasha . . . this is all a misunderstanding. It was the president's intent all along to appoint you premier. As for the oil . . . men of goodwill can always reach an agreement."

Hamedov grunted. Then he looked at his secret ally in the air force uniform. "I do not wish to harm my homeland, my country that I love above all things." He extended a big hand toward the draperies and the uproar beyond. "I would sacri-fice anything for my country. *Any*thing. You must tell that to the president."

"But he knows that, Hassan Pasha. Surely . . ."

Hamedov thumped the table again. *"Oil!"* He leaned forward as if ready to launch himself across the table. "The future of our people depends on oil . . . on pipelines . . . on the moral values of those who will oversee the contracts, the development . . ."

"The president's brother—"

The big fist came down again. "I cannot bear this. I cannot bear to see my country sold like a sheep in a market!" He looked at his air force ally yet again, wishing he could be absolutely certain that the man was not going to betray him as he had already betrayed the president. "I propose a compromise to the president. The president's family retains the executive position in the oil ministry. But a man we all can trust"— he pointed across the table—"General Gandarbiyev, will be appointed as the assistant to the executive. I appoint the chief financial officer. And all contracts go through my bank."

His interlocutor made a dismissive gesture and reached toward his attaché case as if preparing to leave. "The president would never agree to such a thing. The contracts go through *my* bank."

Hamedov laughed and looked at his watch. "In fifteen minutes, my tanks are going to open fire on your bank."

The president's chief representative made a gesture of spitting into his palm. "The accounts are already out of the country. Shoot the clerks, for all I care. Twenty-five percent of the contracts for your bank. Not a bit more!"

"Fifty percent."

"Thirty."

"Thirty on the oil, fifty on the pipeline financing."

"Joint bookkeepers."

"You don't trust me? I'll have your entire family shot."

"My brothers will cut the throats of your sons and the sons of your sons."

"Let General Gandarbiyev decide."

The air force general nodded thoughtfully. For about three

seconds. Then he said, "Joint bookkeepers. Half the pipeline financing to Hamedov. Five percent off the top for the air force."

"Three percent for the air force," Hamedov corrected. "Five for the army. And two for the interior troops."

"What about the navy?"

"Bugger the navy. They're so stupid they backed the Ukrainians."

The president's envoy stood up. Smiling. Hamedov wondered if he had given up too much. But it really did not matter. He could always call out the troops again.

"I will have to submit the conditions to the president, of course."

"Of course," Hamedov said. "And I will be at the airport in the morning to congratulate him on the success of his diplomatic efforts and on the even greater success of his decision to call out the military to suppress criminal activity in the capital." He looked at the covered windows. "I hear it will be a beautiful day tomorrow. Very peaceful in Baku."

They adjourned to the next room for the obligatory round of brandies, and the member of the troika of envoys who had not spoken until then asked, "What about the American girl? The president doesn't want any problems with Washington."

Hamedov shrugged. "I wouldn't know anything for certain. But it is the sense of my heart that everything will be fine."

"She's alive?"

"How could I tell such a thing?" His voice had taken on a warning tinge of anger, but he softened it again. "Anyway, who would have an interest in killing her now?"

"She might have seen a great deal."

"Donkeys see a great deal. How much do they understand?" Hamedov downed a second brandy. "Who among us would want to hurt an innocent girl?"

The presidential delegation left quickly after that. With the larger issues resolved, Hamedov had time now to turn back to the smaller ones. He was weary. But he expected to draw a certain degree of pleasure from the drama he had staged for the next few hours. The foreigners were going to play the parts he directed this time.

He poured himself another brandy and turned to an aide. "Open the telephone lines. I need to make some calls."

"Yes, Mr. Premier. Immediately." The aide turned and barked at an officer still more junior, who took off at a run.

Hamedov watched the bit of military theater patiently. Such things did not happen immediately, no matter how loudly you shouted. It would be half an hour, perhaps longer, before he could use the telephone. The jamming and interruptions would have been imperfect, and now the restoration of communications would stumble. But it had all been good enough, and he could afford a little time now. He was in good spirits, wonderful spirits, despite the exhaustion tugging at him. He savored the bite and faint after-sweetness of the liquor.

"We have the German woman?"

"Yes, Mr. Premier. She was walking the streets like a whore, Mr. Premier."

Hamedov smiled. "And Colonel Burton?"

The aide stepped back a few millimeters and his face changed in a way that made Hamedov want to strike him before he spoke.

"He . . . has not yet arrived at the designated location. There was . . . a confrontation . . . with troops loyal to the president . . . a betrayal. There was fighting . . ."

The first thing Trost saw when he fought his way back to consciousness was the snowfield of the ceiling. The second thing was Ruby Kinkiewicz's powerhouse hair. He was wide awake after that, his mind a bit clearer than he would have liked.

"Heart attack," he said.

Ruby leaned closer to the bed. "You bet your butt."

"Running every day. I never even—"

"Not enough red meat and booze."

He still could not believe it. A heart attack. He had known what was happening to him back in the airport—how long ago had that been?—but it still seemed impossible. He was still young, fit. His doctor had given him a perfect report card not three months before. The whiteness of the hospital room had to be some kind of gag.

"Did they . . . was there . . . how serious was it?"

Ruby made her iron-maiden face. "Didn't even have to cut you, honeybun. Not a single bypass. The Lord was just getting your attention." A smile wrinkled into her cheek. "There's going to be a lot of disappointment in this town, let me tell you."

"I can't believe it." What were the consequences? Had there been any side effects? He tested his fingers, his toes.

"Mitch, darling, you're what, fifty-four now? Fifty-five? It's all downhill from here, sweetie. You're on the compost express."

"It isn't a joke, Ruby." His voice seemed to echo. "I could've died."

"Not damned likely. You're still my meal ticket. You try dying on me, Mitchell Trost, and I'll have to write my memoirs to pay the rent. Then you'll be sorry."

"Good old Ruby."

"Not as old as you, anyway. You look like Strom Thurmond lying there."

"Ruby, if you put any more dye on that hair of yours, they're going to declare you a toxic-waste site."

"The one pussy you never got."

Suddenly she grasped his hand and Trost saw tears in her eyes. It was a day for shocks. He had never seen this woman cry.

"Ruby?" Before she could respond, his heart flickered again. "My God, it's not Kelly, is it?"

Ruby looked away, but waved her free hand dismissively. "It's not Kelly. There's nothing new. Just old Drew MacCauley yapping like a chihuahua. Wishes you a speedy recovery. In a pig's ass."

"I've never seen you cry."

"Oh, damn you, Mitch," she said in a voice of unscheduled tragedy, "you just don't know a damned thing about me."

"So, you see," Hamedov told the telephone, "everything is in the most excellent of circumstances."

"This can't be," the voice at the other end cried. "You *promised*. You—you're supposed to take over the government. The way we all agreed. You can't just—"

"How could I betray my president?" the general asked. "This has all been a misunderstanding, Arthur."

"But the coup, everything was set . . ."

Hamedov laughed indulgently. "What coup? There has been nothing like a coup. The president called out the military to restore order and suppress the intolerable levels of criminal activity in the capital." He looked at his watch. "If you listen, you will perhaps hear a police raid in your vicinity. The tanks are sometimes loud . . ."

"But the rapprochement with Moscow, the pipeline agreement . . ."

"Everyone will be pleased. There will be a normalization of relations. The president is a great leader, a man of vision."

"The oil boys will never forgive you."

"They're businessmen, Arthur. They're—what's the English word for *gibki*?"

"Flexible."

"Yes. They're flexible. Dick Fleming will be the first to congratulate me on my new position. I'm disappointed you haven't wished me well. As a friend and colleague."

"You can't *do* this to me," the American said. "I've already sent the cable."

"Write another cable. Explain the error."

"We had a deal."

"We had a misunderstanding."

"Hamedov, you're nothing but a—"

"Don't say it," the general cautioned good-naturedly. "Some words live long after we wish them dead."

"You could've been *pres*ident in the morning," Vandergraaf said after a pause. His voice was regretful and womanly now, the little vigor gone out of him.

"Me? Hassan Hamedov? President? I'm a simple soldier."

"You've thrown everything away."

It was clear that the American understood nothing even now. Hamedov wanted to hang up, to be done with the filth. But there was one further issue that had to be addressed.

"Arthur . . . we have a slight problem with Colonel Burton."

"That bastard." Then the American's voice grew more focused. "You have him?"

"He's been wounded. Nothing serious. A clean shot. Some blood. A smashed collarbone. I haven't actually seen him yet, but I'm told he's very stoical."

"He knows too much, Hassan."

Hamedov laughed. "He doesn't know half as much as you do."

"That's different."

"I won't kill him for you, Arthur. He may die, but it will not be by my hand."

"He knows too much."

"You sound frightened."

"You have to do it. He'll blow the whistle."

"On who?"

"Are you threatening me?"

"I'm your friend, Arthur."

"Then kill that sonofabitch."

"No. You see, I quite like Burton. I *trust* him, Arthur. If a mutual colleague of ours chooses not to kill him, he'll be back in your embassy before morning. Explanations will be necessary . . . additional cables, I think . . ."

"Kill him, for God's sake."

"Not me."

"What about the girl?"

"She's fine."

"What do you mean, 'she's fine'?"

Hamedov shrugged, although the man on the other end of the phone line could not see him. "Healthy enough. Frightened, of course. Needs a wash."

"She's supposed to be—"

"Yes, Arthur, I know. And I think there is a much better chance that she will be dead before morning than that we will lose Colonel Burton. But we'll just have to wait and see."

"You're talking like a madman. Kill them both. Now."

"Arthur . . . these are your own people. Don't you feel any loyalty at all? Any humanity?" Hamedov meant the questions seriously, but all he got from the telephone was a spiteful laugh.

"You talk to me about loyalty? And humanity? There's been gunfire all over the city. You've probably got corpses from one end of town to the other."

It was Hamedov's turn to laugh. "I'm afraid our soldiers are not very good shots. But they like the sound of gunfire. I don't think there will be so many corpses."

"There had better be at least two."

Hamedov shook his head in inexpressible disgust. He wondered if the American understood death at all. A number of people were going to learn their lessons before dawn. He only wished Vandergraaf could be one of them.

"You know, Arthur," the general said, "this is *my* country. I think I will make the decisions."

"Just get rid of them," the American said. "All right?"

Just before he put down the receiver, Hamedov told him: "Maybe. Maybe not."

CHAPTER 14
. . .

"I know you," Kelly Trost said. Bound to a broken chair, she looked stained but whole. Her eyes were excited, weary, frightened—and hopeful.

The sight of her had been an indescribable relief to Burton. *She was alive.*

He shifted in his chair and the pain from his wound hit him like an axe.

"*Jesus Christ*," he shouted. He could not remember hurting so badly ever in his life. He had screamed when the Azeri medic dumped the powder over his wound, an act that made him think of old history books and sulfa drugs and World War II.

"Are you all right?" the girl asked.

Despite the pain, Burton smiled. Briefly. He had blood all over him and his collarbone stuck up like a spike under the half-assed bandage.

Sometimes, when you were truly badly hurt, your body buried the pain for you. But there was probably a torture chamber in hell where they smashed your collarbone over and over again. The bullet had been fired by a panicked boy lying on the ground, gut shot himself, and it had exploded the bone and skin. Not lethal, so long as the bleeding quit. But miserable beyond anything he would have imagined. He sat bound to a chair with pirate's rope, the enforced posture a torment. They had settled him a good spit from the girl, just where the light began to die, and he was glad she could not see him too clearly.

"I'm all right," Burton lied.

When he spoke, the tendons in his neck tugged at the wreckage of his shoulder and made it hurt in a different way: quick pinches to complement the constant ache.

"I *do* know you," she insisted. She sat fully in the light and Burton could not remember ever facing a human being whose voice and eyes were so complex. Billy Strayhorn had never written an arrangement so elusive. Her fear was as constant as a backbeat, but there was that sudden, soaring, embarrassing hope in her, too.

She looked weathered. Not as young as he remembered her. It was clear that she had been ill. She had the convalescent vacancy.

"Burton," he told her. "From the embassy." His own hurt was brutal and it took his entire strength of will to keep his voice level. But the need to focus on the girl's morale was a good thing. It helped him break out of the selfishness of pain. "Same parties. Face in the crowd at Charley's."

She nodded. Upper arms and ankles tied to a chair, hands fastened behind her, she seemed to take her physical situation as a matter of course. Amazing how fast human beings could become accustomed to things.

"You're bleeding," she said.

"It'll stop."

"There's blood all over you."

"I'm just fine." He wanted to scream it, to shriek and sink his teeth into the pain. "Everything's going to be all right."

Her eyes ached to believe him. She was still absorbing the

education she had received in a very condensed form. "What are you doing here?"

Burton almost laughed again. "I came to rescue you."

She stared at him.

"I guess they caught you," she said.

Burton felt faint with pain. Puking sick with it.

"They caught me."

"So . . . now you've been kidnapped, too."

Burton had not considered his situation from the perspective of that word. That was funny, too.

"Kelly . . . how long have you been here? In this place?"

She thought about it, reinterpreting time from a prisoner's perspective. "A day. Less than a day. We came this morning. Or maybe it was yesterday morning now." She looked at him. "What's going to happen?"

He looked at the stairs. At their vacancy. Now and then the floorboards above their heads creaked under boots.

"Everything's going to be all right," he said again.

"But what's going to happen?"

He sensed a weakening in her, the strain of long weariness. She had been through enough shit for a lifetime and she needed to lean on somebody, to let somebody else drive. But he needed her alert and capable. She looked fit, with lean muscles that did not match the pallor of her face, and the damnable truth was that, at the moment, she was in better physical shape than he was.

"*My fucking collarbone,*" he said furiously. He could not help it. A bull's-eye dart of pain had forced the words out of him. His face would not behave, either. "Shit, shit, shit, shit, shit."

"What did they *do* to you?"

My Azeri pals were giving me a lift. Bringing me to you. And we ran into a roadblock run by the other team. First some yelling, then a little friendly shooting. I honored the Code of Conduct and ran like hell. And a scared kid shot me. A terrifed boy in a rag of a uniform. He was lying on the pavement with his belly turned to spaghetti and meatballs. But he was a good soldier, one of the best. He held onto his rifle. I must've looked like the angel of death when I tried to jump over him. And I was. One of my pals blew the kid's head off. To keep things neat.

"I was in an accident."

She looked down at the dirty cement.

"Listen," Burton said, enjoying a gorgeous, unpredictable break from the pain, "I really believe everything's going to be all right. If anybody wanted to harm you, they would have done it by now. Somebody wants you alive."

"But why? What's it all about?"

Burton gave an instinctive shrug and his collarbone bit him like a shark. "I don't know. I'm not sure they knew when they grabbed you." He tried to order his thoughts through the pain. Good Zen to have someone else to worry about. Fight the self-absorption.

"But what did *you* do? Why did they take you?"

"I was too much trouble."

"They hurt you."

"It was an accident. Nobody meant to hurt me. Nobody with any authority. Listen . . . there's a guy named Hamedov pulling a lot of the strings . . . a general. I do not believe he wants gringo blood on his hands. He's a wheeler-dealer who's strongly oriented on a long and happy life. I can't explain it exactly, but I'm counting on him."

"A general?"

Burton nodded, hurting himself again. The best thing was to keep absolutely still. Oh, fuck you, he told the pain.

No push-ups for a while.

"Yeah."

"There was a guy like that here. In a uniform with a lot of stuff on it. Maybe—"

"What did he do? What did he say to you?" He looked at the girl and watched her face change with memory. It was not a positive change.

"He shot somebody," she told him. "Just over there."

*   *   *

Senator Trost lay in his white bed in his white room. A major siege of flowers had begun and he finally ordered the nurse to remove all of them, give them away, dump them, whatever. He was not in the mood for flowers.

The bastards had learned nothing about Kelly. Not one word. And when he had thrown a tantrum about access to a telephone, the goddamned doctor had given him a shot and asked him, with unforgivable, sensible bluntness, whether or not he intended to live.

Now he lay in a bitter, bedpanned haze, playing a mental film that interspersed his daughter's life and his dreams for her with visions of inhuman cruelty and fear for his own future. The last visitor—and there had been a painful, unexpected hole in the procession—had been shooed away well before the close of visiting hours. The doctor decreed that he needed rest. But the glare of this world would not quit his eyes and he felt he was just beginning to learn how many levels of pain can inhabit one man's heart.

The door opened slowly. Too slowly to be a nurse.

It was Laura.

She wore a smile to which he was not accustomed and her left hand held a bouquet of the sort of flowers you buy from a street vendor.

"Laura," he said.

She closed the door behind herself and came softly across the room.

"The nurses let me sneak in." She laid the flowers on the nightstand, still in their cellophane.

"Laura," he repeated. His battered heart rose.

She adjusted a chair and sat down beside the bed, her shoulders just level with the elevation of the mattress. She was a fine, delicate woman, constructed with hidden strengths for passion.

"Mitch . . . you *know* I'm sorry I couldn't get here earlier. It was the Rafelson case. I couldn't leave."

That was untrue. He knew it, and it hurt him, but he fought to disregard it. She was one of the good ones. Maybe the best. And all of this would have been a shock to her. He knew from his years on the Hill that you could not predict how people would react when the sky fell.

"It doesn't matter. You're here now. That's the important thing."

She took his hand. "They told me you're doing just fine."

He nodded. "Quite a shock. Darling, I can't describe it."

She tightened her grip. Then loosened it again. Letting her hand lie dully atop his. "With all your jogging. And you've always been so careful about what you eat." She looked off through a wall. "It doesn't seem fair."

"That *has* occurred to me."

She turned her face back to him. But there was an unmistakable laboriousness to the gesture.

"Poor baby," she said.

"Laura . . . you know, a man thinks about a lot of things . . . when something like this happens. On top of the business with Kelly . . ."

"Any news?"

He felt a surge of anger that no drug could subdue. "That shit MacCauley. Nothing."

"Mitch, everything's going to come right. There's something about Kelly. She's a born survivor."

"She's as innocent as a babe. I should've put my foot down about this Azerbaijan nonsense."

"She's a grown woman, Mitch."

"She's my goddamned daughter."

"Calm down now. The nurses said I'd have to leave if you got excited."

He did not want her to leave. He forced himself deeper into the pillow, the harsh bed.

"I never realized how much I loved her until now," Trost said. "Funny. I thought I did. But she truly is the most—"

Then he caught himself and shifted lanes. "And I never realized how much I loved you, Laura. Until today."

She looked at the nightstand. As if she found it more interesting than he was.

He moved his hand on top of hers and gripped.

"Marry me, Laura."

He felt the tension quicken in her fingers.

"Oh, Mitch," she said.

"Marry me." There was something dreadful in his voice now. "We're perfect together."

She looked up, and he could tell she had decided to face the issue head-on.

"I can't," she said, looking into his eyes for the first time that night. Then she turned away again. "Damn it all, I love you, Mitch. You know that. I mean, of course I love you." She tightened her grip on his hand now that it was safe. "But what's going to become of you?"

"My God, Laura. I'll . . . I'm still the same man. I'll still be a senator, I'll still—"

"You don't *know*." She shook her head with near violence and flames ghosted in her ginger hair. "You can't say. I mean, let's be honest. That's best, isn't it? I mean, what if . . . what if, God forbid, your health didn't . . . I mean . . . oh, Christ, Mitch. Could you picture me retiring to some horse farm? I mean, that's summer fun. I've got my career to think about."

He looked away from her and just wanted her to go. There was no fight left in him and he was tired.

"And I don't ever want to put myself in a position to be tempted," she continued. "It wouldn't be fair to you."

"Go away," Trost pleaded. And then he told the biggest lie of his life. "I'd like to be alone now."

Arthur Vandergraaf sat alone in the refuge of his office, astonished by the realization of what he had done, of how far he had gone in unintended directions, and, above all, by the possible consequences were he to be found out. In a panic of a sort he had never experienced in his life, he had quit the ambassador's office, almost running from the room. He had not realized until Hamedov's phone call how far he had let things get out of hand, how deeply he had put himself in the other man's power.

It had all begun logically, in service to sensible goals. There were things Drew MacCauley needed done. And Drew, for all his intelligence, could be terribly naive about the kind of people you had to deal with to make certain things happen.

Oh, Lord, Arthur Vandergraaf thought to himself. And haven't I been naive, too? He still could not quite understand how he had arrived at the spot where he found himself.

He had made rash decisions, thinking them bold. Now he feared any attempt to recall those decisions as much as he feared their realization. The business with the girl. And now with Burton. He had never really wanted any harm to come to anyone. He did not even think of himself as a mean man. And he was certainly not a cruel one.

He wondered how easily events could be traced back to him. Could they try him for murder?

Surely not that.

As an accomplice?

Who would have jurisdiction?

For a moment, he pictured himself vagabonding through foreign lands, evading trench-coated lawmen. Lisa would never be able to live that kind of life. Azerbaijan had been horrible enough. The heat was such a strain on her, and the food . . .

He reached impulsively for the phone, then withdrew his hand. He found no trace in himself now of the decisive man he had imagined himself to be. He just wanted to go home to bed and hide himself in the darkness.

Maybe he could still call it all off? Maybe it would be enough to frighten Burton into keeping his mouth shut?

No. Burton was mean. Mean and small-minded. Intolerant. Military. He wouldn't stop until he got to the bottom of things.

Again, Vandergraaf tried to imagine all the possible consequences to himself, painting them ever more darkly as the hour progressed.

He reached for the telephone a second time, determined to call Hamedov back and tell him it had all been a joke, a challenge, a test, and that it was essential to take good care of Burton and the Trost girl.

But he feared that, too.

He feared everything, and it seemed to him that he had always been afraid. As a child, he had been afraid of the bullies and thugs who had haunted the communities and schools through which his father's failures had dragged him. He feared exposure. Losing his career. Losing everything. Humiliation. Drew would not be able to protect him. Not able and not willing. At the end of the day, Drew had a self-righteous streak that helped no one. Drew MacCauley lacked the practicality that true greatness required, and Vandergraaf marveled that he had not seen that until now.

The best bet was to see it through. Ride it out. To finish what he had begun.

What if they put him in prison? What if they put him in prison with blacks and violent criminals? With perverts?

His hand wavered, and when the phone rang, he jumped almost to his feet before losing his balance and collapsing back into his chair.

Would he ever be an ambassador now? It had always meant so much to Lisa. And to him. Their dream. Their own embassy. He would have liked Bangkok. The big house all teak and the cheap staff.

"Vandergraaf."

The caller paused, as if with plotted cruelty. Then a voice without a country said, "Arthur? Dick Fleming here. Been trying to reach you. Where have you been hiding?"

Vandergraaf accepted the oil man's superior tone without a fight. "I had work to do. In the ambassador's office."

The telephone voice laughed. "Is his chair comfortable, Arthur?"

"What do you want? You shouldn't be calling like this."

"Don't be an ass. We're beyond such worries. Things are bad."

"What do you mean?" He felt himself sicken.

"Hamedov. I don't trust him. He's got something cooked up. And that German bitch? He's got her with him. What's going on, Arthur?"

Vandergraaf had no idea. "You mean the Seghers woman?"

"Yes. Her. Arthur . . . our friend may be playing a double game. Or a triple one. Now, I'm asking you nicely: Do you have any idea what Hamedov's up to?"

"How should I know? It's . . . all so confused . . . with the coup. We had tanks right here around the embassy . . ."

The oil man laughed. "Arthur, you have to stand by your friends now."

"Of course, Dick. I'm a very loyal man."

"I mean literally, Arthur. I want you to meet me—"

"I *can't* leave the embassy. It would be impossible."

"Felsher called. From Washington. He's not happy."

"All of my dealings with you two have been aboveboard. It is the policy of the United States Government to further commerce and support—"

"Shut your mouth, Arthur. You're a corrupt, lying bastard." Fleming chuckled. "Just like the rest of us. So spare me the lectures." He paused for a single beat. "We have to talk turkey, as you say, with our associate General Hamedov. He needs to understand that we have . . . alternatives."

"Hamedov's violent," Vandergraaf said in genuine alarm. "He's unpredictable." He was sweating as if he had been out in the midday sun and his flesh quivered.

Fleming laughed a final time. "We're all violent, Arthur. But some of us know how to hurt more deeply than others."

Burton kept her talking. She was worn down, with the vestiges of sickness still in her, but she responded lucidly for long stretches. Until the wrong memory played. Then her ordeal would close in on her again, breaking up her words, and she would look at him with an expression of disappointment no other human being had ever turned his way. But he only bore down again, tasking her mind for the facts. He wanted her focused and capable in case a miracle of opportunity came their way. And he wanted to know everything she knew. If the cards played wrong and he survived without her, he needed the information so he could turn it on their tormentors.

"Tell me again," he said, "how this man Abbas got you out of the compound." His eyes tracked automatically to the brown bloodstains on the floor. Not much more than a shadow. Where Hamedov had gunned down her previous captor. She had talked Burton through it all, letting him draw out the details, until he could distinguish the dried blood from the general grime of the basement.

Even the slightest turn of his head pulled lightning from his collarbone. If he really wanted to hurt himself, he could lower his chin and cant his head to see where the compound fracture pointed up into the bandage. Cold-sweat-and-puke stuff. Why would a man feel drawn to look at the damage to himself?

"Tell me again about calling out. Back at the first house. In the night."

She let her head fall. "I think I did. It's hard to be sure. I was so sick. I never knew what was happening. But I think I remember when he came in . . . why is it important?"

"Try to remember everything you can."

"Please, can't we stop for a while? I'm so tired."

Yes. Tired. Burton understood tired. He had a career full of exhaustion behind him. One of the inquisitors in his soul, one of the hanging judges who did not allow jazz in the courtroom, reminded him of the time an old M-113 had flipped at Hohenfels at the end of a long field problem. The entire platoon had been sleepless for three days and the driver of the last track oversteered his lats as he turned to cross a culvert on the way to the wash rack. It had been a wet autumn and the drainage ditch beside the tank trail was running. The vehicle went over on its back like a turtle and the TC was pinned under the hatch, head down in the wet. First Lieutenant Burton jumped from his own track and soaked himself in a useless struggle with steel and the human anatomy as he watched the young sergeant drown in the mud eighteen inches from his own face. The TC's mouth was just at the waterline, and Burton tried frantically to splash away the water with his hands until a long time after the TC stopped convulsing. Blessedly, the boy's eyes had been under water the entire time and Burton did not have to carry that memory, too. The incident had left him with a long fear of doing much of anything without adequate sleep. Now, with lives on the scales, he had not slept decently for days.

"No. No naps. Not now." He looked at her, trying to appear confident, the way he had often impersonated a better man in front of his troops. "Kelly, something's coming our way. Any time now. Whoever's behind this isn't saving us for Christmas."

She regarded him with sensible suspicion. "How do you know?"

"I don't. Not in the sense of facts and figures. But I can feel it as sure as I've ever felt anything."

Except this fucking pain.

"I can't keep going. It all starts to blur." She looked at him pleadingly.

"All right. Let's try something different. What's the best time you've ever had in your life?"

She accepted the question. Overall, Burton was surprised at how well she had borne up. Tougher than she knew, he thought.

In that hard, bare light, she smiled. And blushed. "You mean the best time I'm not embarrassed to tell you about?"

"That'll do."

"All right. It was with my father. I was, I don't know, maybe eight. I'd have to think about it. Anyway, it's corny.

But I think about it a lot. It's funny. He took me to Disney-world. Just me. And him." She was healthy and far away already, in an immeasurably better place. "See, the one thing my dad never had was time. Oh, he tried. I mean, he did the best he could. And I was a greedy little brat, when I think about it." She smiled, this time for herself. "So he took me to Disneyworld. And the place was fun and all that. But the best part was just having my dad to myself for the whole day. He did everything I wanted." Without warning, tears came. But Burton did not mind. They were good, stay-alive tears. "This is stupid."

"No. Keep thinking about it."

Her shoulder jerked and Burton sensed an instinctive gesture to wipe her eyes. But the ropes held her fast. She sniffled. "I mean, it could've been the town dump. It wouldn't have mattered. As long as it was just him and me." She almost giggled, but it came out as a small, sorrowful laugh. "I hope you're not a psychologist. God knows what you'd be thinking."

"Just that you love your father."

"I keep thinking of how worried he must be. He's really just a big softie."

"I'll remember that if I ever meet him. And yes, he's worried about you. He's moving heaven and earth to find you." Burton smiled, too, imagining his face as a skull, stripped to the bone by the pain. "We all have our duties, Kelly. Right now, your duty is to stay alive for your old man."

She looked at him. "You're hurt pretty bad. Aren't you? You don't have to talk if it hurts."

"It helps me keep my mind off it. If we keep talking."

Flames of pain seared his neck as he spoke.

"All right. Then you tell me about the best time you ever had."

That was good. Let her feel like she was taking charge. Let her know that she was stronger than she imagined.

He smiled and even that hurt him. For a moment, his lips

315

quivered and his eyes closed. An invisible magnet drew wet-ness from the corners of his eyes.

"You mean the best time I'm not embarrassed to tell you about, right?"

She smiled. "How about just the plain best time? I'm old enough. It'd be easier to stay awake."

Despite the ordeal and the sickness and dirt, you could still see an attractive young woman there. And he was not about to go down that particular road at the moment.

"Don't think so."

"You're no fun, Mr. Soldier."

"You weren't exactly all feminist frankness yourself."

"It's different. Guys like to brag."

"Not all guys."

"*All* guys. They just do it in different ways. You're probably one of the slick ones." Then a cartoon lightbulb went off over her head. *"I've got you now,"* she declared. *"I remember. You hang around with that woman from the German embassy. The blonde who always looks like she ought to have pigtails and a swastika armband."*

That was not exactly his image of Heddy. Mostly, he thought of her lying bare-ass on her belly in his bed, with Stan Getz blowing for the groupies. Or Cassandra Wilson moaning. Of course, it was beginning to look as though Kelly Trost might be a better judge of horseflesh than he was.

"Come on," she said. "That's you, right?"

"Guilty. But she's hardly a Nazi."

"Yeah? You should see her in the ladies' room sometime. *Deutschland über alles. Lebensraum* at the vanity mirror."

"You speak German?"

She shook her head. They had her tied high on the arms and it isolated one movement. "I was into this big Holocaust thing. I mean, I even dated Jewish guys exclusively for a year. I went to Auschwitz after I graduated."

Burton nodded, frustrating himself with pain. How I spent my summer vacation. "What was that like?"

"Spooky." She rolled her eyes. "Enough to make you believe in ghosts. I mean, the place is *haunted*." She stared into the shadowy corners of the basement. "I guess that's why I'm here." Burton caught the return of a dangerous note to her voice. "The guilt and all."

"Okay, pal. You wanted to hear about my best—"

"*Oh, God,*" she cried suddenly. "*They're going to kill us.* Aren't they? They're going to *kill* us."

"That's bullshit. Stop it."

But she was shaking so badly it shifted her chair. "They're going to kill us. You're just trying—"

"Knock it off. Stop it, Kelly. *Stop* it."

Instinctively, he leaned toward her, aching to rise out of his chair, and the jagged bone cut into his skin like a knife blade.

"Stop . . . acting . . ." The pain and pain-anger and desperation clenched him. "*Quit it.*"

She downshifted into sobs.

"Get a hold on yourself," he commanded, wishing he could get a hold on himself. "Your father would be ashamed of you."

She looked at him slowly, reproachfully. "You said . . . it's all right to be afraid."

"But you can't let it control you."

"I'm afraid to *die*. I don't want to die . . ."

"We're all fucking afraid to die. But we don't all have a goddamned senator for a father. Nobody's going to hurt you, damn it. They're scared, girl. They're all wishing they never touched you. I'll bet right now they're all just trying to figure out how to get both of us off their hands without crapping in the well."

"I'm so sorry."

"Stop it now," he said, gentling his voice. "Just stop all of it, okay? You're tougher than that. You've been through a lot and you still look like you're ready for the big lacrosse match."

"I don't play lacrosse. I swim."

"All right. The swim meet. It won't be much longer now."

317

"I *hate* this."

"I don't exactly love it. But we have to keep our heads clear. As clear as we can."

Oh, the pain, pain, pain. Running 'round my brain.

"I hate this," she said in a freshly determined voice. Even her spirit had the recuperative powers of youth. "I'm sorry. I'm so damned embarrassed . . ."

"Don't worry about it. It's the stress."

"No. I don't mean that."

"Well, don't worry about anything. Let me worry for both of us."

"No. I mean . . . I have to pee. I don't know . . . crying made me lose control or something."

This was not a dilemma in Burton's repertoire.

"What have they been . . . how—"

"There's usually a bucket or something. Abbas tried to be discreet. I think he was more embarrassed than I was. But since . . . since . . ."

She began to look fragile again.

"*Guard!*" Burton shouted in his best emergency Turkish. He was confident he could handle this situation, at least. "Guard! Come now! Come quick!" The pain hit him so hard he had no difficulty making his voice very loud.

And a guard responded. A boy fresh from the villages, uniform collar several sizes too big for his neck. He clunked halfway down the stairs with his rifle ready, twin to the kid who had shot him.

"*You,*" Burton barked. "Would you treat your sister this way? This woman has private concerns! You bring a bucket and untie her! No self-respecting Azeri man would treat a woman so badly."

The soldier looked at him with idiot eyes, then turned back up the stairs. His boots were too big for him, too, and he went awkwardly. After he disappeared, Burton could hear hushed conversation beyond the cellar door, followed by explosive footsteps overhead.

"You didn't make him angry, did you?" Kelly asked.

"No. I embarrassed him. I just hope I embarrassed him enough."

The soldier reappeared quickly. Bucket in hand. An NCO with a village-Casanova's leer came down behind him.

"Untie her," Burton ordered him. "And then give her some privacy."

The NCO sniffed and his close-lipped smile cut further into his cheeks. Finally, he said, "Lambs don't give orders to the butcher."

Burton did not translate that for Kelly.

But the soldier began to undo Kelly's ropes as soon as he had set down the bucket. The knots were overdone and it took him several minutes. The NCO leaned against a pole and lit a cigarette.

When she was finally free, Kelly had difficulty standing. She had to sit back down for a bit and stretch out her legs, massaging them to bring them back to life. When she finally showed she could walk, Burton said:

"Don't be indecent. Give her privacy."

"We've got to watch you both."

"Go upstairs. We're not going to escape. There aren't even any windows."

"I have orders."

"Aren't you Azeri?"

"Yeah, I'm Azeri. And my mother's a Lezghin." The NCO spit the butt of his cigarette onto the floor.

"Then why are you acting as piggish as a Russian?"

The NCO stiffened.

"It doesn't matter. Whatever you're saying," Kelly said. But the surrender in her voice made it clear that it mattered a great deal.

With a teahouse tough-guy sneer, the NCO turned away and muttered to the bucket boy. "Two minutes," he told Burton.

"And shut the door," Burton called after him.

"What did he say?"

"He said you've got two minutes, girl. Better move."

"Could you . . . turn your head away?"

"Sorry. My shoulder's fucked."

"Then close your eyes."

"They're already closed, for God's sake."

"This is embarrassing."

And it was. It struck Burton that he had never seen a film or read a thriller in which people had practical problems like this.

When he heard her footsteps again, he asked, "Can I open my eyes now?"

"Yes. Sorry."

"What are you doing?"

"I'm going to untie you."

"Sit down."

"We could try to—"

"Don't. There isn't time. *Sit down.*"

But her hands were on the knots.

"*Kelly.* They could kill us. I can't even—"

Her fingers paused.

"Sit down now," he said. "Hurry. We want the guards happy. We'll get our chance."

But she made no move to sit down.

"My God," she said.

"What? What's the matter? Please, sit down."

"Your shoulder."

"I told you it's fucked."

"I couldn't see. From where I—that's the bone? Under the bandage?" He felt her shiver.

"Sit down now."

She clicked off. And moved back toward her chair. "I had no idea," she told him. "My God. You must be . . . you . . ."

She made it back to her chair just as the first footstep hit the top stair. With his shoulder a medieval torture to him,

Burton looked up, expecting to see the guards return. But the trouser legs coming down the steps had a red stripe.

Just as Hamedov's face came into view, Burton saw a familiar pair of shoes appear behind the general.

Hamedov paused the instant he saw Burton.

"*Evan*," he said with what sounded like genuine concern at the sight of him. Then Hamedov went on in his careful, scissored English. "What a terrible night this must have been for you!"

Behind him, Heddy's hips appeared, followed by her torso and more. Her hair framed a doubtful face, and when their eyes met, hers flicked away as if scorched by the contact. Two new guards with paratroop assault rifles followed her.

Hamedov sighed and turned from Burton to Kelly, but said nothing to the girl. The general had the air of a decent boss forced to hand out pink slips. When the little party was assembled at the bottom of the stairs, Hamedov sent the guards away again and told his guests:

"Now it's time for our lesson."

CHAPTER

. . .

"Let the girl go, Hassan," Burton said.

The general raised one eyebrow, then the other. His brows were as thick and dark as Groucho mustaches and they glistened with sweat that had streaked down from his hairline.

Hamedov stepped closer and smiled, leaving Heddy empty-handed at the foot of the stairs. Her expression alternated between fear and calculation, which Burton did not like at all.

The general cracked his knuckles in front of Burton's face. "Your shoulder, Evan. We must get you a very good doctor, I think."

"Just let the girl go. Get her out of here."

The general stopped in front of him, smell close. Hamedov's uniform was dirty, his big face haggard, with a drunken sculptor's grooves cut into the jowls. "We'll see." He glanced at the girl, who sat open-mouthed, then turned his attention back to Burton. "I'm sure you feel much pain, Evan, and I am sorry. You have been my friend, I think. But there are things we must talk about." He wheeled suddenly, stepping toward

Heddy. "Fraülein Seghers, sit down." He pointed toward the bottom steps, then gathered in his hands and popped the knuckles again. Hamedov spoke to Heddy in the tone he might have used with a subordinate who had irritated him. "A man in my position does not like to see so clearly that a woman is taller."

Heddy sat.

"Okay," Burton said, split bone sawing at his flesh. "What's the deal, Hassan?" He could feel sweat greasing his own forehead now.

Hamedov smiled again, then sighed. "Evan . . . there is no 'deal.' You have nothing to offer me at the moment. But do not worry too much." The heavy man dropped to his haunches. He squatted country-style, looking up into Burton's face. The general was tired and he almost lost his balance, steadying himself with one hand on his holster, the other briefly touching the dirty floor. "I have no desire to hurt you. You must understand that." His eyes flicked toward the girl again, did not quite reach her. "And I do not want to hurt this girl. I am not the savage your people take me for." He put on a businesslike face, rubbing his chin with a hand removed from the butt of his pistol. "But, you see, other parties have their own interests." The smile ghosted over his face again. "I have been disgusted by the cruelty I have found in people— disgusted. You, too, will be surprised, I think." The smile faded entirely. "I cannot say how many of the people in this room will be alive in the morning. But I promise you, Evan: *I* will not hurt you or the girl."

"Then untie us."

Hamedov rose with a grunt, adding another nuance to his repertoire of smiles. "In time, in time. I think there is a good phrase in your English, the 'captive audience.' We must talk. About the cabbages and the kings, yes?" The weary humor in his expression disappeared the way sunlight leaves a meadow under a rushing cloud. "First, Evan, you are going to listen to me." He turned around, including Kelly and Heddy in his audience. "You are *all* going to listen to me."

The general worked his gunshot knuckles and began to pace. Then he twisted, suddenly, a *dzhigit* doing a warrior dance from the mountains. He stretched out his hands toward Burton.

"Evan . . . you are the best of them. The best of them all. You almost understand us. I think that, maybe sometimes, you almost have respect for us. Not in all ways, to be sure. But you do not talk to a man as if talking to a dog." He turned again, striding toward Heddy, and his voice rose. "But tell me . . . who are *these* people? These Europeans, these Americans? Who are they to come to another man's country and imagine for themselves a right to control everything? The Europeans want to tell us what we must do, the Americans how we must live." He included Kelly in his lecture, if only for a moment. "You believe you are so progressive. 'Civilized.' Your answers are the only right answers. You imagine that you have a knowledge of everything, and that we . . . that we are stupid . . . incapable of making our own futures. You treat us like the black man of Africa."

He turned on Heddy and shouted. "You do not know the one damned thing, I think. Not the one damned thing." He flung out an arm as though tearing open a drape. "You do not know this country. Or me. Or my people." He laughed, reminding Burton again of a dancing warrior from the mountains, and his voice lowered to a growl. "You do not even know your own people." He eyed Burton. "Even you, Evan. You do not know more than a bit of what happens here. A tiny bit. And you are the best, my friend." The general paused. "Tell me, Evan, you have been believing for some time that I might kill this girl? True? Tell me."

Burton nodded and drew bolts of flame from his shoulder. "What am I supposed to think?"

"I *never* wanted to kill her. When has Hassan Hamedov killed a woman?" He smiled for Burton, but this was catalog number 13, a very bad smile. "Oh, I am glad to use her. A man is a fool not to use every opportunity that comes to him in life. But I have never wished to harm her, Evan." He shook his head. "You think we are beasts. But you know, my friend, Hassan Hamedov has never even slapped a woman. Not a slap. If my countrymen knew that, they would think of me as a weakling."

The general canted his head toward Heddy, beginning to turn away. Then he reversed himself and squatted back down, looking up into Burton's face. With every broken vein in his face, every blister of sweat, every hair visible under the hard, bad light.

"Let me teach you something, Evan. As a friend. Let me tell you who wants to kill this girl." He made the sound of a dog going mean. "First of all, it is your own countrymen. Your oil people. They would kill anybody. You have no idea. Your business people are more intelligent than your government people, you see. They know that the oil is everything. Oil is strategy, power. Who controls the oil of the Caspian and Central Asia controls the next century. Of course, they don't believe that stupid people like Hassan Hamedov can understand that. But *they* understand it. And they think they can buy off the savages with beads and colored cloth." He gestured toward Kelly with a prizefighter's paw. "One girl, no matter which girl, is a small price to them. One girl for a pipeline route where they want it. She is nothing to them. One girl for a strategic advantage in a new century. Evan . . . I do not approve, but I under*stand* this thinking."

"Fleming, right?"

Hamedov shrugged. "Not only him. All those who came late, who had to throw in their lot with the Russians. And, of course, your own embassy is divided. Do you know this? There are people in your own embassy who think it would not be a bad thing for the girl to . . ." He spread his opened palms.

"Vandergraaf."

"Mr. Vandergraaf sees himself as a great statesman, I think.

But he is only a little man in the soul. A bad little man. You see how you misjudge me, my friend? You throw yourself at the conclusion that I want to hurt this girl—and all the time I am the one keeping her alive." He smirked. "I do not pretend to behave out of charity—although Hassan Hamedov does not hurt women. But I do not think it is in the interests of my country for harm to come to her. I do not favor anything that reduces our freedom to maneuver, to set our own course. President Aliev and I share this much: We do not want our country ever to become a prisoner again."

"Who else wants her dead?"

Hamedov shook his head, looked down between his knees. "You should ask me who does not want to kill her, Evan." He looked up. "The Russians would kill her, of course. They want her death to blame on us so they can have your pipeline. I have told you what evil men they are. They betray everyone. It is in their blood." He tilted his head toward the girl again. "The raid on Galibani? All the while Sviridov and I have a deal. On the events of tonight. On everything. But they did not warn me about that raid. They believed they could grab what they wanted. And make a fool of me. When it failed, Sviridov must come to me with more lies. How he has not been informed, how he knew nothing. How this raid was the work of renegades in Moscow. All lies. But I can deal with the Russians. I understand them like a Chechen. They are only whores. I use them, but never trust them. And they are finally very stupid. Tonight, they are the fools." He stood up again and stretched his wrestler's shoulders, fighting the buttons where the uniform spanned his torso. "You must know that the Iranians—your country's terrible enemies—they want the girl alive and safe. Because they do not want the Russians to have your pipeline. A funny thing, yes? On the other hand, some of your most dear friends have not been honest with you." He offered Burton his widest, least attractive smile of the evening.

"No," Heddy said. She had almost gotten to her feet when

Hamedov closed on her with the speed of an assassin. He clamped one hand down hard on her shoulder and slammed her rump back down on the stairs. *"Sit,"* he told her. "I have listened to you while you talked to me like your little boy slave. Now *you* listen to *me.*"

"He's lying," Heddy pleaded.

But Hamedov had not said anything yet.

"Heddy . . ."

"Don't believe him, Evan."

"Fraülein Seghers," Hamedov said in a voice that promised he might just hurt a woman after all. "You must *sit.* And be quiet."

Burton looked at Kelly, who was getting lost in all of this, but he could not read her face anymore. Too many texts printed right on top of one another. Or perhaps nothing at all, the emptiness of shock.

Suddenly, Hamedov unholstered his pistol and jerked back the action. It had already been primed and a cartridge flew out in an arc and clinked on the cement. The general stepped up to Kelly without fuss and settled the muzzle against her temple. Burton expected the girl to scream, but she only closed her eyes and let her mouth hang open, lips trembling a prayer.

"Don't do it," Burton said softly. "I beg you, Hassan."

The general's eyes were on him. But then they switched to Heddy. "How much did you promise if I pull this trigger, Fraülein Seghers? Four million? U.S. dollars, of course. What do you think, Evan? Is that a good price?"

"You'll have to kill me, too."

Hamedov laughed and withdrew the gun from the girl's head. He strolled over to Burton. "Yes. That's the point here, Evan." Another sidelong glance at Heddy. "She is willing to let you die. An unfortunate matter of business. Is that not true, Fraülein Seghers?"

Heddy shook her head. Unconvincingly.

"You see, Evan. Even your German friends are willing to spend this girl's life to place the pipeline where they desire it.

They wish it to appear that the Russians have killed her. So Washington will become angry with Moscow and make the pipeline through Georgia and Turkey. Oh, I do not believe the Germans are so bad. After all, what is one girl against good strategy and good business?"

"You can save her," Evan said. "America will be grateful."

The general put on an exaggeratedly quizzical expression. "How should I think about this? How should I calculate? Like a dirty, greedy Azeri, who cares nothing for his country, nothing for his people? Like a buffoon who does not know how to dress? A clown who has not learned to hide his bad behaviors behind a wall of manners like a European? Should I just think it all out in cash, the way our German friends believe? One girl. Four million dollars. Who would know? What do you really think I should do, Evan?"

Without warning, the general lost control of himself. Waving the pistol so that it almost struck the ceiling, he began to scream. "*Who do you think you are?* Who do you think you *are* to come here full of lessons and false pity and deals full of filth? Who do you think you *are?*"

Heddy had made herself as small as she could. But it was not small enough to avoid the general's wrath.

"Let's find out who we are. All the games. All the lies. Let's find out what kind of courage we have inside." He grasped Heddy by the wrist and tore her from her seat on the stairs, dragging her across the room toward the girl.

"You want me to kill for you. To carry your shit." He pried open the fingers of her right hand and fit the pistol to them. "*Show me.* Show me how a civilized European behaves." He guided her wrist until the pistol touched Kelly's hair. "Show me how to kill, you bitch."

Kelly began to shriek.

Hamedov let go and stepped back, leaving Heddy to decide the girl's fate.

"*Go on,*" the general barked. "Show us your courage. Find out what it means to kill."

Heddy's arm shook, but the pistol did not leave the girl's temple. Digging into the dirty blond hair. Kelly screamed, *"No, please, no,"* crying and struggling to topple her chair, to do anything to avoid death. Burton could see Heddy chewing her lower lip, thinking too hard. She was crying, too.

"Evan . . ." Heddy said, voice a continent away. The continent of Atlantis, going down. "Evan . . . I'm sorry . . ."

In the instant before it happened, Burton saw the future.

"Heddy. Don't."

But it was too late. She turned from the girl and swung the weapon point-blank into the general's face, firing immediately. The bullet pushed into the roots of Hamedov's upper teeth, lifting his nose and kicking his head back for the flash of time it took the bullet to emerge from the base of the skull, dragging brains.

Hamedov fell clumsily, without further drama. His dead eyes looked past Burton.

"Heddy, *quick,*" he called. "Untie me. Give me the pistol."

He had not wanted to touch a gun ever again. But they had just lost their last protector. It was fight or die.

Keeping the girl alive was the most important thing. And Heddy, too. Goddamn her.

"Heddy. Snap out of it. *Move.*"

He waited from moment to moment for the door at the top of the steps to open, for boots on the wood. The only thing saving them was that the crowd upstairs would have assumed that Hamedov had done the shooting.

Heddy stood over the consequences of her action. In a dream. Burton could not stand looking at her, but could not look away.

"Heddy, *please.*"

His lover came to herself and looked at him. With eyes that had held his attention through the jazz of passion, the music of two bodies. Then those eyes clouded again and Burton saw a face he did not recognize at all, and Heddy began to run for the stairs.

"No, Heddy. Don't do that."

It was madness, of course. And he had no remedy for that. She was fleeing. Without real thought. Giving in to an instinct falsely programmed.

She made it to the top of the stairs and through the door, and Burton could not see any of it, though he had it all in his mind: the instant of confusion, the shock on all sides. Then the registry of the foreign woman with the pistol in her hand. He heard the shouts, but they were brief. Then came the shots from the automatic rifle and a pistol. The echoes and exclamations. The sound of falling.

Heddy's body dropped back onto the stairs headfirst, one arm twisted behind her, the bone snapping under the awkward weight of her corpse. The body held briefly in place, then slid downward, gaining momentum. Her legs cleared the door, then scissored out. The shift in her center of gravity pulled her over the side of the steps and she dropped onto the cement floor facedown.

She lay convoluted and still, except for the slow spread of her blood.

"Oh, God," Kelly said in a dazzled voice. "Oh, my God."

There was no time to lie and reassure her. The first heels struck the top steps. Burton felt as though he should say a last prayer, but could not find the words. He looked into his fate with open eyes, determined not to be a coward at the end. But he felt like one inside. He wanted to tell the girl he was sorry, yet could not trust his voice anymore. He had not realized how enormous a thing fear could be.

The first man to enter the basement was Sviridov, the Russian attaché. Dick Fleming of Oak Leaf Oil came next, followed by the awkward, careful feet of Arthur Vandergraaf.

Fabrizio Parma, a young journalist of explosive ambition, could not find the coup. A stringer for Charter House, he had arrived to cover the Kelly Trost story, only to find the airport closed behind him and the sounds of military vehicles and gunshots in the distance. In the eight hours he had spent in Azerbaijan, he had lost his luggage, wandered the streets in mapless excitement, and hired taxi drivers to whom he could not communicate his purpose, but who were glad of his money, coup or no coup. Now he found himself in a local imitation of a Volkswagen van, drinking gasoline fumes and crammed between two older, heavier journalists, one U.S., the other a Canadian who had invited him to ride along. Up front in the passenger's seat, a shrill, thirtyish Englishwoman bossed the native driver, who responded to her every complaint with a senseless turn. The situation out in the dark, grubby streets felt like a coup, and sounded like a coup, and even smelled like a coup. In the midst of a confused, unhelpful crowd, an American who claimed to be a diplomat had insisted it was a coup. But Fabrizio and the colleagues to whom he had attached himself could not locate a center of events.

Twice, they had been barred by men in uniform from entering darkened streets. Once, they came upon a row of parked tanks, but the soldiers perched up on the turrets either did not understand their questions or were afraid to talk to them. Again and again, they found themselves dead-ended in slums or stymied by roadblocks where it cost money just to turn around and leave. Occasionally, a military jeep raced along a boulevard.

Whenever hope sank lowest, a flare would pop in the distance, luring them like a star of Bethlehem launched by a cheat.

"Jeez, this place," the American journalist said. "What a goat rope."

"Fuck all," the female up front cried. "Turn there, turn there!" She had the sort of accent Fabrizio associated with the bleakest quadrant of Britain. Her face was familiar, though, and she had a camera team snoozing on the vehicle's rear bench, and Fabrizio had decided to charm her.

"I think you must know this place," he told her, leaning forward. "You are very expert."

She turned on him with an expression strobed by street-

331

lamps. Her face might have rendered cows barren and cursed fields.

"Who the bleeding fuck are you? Who's this one, Everett?"

"Charter House man," the Canadian told her. "Gwynneth, would you ask the driver to slow down ever so slightly? Street's a bit narrow, eh?"

"Charter House is the bleeding competition."

"You *said* it was all right."

"Fuck-all, I did."

"Anyway, does he look like serious competition?"

She looked at Fabrizio again, judging. "Fucking queer bait."

Fabrizio felt the Canadian tense beside him.

"Hey," the Englishwoman continued. "You. Speak English?"

"Of course," Fabrizio told her. "I speak in several languages."

"Christ," the American said. "Another CNN wannabe."

Fabrizio got the gist of that and it wounded him. His ambition was, indeed, to move up to be a correspondent for CNN. He believed his English to be adequate. And he knew himself to be vastly better-looking than any of the male correspondents on the network. Or any of the females, for that matter.

"That was a tank!" the woman shrieked. "Down that street."

"APC, dear. Personnel carrier. Broken down, by the looks of it."

"I need *foot*age. *Back*drop. Fuck-all, if this isn't abso*lute*ly the worst."

They passed the scene of a collision between two passenger cars that was among the most dramatic sights of their evening. A bloodied man waved his arms.

"Your countryman from the lower forty-eight?" the Canadian asked his colleague. He leaned heavily across Fabrizio as he spoke. "One who claimed to be the ambassador? On the level, eh?"

"That's him, all right. Kandinsky. Interviewed him yesterday."

"Didn't *sound* like an ambassador. I mean, the fellow seemed so . . . so open, so honest. Almost emotional. I thought he was dear."

"Guess they go all to hell out here. White man's burden or whatever. Gwyn, you want to get him to take a left up at that traffic circle?"

"*That*," Gwynneth said, "is the fucking road to the fucking airport. I do *not* want to see the same fucking roadblocks yet again."

"Don't think so."

"On *that* ridge," Gwynneth said, "we are turning downhill. City center's downhill. I want to go back to the center of the city." She jumped, almost striking her head on the inside of the roof. "*Fuck* me dead. *Stop*. Stop the vehicle."

"What is it?"

"Stop, for God's sake. *Stop*."

"What?"

"I saw a body! By the side of the road."

From the rear bench: grumbling.

"Stop the vehicle." She punched the driver on the arm and the brakes squealed. The vehicle fishtailed to a halt.

"Everybody out. No. Dickie, *do* stay with the driver. Keep an eye on the bugger."

Fabrizio followed the American into the street, with the Canadian nudging him from behind. Two bearish men emerged from the back hatch with a camera and wire-strangled boxes.

"Hurry," Gwynneth commanded.

The American stretched in the freedom of the street, paunch rising and falling, and he looked around. "The only local color," he said heavily, "is the color of goddamned dust. Know how much they're rooking me for my hotel?"

Fabrizio let himself lag behind as they approached the body. Death alarmed him. He did not even like the sight of dead animals and avoided butcher shops. He shambled after his colleagues, drinking in the city's hangover of fumes and watching the shifting tints on a horizon where a significant fire had begun. He wondered if there might not be a story there. The fire appeared to be on the ridge, though, and the Englishwoman said the real city was down below.

He forced himself to approach the cluster of journalists just in time to hear the woman shout, "Oh, bloody hell. I could've stayed in fucking Manchester for this."

The man on the ground was not dead. Nor even wounded. He was stinkingly, not unhappily, drunk, and he treated his admirers to an unintelligible song.

"Everbody back in the van," the American said.

"Oh, bloody hell."

In the distance, gunfire snapped and ceased again.

"Should've bought a map, eh?"

"Got a map. Can't read the damned lingo. Funny business."

"There's still the Trost girl story."

"Any leads?"

"Oh, something'll turn up."

The American turned to Fabrizio. "Hey, Luigi. Got anything hot on the Trost girl?"

"Perdoni?"

"Trost girl. Kelly Trost. The senator's daughter."

"Oh, yes," Fabrizio said. "Of course. Do you know something?"

"Christ," the American said to the Canadian. Then he told Fabrizio, "She turned up in a love nest with Michael Jackson. In Vegas."

Fabrizio sensed the rudeness but did not mind it so much. He understood. His own frustration was building to the shouting point. Earlier in the evening it had seemed to him as though he had stumbled into his big break, a story timed precisely for his arrival. But he could not find it. It was heartbreaking.

"Ought to go to the university, if this shithole of a city's got one," the American said. "In a real coup, they always gun down the students. Or bust their chops and lock 'em up, anyway. Great copy. Hey. Hey, Gwyn," he called ahead. "Why don't we try to find the university?" He wheezed toward her manly back.

"Dave covered Tienanmen," the Canadian confided to Fabrizio. "His moment of glory."

The idea seemed logical enough to Fabrizio. It was a tip to file away for the future, too. Find the university, find the coup. Anyway, there were bound to be pretty girls at the university. And it would be a shame to waste the night entirely.

Senator Mitchell Trost sensed that he had wasted his life. He knew it was not true in an objective sense. He had accomplished a great deal by any mortal measure, and he believed he had even done some good. But the intravenous line and the sensors fixed to his skin might as well have been attached to a husk. How could he have had a heart attack when there was nothing inside him?

Only a coal-mine darkness.

His father had taken him to visit one of the company mines north of the mountain. To teach him about his heritage, or perhaps only to give him a thrill. But he had been an unsteady, imaginative child, and they had not gone down the sloping track a hundred yards before the big fire doors began to shut behind them and he started to wail. He had never known such terror. That darkness spotted with the beads of the gangway lights, the sudden cold, the weight of the mountain—all of it or something else beyond had given him his first inkling of death. He had cried and kicked at the steel car and shouted until his embarrassed father directed the lokie driver to stop. Picking him up in his arms, his father carried him out. His father did not speak, but he had sensed the man's disappointment. It was, as far as knew, the only time his father had ever been ashamed of him, so there was a heaviness, a punishment in the memory. But there was something else, too. In addition to the darkness and fear, he remembered his father's strong arms. The strongest arms on earth, the memory iron. Carrying him up out of the darkness into the blue day.

Trost wished he could pick Kelly up like that. To rescue her from the terrors she must be facing. To protect her. But he could not even get out of bed.

None of the things he had done in his life mattered now. And it had nothing to do with Laura. He had already put her out of his mind. Almost completely. He had taken worse than that and gotten up fighting. But now he feared that the better part of him might never get up again. If he could not help Kelly, what was the point of any of it? Even biologically, children were the only thing that mattered, weren't they? Wasn't that why even the most timid parents would fight like lions to protect their offspring? He had been so in love with his own vanity that he had missed what mattered most.

Oh, he had helped her. In all the easy ways. In the things that did not count in the end. But how deeply had he held her in his heart? How close had he let her come? How much had he given that could not be assigned a price tag or written off as one of his perks?

He had believed himself to be a man of the world, of broad and deep experience, knowing. Now he found that he had known nothing of import. God had given him one great gift, a good child, and he had not cherished her enough. His punishment seemed Biblical, terrible . . .

Alone in an artificial twilight, with the occasional footsteps or cart rattle or stray voice sounding from the corridor, Trost had to endure a feeling of powerlessness he had never expected. He had never understood loss before, not really. Even his father's death, the dividing point of his life, had not wounded him like this. When he raised his punctured hand, it seemed foreign and old to him, inherited from a stranger.

If he could not save his daughter, who would?

*　　　*　　　*

Burton sat in the back of the sedan, squeezed between Dick Fleming, who held a very large pistol, and the major he had misused in the Interior Ministry that afternoon. When either of the men shifted, it jarred the spike of Burton's collarbone and tore more damage into the meat of his shoulder.

He did not believe it could be possible to hurt worse.

"Jesus Christ," he called out. *"Please."* He could not help himself. "Don't move. Please."

"Fuck you," Fleming said and jammed his elbow into Burton's ribs.

Tears streamed down Burton's face. The pain was unbearable now. Something had changed. This pain was the kind that made you sweat and scream and want to shit yourself.

"God," Burton told the darkness.

"My hero," Fleming said. "This maggot your idea of a hero, Arthur?" he asked the big man, who had tried to make himself small in the front passenger's seat.

Vandergraaf answered without turning around. His words were barely audible:

"All he had to do was mind his own business."

Fleming gave Burton a lighter poke. "Guess that's a lesson for you, stud."

Dragging him to the car, they had done untold damage. He had tried to talk to them, to reason with them, but the pain crashed his words. And they were not interested. They shoved Kelly into the rear sedan with Sviridov while a pair of gunmen loaded him into the lead car. The major had given his bad arm a wrench as he settled him in, laughing about it.

They were headed south on the main drag. Out of town.

Last trip, Burton thought. Bad end like this.

Think about the girl. Don't be a coward now. Keep your head straight. Use her to focus.

There *was* such a thing as unbearable pain.

How could God or anybody else expect him to focus?

A pothole shot horrible silver electricity through Burton's torso. The pain jabbed into his teeth and his eyes.

He vomited. On Fleming's trousers.

Fleming clubbed him with the butt of his pistol, but Burton could not stop retching. The worse the pain, the worse the spasm.

Don't want to die, don't want . . .

Focus on the girl.

Really going to die? Am I . . .

Belly burning. Throat.

Breathe deeply.

How could this be possible?

"Silk goddamned suit," Fleming said. "You turd."

Burton gagged again.

"Open the windows. Sonofabitch."

The pain was so bad that Burton imagined himself reaching for the exposed bone and tearing it away, ripping out the pain with it.

Focus on the girl. Last mission. Keep the girl alive.

"Kill you," Burton muttered to no one in particular. "Bastards."

Fleming laughed. "Spare me."

Burton groaned and clawed at himself with his good hand.

"You know, I've got a special place picked out for you, Burton. Nobody's ever going to find you," Fleming told him. "Or the girl. And I'm going to see to it that you die ugly. Your body's going to rot ugly. Do you have any idea how much damage you've done? To honest businessmen?"

"He should've minded his own business," the voice from the front seat repeated.

Arthur Vandergraaf. The weak voice. Fear. Fear knows fear. I know you, Arthur.

"Arthur," Burton said, struggling with the shape of his mouth. "They'll find out. You know it."

"Oh, shut up, would you?" Fleming said. He was wiping at the mess on his trousers with a handkerchief.

"No one will ever know," Vandergraaf said. But, oh, yes,

there was fear in his voice. Fear, fear, fear. Burton's fear. Compounded.

"They *will*, Arthur. Kandinsky already knows," he lied. "I told him."

"*Liar.*"

"They *know*, Arthur."

"Shut him up," Vandergraaf said.

Fleming thumped him on the back with the pistol and made Burton scream. Then the major clubbed him to keep things in balance.

"It's going to be a pleasure to kill you," Fleming told him. "I may even do it myself."

They rounded a curve. Through a red veil of pain, Burton saw the night glow of the sea in the distance. Between the road and the water stretched a darkness that reeked evil.

The old oil fields.

The land of the dead.

Burton understood.

They turned down off the highway where it rounded the headland and passed a roadside shrine. Heading seaward, the cars followed a rutted service track into the badlands. The stink of oil and rot, of dead fish and sewage, pumped in through the open car windows. Scrappers had been selling off the metal from the old derricks, but dozens of skeletons still silhouetted against the glow of Baku on their left. Burton had always hated this place, did not even like the necessity of driving by it when he had to head south. It was a swamp of dead earth, with pools of chemicals and waste, where the maze of trails bubbled into quicksand. The oil flats were as terrible a place as man could create.

The car jounced over the buckled surface and its headlights, seconded by the lamps of the trail car, lit a landscape of iron monsters, of blasted ruins and surfaces that gleamed like the skin of reptiles.

"Arthur," Burton pleaded, "save the girl. For God's sake, man."

After a thousand years, Vandergraaf responded:

"Too late."

The vehicles had to slow to maneuver around sinkholes. Burton had heard stories about men and even trucks swallowed by hidden oil sumps in daylight, drowning as comrades watched helplessly. The locals said this earth was hungry and vengeful for all that had been stolen from it.

The major commanded the driver to turn out the lights. As soon as he did so, the follow-on vehicle cut its lamps, too. Now there was only the pink burn of the city back on the horizon and the new-moon immanence of the sea.

"Tell him to drive carefully," Fleming told the major.

"Stop here?"

"No. Closer to the sea. Where the tide comes in over the pools."

"Save yourself, Arthur," Burton said. At least he thought he said it, wanted to say it. He tried to remember something from the Bible, but he only had scraps. The pain was too great. Between shreds of Ecclesiastes and Psalms, Matthew Arnold flickered up and Burton recited to himself, "The sea is calm tonight . . ." mistaking it for a prayer until he caught himself. Yes. A darkling plain. This ignorant one-man army. Dumb shit by profession. Down to this. Heddy such a waste. All of it a waste. Beautiful life. And this pain, as though pain alone might kill a man.

I am afraid, dear God, I am afraid.

He longed to find heroic resolution in himself, reserves of strength. But he was only sick with pain and afraid.

It occurred to him that he had not paid his last Mastercard bill and, after a moment's panic, he laughed at himself.

Will they warn me before they shoot?

Don't warn the girl. Do it so she doesn't know it's coming.

God, let me not be too afraid.

"You'll never get away with this," Burton said as the car gasped to a stop.

Fleming hooted. And yes. It did sound funny. A hackneyed

line on which to end. Burton felt as though he could almost laugh himself. A peculiar giddiness crept into him. Of course they were going to get away with it. That was how the world really worked.

"Please," Burton begged. "Get out myself. Hurts so much."

Is this cowardice? Am I a coward?

I didn't know anything could hurt so much.

Why don't I go into shock?

Aren't you supposed to go into shock when the pain gets too bad?

Am I in shock already?

Hail Mary, full of grace, he thought. A good Protestant boy.

Any God. Please.

Not like this.

They let him get out of the car on his own, even though it took him a long time with the pain. Something had changed now. There was a stillness, a solemnity in the stench of the bad ground.

The death thing.

Even Fleming had gone quiet.

Burton tried to fill his lungs with the scent of his earth one last time. But the air here was laden with oil, sulfur.

He saw the girl, the ambient light off her hair. Jesus, why?

Money, money.

More than that.

How men are.

Killers. All of us.

We love this, as long as the gun is in our hand.

Oh, God. I am so afraid.

"Over there," Fleming said in a low voice. "By the pond."

They began to move. Then Vandergraaf turned around. For an instant, Burton saw how fear looks on a man. The DCM glowed with fear, his face a white slice of horror in the night.

"What's that?" Vandergraaf said. "Who's that?"

"What?" Fleming asked.

"Over there. Behind us."

Burton dragged his crippled body closer to Kelly.

"It's all right," he lied.

"No," she said in a wondrously calm voice. "I know what's happening."

"Just who the fuck is that?" Fleming demanded of no one in particular.

Burton looked. In the middle distance, a third vehicle was searching through the maze of trails that crisscrossed the oil flats.

Fleming turned to the major, speaking bad Turkish this time. "Who's that?"

The major shrugged. "We can kill them, too."

"What . . ." Vandergraaf closed a hand over Fleming's forearm. "Shouldn't we . . . I mean, with Hamedov dead. It could be a message. Aliev . . ."

"Nobody knows about this."

"Dick . . . everybody knows . . ."

"Arthur, get a grip."

"Electric chair, Arthur," Burton half shouted. "Prison."

Fleming whipped around and struck Burton with his left fist. It was an inaccurate blow, landing at an angle to the forehead. Burton staggered against the girl. But he felt fury again. Ghosts of old strength.

Give me a chance. Just a chance. I'll fight you even now.

"They're coming this way," Vandergraaf said. "It could be a message."

"They would've called. Or radioed."

"Maybe there's still jamming. Shouldn't we just wait a minute? If Aliev—"

Fleming turned on the DCM. "Wait? Should we wait a hundred billion dollars' worth? Or just ten billion? This is it, Arthur. Christ."

But Burton did not believe him. The voice was wrong. Just anger, not decision. There was a shade of doubt after all.

"Just see what they want," Vandergraaf said. "What can it hurt?"

They waited sullenly for the approaching vehicle. Its progress was slow, with detours where the roadway disappeared.

"Must've been following us," Vandergraaf said. "Maybe we should turn on the headlights. Maybe they can't see us out here."

"They'll find us."

"Tell him to turn on the headlights."

"For Christ's sake."

"If it's a message from the president, from one of his people . . . we haven't got Hamedov now . . ."

"Turn on the lights on the trail car."

The group took on a life of its own, shifting toward the rear of the little caravan to intercept its pursuers.

"This is a gift," Fleming said suddenly to Burton. "Five extra fucking minutes. Enjoy it."

Burton believed he could run, given the chance. His legs were all right. And the pain might just make him run faster. He wondered about the girl. Looked athletic. But she'd been sick. And she was afraid.

He strained to see into the ink puzzle of the landscape, plotting a possible escape route.

They'd shoot him down before he took ten steps. Or even five.

But better to die fighting. Trying.

The wandering vehicle snorted and turned into the rutted lane where the execution squad waited.

"This better be good," Fleming muttered.

The headlights got them and, instantly, Burton slammed his eyelids shut and looked away.

"Close your eyes," he whispered to Kelly. "Face the other way."

Collarbone screaming at him, he nudged her forward and to the side, working toward the one track that looked dry and had some cover farther along, old ruins abandoned as the sea had risen.

He glanced toward the approaching vehicle, trying to look

around the lights the way they taught you when you learned patrolling as a lieutenant. It had been a long time.

The vehicle did not look, or sound, or feel official. But everything was convoluted these days.

It was a van. It stopped just short of them, dazzling its headlights over their figures, the metal of the cars, the ancient oil scum on the barrier ponds. One figure emerged, then another. Silhouettes, one lean, one wide. Then another figure emerged, and a fourth.

One was a woman.

"Excuse me," a wicked English voice said, "but we do seem to be lost. Anyone speak English? Can you guide us to the university?"

No one answered. But Burton could feel minds and hands reaching toward weapons.

Then a big gringo voice shouted, "*Jesus H. Christ. The Trost girl.*"

"*Fuck me dead. Ian, the camera. Get the lights.*"

"*It's Kelly Trost.*"

More figures poured from the vehicle. And Burton jumped forward.

"Ladies and gentlemen," he declared, squeezing his pain into a cartoon official's voice, "these gentlemen just rescued Miss Trost and me." He pointed with his good arm. "That's Arthur Vandergraaf from the U.S. Embassy. And this is Mr. Dick Fleming, of Oak Leaf Oil. They're the two heroes of this—"

A burly shadow was clumsying up an economy-size gallows: a light bank.

"Miss Trost? Kelly? Over here. Get her, get the girl on camera."

"Just connect it, damn it."

"Get the sat dish."

Burton leaned close to Kelly and whispered, "When I yell, run as fast as you can toward those buildings."

Fleming grasped Burton by his good arm and began to

speak, but Burton tore away, turning into the pain the way you turn into the wind. He plunged across the little stage lit by the headlamps and asked the light man, "Need help?"

"No, I—"

But Burton got the rig in hand just as the spots came on. He turned them toward Fleming and the major, aiming into their eyes. Then he toppled the apparatus onto his tormentors.

"Run. Now."

The one time in his career when it really mattered, Lieutenant Colonel Evan Burton's orders were carried out promptly. Kelly Trost ran, almost tripping over him, heading exactly where he had told her to go. With the pain lashing him like a whip on a horse, Burton followed her.

It was impossible to sort out the shouts behind them. If they were lucky, they had ten seconds. If they were very lucky.

"Stay away from the shiny places," he yelled.

She was, indeed, athletic, and she quickly took a good lead over the man with the butchered shoulder. He stayed low, clutching himself to steady the errant bone, trying to hold in the pain. It hurt immensely. But he felt strong now, too.

The girl fell, then got back up, then the first shots came.

Okay. The first shots would be wild. Even good marksmen could not shoot for shit at night without the proper gear. The problem would be pursuers. Or a dumb-luck bullet.

A long burst of automatic fire poked into the night, but came nowhere near them. There were still plenty of shouts, but no screams. So they had not turned on the journalists. Probably didn't know what the hell to do with them now.

Vandergraaf would cover them with his great big body. Wouldn't want more guilt.

Until he had Burton and the girl again.

Burton thought he saw the girl disappear between the ruins up ahead. But the night was a blur of false shapes. He suspected the pain was making him hallucinate.

Just run.

Don't think.

Run.

He had been dodging evasively until he realized it was a waste of time. Distance was what mattered.

More shots. Had the angle of the report changed?

Wouldn't hear footsteps. Ground too soft. Soaked in poison.

OHMYGODNOTHINGSHOULDEVERHURTLIKETHIS NOTHING . . .

Shoulder won't be worth shit, even if I make it.

Retirement for certain.

Ain't no use in goin' home,

Jody's got your girl and gone . . .

He tripped, blazed with hurt, rose again. Would not look back. Saving instants. And afraid of what he might see.

Plenty of shooting now. Saturday night at the Alamo.

Yelling, yelling.

But no screams. Journalists not yet victims.

We get away, they won't kill 'em.

THISISTHEBIGHURTJESUSTHEBIGONEWANTTO SCREAM . . .

"Kelly?"

The first roofless walls were just ahead now.

Bullets bit masonry, tossing sparks.

Lucky? Or did they have the range?

How I do hurt.

Ain't no use in goin' back,

Jody's got your Cadillac . . .

"Kelly?"

All right. Just run. Go, girl.

And I will have done this one good thing in my life.

Give me the safety of those walls, Lord, and I will take stock.

Feet sloshing in muck.

Did what I told her not to.

Jesus, like glue.

Stay with me, shoes.

Shit.

Ain't no use in feeling blue . . .

He struggled, aching, shouting without realizing it, thumbing the counter of his shoe back over his heel, sliming his hand.

Jody's got your sister, too . . .

"Over here."

Her voice. Girl, I told you to run.

"Please. Don't leave me here."

"Kelly?"

Bullets on old stone and plaster. Close enough for government work.

"Over here."

He found her quickly then. She was lying in a clutter of building stones and ancient metal drums. As toxic a place as any on earth.

"What's the matter?"

"My ankle. I can't run. Can't walk."

He felt along her calf in the darkness. Good muscles. Until she gave a shout.

Oh, yes. Thank you, Fortuna.

The ankle was broken.

Pair of fucking crips on the lam.

"I'm scared," she said.

Not me, honey. What's to be scared of out here?

"It's all right."

"They'll kill us now."

"No."

She began to cry. "They'll kill us right here."

"*No.*" It was the firmest syllable Burton had uttered in his entire life.

"I can't walk."

"*I* can."

"Don't leave me."

"I'm not going to leave you. Come on. Sit up." For a sliver of an instant, he *had* considered leaving her, brain hunting through a variety of excuses with the speed of a supercomputer. But he was not going to do that thing.

"What?"

"Sit up. I'm going to carry you. I just need to get you over my good shoulder."

"But—"

Darling, I am operating on the assumption that the pain cannot get any worse.

"*Just sit up*. Hurry."

Bullets in the air overhead. But they were literally shooting in the dark. It sounded as though their pursuers were firing in all directions now.

He glanced over the broken wall and imagined he saw shapes following the trail behind them. But the night was too dark and ugly to read with any accuracy.

Set clear, simple goals. Make it back up to the highway. Then take it from there.

"Time to go," he said, heaving her into a fireman's carry. She was heavier than she looked: the good muscles. And the pain could, indeed, get worse.

"We're going to make it," he promised her.

CHAPTER 16
. . .

Arthur Vandergraaf ran. He was unaccustomed to running and started out too fast. In less than a minute, he was out of breath and did not think he could go on. But he did go on, panting, gasping, stumbling in the darkness. He was not chasing Burton and the girl. He was running away.

From everything. Everything had gone wrong. Despite his caution, despite the skill and intelligence he had brought to bear.

He stumbled and fell heavily, ripping his trouser knees and cutting his hands. Struggling to his feet, he plunged on desperately, hoping everyone had forgotten him in the confusion, hoping those he had left behind would take care of things. He felt a fear akin to that which he had felt as a child, when his mother would take him down into the basement during his father's long absences and sit astride him, lighting matches, then blowing them out and applying the hot nubs to his wrists or backside, or, sometimes, to worse parts.

Nothing and no one could be trusted.

Except his wife. Lisa. The one person on earth. The only one by whom he could bear to be touched.

She would understand.

Would she understand?

There was shooting. It had been going on for some time, but it came to him through a filter.

Were they shooting at him?

Surely not.

He sloshed into a puddle he had not seen, a pool of black molasses, and when he got out again, he was soaked to the crotch. He felt as though small, slithering creatures had fixed themselves to his skin.

Horrible place. The whole country was a horrible place.

He wondered if there were snakes on the oil flats.

Poisonous snakes, like the one the gardener had killed in their backyard.

He steered toward the glow of the city. Once he got back to the embassy, to his world, he could begin to get things under control.

No.

Things would never be under control again.

He would not be able to stand prison. He knew that.

Surely they would not put him, a diplomat, into prison? With common criminals?

And they could not give him the death penalty. He had not personally harmed anyone. He was a gentle person, a considerate man, trapped by circumstances, by loyalties to his superiors . . .

What had he actually done that was so terrible?

He imagined prison as a place where lurid black juveniles would torment and humiliate him.

No. That was nonsense. They would send him to one of those minimum-security places where financiers and White House staffers went.

He was an important man.

He splashed through another trough of muck and lost both his shoes.

Time wasted. Time thrown away reaching down into the bottomless filth for shoes that had disappeared.

The ground was sharp with stones and his feet were unprepared. He leapt about as if walking on fire, pinched and cut, envisioning terrible infections.

How could he possibly make it all the way to the city like this? It hurt so much.

Behind him, vehicle engines coughed to life.

What if they were coming for him? Fleming had no conscience. What if they regarded him as a traitor for running away? What if Fleming didn't understand? Vandergraaf had learned to be afraid of Fleming.

And the Russian? Was he vicious, too? Drew made saints out of all the Russians, but Vandergraaf had seen a different side of them.

"Lisa," he called to a vision of his wife. "Lisa, help me."

His feet hurt unbearably.

He edged to the side of the trail where the oil bogs began, where the earth was softer underfoot. It was a horrible, horrible place, evidence that the locals could manage nothing on their own. All desolation and waste.

The slop felt cool and almost pleasant under his bothered flesh. If only it weren't so dirty.

Surely the doctors would be able to do something for any infection he might develop.

What if he got blood poisoning? What if he lost his feet, his legs?

He wished he had never heard of this country. Damn Drew MacCauley for talking him into it. "My man in Azerbaijan."

"Damn you, Drew," he said aloud. "Just damn you right to hell."

It was impossible to see the surface of the earth. Black on black on black. He did not see the protruding iron bar that tripped him and toppled him.

Arthur Vandergraaf, career foreign service officer, splashed into the pool with his arms outstretched to break his fall. He submerged entirely before he came back up, and the oil and salt water and mud clung to him with a thousand fingers. He gasped for air and tasted mortality.

His feet reached for a bottom that was not there, and the more he struggled for purchase, the more the heavy liquid pulled him down. He strained to reach solid earth, but there was nothing of substance within his grasp. The service trail receded from eyes stung by chemical poisons. For a flashing, gorgeous instant, his fingers touched the jut of iron that had snared him, but he overreacted and only drove himself deeper into the oil waste.

Up jumped a monkey,
In a coconut grove . . .

Burton sang to himself in a smashed voice, not knowing or caring if the girl heard. The cadence came automatically, prayer to a priest. In rasps and grunts. Challenging the pain. The girl hung over his good shoulder like the rucksack from hell.

He was a mean motherfucker,
You could tell by his clothes . . .

That was what the old cadences were for. Endurance. Mastery of pain. Thumbing your nose at the flesh and the devil.

God, the hurt.

The pain grew so overwhelming he had to put her down, hating himself for his weakness. They lay flat and listened to a vehicle searching for them, to shouts and random shots.

"We're going to make it, baby," Burton whispered.

She looked at him with eyes that had collected all the light left in the world.

And he loaded her back over his shoulder, sure that, even if he got through this, he was going to be a goddamned cripple. He did not know anymore if the wet on him was fresh blood or slime or just sweat.

Lined a hundred women up against the wall,
Made a bet with the devil he could. . . .

She shifted and he barely controlled a scream.

"Sorry."

"Try not . . . to shift . . . your weight . . ."

He steered between ruins and relics, drums and derricks, around stews of poison. Driving by the flats, he had always gotten a chill from the pure, evil ugliness of it. Now the mess and confusion was his only ally.

First get to the road.

Then get control of a vehicle. Somehow.

Get to the embassy.

Plan B, get to any very public place.

He was bent over, bone jabbing the air. He could picture himself all too graphically and would not look down.

But the fuckers hadn't gotten him yet.

Or the girl.

Outlast the bastards. Out-tough 'em.

Fucked ninety-eight till his balls turned blue,

Then he backed off, jacked off, and fucked the other two . . .

"I think they're coming," she said from her vantage point at his rump. "A car or something."

He scurried on weakening legs, heading into a modern sculpture of rusty iron, an old pumping station.

"They see us?"

"Don't know."

He lowered her behind a metal shield, trying to be gentle but suddenly so charged with pain he cast her off him and she landed heavily, making one sharp sound as her ankle hit the ground. She was a good troop, though.

He gulped for air, then dry-retched.

"What am I doing to you?" she said.

One of life's substantial questions.

A vehicle closed toward them. First the sound. Then the jarrring and tilting of the headlights as the car maneuvered over the wastes.

I was wrong, Burton thought. A gun would be just fine. They do have their purposes.

353

On his tombstone, written in green . . .

"They're stopping," she whispered.

But they were not stopping. Only slowing. A bad patch in the trail.

Here lies an airborne fucking machine . . .

Burton let the car pass, let the sound die. Then he snaked around the wreckage to make sure they were not being entrapped.

"Only a little farther," he told the girl.

"Can you—"

"Piece of cake."

VALLEYOFTHESHADOWUNDERFIREWORKSOFPAIN HOWCANITHURTSO?

He grunted and hoisted her and pointed them up toward the highway again. Then he heard the tanks.

"I want that bastard," Dick Fleming told the major, who was none too steady at this point. "It's personal now."

"The journalists? Shouldn't we go back and kill them?"

"Later. Never sell your stock too soon."

"*Over there.* By the derrick."

"Stop the car."

Fleming and the major leapt out yet again and chased another phantom. Feet wet and trouser legs clinging, they returned to the car after wasting priceless minutes.

"I'm going to kill that shit so slow and hard they'll hear him screaming in Washington," Fleming said. He was in a rage he could barely control. He had underestimated Burton, never believed a man in such bad shape could pull a stunt like that. And he had glass in one eye from taking a spotlight in the face. Hurt like hell. Burton was going to pay.

As was Arthur Vandergraaf. Took off like a flushed bird. But he wouldn't get very far. Vandergraaf was going to take some serious dictation before he went back to his embassy.

And Sviridov. The Russian had taken the second car and bolted.

Even the major was a bit shaky for Fleming's tastes, with his mentor Hamedov a sack of dead meat. Too many calculations steaming out of the guy's ears.

In the end, it was him against Burton. And there was no doubt in Fleming's mind about who was going to win.

He saw them. At the far reach of the headlights, struggling up the embankment to the highway. The slope was steep and bare and the motion showed immediately, although the forms confused Fleming at first.

"Stop. *No.* Drive up there, *up there.*" Fleming struck the driver on the shoulder, pointing.

The major roused and saw the movement, too.

"We'll have to get out. Go after them."

"Stop the car."

"Give me the rifle."

Fleming jumped out into the muck and alerted to a sound that had been there for some time, waiting for him to acknowledge it. Once he stood separated from his vehicle, the noise came hugely.

Tanks?

"What's going on?" Fleming demanded of the major. "I thought all that crap was over with."

But this was a country in which majors, even very privileged majors, had limited knowledge. The officer looked baffled.

"Maybe . . . perhaps they're going back to their barracks."

Fleming scanned the horizon. With his back to the sea, the halo of Baku rose over the headland, and only the city's first structures showed where the highway traced the curve below the promontory. Then the road wound southward, dividing the oil flats and the shanties of desperate pioneers from the settled patches that clung to the hillside. The road made a great horseshoe around the headland. Burton and the girl were climbing toward its apex.

Fleming ran, pulling the major behind him by strength of

will. "Christ," he said. "He's goddamned *carrying* her. We've got them."

But as he ran, he scanned further south. And he picked out the long line of running lights creeping northward.

He stopped again and reached out toward the major, not quite touching him.

"Down there. Toward the salt flats. What's that?"

It looked like a jeweled serpent inching toward the city.

"The tanks," the major said. "Running lights."

"But . . . they're heading into the city. That's the wrong way."

The major looked at him in the bad light and his face changed for the worse. His mouth opened to speak. But Fleming was quicker.

"That bastard Aliev. The deal was a fake."

It was a countercoup. The loyalists were moving in.

Not three hundred meters away, Burton and the girl seemed fixed to the side of the embankment, unable to make any progress.

"I have to go," the major said. "I—"

"Shit. You stay right here. First things first."

Fleming raised the rifle, aimed, and fired. But the clot of figures on the embankment did not respond. In the darkness, Fleming could not even judge how far off his aim had been. He fired again.

"Too far," the major said. "It's not accurate at that range."

"Nothing in this fucking country's accurate. Come on."

The driver of the car did his best to follow them on the trail. But men on foot were quicker. Long shadows ran ahead of them.

"I don't want those tanks getting between us," Fleming said.

"Careful. The ground . . ."

But Fleming was not fated to follow Arthur Vandergraaf. He closed the distance to the fugitives to a hundred and fifty meters, watching all the while as Burton struggled pathetically to drag the girl up the slope. They had come to a steep place and she was off his back now, scrambling up the bank like a cripple, with Burton tugging at her arm.

Dumb shit. Had to play the hero. It was going to cost him.

Fleming stopped, took a controlling breath, aimed, fired. Then he fired again. Burton twisted to look behind. That meant at least one round had come close.

The lights on the leading tanks had disappeared as the vehicles closed on the side of the hill and began their turn to follow the horseshoe road. Fleming and the major came under the lee of the embankment.

The noise was enormous now. Ten thousand steel devils.

If Burton got her across the road before the tanks began to pass . . .

Fleming surprised himself. He shouted. Screamed into the night.

"I'll kill you, you bastard. I'll kill you."

Just at the base of the slope, he and the major found themselves at the edge of a long, hidden channel whose surface glimmered like liquid anthracite.

The major grabbed a long stick and tested the murk.

No bottom.

"Goddamn it. Goddamn it all," Fleming said. Then his language shifted from English to the Brussels underworld tones of his youth.

It was hateful. He could pick out the details of their limbs by the light of the highway lamps now. He could see their torn clothing flap. Almost close enough to grasp. He raised the rifle, aiming as carefully as he could at the clumsy shapes on the slope. He fired until the weapon was empty. Without dropping his prey.

He turned to the major.

"Get in the goddamned car. We can still get up on the highway before that bastard."

*　　*　　*

Burton fell forward onto the slope. Slick with sweat and blood. The earth felt wonderful under his body.

"I can't. I . . ."

"They're shooting at us."

"I can't . . .'"

"Please."

He rolled over, bad shoulder a write-off. He could not get a clear fix on their pursuers. The intermittent flashes down in the darkness were elusive, his vision and judgment addled. How close? How many? He believed he heard only one weapon. But it was getting weird inside his head. He was seeing things. Dancing rocks in front of his snout, a shimmering world. Maybe going out soon. Hell of a time for the shock to kick in.

The girl looked bad when he focused on her. Fresh round of fear. Nothing constant, emotions all shifts. Bravery and fear, desperation and despair, all going around in human beings like carousel horses. She looked even younger to him now. Last woman he would ever hold. Odd, he sensed that he already knew more about her than he had known about women with whom he had spent months or even years.

Certainly more than he had known about Heddy.

By the quay side in Cologne. Walking in May. Kisses. And the thin, cool beers in the alley bars.

Fucking bitch.

"Let's go," he said, forcing himself back into the survival mode. Amazed at his own ability to do the impossible. "Crawl. Anything. Move."

Yes, Drill Sergeant.

Wordlessly, she began pulling herself up through the rocks and dirt. He half rose and staggered up the bank beside her, hunched like an ape, propping himself up with his good hand.

The symphony of the tanks was nearing a crescendo. Beautiful music. Rolling down memory lane. This is your life.

Even in the madness of pain, Burton realized exactly what was happening. Aliev had bought time, flushed out the conspirators. Now the trusted forces were coming in to mop them up. Burton could imagine a thousand threats, promises, deals. In the end, the tanks decided.

Easy now, with Hamedov gone. Aliev was incredible. Headed for a longer career than Louis Armstrong. The eternal president.

Even if they killed him and the girl, Fleming and his crowd were going to lose. Aliev would never give his oil to the Russians. Fleming, Vandergraaf, Sviridov. Screw 'em all.

Kelly looked like a cripple on a medieval pilgrim's trail.

"Come on, girl." It was his turn to beg her. A sorry team. "You can do it."

He expected her to complain of the hurt in her ankle, the misery of the effort. But she did not say a word. Hardly even looked at him. She kept her focus up on the lip of the embankment, on the twisted guardrail that marked the road. A real fighter. But she was too slow.

"Come *on*."

The ground had begun to shake under them. Tanks closing. The sound massive.

"Come *on*, Kelly."

They had to get across the road before the convoy cut them off. They were in no shape for a quick dash between tracked monsters.

The last bit was too steep, and they had to correct the angle of their climb, losing time they could not afford. With ten feet to go and the tank treads grinding up to the big curve, Burton reached down and grabbed her under the armpit, dragging her in a fury, losing his balance, raging, screaming at her now, overwhelmed by the desire to survive and take her with him.

"Come *on*. Move, *move*."

She clawed at the earth, hands bleeding. He pulled at her. She was crying and shouting and cursing, too.

"Trying . . . bastard . . ."

"Come *on*, goddamn you."

"Bastard . . . *bastard* . . ."

An earthquake had begun. Rocks broke loose and wandered down over their outstretched hands. Tanks breaking the road, the earth.

"I'll fucking leave you here," he told her. He was crying, but did not realize it. Vivid with fear and anger and determination. "I swear to God I will."

Her clothes were torn and it was horrible to watch her pulling at the earth, fighting him in her mind and trying to help him help her at the same time. She lofted her bad leg in the air whenever she could, trying to reduce the pain, but it only crashed back down again.

By the time they reached the guardrail, they were both groaning and they would have hurt each other if they had possessed the strength.

Burton pulled her over the warped metal onto the blacktop just as a great machine wheeled into view, its long gun barrel testing the air like the nose of an animal on the hunt.

She landed on her ankle and screamed. But Burton had her now. He grabbed flesh and rags of clothing and dragged her into the middle of the roadway, racing the tank and hoping the machine gunner was not trigger-happy.

The vehicle was not going to stop.

He wanted to shout at her, to tell her to come on, to kick with her good leg, help, do anything. But all he could manage was an inchoate scream.

With the tank almost on top of them, Burton saw a black car turn onto the roadway.

Fleming saw Burton and the girl the moment the car gained the highway. The American, God's own fool, was stumbling and dragging her by the arm. The girl was crawling. And a tank was about to crush them.

Fleming aimed the reloaded rifle out through the window. To make sure.

The range was short enough to hit them with a rock.

"Dead meat," Fleming hissed, squeezing back on the trigger.

A wild shout in his ear stopped him. The major grabbed his arm.

Look.

On the other side of the automobile, on the northern loop of the curve, a second column of armored vehicles was closing from the north.

They had driven into the middle of a tank battle.

Fleming saw the tank that had almost solved his problem stop short of Burton's twisted back. As the long gun traversed, Burton pulled the girl toward a gully on the far side of the highway. Fleming fired, with his weapon on full automatic, but it was too late. Burton won by seconds.

Firing at Burton was the wrong thing to do. It meant he had fired in the direction of the lead tank, whose gunner would not have seen the two half-human creatures fleeing through his dead space. But the gunner did see the bullets sparking from the car.

Before Fleming, or the major, or the driver could jump out, a tank round fired point-blank tore into the car, slamming it backward over the embankment in the fraction of history before it exploded.

Burton lay atop the girl in the ditch, a battle roaring in his ears. The ranges were preposterously short and the combat was a big steel bar fight that bore no resemblance to the finessed maneuvers he had studied at Fort Leavenworth. He could feel the heat of the fires and smell burning fuel and metal and the girl's flesh under him, and he did not look up. Terror held him down like a weight.

The noise was incalculable. In a fit of instinct just short of thought, he shifted to cover as much of the girl's body as possible, screaming in pain at his own contortions, bleeding into her hair. He did not think to ask if she could breathe.

Every millimeter of cover mattered now. Every second they remained alive was a miracle.

He heard the grisly bell sound of SABOT rounds piercing turrets, imagining the slaughter inside the crew compartments. Coax machine guns stuttered and the rounds chimed on steel. But there were no human sounds.

The roaring grew so loud he wondered if he would ever be able to hear music again and his head thumped with pain. He waited for an errant shell, or shrapnel, or a spray of machine-gun fire to find their hiding place.

A magazine blew in the roadway just beyond the ditch. Burton cringed even lower, snubbing his face into the girl's shoulder blade, his good hand shielding her head.

She was shaking. So powerfully it moved his weight atop her.

"All right," he tried to tell her. But the words were all gone. He felt as though his ears were bleeding.

The Azeris made notoriously bad tank crewmen. But the ranges were so short that it was virtually impossible to miss, and every vehicle in the national inventory seemed to be firing as fast as it could. Even with his eyes closed, the world was bright red. Heat scorched his back. When a corpse-size twist of metal fell out of the sky an arm's length down the ditch from where they lay, the shock of the impact opened Burton's eyes and made him cower. His broken shoulder prodded against the girl and he recoiled differently. Then a main-gun round smashed into the hillside above their heads and a fall of earth tried to bury them.

The fighting was over in minutes, but the minutes were very long. First the big guns stopped, then the coaxials drizzled off. All Burton could hear was the grunting of engines as vehicles maneuvered well in the background, safe behind barricades of destruction. Flames snapped, and another magazine cooked off in a tank turret. Danger close. He waited for the heavy metal rain. But nothing touched them except the heat.

"What's happening?" the girl whispered—or maybe shouted—against his face.

"Local equivalent of an election."

"Are they after us?"

"We don't count anymore."

Just a little farther now. Just a little more pain. He breathed deeply, imagining it might help.

"Just stay put," he said.

He scrambled up to the lip of the ditch, trying to go easy on the wrecked side of his body.

On both the northerly and southerly curves, burning armor blocked the highway. Dense as a Manhattan parking lot. The engagement had stopped when the shot-up vehicles became so tightly packed no one else could get close enough to get a shot in.

It wasn't hard to picture it: the rear vehicles moving forward on inertia, the radio net clogged and confused—and half the radios not working, anyway—and the road too narrow for evasion, the slopes too steep for armored flight. Buttoned-up and ignorant of what was happening to their front, the crews in back would have kept nudging forward, trapping everyone ahead of them until they trapped themselves.

It was a metal massacre. With human flesh roasting inside the steel carcasses. Burton figured most of the crewmen—crewboys, better put—had been younger than the vehicles with which they had been entrusted.

No bodies on the ground. The crews had made the classic mistake of staying on board too long. So they cooked themselves.

There was a black stretch of night out over the oil flats and the sea, a dark path between the firestorms that marked the head of each column. The peculiar emptiness between the flames reminded Burton of Charlton Heston's parting of the Red Sea. Odd how the mind worked. Let my people go.

But not back down there.

Well, he had seen the sedan go. With Dick Fleming's happy

face. He had known that satisfaction. And just put all feelings of humanity on hold until tomorrow.

Unwillingly, he recalled Heddy. Lying in an embarrassing sprawl where she had fallen, dead, to the basement floor.

A waste.

Burton slithered back down to where the girl lay. He nearly blacked out from the little effort it took.

He was not going to last much longer now. He'd used it all up. The nine lives, the luck, the energy of fear.

"Let's go," he said. Forcing out the words, hoping he could live up to them.

"Where?"

"Up that ravine."

"How far is it? My ankle . . ."

"Far enough to keep us alive."

"Won't they . . . shoot at us?"

"We'll find out."

"Shouldn't . . . can't we just wait here?"

He looked at her. Bloody. Grimy. Bruised. And, at the end of it, one tough sister. Give the girl credit.

"Miss Trost," Burton said, determined not to faint from the sheer fucking pain, "you have me . . . in an embarrassing position."

She looked at him with great, clean eyes in a dirty face. So wonderfully alive.

"I don't think I can make it without you," he told her.

EPILOGUE
∎ ∎ ∎

Drew MacCauley sat in his office on the seventh floor of the Department of State. Watching the autumn come to Washington. His days were full—unbearably full—and he had wielded the strength of his personality to bring an interagency working group session to an early close. He had experienced a sudden, commanding, almost physical need to be alone for a time. Had he been elsewhere, he would have stretched out on his back. There was an inexplicable downward pressure on his soul. The fingers of one hand stroked an inscribed paperweight he had received as a reward for well-bred journalism in his days of lesser privilege.

It was an ungrateful town. Damnably so. A man gave heart and soul to a good cause, only to see his actions misinterpreted and his name sullied. It had gotten to the point where the Republicans on the Hill blamed him for every little thing that went wrong in Russia or the comic-opera states sucking at its borders. As if nations could be reborn without pain, as if history were not created by fallible human beings.

He stared out over treetops erupting with color and a roofscape that led to the garden of the Mall. And he stared into a vision of the future, his vision, one that might forever be credited to his name, a conception of a Russia made firmly European and upright, a monument to perseverance and faith, a triumph of civilizaton.

More than anything else, Drew MacCauley wanted to be remembered well. Now legions of small men were fracturing his dream.

The entire Azerbaijan thing had gone off the rails, and damage control was the order of the day. Difficult, without his own man on the scene. Poor Arthur Vandergraaf had died a heroic, if unpleasant, death in his attempt to rescue the Trost girl. Not an athlete, Arthur. A man really did need to keep himself in condition. Still, a tragedy. Arthur would be missed.

The military had tried to twist everything. They were monstrous. Besmirching a dead man's name. And then Kandinsky—a traitor to the department—had put his smear in. The fellow was even jealous of the dead. Careerist of the worst sort. Ungentlemanly.

Well, Kandinsky had no future. Baku, then bye-bye. He could go teach and scribble down his memoirs for some university press. As for the military, they would never have the President's ear. Although he did like to pose with them.

MacCauley clutched the paperweight in his tennis-strengthened hands as though it were a last weapon and his office under siege. He had even been misunderstood on the matter of the analyst's suicide. No one could have predicted an overreaction of that sort. The girl had clearly been unstable. But the hounds were out for blood.

A flight of birds skimmed crimson treetops. With a sigh, MacCauley dropped the paperweight onto his desktop and leaned back, locking his fingers behind his head. Staring into heaven.

At least Trost had backed off. Once he got his troublemaker daughter back. Old Mitch was up on the Hill again, up to his tail in domestic policy and little-people programs. Blessedly no longer interfering in things he could not understand.

A rally of wind stripped the branches outside his window, tossing a celebration of leaves into the sky. MacCauley felt as though he could just sit and watch those trees all day. There was so little time for the beauty of the world, for poetry, for the things that mattered. It was a hard, mean-spirited, ungrateful town. Only his sense of duty kept him at his post.

His secretary buzzed him. Reminding him, cruelly, that it was time to return to fixing the world.

Evan Burton was far from mastery of the tribal dialect and he used his interpreter to explain how to continue the work on the irrigation channel. Then he broke away in midmorning, walked the paddy walls to his jeep, and drove back to the village. Gray clouds had wrapped the mountains to the east, where the Laotian highlands arbitrarily became Vietnamese highlands, and he asked the rain gods out loud to hold off a bit, just long enough for the resupply helicopter from Vientiane to land and off-load its cargo.

He parked in front of the enclosure where the aid organization had built him two cement-block rooms and he goofed around—more briefly than usual—with the kids who hung out at his door, waiting for a moment's attention from the funny-looking fellow from far away. Inside, he looked around again to ensure that everything was clean and that no animals had come to visit in his absence. He tidied the stack of books by the hurricane lantern, laying Milan Kundera on top of Marcus Aurelius, then stripped off his clothes. Peeking to make sure he was alone, he stepped out back to the shower he had rigged from a barrel, a few planks, a pipe, and an old tarpaulin. It was already cool in the highlands and he had always been a sissy about cold water, but there was no avoiding it. He had been down in the ditch with the locals and he had done his fair share of sweating.

He soaped over the hachure of scars on his left collarbone

and shoulder. He had a good seventy percent use of his left arm and believed it was still improving. Manual labor was good for it. Manual labor was good for a lot of things.

The project he had joined built small dams and weirs and corrected channels to control local flooding and help turn poppy fields into rice paddies. Not long before, the valley had been gorgeous with opium poppies. Now it shimmered silver and green with rice. Once completed, the little dams generated electric power, too, and the dirt roads that the Department of State had funded in a fit of rationality took the rice to market and brought in bright clothes and medicines. There was even capitalism to show off in these Ozarks of Socialism. For the first time, two little stalls had opened—side by side—in the village, selling goods for which the villagers had once had to walk three days.

The living was hard, and there were the inevitable bouts of sickness, and the batteries for his boombox always seemed to be running out. Yet the clarity of purpose outweighed the discomforts. And once a month he would drive the four-wheel down to Phonsavan and hitch a chopper ride to Vientiane for a weekend of French cuisine once removed, a major purchase of chocolate bars, and some chat with the other expats who had washed up beside him. But he would have forgone even that last luxury to do what he was doing. Making a difference. His penance. And his joy.

He dried himself hastily and put on a clean khaki shirt and jeans. The aid project was a mix of official and unofficial U.S. aid, and he was proud of his small part in it. It was especially important to him to show his country at its best here, because Laos had already seen it at its worst. When you flew up from Vientiane in the wheezing MI-8 choppers the Russians had left behind—each and every ride an adventure—you flew over the Plain of Jars: hundreds of square miles of devastation that nature would need centuries to reclaim. Villages had re-arisen amid the craters, their farmers intermittently surprised to death when they plowed the wrong line and harvested a bomb that had failed to detonate on impact. During his country's Indochina wars, the bombers based in Thailand had used the Plain of Jars as a dumping ground for any ordnance they had not been able to deliver over Vietnam. For a decade, tens of thousands of tons of bombs fell on the most fertile valley in the Laotian uplands. In theory, there had been some Pathet Lao guerrillas in caves in the vicinity and that made the indiscriminate bombing all right. But every time he had to fly over it, a quarter of a century after the last bomb had fallen, Evan Burton felt something to which he was unaccustomed: shame at being an American.

The vanity and arrogance of what his country had done here was indescribable. Every time the geriatric Marxists in Vientiane angered him with their suspicions and bureaucracy, he made himself think about the Plain of Jars. It was astonishing, part grace and part desperation, that the Laotians would even talk to an American.

He heard the helicopter throbbing in the distance and hurried out to the jeep. The field where the pilots always put down was only a two-minute walk, but there would be things to carry today and his shoulder was still cranky. He drove down the bumpy track, with first the village children, then the adults, too, hurrying to admire the flying machine.

The Hmong were Stone Age. But they were Stone Age with a smile. Burton genuinely liked these people. Perhaps loved them, as Christians were supposed to do. He felt he was learning about the world at last.

He would not stay here forever, of course. He did not romanticize their misery, but ached to reduce it. When the project was completed, he would move on. God knew where. But, for now, he was almost a happy man.

He parked and jumped out to guide the potbellied helicopter to a safe landing. Hair whipped by the prop wash, he planted himself with both arms raised—one a bit higher than the other—and a kid's smile on his face. The overage engines growled and burped, and the machine settled, one of the pilots giving him a thumbs-up from behind the bird's glassy snout. Then the rotors began to sag and the hatch opened. Rough hands dropped a ladder into place.

Burton jogged over, still smiling. First a duffel bag hit the earth—a large, tightly packed green sausage—then hiking boots and jeans followed. It was a pearly, overcast day. But Burton had never known a brighter one. Kelly stepped clumsily onto his earth. She was smiling, too.

"I couldn't wait any longer," she called to him, sweeping her hair from her face. It had grown out since the last time they had been together.

Public shows of affection were not customary among this tribe. And Burton was generally one for playing by the rules. But after an awkward moment, he found himself holding Kelly as tightly as he had ever held anything in his life, and he instantly remembered the feel of her and the warm smell of her hair from their goodbye in Washington.

"You brought a lot of stuff," he said unimaginatively.

The embrace loosened itself and Burton glanced around at the hundreds of very curious onlookers. Their smiles needed no translation.